Tug of the Wishbone

Tug of the Wishbone

by Katherine L. Holmes

Couchgrass Books

Couchgrass Books
PO Box 3481
Duluth, MN 55803
couchgrass-books@centurylink.net

Cover by Bradley Wind

Interior ornaments © Elena Andreeva/Dreamstime.com

ISBN-10: 0991091157
ISBN-13: 978-0-9910911-5-7

Grateful acknowledgement is made for publishing excerpts of this book: *Frigg, Phantasmagoria, The South Dakota Review, whimperbang,* and *WordWrights.*

Prologue

Before Her

Inside, the cedar chest smelled like trees. Maureen found animals tucked under a blanket, two animals connected to each other. Their mouths leered but they didn't bite, nodding at her with hard eyes. Handkerchiefs held ribbons - ribbons with blossoms on them, ribbons with coins, ribbons with rainbows. They spilled onto a storybook of pictures, its pages black and the words white as milk.

The shiny story started with a lady on a bench. Her straight hair glowed like candles and the building behind her had church windows. Her teeth were strong, unafraid of the animals that crept on her shoulders. Then a man came to find the animals nosing the lady's purse. His dark hair rippled like grown-up chocolates.

On the next page, the man and woman sat together on a hewed bench in the woods. They both wore swimming suits made of scratchy material. Their skin was pale as springtime and they both looked embarrassed.

Next, the woman sat on a dock, dangling her legs and smiling at the smiles her toes were making in the water. The man went to the deep end where he looked out on the lake.

Then the man put on a hat with a bird's crest and a jacket that was like a mailman's. But he grinned in a cocky way, not like a mailman. The woman was downcast, her head and coat drooping near a mailbox. Then she crouched and hugged a suitcase that was drenched in leaves. On the next pages, letters folded out like paper airplanes.

In a garden where flowers strayed from their beds, the lady hugged a baby. Her hair was shorter, puffed like a strudel and her mouth was saying *cinnamon*. Across from her, the man wore a hat big enough to have letters hiding in it. Ribbons with blossoms, ribbons with rainbows, ribbons with coins covered his jacket.

"Maureen, what have you gotten into?"

It was her mother.

PART I

1   White Flag

Kindergarten, 1961. A disembodied, deific voice rang out, "Not one of you will win!"

Miss Nettleton had returned from her storeroom with flannel pictures of Thanksgiving. Thanksgiving was in one week and their town's products were Thanksgiving food.

"Who started it?"

Maureen Berwick righted herself from the classroom siege. Five minutes before, the boys were lined up at the flannel board and the girls were huddled near the piano. Red-haired Kevin, easiest to follow, shouted, "Maisie's a gobbler!" Hardest to catch, Maisie ran at him and then the sexes charged at each other, slapping and capsizing.

Everyone watched as Maisie spit out "Kevin!" at the freckled boy. Seeing the answer, Miss Nettleton grasped Kevin with her right hand and Maisie with her left until she could shake them as if she were the beanstalk giant.

All the girls were mad at all the boys. Maureen was mad because Jerry R. discovered her red underpants. They went with her kilt skirt but she wasn't wearing it that day.

"Maureen's got red underpants on!"

"It is the most natural thing in the world for boys to side with boys and girls to side with girls," Miss Nettleton said in her new frightening voice. She understood because she didn't live in a house with a man. She gave each of the kindergartners a white flag, the note pinned on Maureen's collar when she went home. Whatever was in it, the mothers would side with Miss Nettleton just as they sided against Uncle Jake of "Uncle Jake's Ballpark."

Uncle Jake gave the children in Wanatin, Minnesota, the chance to be on television. A wheeling camera showed them laughing on bleachers as he divulged useful hints to the home audience. He demonstrated signals with window shades and how change fell out of men's pockets while they sat on a chair cushion, "finder's keeper's" coins. Kids could also look for the place on a treasure map where cans of waxed beans and peas were collected for the local tramp.

Waiting for "Uncle Jake's Ballpark" to come on TV, Maureen paged through one of her favorite books from the living room bookcase, *The War Between the Men and the Women*. It was full of cartoons. She gazed at the snowball fight where the women sided against the men and snowballs separated them.

Maureen's fifteen-year-old brother, Hugo, asked, "What day is today?"

"Monday, Tuesday, Wednesday, Thursday."

Their eleven-year-old sister Lydia wouldn't come home until supper. Maureen accepted the Thursdays of the past year the way she accepted chocolate sundaes after Sunday dinners.

After watching an "I Led Three Lives" re-run in the backyard room, Hugo usually went up to his short wave radio. He was too old for Uncle Jake's umpire shirt and his cliffhanger glasses. But he wanted to find out if the rumor about Uncle Jake was true – whether he had gotten a girl in town pregnant or not. Lydia hadn't found out anything. She and her friends ogled the windows of his apartment, said to be above a sporting goods store downtown.

"What's in the note?" Hugo leaned from the wicker chair and undid the note from Maureen's Peter Pan collar.

"It's for Mom!"

Since it was Thursday, Hugo read the note but then he mimicked Uncle Jake's goofy voice. "It says the boys and girls aren't getting along in your classroom. You're supposed to wear cleats to school tomorrow."

Beyond the windows lining the backyard room, the Berwick blue Ford Impala rippled through the alleyway. Before Thursday meant anything, Clive Berwick talked of moving to the country and, gleaming like a horse, he promised one. *Your father is up for a promotion, a vice-presidency,* Joann Berwick glowed. But when her husband wouldn't talk about the horse, she explained, *Your father is too young for that. He has so many ideas but the promotion wasn't his idea. He can't have everything he wants unless he wants to be alone at home.*

They stayed in their old Wanatin house, once a dentist's house and office. In the neighborhood were employees of Country's Plenty, doctors, and old ladies who could pickle with their looks. Clive Berwick probably caused as much wincing these days as the dentist had.

Because of what happened on Thursdays. After the back screen door whined, Clive glared at Hugo. Even Tucker, the family's springer spaniel, made a Thursday retreat. Clive set his hat on the divider and then he removed the rubber liners from his shoes.

"What are cleats?" Maureen wondered from the wicker settee.

She didn't interpret her father's glare, green as a tornado sky. Without answering, he went into the kitchen with his coat and hat.

"So why are Thursdays Thursdays?" Hugo wondered.

Maureen couldn't remember when Thursdays were like any other night of the week. That was when Joann frothed like her summer strawberry jam, saying that her husband was so reliably rational.

But after Maureen's father went to his room today, night monsters might be real. If Maureen knocked on the door, she might receive a snarl in answer. Her parents' bedroom was gloomy with purple orchids on the wallpaper. The mossy carpet reminded Maureen of dark woods. Still, their bedroom was better than Maureen's room. It was once a dentist's examining room, a place where children suffered torture, Hugo said. Moonlight made the curtains look like a patient smothered in a dental chair.

Thursday evening, the smell of Scotch usually emanated above the potato chip casserole. Any smell of Scotch was too much for Joann Berwick. She attended cocktail parties before Maureen was born and now, she said there were too many "snideties" amongst the niceties. In *her* family, deciding on a cocktail was like Catholics discussing birth control.

If she mentioned the Scotch, Clive might retort, "Teetotalers don't need a drink to say their snideties." On Thursday nights, he opened his mouth as if it were a complaints box. The people at work respected his complaints, he was proud to say. He was the first executive to sport a pin-striped shirt instead of a white one. He had taken a course from Lillian Gilbreth before anyone in Wanatin had heard of time study. But on Thursday, it didn't help for anyone to bring up the book Lillian Gilbreth wrote, *Cheaper by the Dozen.*

If Hugo grimaced at his mother, his father might complain, "Hugo is just like his Grandpa Bensen." Lyle, two years younger than Hugo, shrugged at the Thursday Scotch because he wasn't like his Grandpa Bensen.

After Clive Berwick came back from the War, he treated Hugo as if he were his Grandpa Bensen's boy while Lyle was *his* son. Then Lydia became her mother's daughter and Maureen was noticeably her father's daughter. They sat in that formation around the yellow Formica table. Sometimes Joann looked past her husband, through the dining room and living room to her sunroom where dusk marbled the bookcases. Clive looked past Joann to the yard and the tall nodding trellises that he tended.

After the Thursday Scotch and the dessert, Clive's eyes gleamed like fluorescence. Last Thursday, he took an egg from the refrigerator and, gripping it in the palm of his hand, said, "You see how hard I'm squeezing this egg? It won't break. Any more than honesty does."

He stood up tonight, beginning his tirade as his wife stacked the dirty dishes. "Coming to this town was your idea, Joann! You couldn't live in a trailer house for two years. She couldn't wait for me to finish graduate school!" He glowered at his children as if they were his students.

Though Hugo hardly remembered it, he lived in the trailer house. Of course he didn't remember what his mother blurted out one Thursday. The trailer house was so suffocating that his father made a new trail in the trailer court, helping out a tragic woman.

She might bring that up now. She was on her way to the sunroom but Clive was ahead of her, trapping her at the dining room table.

"You wanted money when you came back from the War, Clive," she protested. Sometimes when he blocked her under the framed antique road map, she ran into the hall and locked herself in the bathroom.

Lydia left the dishes, shouting, "Who could stand living in a trailer house?"

Instead of going upstairs, Hugo stood near his mother. Lyle and Maureen drifted to the border wainscoting between the dining room and the living room.

"You're getting as spoiled as your mother," Clive snarled at Lydia. "Your mother with her lake property. Bensen made me feel like a trespasser." Strangely calm and green, his eyes landed on Hugo as if he were Grandpa Bensen.

Lydia cried, "How do you know Grandpa doesn't like you? You never talk to him!"

Their Grandpa Bensen was so quiet that he was promoted to Postmaster in his town.

"Because he sold lake property to someone else. I was ready to buy it! You, Lydia, have never received a single letter from him."

He had shut up Lydia. Lyle and Maureen came closer to the dining room table where they stood on either side of their father. They might calm him even though his eyes were like a tornado sky. One night when Joann locked herself in the bathroom, he threw beer on the wallpaper across from it.

Joann hazarded the eerie atmosphere. "You wanted to work at the Thanksgiving company. That's what you called it. You said your father's family went back to the wild turkeys."

Hugo went upstairs before his father started in on him and how his upbringing was based on Grandpa Bensen.

"Grandma Rhiann came from the whales," Maureen piped up. Her father was angry after her mother mentioned turkeys. He usually smiled if anyone asked about Grandma Rhiann.

"Her parents came from Wales! A country." He was still glaring. Maureen's mother looked as if she had a secret up her sleeve.

"Maureen, you shouldn't be here," her mother said. Then she told the secret. "I don't think you're stable enough for marriage, Clive. Maybe your family had trouble settling down. Your father on the road."

"My father was a cartographer!" he yelled.

"Go to your room, Maureen," her mother said.

Maureen left the door to her room open. Sitting on her bed, she thought about another secret. One day, she and Lydia were watching Uncle Jake in a catcher's mask, throwing popcorn balls at the kids on his bleachers. Lydia said, *Mom was afraid that no one else would ask her to get married. She was too tall. Mom didn't fall in love with Dad at first. The first thing she noticed about him was his acne scars.*

When Maureen asked her mother about acne, her mother said that acne came from the peculiar side of Clive's family, Grandma Rhiann's side. But Grandma Rhiann stayed beautiful because her skin was oily, her father said.

Maureen wished Grandma Rhiann was visiting. She imagined that her grandmother came from mermaids in the country of the whales. Grandma Rhiann lived in Minnesota with Grandpa Berwick but after he was gone, she went back east to live with her relatives.

When she visited, she told stories about Maureen's father. At Maureen's age, he followed water trickling in the walls and pipes. He trailed cords and played with danger. "He would have loved these Seuss contraptions," Grandma Rhiann said, her eyes gleaming and her wavy hair glistening with spray. "When Clive was a teenager, he worked with bottling machinery in the summer. They called the lake Lager Lake. Clive used to swim across it with a girl, Anastasia."

Maureen's mother had never heard of Anastasia. "It's time for your nap, Maureen," she snapped.

In her room, Maureen played with the plastic flowers that came with Grandma Rhiann's present, a toy cake that could be frosted with Play Doh. Then she crept to the hall and sat on the stairs.

"Clive was too easily bored," Grandma Rhiann was saying. "At least he didn't marry Anastasia."

"Oh, my dough has risen," Maureen's mother said.

She was pounding dough while Grandma Rhiann, in the living room, riffled a paper at the desk. *She whispers in her letters,* Maureen's mother said. Maureen crept up the stairs to look at Grandma Rhiann's belongings. They were like presents with straps and clasps, not to be opened. Then she went into the large room where Hugo and Lyle slept, Lyle in a cove under the eaves. Riches were strewn everywhere – a stopwatch, a Brownie camera, a mechanical pencil, a transistor radio. Maureen hung the camera around her neck and then she slipped the other things into her overall pockets, pretending she could go away with Grandma Rhiann. At the top of the stairs, Maureen felt as heavy as if she were carrying a suitcase. She tottered and tumbled down the waves of the staircase carpet.

"Maureen, is that noise you?"

Grandma Rhiann was investigating the spilled trove. Then they made a game of putting it all back in the right place.

"They were for my suitcase," Maureen explained.

Grandma Rhiann's lips held another mysterious thing until she left, the next morning.

Upstairs, Hugo heard something he heard before.

"You can learn respect, Lydia! You and that mother's boy upstairs can respect a selfish lunatic!"

At least his father didn't call him a mother's boy in front of him. Hugo turned up the volume of his short wave radio. A Canadian announcer was being rational.

Downstairs, a scuffle sounded and then there was a crash. Hugo shambled to the kitchen where his father loomed with eggshell in his hand. He looked as if he could destroy a geodesic principle. The raw contents of the egg dripped on the yellow wall tiles and a chair was splayed across the floor. Maureen stood between her parents, fascinated as if she had seen a funnel cloud without comprehending it.

Hugo might have throttled his father, especially because he was now an inch taller than him. But Lyle was already talking to him while Joann ran to the telephone.

"I'll move to a trailer house!" Clive answered Lyle. "Your mother wouldn't care if I died driving to it." He sideswiped his sons, going to his bedroom and returning with an armful of suits. All the while, he yelled about the trailer house until the screen door screeched, Tucker barked, and he was facing the neighbor man, Mr. Cassidy.

"Clive, are you going on a trip?"

The doorbell rang and Mrs. Cassidy came in from the front porch.

Hugo wished he could find Thursday night religious broadcasts on his short wave radio. Everything would be peaceful on Sunday, his parents keeping their roles the way they used to. Though the Cassidy's were helpful, no one in Wanatin could stop the twilight zone lecture of next Thursday, Thanksgiving, if his father drank that day. Not the minister, the police, the psychiatrist his mother whispered about, nor his father's colleagues. They didn't believe he could be so bad, his mother said.

Some Thursdays, Hugo's parents talked about divorce as if it were a vacation spot that no one in Wanatin had visited. Because of a bus trip Hugo took when he was ten, he made sure to find out about places he would like to see.

"You must stay in the Minneapolis bus depot during the layover," his mother warned. "You have your comic books."

Fearless then, Hugo read the movie marquees on Hennepin Avenue before the bus pulled into the depot, one block away. According to the Minneapolis newspaper, people went to the movies on weekday afternoons. His parents raved to the babysitter about *The African Queen*.

In fact, the afternoon movie was as disappointing as a babysitter because Bogie was stuck on a chugging boat with an old maid missionary. Hugo expected a safari. A man who looked like a better deckhand sat down next to Hugo and called him "Kid." He offered Hugo popcorn and put his arm around Hugo's plush chair, explaining about tsetse flies and torpedoes. When Hugo squirmed at his shoulder being squeezed, the man took his popcorn back, grabbed Hugo's hand, and said he had a torpedo.

The old maid was shrieking and the popcorn toppled. Hugo ran from the theater to a terrifying amnesiac moment. Everything on Hennepin Avenue seemed re-arranged.

At the Iron Bluff bus depot, Grandpa Bensen was so taciturn that he didn't ask why Hugo was speechless. He was so taciturn that Hugo remembered everything he said.

The Bible doesn't say divorced people go to hell, Grandma. It says the rich do.
Grandpa Bensen really didn't like Hugo's father.

On Friday, Maureen wanted to tell Miss Nettleton that she was the white flag. Last night, she saw her mother holding a kitchen chair like a lion tamer and her father pulling it by the legs until it fell on the floor. Maureen ran between them. Her father looked at her and her mother said, "Clive!" Then they stopped fighting.

Friday was Forgive Day. After school, Lydia sat on the wicker chair until Lyle came home. He switched the television to "I Led Three Lives", and then he pulled the back of the wicker chair until Lydia toppled out of it. When she was sitting on the wicker settee with Maureen, their father came in. His suit was like the spy's suit in his third life.

"Hi kids," he said, cradling his hat above Tucker. After he set it down and removed his rubbers, he asked, "How's Maureen?"

Maureen had a square of Chiclets gum in a blonde curl and another in her ear.

"One for Lydia."

Lydia sat silently as if she were under punishment. Besides, Uncle Jake was going to make an important announcement. When he did, the kids started crying on his bleachers.

"If you see my summer re-runs and your own old faces, you'll know I've headed west to the radio of the rustlers. As you all know, I'm not that handsome to look at, Kids."

Lydia erupted, "He's supposed to announce his wedding! Mom said that if it's all true, he'll marry the girl!"

Having greeted her husband, Joann announced, "Friday hamburgers are on at six. Pie crust cookies are ready."

Lydia ran to the kitchen and returned with the plate of piecrust pieces baked with cinnamon and sugar.

Soon, their father appeared in his fuzzy button-down sweater as he did every Friday after "Uncle Jake." He was ready to take Lydia and Maureen with him to the drive-in bank. Lydia couldn't turn down the invitation because she and Maureen loved to watch the teller press a button that sent an automated vault to their car. After that, they went to Woolworth's and picked out a game or a small toy.

When dinner was over, Lydia put a guitar charm on her bracelet while Maureen nudged her new slinky towards the apple dumplings. Then Maureen sat on her father's knee so that she could count out the Friday allowances. Hugo came downstairs from his short wave radio, having eaten his dumpling faster than anyone.

"Who's winning?" his father asked.

Hugo took his three dollar allowance and said, "Warren Spahn's pitching for Milwaukee. Gotta tell the guys."

After that, the front door crunched shut.

"Are you going to practice your back dive at the Y tonight?" was the question for Lyle.

"Tonight's family night at the pool," Lyle replied. He snatched his two dollars.

Soon the back door creaked and closed.

Maureen squeezed her father's egg-shaped coin holder for Lydia's allowance.

"Uncle Jake is going west to be on rustler radio," Lydia said. "I guess *all* the mothers will be glad."

Since her salad, Joann Berwick's mouth was as tightly closed as the coin holder. But after Lydia told her about Uncle Jake, she began laughing as if she were the coin holder racked with money.

"I've got to get over to the Cassidy's," Lydia said. "I'm going to play

'The Flintstones' on the piano for Donna." Urgently, she grabbed the coin holder from Maureen. More than her three quarters spilled on the floor.

"Finder's keeper's! That's what Uncle Jake says." Lydia was already on the floor so Maureen crawled under the table to make sure she got her dime.

Every Friday, there were treats during "The Flintstones", usually a Hershey's bar and Dr. Pepper pop. Tucker usually sat near Maureen's mother but tonight, Maureen's father teased him. The dog food dish was on his knee and, while Maureen opened her Hershey's bar, her father tossed a chunk of dog food down the basement steps.

Tucker was trotting around the dark cellar for his fourth chunk of dog food when Maureen's mother stuck her head into the backyard room.

"Is Hugo coming back for the end of the Milwaukee game?" she asked, breaking her silence.

"I can guess the victor if Spahn's pitching," her husband said.

Tucker sprang up the stairs and into the backyard room.

"Watch this, Joann! He can have dog food without doing this."

Another chunk of dog food hurtled into the basement. As Tucker leapt after it, Maureen's mother said she would be in the sunroom, reading a longer-than-usual novel for her library book club.

Maureen broke off another square of Hershey's chocolate. While Wilma Flintstone talked on her prehistoric horn telephone, she suddenly felt happy, as if she had won.

2   The Wishbone

Somewhere between Duluth and Iron Bluff, 1963. Maureen was still at the age when the question "How long until we get there?" meant "Where are we going?" The trip north was unfamiliar because the highway was a tightrope between snowdrifts. Outside the bus, the land was like the days after Christmas, sparkling as her mother's diamond but otherwise featureless.

Maureen hadn't ever visited her grandparents in the winter. Her mother was proud of Grandpa Bensen being a self-made man. If he had to, he could live without conveniences and eat the duck he shot for dinner. The outdoor furniture he carved from pines made Maureen feel as if she might be carved into someone else.

Her mother's head reeled as the bus bumped against a billow of snow. Maureen couldn't nap, sitting up. Lately, dusk made her jittery as it crept into darkness like the word *divorce.*

"Can I trade places with you, Mom?" she whispered. Murmurs flickered in the bus. Before napping, her mother chatted with the lady across the aisle.

"Oh, alright," her mother replied. She was overly polite with the Eeyore donkey that Maureen's father gave her for Christmas. Then she flipped on the overhead light. Strong as a flashlight, it illuminated the things Maureen brought for the bus trip – a paper sack of spritz cookies, a Doctor Dolittle book, riddles for her grandparents, and her special drawing game. At home, she crayoned colors in stripes or circles or blobs on a sheet of paper. Then she colored over the whole paper with black crayon. With a bobby pin bent straight, she drew on the black crayon. Already, between St. Paul and Duluth, she had drawn a bus that turned out red, blue, yellow, and purple. Next, she would put passenger heads in the windows.

Joann Berwick craved sleep. She was traveling from one county of dread to another, the dread of telling her parents about her separation. Its process was gradual but unstoppable, like something being altered in a factory. Though Maureen suffered from this reassembling, she knew Eeyore was an ass of sadness. Perhaps Joann could wait. She only had to lean near Maureen and whisper, *Don't tell Grandma and Grandpa about Daddy's rented rooms.*

They wouldn't understand because of the equilibrium between them.

But the emotions between Joann and Clive became immoderate and wrong. Clive's eyes glinted with that process behind them when, outside the house, he was as charming as he used to be. Her best explanation for her marriage being an unbearable mismatch was that Clive's mother was Welsh. Clive drank! Her parents might think of mines and the actor, Richard Burton, currently being exposed for alcoholism.

"Can I see your picture?" asked the lady across the aisle. "Why, it looked like a camera picture that didn't turn out at first. It's very pretty. See that, Dad? There's color under the black crayon. A bus!"

"I have a toy camera," Maureen said. "But it doesn't work." She rose in her seat to look at the other passengers, huddled like laden trees. A woman plump enough to be Mrs. Claus was knitting in her bus beam. A boy looked as if his hair was cut in cowlicks. There was a man who rushed onto the bus, wearing suit slacks under his wool coat. He tried to help her mother hoist her traveling case but she flinched at his attention. Smoke was shading another man while across from him, a grown-up girl coughed.

The lady across the aisle returned the crayon picture, saying, "Your mother told me that you're from Wanatin. We got our Christmas turkey from Country's Plenty."

With her bobby pin, Maureen found out that the boy's cowlicks were green and blue. "They sent stuffing to the stores this year too."

"I saw it at the supermarket. It has a picture of a boy and girl pulling a wishbone."

"Uh huh." The man in suit slacks had a purple head. Maureen opened up her sack of spritz cookies and bit into one. Then she offered a wreathed cookie to the lady.

"Do you want one?" the lady asked the old man next to her.

"No, that's OK." His hand flapped up.

"I'm bringing my father up from Duluth for a visit," the lady said. She wore a fuzzy peach cardigan. "Does your family eat turkey all year around?"

"Uh, no," Maureen replied. She wasn't fond of turkey, having watched the turkey trucks at the edge of town. Her brother Lyle called them tumbrels because the gobblers were going to the chopping block. "We ate a lot of stuffing this year. They just started making it. My dad said they have to run things like clockwork."

"I guess. The timing a turkey dinner needs," the lady said and then she turned to her father. "It *is* just dried bread. They have to preserve it though."

"The room where they make it is like the inside of a clock," Maureen said.

"So how does your family decide who gets to pull the wishbone?"

"We take turns. This Christmas, my brothers, my sister, and me were all wishing the same thing. We got into a fight about who had the strongest wish power. Once, one of my brothers wished to be noticed and the next day, he was in the newspaper. Walking near the turkey mascot. The other one can Indian wrestle better."

"Did you get your wish?" The lady had a mole the size of a watermelon seed on her jaw.

"I don't know yet," Maureen said. When Hugo tugged off the long end of the wishbone, he looked as grim as he had when some girls elected him vice-president of the Luther League.

Listening, Joann stiffened. She would have to be superficial if she gave her children their wish. Clive wouldn't keep up his role in such a household skit. It would only become a canker of dishonesty to him and then the trouble would begin, spilling in a concentric way that involved the whole family.

Experienced at keeping her body inert, Joann wondered what else Maureen would say outside the house. Maureen was more easily awakened than the other kids. She was the first to find her mother exiled to the couch, bucked out of her own bedroom. "Daddy's been exhausted lately," Joann explained.

Maureen should understand. Her room adjoined the room of her domineering sister and she was barred from the upstairs domain of her brothers. But her father renting a place of his own wasn't fair. When he came over unexpectedly one night, Maureen discovered them clasped in their inconsistent way. Leery, Maureen counted the ties that were still in the bedroom closet.

The incompatibility went as deeply as their concepts of love. Clive thought marriage should be second nature. They should be correlated like a clock with bells, chimes, cuckoos. She was stupid. *He* was unstable. They couldn't love each other anymore but the question was, did they ever? So there were rotations to the couch, to another bedroom, similar to the rotations Clive arranged for workers who wearied of the slaughter room.

"But how would Santa have your house key?" the woman across the aisle was asking.

Maureen was telling her father's explanation of Santa Claus. Of course a fat man with a weakness for sweets couldn't fly the entire United States in one night. Claus was a corporation of uniformed look-alikes reporting to the North Pole. Maureen finished, "I thought I would hear him this year because I hear when my father comes at night."

Joann would have to broach the subject soon after they arrived. There was no refuge, no hiding out. The week would be glum, her father's "I told you so's" overriding everything. She had eloped.

"Santa is still magic to me because I haven't caught any of his look-alikes at night," Maureen said.

The bus was slowing as she told about her bell-ridden stocking. Amidst the serene, virgin snow, the bus sidled at a snowdrift and then it abruptly stopped. Maureen's slip in conversation wasn't the pressing riddle anymore.

The bus driver heaved on his jacket and then he pulled on a wool hat. But he belied his helplessness, sitting again to try the starter. It only gurgled. "It's engine trouble, Folks. Fifteen miles to the next town."

Already, the below zero weather possessed the bus. Maureen put on her coat and then her mother found her muffler.

In a huffy voice, the lady across from them asked her father if he could eat a sandwich. The boy yelped to the bus driver and then he was stifled. When the bus driver spoke again, Joann crushed Maureen against her long camel coat. Joann could withstand cold the way a camel withstood the desert.

"Folks, another bus is due for Duluth in about an hour. I expect a patrol car before then. Anyone needing special attention to their health should go with them."

Maureen's mother sat stoically as the cougher behind them rasped and the lady across the aisle shrieked about her frail father. Maureen wriggled, watching the bus driver going out to the engine. Down the aisle, the knitting woman draped something over the coughing girl. The boy had turned into a ghoul, wearing a stocking mask. Other passengers sat like people at church, hearing that they were sinners.

"I had to talk Eeyore into coming on this bus," Maureen said.

Her mother sat attentively but her eyes flared. *The look of the martyr*, her father said.

Growing numb, Maureen couldn't look at her picture anymore, the colorful bus and the highway a rainbow in the dark. She felt she was being made into someone more like her mother, like her grandparents with their self-made furniture and their lace. Maureen didn't think of her grandparents as being married. They went on like trees without leaves. A stocking doll with a fishing pole stayed year-round in their boathouse, never known to complain like Eeyore. If Maureen's father found out about this, he would probably yell.

When the bus driver stamped his boots inside the bus again, a man's voice called hoarsely, "Any luck?" Then a flecked wool overcoat passed Maureen, that of the man who looked as if he were on his way to work. He told the bus driver that he worked with airplanes and then, putting some gruff into his voice, said, "Do you mind if I have a look at the engine?"

Maureen's mother glared at the two men as if they were to blame for the calamity and the cold. "It probably can't be repaired here. He's not a mechanic," she said. "You've spent a few hours in below zero weather."

"Only when there was a warming house," Maureen said.

Maureen's legs had gone from numb to stiff. The knitting woman was talking in high hysterical tones, tones like turkeys. She was telling about furnaces that quit in the winter and about building fires. When the bus driver stepped inside the bus again, the boy behind Maureen unleashed himself from his mother. Looking like a ghost that wanted its body back, he beseeched the driver to open up the luggage compartment.

A second pair of socks, her spare mittens, a sweater, Maureen reminded her mother. On someone else's feet, Maureen followed the boy and the smoker in his leather jacket. Outside, the glazed view demanded her to adjust. She didn't know where she was, only that she was somewhere between her father and her grandparents.

The boy had gotten words out of the man while his head was in the engine. The words came from the mouth opening of the boy's stocking hat, making white patches in the air. *Piston. Ring. Pin.*

Then the bus driver displayed the huge gray drawer where the luggage was kept. As the boy searched for his suitcase, Maureen saw how the moon was shaped like an egg in the glassy sky. She shuddered at its unbalanced position, that even the moon might have a great fall. Anything could break now. All the king's horses and all the king's men could wish on stars spread like wishbones while the earth turned cold.

"Can you see what you want?" the bus driver was asking Maureen.

"There." His flashlight halted at her sister Lydia's suitcase. Tan as farm eggs, it was balanced on heftier luggage.

Her mother helped her with the suitcase key and its cold latches. "Can you feel your feet?"

"A little," Maureen lisped. Numb was better than feeling now.

The bus's breakdown, this stranding, was all Joann needed to explain, and then with the word *marriage* substituted for the word *bus*. Her qualms seemed of secondary concern now. This was appalling but the misfortune would cause immediate comforting.

The hexed bus driver and the man who flaunted his expertise were lumbering in, probably defeated. Sick of seeing a man downcast and beaten,

Joann buttoned Maureen's coat over her second sweater.

Then the driver ground the starter as if he could drill for heat in the packed snow. Wallowing, the engine rolled over like a besotted man. And there was that too, how long people had to wallow, fizzling in misery.

But after the bus driver floored the accelerator, the bus transmitted a pulse. The exhaust raged open and the bus snarled into consciousness.

"Oh, I'm so glad. It's wonderful!" Joann Berwick cried, ecstatic with the other passengers. "We're moving!"

Lowering the visor of his winter hat, the hero made his way back to his seat. He was a genius, Maureen's mother said. He knew how airplanes were made. Maureen thought he looked ordinary for being the bus's wise man.

The boy was peeling off his ghost face. He chattered with the man's words as if they were a tinker toy riddle. *Bad installation. Pin. Piston. Ring. Slipped belt.*

As they swung into highway speed and the heat became tantalizing, passengers actually clapped their smarting hands.

"Are you feeling alright?" Maureen's mother asked.

"He must have known the bus engine like the inside of a clock," Maureen said. Her toes were beginning to hurt.

"The way a clockmaker knows a clock. Do you know what's in a clock that makes it go? An escapement," her mother said.

Maureen was tugging off her second pair of mittens when something flew out, flicked her mother, and landed on Eeyore. It was the long side of the broken wishbone from Christmas. Hugo let her keep it. Their table was shaped like an egg and each of them sat around it like a number on a clock, the whole family.

"What does Eeyore have there?" Maureen's mother asked.

"His pout. It fell off," Maureen said. She put the broken wishbone back in a mitten. "Eeyore has a riddle. He says, 'Is a family more like a clock or like Humpty Dumpty?'"

Her mother hesitated. "I don't know. Maybe it depends on how a family is made." Her face looked numb, as if she weren't happy anymore about going on, as if she weren't sure where they were going.

3   Eggs in a Basket

The weekend of a swimming meet, 1966. Maureen's father said the name of the restaurant, "Rudolpho's", in a soaring voice. It was painted in orange spaghetti letters above its entrance at the edge of Owatonna.

Rudolpho had charcoal hair like her father's. "Are you going to have some spaghetti and meatballs?" he greeted them.

"How many times have you had real spaghetti, Maureen?" Her father's voice in public reminded her of Bay Rum.

"I only had it once. At Dee Dee Guccinni's house. Unless you count Mom's," Maureen mumbled above the checked tablecloth. Her mother was an officially divorced woman now and she would think they were pushing checkers forward with Catholics. She put her sunglasses on. Her father was going to drink a glass of wine.

"Dee Dee and Maureen are both swimming in the meet this weekend."

There was lemonade on the menu. Maureen stared at the photographs on the wall – the leaning tower of Pisa, a silo with people smiling in front of it, and President Kennedy, dead now.

"Are you going to eat spaghetti with sunglasses on?" Rudolpho inquired.

"My eyes are sensitive from chlorine," Maureen said. Since the divorce, people were always peering at Maureen to see if she had been crying. Because she swam a lot, she often looked as if she had been crying.

"For crying out loud!" her father exploded. "Can Maureen eat all of that?"

Already, a teenage girl was putting plates of spaghetti before them. Meatballs perched on it like the ratted curls on the girl's head.

"Are the other swimmers coming tonight?" the girl wondered.

"They're still swimming," Clive Berwick said. "Maureen's done for the day. She swam the backstroke in a relay."

He was as jovial as he used to be, telling about being a lieutenant in Italy. If his voice didn't have alcohol in it, he skipped the entire war and described its happy ending – feasts that lasted until midnight. Now that Maureen's mother worked in the public library, her father came over with his Bay Rum voice and only for the pineapple upside-down cake. He discussed

Maureen and how she was caught filling out a questionnaire in a women's magazine.

"I thought she liked looking at the photographs," her mother said, frowning.

Talking about Maureen, they agreed on something. She should go out for swimming. She floated on water like cranberries at harvest time. Her brother Lyle dove for the summer municipal team and her friend, Dee Dee Guccinni, could cause a ten-year-old tidal wave.

"Repeta per favore. Catch-a tori." Maureen's father was showing off his Italian for the waitress. "It's easier to read a spaghetti menu than a magazine for women."

When Rudolpho wasn't looking, Clive cut some of Maureen's spaghetti. "During the War, I watched the Italian women in their kitchen. They were sculpting pasta into all shapes and sizes. Sizes to fit on your fork."

He showed her how to loop the smaller strands onto her fork and told her about Italy. He hadn't planned on returning to farming country until he stayed with a family there. He wanted to invent, having begun a course in engineering. But the inventions of the Germans made him as jittery as people in Wanatin could become.

He couldn't say how he began to drink, fifteen years into his marriage. Other men drank and on Sundays, they went dazed to church. The first church in the Bible was like a brass slaughterhouse where priests twisted the sacrificial bird's neck just so. Wanatin children were told how well turkeys were treated before being trucked into town.

Even though Wanatin was like provincial European life, he felt like the Grim Reaper when he had the jitters. Clive hadn't planned to stay there long. He was promoted quickly but that lead to a psychiatrist, then a marriage counselor, and finally, they'd trapped him. He slipped in the management drift while men above him squabbled like turkeys about future farms, warehouses of livestock instead of "Turkey in the Straw."

"I'll bet you haven't had real spaghetti for a while," he said. Maureen begged her mother for it after she ate it at the Guccinni's. Poor Chef Boyardee had been found out for mixing tomato soup concentrate with limp pasta.

"Not since…" Maureen stopped because her mother hadn't made spaghetti since her father ate dinner at home. "Mom says that Italians make spaghetti. There were Italians up north when she was young."

"That's right. But they didn't eat in courses like the people I knew in Italy," Clive quoted his ex-wife.

When Maureen became a backseat grocery cart pusher, Joann relented and made real spaghetti. She distributed handfuls of napkins with her tidy, herbless sauce.

They made a circuitous elopement that way. He had been recruited but when he met Joann's father, he might have been Italian. Joann was willful too and she didn't want to wait. It was as if they'd switched on the contraption he built in college, what produced eggnog without spilling any eggs.

Maureen was examining her spumoni ice cream. Her sunglasses were folded on the table.

"She's had a hard day, Rudolpho. Playing casino and eating frozen Snickers bars."

"Casino?"

"The card game. They don't bet." Soldiers played the card game in Italy when they didn't dare bet on the city Cassino. "We'll be back tomorrow night with the boys. That's a promise."

On the way back to Wanatin, the rows of corn were like seconds between the windbreaks of poplar.

"Your mother and I," Maureen's father began.

Maureen nodded. He probably wanted to explain more about the divorce.

"Your mother and I were separated during the War."

But the letters in their old scrapbook had romantic rhymes in them.

"I suppose nobody ever told you this. That Italy has the oldest swimming pools in the world. Romans built them and they also built canals to transport water."

Relieved at not having to follow her father's conversation like a windshield wiper, Maureen turned towards him. When he talked of the new arrangements, tears sometimes rolled down his face. He spoke of failure as if he and her mother were last in a race. But the answer was as simple as a mismatch. When her mother wore high heels, she was taller than her father.

Her parents attended a ceremony at the courthouse, the opposite of an elopement. After it, her mother drove out to the countryside by herself and screamed where there were only ears of corn to hear.

"I probably got my Roman nose from my Welsh side," her father continued. "You see, Romans lived in England about the time of Jesus. They built swimming pools there too. Still, I've never seen a woman with a Roman nose."

Maureen laughed at his joke because his jokes were no longer like Don Rickles television jokes. Her father used to tell Norwegian jokes and when his voice veered with Scotch, he said that Grandpa Bensen was an old Viking who taught his daughter to enslave British men. Maureen had never seen anyone so angry until she watched the swimming coach thump back and forth on his thongs, blowing his whistle. That yanked boys out of the water so that they could hear his insults.

Her father continued, "Roman architecture, its bridges and buildings, is a grand example of human creation. When men aren't imitating nature, they create patterns of geometry – arches and cranes and revolving disks. Humans like order."

While her father talked, the road seemed like a factory line surrounded by crops and cows and fences. But he didn't tell about a widow who worked in the packaging department at Country's Plenty. He wrote rhymes during the War because he couldn't tell her mother what he was doing. Now he was telling Maureen about geometry because he couldn't say that he took a widow out dancing.

When they got back, Maureen's mother acted as if her father had taken her to Italy.

"Lyle's an egg in another basket today," he said.

Her mother's blue glance said that she understood. Clive felt better if his children didn't travel in the same car. It had to do with the War.

He left for his apartment, a somber place with burgundy furnishings. He no longer needed to lecture about the librarian's clutter in his house and how Joann should place ladles and stamps so that she didn't have to take extra steps.

The next day, Clive drove his kids and Dee Dee back to the meet.

"Breathe now. I'm passing on a two-lane highway. It's more important than passing a swimmer in the next lane." He inhaled. Lyle was scheduled for a back somersault that afternoon.

"At least we're not in a bus. All the eggs would be in one basket," Maureen giggled.

"Breathe, Cranberry," Lyle said, stretching his neck backwards. "Before the coach tells you to walk the plank," His best dives were back dives.

In the back seat, Dee Dee giggled with Maureen. "That guy on the green suburb team," she said. "He sways back and forth with his eyes closed. The city turkeys call him Twinkletoes."

"I saw him do a turkey dive," Lyle said. "Where did the green suits find those Amazon girls?"

"They don't look my age. At least you don't have to be bigger for diving, Turkey," Maureen said.

"No more calling people turkeys," Clive said. And Maureen knew he was fed up with it. So much that he would move if he could and travel for his visitations. He had threatened to apply to a dairy company or any company that would hire a man that left his wife and kids – a company run by a military man! "Dee Dee, does it help to breathe before you get on the racing block?"

"I feel like I've been shot when the gun goes off," Dee Dee replied.

"I can't think about breathing," Maureen said. "When I'm hunched up for backstroke starts."

"A boy hears his own breathing when he aims a rubber band," Clive answered. He had aimed airplanes like jacks into the sky and, in the way of boyish conquests, he wanted to learn sleight of hand. He was the turkey that didn't fly the airplane.

"There's Rudolpho's!" Maureen shouted.

"We're going there after the meet, aren't we?" Dee Dee chorused.

At the pool, Clive took his assignment from the coach, a history teacher with a sinewy British lip. He kept Lyle from any daredevil diving. Swaggering on his thongs, he was as trenchant with teenagers as a commander. After all, he knew a man who used stopwatches on the job. Clive had been timing moving objects ever since the Air Force.

"We'll have you at lane five during the boys' heats. I think Lyle's got a good judge for his back somersault today, Clive. I'm sorry we've had so many twist experts lately."

"In and out of school," Clive replied.

Warming up, the swimmers bounded like dolphins in the Mediterranean. The coach answered him with his sensible smirk. The sort of man Joann thought she was marrying before she met Clive's Welsh mother, a woman who was suspicious of decorating plans when half the world had crumbled.

"Let's get the ropes ready," the coach said.

Clive and the other fathers took their places, preparing for the parade of swimmers that would take the ropes across the pool. Where was Lyle? Playing dead, stretched out on the low diving board. Didn't the coach ever get scared?

Maureen didn't look like a mermaid but when she was submerged in the aquamarine water, she felt like one. In the wading pool downtown, she used to walk to the center where she was almost underwater. Once, she dipped beneath the surface and stayed where the sunshine was dreamy instead of glaring. The wading pool lifeguard, a hefty woman who probably lost her husband, lugged her into the air where happiness and sadness were separated.

She was scheduled to compete in the 50-meter backstroke. When she came up for air, an annoying boy was in her way, burping his warm-up backstroke. If there were underwater swimming races, Maureen might win one, she thought, diving into the water again. But then she saw a circle of feet and, not wanting to pop into the midst of big suburban girls, pivoted towards the pool edge. Emerging, she burst into the boy as he threw himself backwards in a backstroke start. Something solid hit Maureen's front teeth.

"You bit my back!" the boy spat out under his white-painted nose.

Maureen dove away and then she stretched herself into a dead girl's float. She had never won a swimming race, not like the oldest girl on the Wanatin team. Their star swimmer developed biceps from swimming the butterfly. Once when she burst up from the water, her suit strap slipped, showing that she was a grown-up girl, not Tarzan. The older boys just laughed at her. They didn't date her, not even after the coach sneered at girls who traded in their tank suits for bikinis. Maureen and Dee Dee couldn't laugh at the boys and their scant suits unless they were in the locker room. It all made Maureen wonder if it worked out to win. She watched her tall mother win a house and self-respect when other people thought she had failed or lost.

Dee Dee already had a banana Popsicle when Maureen shambled out of the pool.

"It's good luck! A banana Popsicle before the race," she said.

They skimmed a cooler across the lawn that sloped into a park. Under their team tent, they arranged their towels respectfully near two teenage boys, Fallen Arches and The Statue. Maureen put on her cat sunglasses and listened to Fallen Arches, the sauntering lifeguard who would be 4-F in running sports.

"After the swim meet, we're going to Rudolpho's for spaghetti. Is your car going?"

Maureen acted as if she were underwater, deaf to Fallen Arches. She drank her pop and wondered about his real hair color. Chlorine made his hair glamorous, streaked like tinsel.

"I don't know," the Statue spoke. "I guess it depends on Coach's mood." He was often mute, awesome on his lifeguard pedestal.

Because Dee Dee was getting somewhere as an athlete, she stood up and stared at the card game.

"I said I might drive over to Janine's tonight," Fallen Arches said. "She came over with the chip cookies."

Maureen refrained from turning her head. The chip cookies were like a racer, passing her.

"She had on her red pedal pushers. Hey, did you notice the arches on the Torpedo? Do you think that's why his turns are so good?"

"Any excuse, Fallen Arches," the Statue replied, flipping a card. "Those girls wearing red with their old excuse. Any excuse is a loser, coach says. That Torpedo's got a jag in his stroke."

Having finished her Popsicle, Dee Dee started jumping around and flinging her fingers to loosen up. "How can you just sit there and breathe, Maureen?" she demanded.

"She's the cranberry," The Statue said, exhilarating Dee Dee. "Too bad swimmers can't get anywhere with a bunt, huh Maureen? Hey, Dee Dee. Maybe we can get you a brown hula skirt and you can be the turkey mascot."

"Dee Dee. Don't waste your energy."

The coach had come with his pep talk. His personality had little pep in it but at the frill of the tent where he stood with his arms crossed, he kept his eyes on swimmers.

"If I think about breathing, I can't breathe!" Dee Dee complained. "What do you think about, Maureen?"

"I think about supper later. Spaghetti. Spumoni ice cream. Get there first." Maureen opened her mouth with boldness because Fallen Arches and the Statue were playing casino, the game Maureen's brother taught them.

Dee Dee screamed, to the coach's disgust.

"Dee Dee, you're on the block in fifteen minutes," he said.

"Maureen's got blood in her mouth!" Dee Dee screamed again.

Startled, the lifeguards leapt towards Maureen only to find that they didn't know whether she needed a doctor or a dentist.

Maureen dabbed blood from her tongue to her finger. "It doesn't hurt," she said.

"Get to the starting block, Dee Dee," the coach said. "One swimmer out is enough."

"I saw the boy. The boy who hit her," Dee Dee cried.

"They might be dead," a dentist muttered with dental chair confidentiality.

Nerves in Maureen's teeth were possibly damaged. Dead teeth could mean root canals, perhaps darkened teeth. The teeth weren't broken.

"It doesn't even hurt!" Maureen protested.

"Dead teeth," murmured The Statue. He had found a dentist in one of the tents.

Clive had to give Maureen's mother the bad news. While they drove back, he would worry about Lyle and his back somersault.

Lyle was saying, "At least all the eggs aren't in one basket. Gees, injuries like that usually happen to divers."

Clive was the one to say that! He was the one who sent a planeload of paratroopers over Sicily when the air was swimming with Nazis. All the boys went down as if it were natural to shoot down the ones you know. That blue disillusionment, his wife saying, *You're wrong.* As if everything he did was wrong. *You weren't the one who gave those orders,* she said after the psychiatrist discovered his guilt.

"You promised that we'd go to Rudolpho's!" Maureen said. "It doesn't even hurt."

He extended his service in Italy. They'd watched one of their oldest monasteries demolished by Italians when there wasn't a Nazi in it.

"We'll go another time."

He'd wanted to go down alone. He'd felt that the entire family would go down if they all stayed in one house.

Between the garlic bread and the minestrone, the antipasto and the spaghetti, the shrimp and veal, the ricotta cake and the fresh fruit, during the wine and the wine and the wine, he forgot about any scheme of sacrifice as a young widow did. She knew what kind of hero he was and how a broken spirit couldn't be resurrected to its former state. He couldn't even watch his son dive this afternoon. Still, he wasn't very efficient at leaving behind what could be annihilated in the air he breathed.

4   Rite of Spring

Spring, 1968. Lying out in the sun with her new best friend, Maureen heard a rolling pin thud from the Magnuson's kitchen window.

"I invited Heidi to the bunking party," Jayne said, twirling a picked pink tulip on her lawn chair. "I suppose the white rabbit won't be able to come."

"She could hardly go to the Mad Hatter's tea party, missing rehearsals," Maureen said. As Alice's sister, Maureen could skip some of the *Alice in Wonderland* rehearsals. But she had inherited her Grandma Bensen's Brownie camera and practicing, she took pictures of the seventh grade cast.

"Heidi's mother really is The Wicked Witch of the West." Jayne peered beyond her backyard, not caring if her mother heard this from the kitchen. Heidi lived down their block.

"She's been a scared rabbit since grade school." Maureen recalled waiting outside the school door with Heidi after lunch one spring day. Heidi must have walked home and walked right back. Maureen ate in the cafeteria after her mother went to work at the public library. That day, she didn't think she needed a coat but the weather turned chilly. They were supposed to stay on the playground. When a cold rain shower started, Maureen opened the door and tried to talk Heidi into waiting inside with her. But Heidi mutely remained where she was.

"A rabbit with a sunburn," Jayne said. "Her mother used to slap her so much that she had welts."

"Is that why?" Maureen was stunned.

"My mother reported her. It's been better since the social worker visited their house."

Sizzling sounded from the kitchen. Mrs. Magnuson probably never screamed at Jayne. Her nonchalant, dreamy mind seemed to dwell on Mr. Magnuson, the town's soft water provider.

Jayne's smile was like her father's, sudden and intact when a minute before, she looked sullen. "Let me look at your ring again."

Maureen put a plum-colored tulip across her legs and showed Jayne her braided silver ring. Roy Von Fischer put the ring in one of the letters he mailed into Maureen's locker. They sat next to each other in the back row of Mr. Gleason's science class where Maureen found out that Roy's IQ was one point higher than hers, comparing home room forms. Since the play, she sat next to him at Saturday matinee movies.

Jayne was still playing musical chairs at the matinees although last Saturday, she sat next to Cal McConkey, one of the cutest guys in their class. "I don't think Cal will give anybody a ring," she said, sullen again. Spindly and taller than most boys, Jayne played the caterpillar in *Alice in Wonderland*.

"We'd better go and get ready," Maureen said, beginning to put on her blouse and jeans over her bikini. The Saturday matinee started at two and they were picking up Dee Dee and Betty. Dee Dee played the Mad Hatter in the play and Betty was the Duchess.

It didn't matter to Jayne if her mother heard them. Mrs. Magnuson once shared rooms and rent with working girls in Minneapolis. Jayne could tell her about the movie matinees and how they sat boy-girl, girl-boy, watching a grab-bag of failed films. Mrs. Magnuson probably knew that Maureen was going steady.

"It's such a nice day. Are you going to sit in a dark theater?" she asked them. Her voice sounded as if she'd been eating honey.

Jayne nodded and Maureen looked into a salad bowl. Green olives were in Mrs. Magnuson's coleslaw. "You don't put mayonnaise in your coleslaw?" she said. She and her sister Lydia were making dinners that summer.

Mrs. Magnuson pulled a dish from the cupboard, perhaps hoping to waylay them. "Would you like to try it? I found the recipe a long time ago. When I worked in a store that sold radios." She helped Mr. Magnuson downtown with his soft water accounts.

Mrs. Magnuson liked to tell about her life in Minneapolis. It sounded as strange as a caterpillar's but with her dark auburn hair, she was more like a moth than a butterfly.

"Did you get a commission?" Maureen asked to egg her on.

"No. I worked in the backroom with the bookkeeping." she said, "When the war ended, I had to train in a man. I was without a job for a while. I couldn't afford meat." She rolled her ever-present cigarette in her kitchen ashtray.

"You must have been good at math," Maureen said, puzzled. In Wanatin, the fathers usually complained about the hard times they endured.

As Maureen tried coleslaw doused in oil and vinegar, Jayne left the room. But she soon returned with a piece of notebook paper that she slapped on the kitchen table. "You know Mr. Gleason, our science teacher?"

Mr. Gleason's overhanging eyebrows made him suspect for being the missing link man. They were doing a unit on transformations - caterpillars into butterflies, nymphs into dragonflies, tadpoles into frogs, and the evolution of man.

Jayne explained the stages of man in her homework: *They have not found that Neanderthal man changed into Cro-Magnon man. But they found the bones of ogres, giants, and creeps. Others grew wings. The scientists dug up rings and bells from their fingers and ankles. The fairies cremated at their funerals so they didn't leave any skeletons.*

"Look at my score. Ten out of ten. I got full credit," Jayne gloated.

Mrs. Magnuson was nonplussed.

While Jayne changed into her bell bottoms, Maureen used the downstairs bathroom to comb her hair and put on frosty lipstick. She wondered about the Magnuson's more than Mr. Gleason. Jayne's family could move over to Lombardy, the nicer side of town, if Mrs. Magnuson wanted.

Living near the river and Baisley Park, Jayne was a park ringleader. Maureen got to know her at the swings when they took off from picnic tables. She knew the boys who played baseball, Cal McConkey and his gang.

The park neighborhood was only four blocks from Maureen's house. Three-story brick and Victorian houses lined Maureen's street to Baisley Hill. Beyond that were houses built for the workers at Country's Plenty. Near the river, many of the houses were close-set and clapboard.

Jayne lived in a chrysalis compared to most of her friends. Heidi's mother was a case. The well-groomed Betty was one of ten children in a house sided with tattered, glittery gray shingles. Their living room usually looked like a laundry service. Dee Dee shared the second floor of her house with five brothers and sisters. The first floor was full of musical instruments because her father directed the high school band. Maureen had enough room but her parents were divorced.

Since the play, they met boys at the Lombardy Plaza movie theater, often boys from the Lombardy side of town. Roy lived over there. Two weeks ago, they played touch football on a vice-president's lawn and since then, the vice-president's son "liked" Dee Dee. One of his friends held Betty's hand while a Cyclops tossed bodies around on the screen.

The next time Maureen went over to the Magnuson's, she avoided the river road. She was surprised that the bunking party was still on.

After the Saturday matinee, Jayne was walking alone on that road when a man called to her from his car, wanting directions. He called from the open window at the passenger side and then he yanked open the door, asking her to sit on the car seat. Jayne ran behind his car, memorized his license plate, and then she kept running.

Mrs. Magnuson called the police and Jayne had a conference with the school principal. Everyone Jayne knew was looking for a beer-bottle brown Dodge with the license number she memorized.

"My mother said it *would* happen to me," Jayne said. "When we went shopping in Minneapolis, she showed me where she used to live." Jayne described a building that looked as yellowed as the teeth of a cigarette smoker. Windows in the neighborhood were boarded up. "She roomed with a telephone operator and a lawyer's stenographer. The stenographer didn't know she was dating a married man until his wife turned up at the sidelines of a tennis game. And he was some kind of tennis champ."

Besides feeling bad about Jayne walking alone, Maureen had to keep Jayne's party idea a secret.

"Did you walk over here alone?" Mrs. Magnuson asked when Maureen showed up for the party first.

"I'm helping Jayne get ready," Maureen replied, unloading her sleeping bag and Lydia's album, *Surrealistic Pillow.*

Mrs. Magnuson put out her lipstick-smeared cigarette and led Maureen to their TV room where Jayne was sitting with her father and her older brother.

"Do you think Jayne will turn into a butterfly or a moth?" Mrs. Magnuson wondered.

In the light of their color TV, Jayne's frosty lipstick was chartreuse. Besides that, she resembled a caterpillar, wearing a quilted robe and bristle rollers in her hair. The drama teacher turned Jayne into a silk-spinning caterpillar instead of having her smoke a water pipe.

"I think her teachers know that butterflies don't spin silk," Mr. Magnuson said in his teasing singsong.

"Maybe a Luna moth," Mrs. Magnuson replied.

Sassy as her father, Jayne gave her instant dimpled smile.

Her brother looked up and said, "You could turn her science teacher in to the principal. Giving Jayne a ten for putting creeps into evolution."

"They might think she's the girl who called wolf," Mr. Magnuson warned, mild as ever. "Think about all the homework Mr. Gleason has to correct."

"How many of those looking glass girls are invading our house?" Jayne's brother demanded.

"Seven instead of six," Jayne said. "We had to ask Char."

Char played Alice. Alice had two songs in the play and Char had the soprano voice that swelled and fluttered. Maureen's mother said that Char looked like the girl who inspired *Alice in Wonderland.* But Char was the biggest joke. At the Saturday matinees, she sat near the seventh graders with an older boy, her date. When the movie was boring, everyone watched Char. Her date usually felt her up at least once.

"Soft water would be good for Char's voice," Mrs. Magnuson said.

"She'll try anything," Jayne replied.

"At least she's not trying to be skinny like that model, Twiggy," Mrs. Magnuson said. "I can't imagine why anyone would want to look as if they were starving."

After they brought Maureen's sleeping bag to the basement, Jayne said, "Roy wants to marry you."

"In a play wedding," Maureen retorted. She didn't know how it started. The girls with steady rings were going to be in a play wedding ceremony.

Jayne arranged the bunking party entertainment in the cafeteria after Maureen told her about going to Roy's house on Saturday night. Roy was weird, maybe because his real name was Royce. He liked kissing Maureen's earlobes and then he started playing with her shoes. He took them off but then he found a hole in one of her stockings. "I'd like to take care of you," Roy said.

"I wish we lived a hundred years ago," Jayne said in the cafeteria. She and Maureen were both reading *Pride and Prejudice*. It was only five days since the man in the beer-bottle brown car wanted directions.

The other girls wanted to do the play weddings. What was really a gas was that the boys who gave steady rings agreed to be in a pretend ceremony.

"I'm going to be the minister," Jayne decided.

The Magnuson's had a typewriter in their basement and Jayne had already typed three marriage licenses - Maureen's, Dee Dee's, and Betty's. She only had to do Heidi's. Heidi was going steady with the only boy in the play, the Knave of Hearts. She usually left her ring in her locker and so far, she could come to the bunking party.

"Jayne, are the snack tables ready?" Mrs. Magnuson called from the kitchen.

Maureen shook out paper tablecloths and then she set out paper cups and plates on two card tables. Jayne put the licenses in her windbreaker.

Upstairs, Maureen felt as if the sleek lines of her bell bottoms were forming an evening gown. After Dee Dee and Betty arrived, she sat with them on Mrs. Magnuson's couch. It was creamy with damask catalpa blossoms. They all stared longingly at the Magnuson's stereo.

"Are you taking your windbreaker, Jayne?" they heard Mrs. Magnuson ask Jayne in the kitchen.

Jayne answered her with a yank of aluminum foil.

"Did I ever tell you about the night I didn't take a wrap for a date?" she said to Jayne.

"Uh uh." Jayne came to the open kitchen door and winked at them.

Betty and Dee Dee nudged each other because Mrs. Magnuson

treated her daughter like a girlfriend.

"I couldn't decide what dress to wear for a week."

"You wore a dress on a date?" Jayne asked as water gushed.

"I wore all the wrong things. A blouse that showed my shoulders. Open-toed shoes. I didn't know where we were going until I got into the sedan."

The Magnuson's garbage disposal gurgled. When it stopped, Dee Dee was laughing. Jayne's mother once dreamed of being in radio plays.

"Was it Dad?"

"No, honey. I hadn't met your father yet. This date was the nephew of the man who owned the radio store. He was wearing his college sweater because we were going to a country club. The dancing was outside." Silverware sounded as if it were shivering. "My shoulders were so cold that it looked as if I was wearing dotted Swiss. So my date let me wear his sweater. In those days, wearing a guy's sweater meant that a girl was going steady. But after a while, he was shivering for all his chivalry. You just don't know when the weather's going to change."

The girls on the couch covered up their Woolworth rings. Then the doorbell rang and the other girls brought in their sleeping bags.

"Where are you going?" Mrs. Magnuson asked after they returned from the basement. She was pulling a record out of her console.

"The Dairy Queen," Jayne said.

When Perry Como crooned "Don't Let the Stars Get in Your Eyes", Mr. Magnuson came in from the TV room in his stocking feet. He and Mrs. Magnuson danced and then they made finger waves at the girls.

Maureen went straight to bed after she got home from the bunking party. When she woke up, her mother and Lydia were waiting with the play marriage license. She'd tucked it into her sleeping bag.

"What does this mean?" her mother demanded.

"Nothing. It was just for play," Maureen said.

But Joann Berwick didn't want to hear any explanation. Maureen could hear her calling Mrs. Magnuson in the dining room. "Was Maureen at your house last night?" she said in her stricken divorced voice.

The play ceremony was on the steps of an Episcopal Church, one block away from the shopping plaza. Its entrance was thickly terraced with juniper and cedar so that they were shrouded in the dusk. The other girls were bridesmaids except for Char who sang the Beatles song, "Do You Want to Know a Secret?" When she got to the line, "I'm in love with you", the boys started laughing and the play was over.

When Maureen's mother returned, Lydia tore up the play license for her.

"You didn't call anyone else, did you?" Maureen asked, fearing that her mother called Roy's mother.

"Where were you last night?" her mother demanded, still dumbfounded.

At 9:30, they were all back at the Magnuson's. Mrs. Magnuson showed them the shag dance and Mr. Magnuson made a boyfriend of himself. "What did Mrs. Magnuson say?" Maureen asked.

"She drawled. She said all the girls were at her house, dancing to the record player downstairs. She said that she was awake most of the night and that she checked on you from the kitchen."

Joann was so angry that she made Maureen give her the steady ring. In chagrin, Maureen called Jayne.

"Stay on the phone in case anyone else calls," Jayne said. "At least Heidi left her license at our house. But my mother found Char's bra in the freezer. She was eavesdropping."

"Char was so loud," Maureen said. "I thought she took it out of the freezer."

Char had the biggest bra. After she put on her nightgown, the other girls confiscated it and dangled it from the basement ceiling light. Then they danced in a ring around the bra and sang a new song from the album that Maureen brought - "White Rabbit." "One pill makes you larger", they chanted, but they changed the last line to "Ask Alice, when she's D-cup large."

Char's shrieks surmounted the singing, her voice mature and rapturous. They danced like nocturnal moths around a streetlight. After they spread out their sleeping bags, Dee Dee doused Char's bra in water and stuck it in the Magnuson's freezer.

"Char left without her bra," Jayne said. "She went home bra-less! It wasn't in the fridge."

"Where was it?"

"It was hanging in the downstairs bathroom."

"Did you tell your mother why we made fun of her?"

"My mother knows why," Jayne said.

"My marriage is annulled," Maureen informed Jayne. "And I have to return the ring to Roy. I'm grounded."

"Do you think your mother will tell Dee Dee's mother?" Jayne asked.

"No. She's too ashamed. She knows we didn't do anything."

5   Lydia's Leave-taking

Ninth grade, 1969. A burglar banging at the back door was far-fetched, especially in Wanatin. Maureen stood at an impasse, ready to call the police. Just a few minutes ago, a strange man had come to the front porch and that made her scream in an unfamiliar voice - primeval and before towns. Before cameras, she realized, running for hers. The other day, Maureen's mother shushed her out of the living room because a stranger in a dark suit was visiting. Afterward, Joann walked around as if she were Mrs. Hitchcock and having an affair with Rod Serling.

Only the females inhabited the Berwick house now that Hugo and Lyle were in Minneapolis, Hugo at a Lutheran college and Lyle at the university. Maureen's father hadn't visited for weeks because he married the widow who worked in packaging at Country's Plenty, Poppy.

With relief, Maureen opened the back door for Lydia. She was pummeling it as if it wouldn't admit her ironed hair, her hippie beads, and her odd odors.

"Why was the door locked?" Lydia demanded. "*Don't* take a picture of me."

"A man was sneaking around," Maureen answered. "He came in the front porch and put his face at the porch window!"

The dauntless Lydia went straight to the front porch. "Maureen, it must have been Mr. Tollefson. Joyce's father."

Since Hugo's first year of college, he had become steady with Joyce Tollefson. This year, they were unoffically engaged.

"He left this box for Joyce. Hugo is coming down from Minneapolis." Lydia pointed to the box. "Mr. Tollefson drove all the way from his farm. You probably scared him."

Evenings had become the stuff of bunking parties. Lydia started making cream puff dough and after she baked blobs of it, Maureen would eat some of the hollowed-out insides.

Lydia was in danger of inflating like a cream puff. She had spent hours on a piano bench and then on the organ bench at the church, exercising her fingers. In high school, she dated only one boy, but when he serenaded her with a guitar, she treated him like a hymnal. At home, Lydia made bowling pin crashes when she played chords. Her first year at Wanatin's junior college, she tried out for the play *J.B.* and accepted the part of a prostitute. This year, Lydia went out with her psychology teacher. He hypnotized her in class and, even though he'd been warned about bringing students to his apartment, Lydia often came home in a trance.

As Lydia surfed whipped cream with the mixer, she said shrilly, "Are you going out to eat with Dad next weekend?"

Not that Lydia wanted to eat with Poppy. She refused to attend the small wedding.

"Poppy wants you to come," Maureen said, having to raise her voice.

"Dad's afraid I'll tell her about his drinking," the forthright Lydia said. She opened the kitchen window and took a cigarette out of her macramé purse. "Now that he's so dedicated to the Freemasons. And Poppy being a Job's daughter."

"Tucker's barking again."

When Joann Berwick came in, she sniffed for cigarettes, patchouli, and marijuana. Then she collected a cream puff.

"Maureen might have insomnia tonight," Lydia said. "She was scared of Mr. Tollefson. He left Joyce's box on the front porch."

"I didn't know what he looked like," Maureen said.

That fall, Maureen felt marooned after midnight. When she complained to her mother about it, Joann told her to clean out drawers or to paste Green Stamps in their books. One night, Joann sat up with Maureen, reading *Cannery Row* aloud. Then she made an appointment with a man not known to exist in Wanatin, a school psychologist.

After Maureen claimed that she was cured, Lydia wanted to tell Samuel, the psychology teacher at the junior college, about Maureen's session. She offered her two cream puffs. "I thought you couldn't sleep because of the *Look* war photographs. Or because of *Rosemary's Baby*," she said.

They were in the sunroom where the strewn fiction was no longer under their father's censorship. Maureen didn't tell Lydia that during her insomnia, when the night was like outer space and time slowed down, she knew that her birth was a mistake. Her mother confirmed that she was a mistake, born despite the rhythm method.

"What did you tell the psychologist?" Lydia prodded her.

"Nothing. I was only there for about fifteen minutes."

The school psychologist wasn't anything like Lydia's psychology teacher. He was short and his hair was sparse, like wires.

"Did you want Samuel to come over and say, 'Are you getting sleepy?'" Lydia accused Maureen.

"No! I didn't want to go to a psychologist. He asked me if Dad was re-married. Then he said I shouldn't bottle up my feelings."

Disappointed as if she were hearing old gossip, Lydia munched her cream puff.

Maureen told her the good part. "He asked me if I had any friends who were boys. Then he made a prediction. He said, 'You will probably have a boyfriend in the next two years.' And that week, I was asked to the Homecoming Dance."

"You can't go to Homecoming, Maureen. Ninth grade is technically junior high."

"I said no. To the dud, Sid Ciel from the swimming team. The one who has skull curls like Julius Caesar."

"He might have given you a French kiss," Lydia surmised.

Sid Ciel's last name was pronounced like an ocean mammal and he looked like one, clean-cut and known at school for his swimming and his grades in math. Maureen liked long-haired boys better. She liked Eugene McCarthy better than her father because he wanted to prevent the long-haired boys from going to Vietnam. If Sid came to their door, he might encounter Lydia in a bitchy mood and wearing a towel turban because she didn't feel like washing and ironing her hair. He'd probably encounter Maureen's mother, suspicious of him and shabbily dressed.

"Sid Ciel wouldn't have any fancy kiss," Maureen insisted.

"Don't you know what a French kiss is, Maureen?"

Maureen was so ignorant about the gastronomy of a French kiss that she gaped at Lydia's description. Mr. Tollefson might have stuck his head at the front door windowpane again. But Maureen's body was already honed into curves from swimming. And she smiled mysteriously as if she were the Mona Lisa, hiding grayed front teeth, her swimming injury.

"Why don't you get sleeping pills for Maureen?" Lydia asked their mother.

"I am not giving Maureen drugs."

"Everyone needs the sandman's sand," Lydia said. "Samuel says that they're like penicillin in a crisis. Nance's mother takes sleeping pills."

Nance also played a prostitute in *J. B.* When Lydia came home in a trance, she often said that she spent the evening at Nance's Lombardy house, listening to Steppenwolf.

"Artificial, expensive means are not for girls Maureen's age." Joann said, stoic as her cloud-watching Scandinavian father.

"Samuel could probably hypnotize Maureen."

There used to be coffee cake conversation between Lydia and her mother. That was before Lydia displayed her cream puff nourished cleavage on stage, one hand supporting her back as if she had been sleeping on desert sand. How the director wanted her to stand.

"Maureen has just started, Lydia."

"Started what? Menstruating? So what did *you* start? Masturbating?" Lydia was screaming. After her mother gaped and glared, she slammed the doors on the way to her bedroom. A door was Lydia's last word. Then Iron Butterfly bellowed out "In-a-Gadda-Da-Vida."

"Maureen, are you wearing Lydia's mascara?"

Timid to say what really disturbed her, Joann glared at the McCarthy buttons on Maureen's dark sweater. "I shouldn't let you go out like that!" But her voice was feeble.

"You're just unhappy because you don't have anything to do after the library is closed," Maureen countered.

The girls had come for Maureen. Although the Berwick's house was messy from melancholy and the space to spread that in, Jayne's dimples were off-the-record. Dee Dee inquired, "Are you going to listen to the game on the radio?" Her father's marching band would be on. The Guccinni's talked of divorce as if it were 5/4 time and atonal.

After they all said goodbye to Maureen's mother, the girls tramped through the crepe of maple leaves. They laughed about their new math teacher although he sent Maureen and Dee Dee to the principal's office. Dee Dee couldn't pronounce his name so she spread sneezes around the class, trying to. Maureen simply called him by his first name, Peter. After he complained that the two were walking over him the way Nancy Sinatra walked in her boots, they talked the other kids into outlining their shoes on a paper banner. Then they taped it above his chalkboard.

The boys in math class called Maureen "Candid Cheese" because she took pictures for the junior high newspaper. She was known for a close-up of a boy's sole and for the article, "Say No to Athlete's Foot." They called Dee Dee "Goose Lips" because she was the only oboe player in the band.

Because of that, the girls spent the first half of the football game behind the bleachers, getting to know some kids from the Aspen side of town. Maureen might take a cigarette from a tall boy with a name almost as hard to pronounce as Peter's – Czubinovski. Last summer at the county fair, he asked her to go on the parachute ride with him. Since, they stood in the school halls or at a football game, peering from behind blonde blinders. But Czub wasn't shy about calling Maureen on the phone. His older brother had a garage band and he whispered the numbers they played until Maureen laughed.

The crowd from the Aspen neighborhood called one another by last names. Zarvas' mother worked at Finch's Boutique downtown. Zarvas was jet-haired, spectral as a black and white TV, and she dated a boy who appeared to be prematurely adult. Her friend Ronning smuggled *I Am Curious Yellow* past Maureen's mother at the public library. Ronning wrote R-rated stories, the funniest about Burt from Burt's Burgers and how he prevented his wife, a movie magazine worm, from eating too many Cheetos. Maureen wanted to know if she could describe a French kiss.

After the game though, Maureen was walking with her regular friends to the logical place for ninth graders, the weekly Methodist church mixer. She and Czub hadn't gotten past cigarette smiles.

Dee Dee asked Maureen, "If we don't see anyone at the mixer, do you want to be a go-go dancer?"

"That's not why I'm wearing my Eugene McCarthy buttons," Maureen said.

Jayne hummed the Nancy Sinatra boots song.

In the Berwick's neighborhood, children regularly ran away. Like the others, Lydia once tied peanut butter sandwiches into a bandanna, tied the bandanna to a stick, and set out for Baisley Park. A wood-planked swinging bridge took her far from home.

While Nance whirled on a swinging gate covered with leaves, Lydia undid the paisley scarf that she was wearing as a headband. A baggie of marijuana flumped out of it. "Let's go down to the river. The weed looks like algae. One more thing would kill my mother."

"Step on a crack, break Mom's back," Nance said. "I've got to get out of this town too."

Nance's parents chaperoned her at the TV, especially when she watched the channel with the cola nut man commercial. She'd met a black man in Minneapolis when she stayed with some hippie friends there.

They sang "MacArthur Park" until the creek bank stretched like a road shoulder and the glimmers going downstream looked like car rooftops in the sun.

"I used to sing 'Moon River' here with Maureen," Lydia said. "Maureen was in love with Perry Como and Dad adored her. She might make more trouble than any of us."

"I'd probably cry if I sang 'Moon River'," Nance said.

To find out for sure, they fell on their backs and sang it. Lydia threw in an unsentimental syncopation and then, sobbing, she told Nance that she'd missed her period again. "I have to tell you about Samuel," she said.

In the junior college canteen that day, Lydia felt as if she and Samuel were sitting on a swinging bridge. Students were still ogling her for her performance under hypnosis. She heard it on tape:

I am six years old. I have all the little things. The little tea set is mine. I want more little books, not just Peter Rabbit. I have a little piano and the baby is mine. My cereal is the little box but my mom won't get me a little pint of milk. There is a small seed on a shelf. It's from a Chinese country. It has the littlest ivory animals in it. They run in the palm of your hand. I have hidden it.

In her mini-jumper and her Mary Jane heels, Lydia was ready to tell Samuel something that might really shock him. Some days, Samuel's hair seemed to recoil from his own thoughts.

"Me first," Samuel said. His sad smile seemed to concede that some things never change. "Lydia, when I was in graduate school, I had a girlfriend. Because of old times, out of a wish to get high, I visited her between terms. She's finishing her M.A. in Ohio. The other day, she called and asked me if I could see my anima. Remember the Jung anima? I thought she was high. It became a long blind call, full of speculation because she is pregnant. Amazing. She's sure that I'll recognize something of my hidden self in the child. Seeing her has kept me clear with the college officials."

Samuel had snapped Lydia out of a trance. He was like her father, phasing out workers from the gravy line.

"Don't you wish we could have a draw on a water pipe?" Samuel whispered so seriously that he might have been quoting Carl Jung. "I don't want to get married right now, Lydia. So what did you have to tell me?"

Lydia repeated what Nance said the last time they spiraled out of Nance's neighborhood. "I've decided to move to San Francisco. I'm going to drive out there at the end of the quarter. With Nance. We'll transfer after we get residence. I'm sorry, Samuel, but it's gotten pretty bad at home."

Hugo and Joyce were in the kitchen with Maureen's mother when Maureen came back from the mixer.

"Dee Dee and I danced the swim like go-go dancers," Maureen reported.

The screen door slammed like a grace note before the back door slammed shut. Coming into the kitchen, Lydia snapped at Hugo, "I suppose you ate all the drumsticks."

Hugo nodded no and began sorting old maids from the popcorn. Joyce kept crocheting an afghan.

They listened for the doors to slam, the bathroom door and then Lydia's bedroom door. Soon she was stamping back to the kitchen where she slammed the refrigerator door and settled herself at the kitchen table, eating a chicken drumstick.

"I'm going into the armed services," Hugo announced.

"I thought you might go to the seminary," Lydia paused. "If you could talk your way into it."

"The draft doesn't have to believe me either. Besides, I have loans to pay."

"The FBI contacted Hugo," Joyce said, hysterical.

"They were looking for Lyle," Hugo said.

"A man came here. You saw him, Maureen," Joann said. "It's because Lyle subscribed to *Pravda*, the Russian newspaper. I explained that he's taking a course in Russian at the university."

"Was that the man Maureen saw? As if Dad would have a communist son," Lydia said. "It's because Lyle went to the anti-war demonstrations in Chicago."

"Lydia, Hugo might want more chicken," Joann sniffed.

"My mother, the chauvinist," Lydia complained.

"You're getting fat, Lydia," Hugo observed.

"Just think," Lydia said airily. "If Hugo got killed in Vietnam, it's as if his country aborted him."

Joyce paused from the hobby that she referred to as her trousseau. She and Hugo were still members of the bobby sox party. Hugo was taking pre-seminary coursework and he helped a church with their Sunday radio broadcasts. Joyce and Hugo ate dinners with a church club.

Joann sniffed, commiserating with Joyce. Joann was like a knotty tree lately, not knowing which way to bend with the breezes.

"Do you have a cold, Mom?" Maureen said.

"Lydia, you've been smoking that stuff again!"

On Saturday, Lydia agreed to eat lunch with her father, Maureen, and Poppy at the Harvest House, a new restaurant that gripped an intersection of highway like a UFO.

"Lydia should try a club salad," Clive said. "It's Country's Plenty turkey. The croutons are fresh. Poppy supervises in packaging, you know."

After they ate, Poppy clasped a cigarette and flicked it into an ashtray tiled like Indian corn. Lydia lit up but she tapped her cigarette ash onto her dessert plate. She told her father, "First, a man from the FBI frightened Maureen because Mom didn't introduce him. Then Maureen thought Mr. Tollefson was a burglar. He was dropping off a box for Joyce."

"Where were you, Lydia?" Clive inquired evenly. His hair had more white in it than gray this year.

"I was discussing hypnosis for insomnia with my friend, Samuel."

"I thought that psychology teacher was disciplined for fraternizing with students."

"He can't have them over at his apartment," Lydia said.

"Did he really put you under or did you act?" Clive turned to Poppy. "My daughter can act."

"I went under." Lydia gazed at her father until he looked as if she had blown smoke into his eyes.

"A man who can put girls under like that," Poppy said. Her hair looked as glossy as cellophane and her clothes crackled when she moved.

Lydia missed the plate, her ash dripping onto the tablecloth. "No, I won't be seeing Samuel anymore."

They dropped off Poppy at Clive Berwick's new house, a puzzle brick bungalow on the Lombardy side of town.

At the old house, Maureen's father raked in the backyard. Until his wedding with Poppy, he tended his trellises of morning glory during his visitation. Hugo raked near him while Maureen carried dug-up bulbs to the basement. She returned with her camera, a Christmas present from her father.

"You might get some valuable experience in the military," Clive said for the second time, piling basswood leaves with his rake. "Be sure to tell them about your church involvement and your short wave radio. I'll bet they don't send you into combat."

Lydia came out of the house with Tucker. After she leashed the dog, she went up to her father and hugged him, startling them both. "I'm planning to drive out to Berkeley with Nance, Dad."

After the snapshots, Lydia went back inside, knowing that her father didn't believe her. She slammed doors all the way to her old room where she stayed until the end of fall quarter, tiptoeing around Maureen's insomnia to keep her mother company in the evenings.

6   Last Dive

September, 1970. The news was that Roland Werff had a crush on Maureen. Louise Ogland told Maureen about it in the school newspaper office after Roland told everyone in Louise's English class.

Louise was a new friend now that her parents had moved into a Victorian house two doors down the block from Maureen. The two picked up Jayne on the first Friday night after school started. Then they met Cal McConkey at the Cool Point in the Lombardy Plaza.

"You mean, you didn't remember Roland from the picture you took last spring?" he asked Maureen.

She'd taken a picture of the ninth grade baseball players but she didn't attend their games. "I've never been in a class with him," she said.

They were hoofing it to the Lombardy house of another baseball player, Dave Battaglia. Jayne and Louise wanted to know how Cal was preparing for his driving test.

When Dave joined them, he said, "My sister's home but she's going out. No one will be home in half an hour. Let's pick up Roland."

The boys jostled the girls along a road that rounded a creek and Clive Berwick's new house. Cal peered through the lawn willows as if he were watching a melodrama.

"My dad must be home," Maureen said. "Let's get going."

Jayne and Louise admired the snug puzzle brick and then Dave said, "We'll give Roland time to get ready. When I called, he was in his jammies, watching TV."

This made Louise shriek. It was only nine o'clock.

"He didn't think Maureen was coming. After she figured out who he was," Cal said. "He's got to get up tomorrow and work out at his uncle's farm."

This made Jayne laugh along with Louise.

Roland was in his garage, putting apples into a paper sack. He lived on Cedar Avenue, the widest street in Wanatin. Across it, floodlights from Our Lady Catholic Church and Gethsemane Lutheran shone, causing the plain green siding of the Werff house to look garish.

"You're going to chance it?" Dave Battaglia said, pulling an apple from the bag.

"Are we having an apple party?" Jayne wondered.

"They're windfalls," Roland said.

Then Cal led the girls across Cedar Avenue, his eyebrows lilting in the church lights. Under the luminous robes of Our Lady's, they watched Dave catch an apple as he ran towards the Lutheran line drawing of Jesus praying. Cal waved to Dave.

"Do you want to play catch or watch Roland throw?" Dave said.

Roland approached, holding an apple like a baseball. Coming through the lights, his eyes looked silver.

"It's a long fall season, forfeiting to the fricking football players," Cal said. As Roland turned and wound his arm, Cal called out, "Corvette!"

"The quarterback's helmet!" Dave yelled.

Roland took a step out of the shadows, wound up again, and then he slung the apple as the Corvette whizzed to the outskirts of town, where Cedar Avenue turned into Interstate 90. A metallic impact followed.

"The fender! Strike!" Cal called, having run out towards the curb.

"I didn't believe it. They told me about this in class," Louise said.

Then another apple ricocheted.

"Foul!" Dave yelled. "It's low."

Maureen watched a Chevy slow down. At least the license plate wasn't a Minnesota one.

"Another low one," Cal warned.

Roland wound up and stepped towards the lights.

"This one's gonna bunt," Dave warned.

"That's my brother's new car! Used car!" Maureen shrieked.

They watched the blue Volkswagen slowing down but then Louise screamed.

"Shut up, Louise," Roland said.

The hood of a police car was creeping out of a side street. Because Louise wasn't Catholic, she ran to the Catholic Church and disappeared into it. Maureen and Jayne followed, relieved that the boys weren't behind them. They knew the neighborhood.

Prostrated under a dark pew, Maureen could hear Louise praying. Behind the next pew, Jayne pulled a kneeler down.

"Louise, there's enough room for you to lie down!" Jayne interrupted her.

Hearing the sanctuary door open, Louise rolled under a pew and pulled a kneeler down. Footsteps clicked along the main aisle and back again, hushed as an usher's. The beam of a flashlight roamed.

Finally the footsteps waned, a door swung shut, and Maureen lay paralyzed in five long minutes of silence. Then Jayne whispered, "It was a policeman."

Louise crept out and sobbed at a kneeler, "Oh God, we're innocent!"

While Louise prayed, Jayne ducked down a pew. "What if they come back?" she whispered.

"They knew a guy threw the apples," Maureen said. She felt like a snake, lying on her stomach.

Contrite, the girls eventually crept to the nave and stood in shadows near a huge basin of holy water. They'd seen the basins in the summer, giant birdbaths to the Protestant girls. Dee Dee Guccinni was horrified when they bathed their sunburnt faces with the water. Now they felt like jittery geese. They painted dripping crosses of holy water on their chests for good luck and then they set out into the seven-foot shadows.

Driving along Cedar Avenue to the western edge of Wanatin, Lyle Berwick felt a bump on his fender. He veered onto the service road where, in his rear view mirror, he saw an apple rolling and boys running. Then he glimpsed a police car. By the time he reached his father's new house, Lyle could hear his own breathing.

His father offered him a beer and then, demonstrating the electric fire at his puzzle brick hearth, he said, "No one can be a pacifist with a woman." His second wife, Poppy, was at an Eastern Star meeting.

They might have been talking twenty feet underwater. Lyle had to explain twice how the Russian language defeated him at the University of Minnesota. He'd lost his draft deferment. Because his father sat uncomprehending, he tried again. "Where do the Freemasons stand on war? Are they anything like Quakers?"

"No one in court would think so. My great-grandfather was a Freemason and he fought in the Civil War." His eyes still stared like a fish's.

"Remember Nance? The chick who went to San Francisco with Lydia?" Lyle changed the subject. "Her parents live a few blocks from here."

"The chick?" His father was powerless to comment on Lydia. She had an illegitimate son and lived in a Berkeley commune.

"It's really hard, Dad, having been trained as a lifeguard and then watching those guys flailing on the battlefield. No one putting out a hook."

"Your brother Hugo played around with a short wave radio and now he's in a military office," his father replied. "It's part of being a man Lyle, doing things you don't want to do. The military is an employer like any other."

"I sincerely hope that's not true, Dad."

Lyle avoided a summer job at Country's Plenty, an initiation rite. Guys went into the factory in white coats and came out with turkey slaughter on them. "Yeah, those guys who go to court over the draft. They don't really want to."

"It's no use, talking to a judge." His father grimaced over his empty beer. "I tried to tell a judge that marriage is about feelings. Sometimes a marriage feels over. Judges don't even accept a scientific fact, that a man is related to his children, not his wife."

"Meditation, Dad. You should try it. It's like taking a dive underwater."

"A man just has a love affair!"

Lyle's father was on his next beer.

If anyone told Lyle that children in Wanatin were assembled with a stork-like crane, he might have believed them. They were conveyed through linear neighborhoods and hallways, bounced by the bunch in classrooms, and then spurted out of high school.

Policemen chasing boys for throwing fruit at cars was a manufactured lesson in a company town. Boys learned that they needed to be supervised and if they didn't cooperate, they could get stuck in a room with a routine.

Houses repeated like a cartoon background. Ranch house, hedge, driveway, ranch house, hedge, driveway. After the shopping plaza, Lyle rattled across ruts and past a picket fence, another rut, and a picket fence.

Beyond Baisley Park, Lyle toured the nostalgic Aspen neighborhood where nursery pastels jumbled in tent-like forms, pink and green and blue aluminum. The Berwick's first house was in Aspen and when Lyle was little, Before Television, he looked out on prairie grass and corn from the backyard.

On the laborer's route to the factory, gas and cigarettes were cheaper. A polluted moat separated the factory from a horseshoe park and the swimming pool. Lyle used to dive and dive until he no longer smelled the turkey slaughter in the air.

At the swimming pool, a lifeguard was raking the concrete bottom. Smart Kid Sid made sure that the person stamping out homemade smokes wasn't one of the noted lechers who sat on the bleachers outside the pool.

"You're still staying open Fridays?" Lyle greeted Sid at the wire fence.

Sid let him in and surveyed his frayed hair and his frayed bell bottoms.

"Under these patches, I'm in my swim suit, as usual."

"How can you dive with long hair?" Sid's hair was still clipped like Julius Caesar's.

"I want to sit on my old pedestal," Lyle coaxed Sid. Sid knew that he'd given up competitive diving.

On the pedestal, he was high enough to view the factory and the social track on Main Street. He could see darkness seeping like waves over people who couldn't be on top of things. The huge cane at his side gave a lifeguard an inane sense of power when every diver knew that consciousness could crack like an egg. Yet he'd dived from the throne so many times, landing nicely in the clean cool cave of the deep end. And then a freestyle race with Kid Sid before he was the old Lyle, duck-back hair, saying, "Stay cool, man."

When Lyle came downstairs with his backpack and bags, Maureen was in the sunroom flipping through magazines. He had been home for two weeks because he wasn't going back to the university. She hadn't known when he would be leaving though today, he wasn't in a hurry. He joined her in the sunroom.

"Lady Bird's still chirping," Maureen said, closing a woman's magazine. She put the magazine over an old cover with the Chicago Democratic convention on it.

"In the McCall's cage?" Lyle replied, moving the magazines from a cushion. He sat down. "So what's the groove in Wanatin tonight?"

As if Lyle was interested in Cal McConkey getting his driver's license. Maureen couldn't tell him that she knew about his Volkswagen getting hit with an apple.

"Need to tell you. I'm taking off. I'm going to trip across country. Maureen, I don't know when I'll see you again."

Ever since Maureen looked for Lyle in the TV coverage of the Chicago protests, she'd been cautioned about this.

"See you sometime, Cranberry," he said. But standing now near the sunroom curtains, he was watching the street. Then he did something extraordinary. He kissed her cheek.

Maureen drifted after Lyle. He heaved up his bags, picked up a paper sack in the kitchen, and went into the backyard room where he put an arm around his mother. Vaguely, Maureen and Joann followed him to the alley. To ask Lyle where he was going was like asking him to remove his sunglasses.

The leave-takings were getting more difficult, especially since Maureen had emotionally taken hers. During an argument with her mother about Yardley products and the sensational F she got in gym class for refusing to do cheerleader jumps, Maureen promised that the grades she got in high school would eventually separate them. Lately, they'd been living like roommates.

In the alleyway, Maureen and Joann agreeably took turns with their cameras. Then they waved and waved while Lyle pulled out of the alleyway and splashed into September.

Cal McConkey honked his father's station wagon outside Maureen's house, picking up Jayne and Louise there too. Roland Werff wanted to see Maureen again.

It sounded like a triple date when Louise told Maureen about it. "You talked with Roland all through the football game last Friday," she said.

Some girls liked Roland for his sad silver eyes. In fact he didn't hold his chin up, Maureen noticed, because her father was always telling her to hold hers up. According to Louise, Roland could have a starlet-blonde date, a popular girl who had a crush on him. But he kept telling kids in his English class that he wanted to go out with Maureen.

"Roland and I have something in common," Maureen explained. "We both hate football."

"I'm not dating Dave or Cal," Louise said, although every girl in the tenth grade wanted to date Cal.

In the summer, Louise went out with a guy from Hay Valley. He'd hung around her at the Dairy Queen, asking for something slender and frosty. Louise was slender but top-heavy which confused both her and the boys at school until she drove to the sticks with a rural boy.

Louise quoted her mother: "Anyone can get married if they look low enough." She filled out a magazine frigidity test for her mother after Maureen filled out one for hers. Maureen quoted her mother saying, "My divorce wasn't because of sex. It was because of what happened outside of bed."

Joann Berwick was alone and the Ogland's arranged two double beds in the huge master bedroom of their new Victorian house. When Maureen admitted that kissing boys was cuddly, Louise worried that she didn't even feel that. Louise was afraid that she wasn't normal.

But when Cal McConkey yelled from the front seat of the station wagon, "Louise!", she jumped in beside him. Roland Werff let Maureen into the middle seat and Jayne went to the back seat after Dave Battaglia opened the door for her. Soon, Cal was speeding along a concrete road into the country.

"Where are we going?" Maureen demanded.

"Out of the stadium," Cal said. "Did you want me to show off my breaks on Main Street? Hey, Rolla Rolla's gonna have a lucky day."

"Rolla's way way way throwing himself to the Milky Way," Dave said.

"What are they talking about?" Maureen asked.

"It's the baseball infield chat," Roland said beside her.

"Ten nine eight fire the rocket rolla rolla rocket away," Cal chanted. "We're driving over the football coach's bald streak."

"Sam Strole's got a big head," Roland said. "All his guys wear his bald streak."

"No more baseball. Not for months, except on TV," Dave lamented.

"I'll hit this engine," Cal said. He gunned it until he came to a dirt road. They drove into a dead-end cow meadow.

After the car stopped, Roland and Dave rolled celebration bottles of Boone's Farm apple wine from under the middle seat.

"Cal catcha catcha catch-em crawling to McConkey country," Dave said, tossing a bottle to Cal.

"They keep me primed," Roland said. He was toeing the cow path, looking for cow pie bases.

"Do you really say this stuff during games?" Maureen asked.

"Ba-ba-Battaglia, have you any third?" Cal asked.

"They don't need cheerleaders!" Louise scoffed.

"Hey! That's only a bottle cap, Louise," Cal said.

"Ba-ba-Battaglia, have you any balls?" Roland called. He'd discovered a cow pie.

"Ohhh!" Louise spit out her apple wine. "You're too rude."

The boys in Louise's English class were too rude for feelings, she'd said. Even though she was thrilled like any other tenth grade girl to sit with Cal, he was probably interested because she was top-heavy.

"The police!" Dave yelled.

Maureen fled towards the trees while Dave yanked Jayne's blonde head in the crook of his elbow. Cal confiscated Louise's headband and, pretending it was a magnet, attempted to control her. From the trees, the McConkey station wagon looked like a primitive mastodon husk, still lit up inside.

They passed around the Boone's Farm wine before they ventured out of the darkness to sit on the car seats. The doors were open and the radio played. It didn't take long for Maureen to feel as swoozy as if she were swimming. When Roland grasped a hank of her sandy curls, what he must be in love with, he started kissing her in a way that made kissing the essential. Never having experienced that before, Maureen became enveloped in this for as many seconds as she could stay underwater. Eventually, she found that she had surfaced in the backstroke. She was lying across the middle seat of the station wagon, clasping Roland's dark curls. Jayne and Louise were hanging over the back seat, laughing at her. Maureen shot up, feeling like a dog thrown into water and forced into a swimming lesson.

In Berkeley, baby Lonnie made a face like his grandfather after he'd had a few drinks. Then he babbled to a tall avocado plant from his hump of India print.

Lydia said, "He looks like old snapshots of you, Lyle."

"Lonnie's talking to an avocado plant," Lyle replied to his sister. Lydia took classes to be a music therapist, whatever that was. Another woman in the ivy-lawned communal house made rag rugs for Lonnie's naps. "What if it talks back?"

They were doing something immoral out here. In Wanatin, people kept on their side of the peek-a-boo saplings. Once upon a time the Midwestern grass was high and went on forever but now the grass there exposed people. They pondered it, selected it, rolled it out like carpets, and trimmed it. In the Bible, bad people were stoned and that could be painful if the ground weren't covered with grass. Grass made people safe.

"Maybe I'll camp in a Never Land park tonight. That park we passed, Lydia." The desert was hellish for a diver; Lyle had to take mescaline to get across it. The sand became a long, grainy diving board that led to the suspense of smog and ocean. If Lyle looked back, he could see Captain Hook and the crew. "I don't care if I see crocodile teeth, Lydia. I can swing across water like Tarzan." He swooped down to Lonnie and pulled on his little arms.

Lydia's new boyfriend, Emory, strummed about Tarzan and Never Land. He'd already sung about a prospector who found the California gold was gone and that a government used the gold to blast holes in Vietnam.

Nance from Wanatin came with curried vegetables and a friend with a mantra.

At supper, Lydia said, "Did you know that the Waves wanted to recruit Lyle?"

"I never could cooperate with the military," Lyle said.

"The year Lyle graduated, mail came for Lyla Berwick to join the Waves," Lydia continued. "When I graduated, they got my name right."

"They'd probably take a guy into the Waves. They'd take anyone," Nance said.

"That reminds me," Lyle said. "I have an appointment tomorrow with the barber."

Nance's friend recommended the Berkeley barber. He had a reputation from San Francisco to Vancouver.

"Don't cut your hair," said the rag rug maker. "I'll make you a cap that a religious man would wear."

"Do you like *this* hair?" Lyle asked, showing the others a magazine picture. A man was standing in front of an old world wharf. His blonde hair was cut in short bangs and clipped straight at the nape of his neck.

"It's Euro," said the rag rug maker. Her name was Nebbie. "Where is he?"

"Amsterdam," Lyle said. "So you think the barber can do that?" He didn't want to look like an American when he drove to Canada. "Do you like that, Lonnie?"

"He can do cool. He's got the evolution of hair in a mural across his wall," Nance said. "Long and scraggly, bowl cut, long ponytail, waxed back, crew cut, and him, receding long hair."

With duck-back hair, Lyle could walk the plank blind and alone, as if nothing were behind him except Captain Hook's sneer. Even his father was back there with the yo-ho-ho's. Once he had walked the diving plank, he could do it again. He had to do it fast in order to elude the crocodile teeth. Someday, the only command he might get from Captain Hook would be a message in a bottle.

All Lydia could write home about was how Lyle left with Nebbie that evening. In a San Francisco house painted lilac and green, they rode on a woven carpet to the nebula and their hopes. Nebbie could be trusted to say that Lyle spent the night with her but she didn't want to talk about it. He would send his mother a picture of his Euro haircut once he reached Vancouver.

The next Friday night that September, Louise and Jayne came over to Maureen's house but Maureen wouldn't open the door for Roland Werff. When he hovered on the porch, Louise cracked the door. The temptation to relay messages from him was too scrumptious for her.

"He says he's not leaving until he can apologize," Louise said.

"He doesn't need to. I don't want to go out with Roland."

Jayne stuck her head out the door. "He's got a book," she reported. "He says he's going to read Kurt Vonnegut under your porch light until you talk to him."

At the window of the door, Roland mouthed something with his mule-like lips.

"Tell Roland I won't talk to him until he gets through Steinbeck," Maureen said, switching off the porch light. In a half hour, her mother would be home from the library. "We could call the police."

Louise and Jayne were disappointed that kissing could lead to this. Besides, Cal and Dave were sitting on the front steps between the geranium pots.

"Look! Roland's doing the turkey!" Louise shrieked at the sunroom window.

Under the streetlight, car passengers could view Roland Werff stepping high with his arms tucked up in his armpits.

In most Wanatin homes, it was ritual to let the guy win.

7   Chapel Wedding

Before Homecoming, 1971. When its lichen green carpets were freshly vacuumed, the Berwick's house had a patina now. Coming in from a summer night out, Maureen knew that Joyce Tollefson had arrived for the weekend. Although Maureen's family had finished with the house, the red-haired Joyce made its living room feel refined. She was planning her wedding and besides that, she was a talking tranquilizer for Maureen's mother. Joann hoped that her future daughter-in-law might someday be a minister's wife.

Joyce admired the silver sconces, the colonial hutch, the Wedgewood china, and the felt-lined box of Sunday silver. She was kind about Joann's slackness now that everyone but Maureen had gone. Tucker, their old springer spaniel, treated the kitchen table like a doghouse. The cave under the basement stairs was stacked with junk and bags of garbage, a missing person's chore. Joyce had discovered canine emergencies in the basement when she did laundry. She stayed in Hugo's bedroom among his things, his short wave radio and his books - old Zane Grays, *The Great Divorce*, and *The Crucible*, the play he'd acted in.

Joyce's father usually drove her into town. Out in the country, Mr. Tollefson bullied Joyce and her mother as they sat with their knitting needles, scissors, and crochet hooks. Joyce wasn't very disturbed about the Berwick divorce.

In stocking feet, Maureen heard the Tonite Show from the kitchen. Then Joyce said above Johnny Carson's voice, "I wouldn't worry about Maureen. She's not getting anywhere with her crush. The girls are all calling her since she got that photography award."

Joann was afraid that Maureen was becoming like Lyle, exiled now in British Columbia. Maureen's prize school newspaper photos were of dancers in black leotards and combat helmets performing at the Methodist church. The liberal pastor there had already been called to a city church.

Joyce's laughter in the backyard room was like sighing. She laughed like that when Maureen became grossed-out at the four-finger stretches in her marriage manual, what prepared brides for their wedding night.

"Oh, I can't stand it!" Joann shrilled. "Dean Martin's drunk! Is he going to sing?"

Maureen was now standing quietly at the backyard room door.

"See, Maureen's back," Joyce said.

Her mother was glued to Dean Martin and the signs she knew too well. "I talked to Lydia this week," she said. "She offered to play the organ at the wedding."

Startled, Joyce replied, "I thought Lydia gave up the organ. Unless it was electric."

As Maureen settled into a wicker chair, she could see that her mother was satisfied. The winter wedding would be a small one. Hugo's official engagement to Joyce was planned with more ceremony - a velvet dress sewn with small faux pearls for the penthouse Radisson Restaurant in Minneapolis. The Golden Strings played as Hugo presented the engagement ring.

"Where were you tonight?" Joann demanded. Dean Martin had begun to croon "Everybody Loves Somebody Sometime."

"The Balcony, dancing. I have to go out with Roland Werff."

"What do you mean, you have to?" Joann didn't wait for a reply. She shuffled away from Dean Martin's voice in her worn-down cocoa chenille robe.

Joyce pushed a plate of rocky road fudge towards Maureen and said, "How can you *have* to go out with somebody?"

"Maureen!"

Maureen peered through the simulated moonbeams at the Balcony. The band was on break and she was sitting with her friends at the wall. Four chairs down the row, Roland Werff stared at her, his eyes glinting like a husky's in the lights.

Maureen hadn't meant to keep Roland interested, trying out her discussion strategy. If a boy had an opinion about Vietnam, *Rolling Stone* magazine, or the ending of *Butch Cassidy and the Sundance Kid*, he might not mind her perplexed personality. Girls said she was too quiet, like a camera, around boys.

"Why is everyone looking at me?" she asked.

At least Jayne, Dee Dee, Kezia the clarinet player, and Cal were blocking out Roland. But then they sat back against the wall. Roland's fist was curled under his chin.

"Roland just asked you out," Kezia said. Kezia came from one of the few Jewish families in Wanatin. She'd probably heard about Roland's exhibition kiss in Cal's station wagon, the kiss that turned ice into wine.

Chairs between Maureen and Roland were emptying as amplified pangs sounded from the stage. Maureen would probably sit there if she didn't dance with Roland. Somehow, they were paired up for the weekend although they all went to the same party.

The last month before Maureen became a social security number, she sat in front of the garden sprinkler like a spoke. At another spoke, Louise Ogland admired Joyce's diamond set in filigree. Then she asked Joyce, "How should I dress for an interview when it's about cleaning cages?"

"That's a hard one," Joyce said, although she had easily obtained a part-time clerical job at the Wanatin clinic. "I guess if I were going to interview with a veterinarian, I'd wear one of those sack dresses with a belt."

"With knee socks? I'm afraid I won't get the job if I wear nylons," Louise said.

"It's time for 'Dark Shadows'," Maureen said.

Joyce flinched, getting up from her lawn chair. Roland Werff was approaching on the backyard sidewalk in his soundless chukka boots. His untanned legs were as singular as Hugo's and he looked as somber this afternoon, not expecting Joyce. She'd already asked about the vampire-like hickies that Maureen covered up with Clearasil.

The hickies were from a good night kiss at the back door. As if her body had been waiting for this or Roland, Maureen's limbs lost consciousness and she drooped under his six-foot frame. She hadn't been drinking wine, what she thought caused their first kisses.

Joyce flung a terrycloth shift over her bubble top swimsuit. Roland followed them all to the backyard room where Maureen and Louise, in their bikinis, crossed their legs. They watched the vampire Barnabas dissolving into the fine New England foliage and then, during a toothpaste commercial, Maureen opened a card Roland gave her.

Roland had drawn a tall tadpole interviewer. It was asking a girl how she would keep kids without memberships out of the swimming pool. As if Maureen needed a good luck card when she was applying at the YMCA. Her father bought a foundation brick for its new building.

Joyce read the card and said, "Are you looking for a job too, Roland?"

"Nah, I don't interview with my uncle. Farmers have to mow their ditches. I already have experience on a tractor."

"Roland has his own car," Maureen said.

Feeling outnumbered, Roland said, "Adios" and went out to his car, a Ford Galaxy 500. Then they all slouched in the humidity as if they were embalmed.

After "Dark Shadows", Joyce said, "I want to order cloth napkins from the Sears catalog. I thought I might embroider them. Do you want to come?"

It wasn't far to walk. At the Lombardy shopping plaza, Louise and

Maureen went up to Elliot Gould's poster outside the movie theater, neither of them mentioning that Roland vaguely resembled Elliot. They talked Joyce into stopping at the Cool Point for cherry slushes, betting on what the Sears catalog lady would do about it. She'd probably stretch her neck like a turtle, peer behind her tortoise shell glasses, and clear her throat. She could stretch her neck across pages of models in brassieres and men in briefs as if they were table settings. When she wasn't in the catalog booth she sold nylons, wearing support hose that was as thick as a homemade doll's.

Joyce unnerved her as she surveyed the cherry slushes. "Is it possible to order these napkins separately from the tablecloth? I'm not sure about the table sizes yet."

"There aren't many napkin sets in the catalog. You could order the set and make napkins out of the tablecloth. Or alter it." The catalog lady had forgotten the cherry slushes.

"That's an idea," Joyce said. "I also want to order a long slip."

After this Wanatin entertainment, Maureen and Louise tight-roped the softened seams of blacktop on the walk back. Maureen lost her balance when Joyce said, "I don't think Mrs. Werff knows who I am. My mother knew her from church. Out in the country. She still does clothing drives with them."

"She's Roland's mother?" Maureen said. She'd been a pillar at the Sears catalog center for as long as Maureen could remember.

"She's got three boys and they live over in Lombardy," Joyce said. "Across from Gethsemane Lutheran Church."

"Maureen didn't know!" Louise grinned at Joyce. "That's why Roland's school clothes are like an ad for someone he isn't."

Joyce paged through Maureen's first graphic design project – the family scrapbook that Joann couldn't complete. It was already October and Joyce was thinking about her wedding guests, whether they would talk with Joann or Clive Berwick, and how they would react to Lydia and Lonnie. The small ceremony would be in the chapel of St. Matthew's Lutheran church, the downtown church that Joann attended.

In the scrapbook, Joann's permanent became more frazzled each year. Mr. Berwick became snazzier and sometimes he looked as suspicious as Dean Martin. Hugo stood out with a stunned expression, being the tallest in the family.

Maureen complained, "The Lombardy kids call me Split House behind my back." She explained how, driving in their cars, kids looked for a house by feature and that became a nickname - Lantern, Breezeway, Flamingo. The Berwick's house had two front doors from the time it was owned by a dentist. "Roland is Corral Fence. His father built the corral fence around their backyard."

In fact, Roland's father once had a business building fences. Roland came from four generations of farmers but with more Werff's, the larger farms were split. After World War II and an injury to his hip, his father leased his small farm to Roland's uncle and partnered with a construction company, calling his business Werff's Fences. But after a few bad winters, he took a union job at Country's Plenty.

"Are you still going out with him?" Joyce asked.

"Not much. Louise heard a rumor that Duncan Nichols wants to ask me to Homecoming."

"The boy you want to go out with? The one who works on the school newspaper?" Joyce smiled but when she turned a page of the scrapbook, she started. "Who's this?"

A flirting woman was perched on a bed, her hand at the hip of a tousled dress. On the opposite page, Maureen's mother was lying supine on the bed, wearing pedal pushers, a blouse, and a sunhat over her face.

"That's Aunt Gilly, Dad's sister. She and Uncle Wally went on vacation with us the year before the divorce." Maureen turned the page. "There's the bear. If Uncle Wally acts mad at the wedding, remember that he was a grouch on vacation. Strawberry pie makes him mad. He's like Mr. Wilson, mad because he hasn't seen Dennis the Menace lately."

"I'd rather your dad came with him than with his new wife," Joyce worried.

"He hasn't said anything about Poppy coming," Maureen said.

While Joyce planned her wedding, she taught Maureen to crochet. Maureen started an edging that she might sew to the neck and the wrists of her new wool tent dress. That helped her to sit near the telephone in case Duncan called. But on the Saturday before Homecoming, she was embarrassed to tell Joyce that Duncan hadn't called.

"He might have called and no one was home," Joyce suggested.

Maureen worked that afternoon at the YMCA, handing out locker room baskets. She had succeeded in forgetting about Homecoming when Roland showed up at the basket window. "Want a ride home?" he asked.

After she got into Roland's car, he asked her to Homecoming for the third time. When she paused, he said, "I was afraid you were going with Duncan Nichols."

"I wasn't," Maureen answered, feeling resigned.

"I was. I started that rumor," Roland said as the steering wheel slid through his big hands. "Then I was afraid that Duncan would believe it. I didn't want you going with anyone but me."

Maureen just looked out the car window.

When Roland parked at her house, he wanted to show her a cartoon he'd drawn. Rather than sit outside with him, Maureen let him come in where he would be subjected to Joyce's scrutiny and amusement.

His cartoon was the dance floor at Homecoming, split up like a football field. Guys in suits and glasses were on one side, dancing with girls wearing flips. But they were colliding with large-shouldered athletes wearing sweaters and girls whose hair flew like shrieks. In the margin was a winter ski jacket for girls. Arrows pointed to double snaps, locks, and a zipper with jagged teeth.

"Are you trying out for the school newspaper, Roland?" Joyce asked.

"Nah, I've got hockey and baseball."

"What's your favorite class?" Joyce wondered, staying off the subject of Homecoming.

"Hogan's Heroes," Roland said automatically.

"His favorite columnist is Charles Schulz. It's almost time for our hoagies," Maureen said, threatening Joyce with a cigarette. Maureen's mother was at the library that afternoon.

"Isn't your mother expecting you for supper?" Joyce asked Roland. He hadn't taken the hint.

"Nah, they'll think I'm at the Battaglia's. They're my second family." Then Roland confessed, "This morning my mother set out a cigarette with my silverware. She found it in my letter jacket. My brother Arch and my dad sat there with their breakfast sizzlers. I suppose I should have lit up before I did the chores. But I might not be here now."

"His brother is so square that his eyebrows look like glasses frames," Maureen said.

While they made hoagies, Joyce told Roland about Hugo's job in the military. He interviewed soldiers who returned from Vietnam in order to identify cases of war fatigue. Sometimes they used Hugo's tapes for basic training.

"I think Hugo might like giving confession better than giving sermons," Joyce said, pitying Roland for the Lutheran strictness in his family. She allowed him a last cigarette before he went home.

After showing more stamina for slow dancing than the other eleventh graders, Roland kept Maureen up, parked on the dark side of her block. She drank coffee mixed with brandy from a steel thermos. Soon, Roland was warming his hands under the hem of her Homecoming dress.

"You've got to live down the rumor about Duncan Nichols," he said, as if kissing her and tracing the crochet edging at her neckline would dispel it. "I didn't mean to hurt you, Maureen. I want to marry you."

The brandy hit Maureen's head like a cartoon bubble that was bursting. She laughed so hard that she was turning the thermos mixture into a shake.

"I'm serious. I want to marry you someday."

"Roland, you're only sixteen. And I'm going to college."

"My parents got married when they were eighteen," Roland replied. "A lot of farming people get engaged before they graduate from high school."

"My dad and mom went to college." Maureen pulled her pea jacket around her dress.

"Those dorms look like camps," he complained. "My dad says it's enough to scare him, all those lies about college. It's better to have land."

"If you keep making the honor roll, Roland, you'll have to leave Wanatin," Maureen informed him. "They're not hiring guys in the factory if they can go to college."

Joyce waved from behind a veil of snowflakes as she and Hugo made their getaway. The reception was stressful. Clive Berwick brought his home movie projector. Uncle Wally looked mad after he took the long distance phone call from Lyle, exiled in Canada. Aunt Gilly and Joyce's girlfriends acted like floorwalkers, making sure to separate Joann and Clive. Lydia played a crashing recessional piece in her long boots and then, her illegitimate son threw confetti over every guest. At least snow covered the cross and circle sign of woman, sprayed on the left fender of the Corvair that Hugo rented. As soon as the windshield was cleared, Joyce pointed at Roland Werff's Galaxy 500. He was walking from it and soon, he was kissing Maureen behind an evergreen tree. The worst stress for Joyce was that chapel brides were usually pregnant.

8   Blindman's Bluff

Spring of eleventh grade, Maureen and Jayne established a smoking route. Along rural roads and pussywillow, they set their drive to two cigarettes and seven chances to hear "Snowbird" on the radio. A turn off from their route could become an odometer warp.

"When the corn's grown, we'll feel even more lost," Maureen said. Then she pointed ahead at a shield-shaped sign with a county road number on it. "I'm sure this is the road Roland takes." Nights, she couldn't figure out the route he took to their parking place. Even his best friends, Cal and Dave, didn't know exactly where it was.

"It probably goes near his uncle's farm," Jayne said, slowing her parents' Grand Prix. "I wonder if I'll ever find my way out of Wanatin."

Jayne's mother worried that she'd found something *in* Wanatin – a boyfriend named Garth and a job at the Trampoline Center. Down their block, a gas station owner dug the first trampoline pit in his back lawn. A few years later, after Jayne had bounced on it, he began his trampoline business. He hired Jayne to punch tickets and spot jumpers once the twelve trampolines were dug into a lot near the Lombardy Shopping Plaza.

"Roland turns right on a road after the Hutchinson horse stables," Maureen said, craning her head to see if the horses were grazing.

They gazed at brick stiles and a grove of May apple behind which a long low building appeared. Mrs. Hutchinson was married to a director at Country's Plenty and she was a star of the society news, her pale hair sprayed into a flip. She made pleas for library funds when librarians like Maureen's mother might be ignored.

"Garth can ride standing on a horse," Jayne said. She met him at the Trampoline Center the week it opened. He was a gymnast from out-of-town, Albert Lea. Last month, Maureen double dated with a friend of his, the son of a drug store owner. Maureen and her blind date, a nice-looking sandy blonde, talked about film processing. But kissing him was like getting a roll of film back without anything on it.

The blind date was a secret Albert Lea evening because Maureen had been going steady with Roland since February. She stayed at Jayne's on a winter weekend when the Magnuson's were celebrating their anniversary in the Twin Cities. On Saturday night, Roland and his friends showed up with wine bottles that they spun for chance kissing during *Horsefeathers*, the movie on the late show. The next morning, Jayne found Maureen and Roland in her brother's old bed, fully clothed except that Roland's man-sized shoes were on the floor. Roland mashed his mouth like Harpo Marx and said, "I was afraid to go home. My brother smells my breath."

Roland as her first sight in the morning was a mistake, Maureen felt. But a high school steady might as well be a mistake. He was solid and from a stolid family, something she'd wanted to know about. She doubted that he could ever hurt her. In the spring, he was really an ace pitcher and Maureen could fall in love.

The steering wheel slithered under Roland's sure knuckles as he won again at Blindman's Bluff. He turned the square corners of so many cornfields that, on her own, Maureen still couldn't have found their parking spot, a tractor-wide drive near an out building.

And her eyes were propped open as if she were focusing a camera. She had insisted on leaving the movie *The Night of the Living Dead* and then she insisted on Cheese Frenchees at King's Food Host. Roland hadn't argued and he paid for it all.

"You're not scared, are you?" he said.

"No. The safest place in that movie would be in a car."

Roland put his arm around her. "My uncle promoted me. I'm going to mow the county ditches this summer." His summer job was hazardous since the tractor he drove could tip. He was planning to escape his hired hand job with a baseball scholarship.

Maureen wasn't sure how she would make her escape from Wanatin except that she grabbed up printed materials as if they were C.A.R.E. packages dropped from helicopters. "That movie was like smelling something bad. It was like smelling turkey in the morning." She was feeling nervy, the way she did before a bout of insomnia. "I'd rather be here than watching it."

"More time with you," Roland replied. "She wakes up when I get home."

"Does Minnie bark?" The Werff's had a high-strung cockapoo.

"No. My mother has insomnia."

"Your mother?" Maureen jerked up the way she did when she was falling asleep. She thought the Werff's were ultra-normal even if Mrs. Werff was getting a double chin. Since grade school, Maureen was curious about families that seemed cheerful about being cooped up in their house. There weren't so many that were cheerful inside, she discovered, visiting anyone who invited her over. The Werff house was utilitarian and it could feel cramped because of the hunks of furniture they'd brought from their farmhouse. Otherwise, there was little adornment except for a few ceramic dogs.

One spring evening, Roland wanted Maureen to see the vinyl-covered bar his father had built in their basement. As soon as they drove into the garage though, Mr. Werff asked them to sort out a bunch of nails and put them in jars. "My dad was wondering if you're lazy," Roland said. "He already knows that I'm lazy."

In the basement, they were served cokes with a tad of rum as they sat at the bar. Mr. Werff fixed a Bloody Mary for Mrs. Werff and then she invited Maureen to a game of Five Hundred. Before Roland could ask for another tad of rum, the card table was set up. Mrs. Werff flirted with her graying husband. He had maintained his physique and looked as if he played baseball with Roland.

"She needs a psychiatrist," Mr. Werff said while Mrs. Werff dealt cards.

Bewildered, Maureen saw that Mr. Werff meant Minnie. Their cockapoo was in the room, forgotten until her little nose emerged from under a settee.

"I've had insomnia," Maureen told Roland. "I first got it after seeing *The Time Machine*. Then I couldn't sleep for about a week after reading *Lord of the Flies*. I'll probably have it tonight from that movie."

"Is that why?" Roland wondered. "Isn't there cannibalism in *Lord of the Flies*? There was in *The Time Machine*. You had to leave the movie tonight when the ghouls got hungry." He made a bite at her.

Impressed at this analysis, Maureen wondered, "Does your mother take sleeping pills?"

"Yeah, she takes pills."

"Where did she get them from? A psychiatrist?"

"Hell no. Are you crazy? Only one thing works for her and she knows that."

Maureen had been sleeping better since she'd been steady with Roland. She associated his baseball uniform with pajamas and he often had a post-shower aroma. His frame was strong as a bed's and he could be sexy. In the daytime though, she doubted him as a date.

At school, boys often treated her like a beach ball. She was blunt and soft with them, flirting at the YMCA. She might as well go steady with Roland. She wanted to know more about sensations that were as bad to her as floating on a water mattress. Even if she reached them with wine or on a lost tractor trail, she craved this doze-like state. Grasses swayed and the air spilled like lake water into the private places. Roland was an underpinning, sinewy and nudging.

She realized she was drifting into being chronically attached when liquid seeped down her neck. Roland threw his head back before she could ask why he was crying.

"Get the Kleenexes. The box."

Switching on the light in Roland's car, Maureen gaped as he soaked a nosebleed with swatches of Kleenex. "I'll drive to the hospital. How do we get back to Wanatin?"

"Nah. They might try to give me a nose job. I got hit in the nose with a puck. That's why I don't care if I sit in the foul box because of a little sticking."

"You mean, this has happened before?"

"They cauterized the vein. It would look bad if I went in every time." Roland was as calm as his father was, talking about a cockapoo needing a psychiatrist. "Don't go around talking about it."

"Roland has an Achilles nose," Louise gloated.

She loved a glass of gossip so much that she probably wouldn't spill this one. They were taking Joann Berwick's new Toyota on the smoking route and when they picked up Jayne at the Trampoline Center, Louise didn't tell her anything.

Jayne complained, "The owner got a call about an X-ray for a kid with a sprained ankle. He's already talking about buying a motel. He asked me if I'd like to change mattresses instead of people on tramps. And Garth is teaching me the half-twist."

That reminded them of prom.

"Do you know what you're wearing, Maureen?" Louise asked. Louise and Jayne's mothers were sewing their dresses.

"One more YMCA paycheck and I can afford Finch's Boutique," Maureen said. Her mother's budget was for Penny's or Sears.

Louise waved the cigarette smoke out the window and opened up a box of Hot Tamales, her addiction. She'd succeeded in pushing them on a guy in her Spanish class. Monte had a rabbit and when it got its shots at the veterinarian's office where Louise cleaned cages, he asked her if she was going to prom. Her mother was afraid that Meadow Bullet was the Mustang he drove, not a rabbit.

"Did you ask Roland about triple dating with Jayne and me?" Louise asked Maureen, handing her a Hot Tamale.

"He's got to go to prom with his baseball friends."

At least they could eat at the same restaurant, they schemed.

Prom wasn't about a dress anyway. Maureen and Roland were planning to lose their virginity prom night. They decided that at the parking place where, triumphing over her, Roland handed Maureen the Kleenexes. "I thought you were feeling good. The erogenous zones are innocent," he said.

Maureen's skin felt like a cloud condensing into tears. It would be better if they planned this instead of being taken by surprise. Roland suggested a rehearsal.

During the ten o'clock Sunday church service, he and Maureen drove to the cow path where they first made out in the McConkey station wagon. The woods were shy with blue phlox. Other wildflowers were like the veils old ladies wore on their Sunday hats.

They had a picnic of Kentucky Fried Chicken and Maureen's chocolate-iced Rice Krispie bars. Then Roland took off his shirt. The sunshine was as bright as a chalice and muggy as a sermon. "My parents approve of me visiting your church," he said. "It's all virgins and sins and babies."

"Prom night will probably fall on a safe day," Maureen said, unclamping her sticky nylons from her garter belt. Her period was so regular that she argued with Roland every twenty-four days. "My mother said she was using rhythm when she got pregnant with me. But she acts so surprised when the monthly bills come."

"They all lied in her time," Roland claimed. "You're the only honest girl I know."

"Your mother lied?" Maureen couldn't imagine Mrs. Werff lying at Sears.

"Sure. She said padded bras and falsies were for warmth."

Hippies were having pre-marital sex and everyone at school speculated about the steadies. Maureen's mother said she was a virgin when she married and that she didn't really know her father. The Ten Commandments forbid adultery, not pre-marital sex.

"We won't be runaways like your sister," Roland planned.

The little girls sat on the curb across from the Crescent Ballroom. They cheered when Roland, Cal, and Dave Battaglia led their dates in long dresses. Photographed every week for the Wanatin newspaper, the baseball players were spring stars.

Louise's date, Monte, preferred sitting at a table near the dance floor. "They're saying it might be the last prom," he said.

"That's just an ultimatum," Louise said above the snifter candle. She had written an article on this for the school newspaper because a few high schools in the state suspended their proms that year. Proms were from the

Fifties, many students felt. Louise's survey had predicted malingerers and now, The Crescent Ballroom wasn't crowded.

After their dinners in the converted train cars of a Rochester restaurant, the dance was mostly a fashion show. Garth would rather be on a trampoline with Jayne than confined between the dancers. Roland made fun of the Beach Boys, doing the swim in an Egyptian-type dog paddle. And Maureen smuggled in her camera. Everyone wanted a picture of Char, the star of the musical, *Little Merry Sunshine*, arriving with a soldier home on leave. So far, she could still perform without showing a pregnancy.

Roland and Maureen were one of the first couples to elude the chaperones and sneak off to the celebration games at Baisley Park. Beer cans were stashed there as if they were Easter eggs. Eventually, an orgy of lilting Carpenters music came from cars parked near the woods, one of them Meadow Bullet the Mustang. Louise and Jayne emerged, looking for Roland's car.

Maureen and Roland were over at the sandbox, fishing up beer that was buried there. Then they spun on the revolving gate like a pair on a wedding cake. They drifted slowly across the swinging bridge that creaked and rippled after they were gone. Louise pointed at a taillight creeping towards the country. "Does it feel like you're losing your best friend, Jayne?" she said.

The plan began at a farmhouse that Cal's older brother lived in with some other junior college students. There was more beer besides bedrooms to crash in. But the noise, music, and Meadow Bullet's arrival were as profane as expected. As soon as Roland and Maureen wanted to be alone, they drove to Rookie's Truck Stop on Highway 2. The waitresses celebrated their prom clothes; Maureen and Roland often ate a late night breakfast at Rookie's.

Next, they roamed in Roland's car to a new parking place, a gravel road between two windbreaks of wooded trees. At four in the morning, a silhouette farmhouse appeared in the moonlight. Maureen watched the streamers of poplar and maple as if spring happened every morning.

"I could marry you in this dress," Roland said, kissing Maureen. She'd found a gray and blue empire-waisted dress at Finch's. And she crocheted a silver colored windowpane shawl for the parade into the Crescent Ballroom. But the dress was an encumbrance and Maureen, not having anticipated this in the plan, found herself wading in its fabric. "We should have stayed at Cal's farmhouse," she said.

"Cal Interruptus." Roland fought with his tux shirt. Wanting Maureen to strip to her slip, he peered at the farmhouse and its dark vehicles. A tinny silo signaled a more economical farm. "They got up," Roland said.

While the farmer was probably eating breakfast, Roland hastened his plan. But instead of experiencing new sensations, Maureen flinched at a floundering dive, a belly flop.

"Any other time," Maureen chided, secretly glad that she was still technically a virgin. She'd had her last argument with Roland exactly twenty-two days before. Tomorrow she would try to break up with him and the next day, she would get her period.

They watched the clouds turn into corn silk and listened to the trees swaying over the narrow road. Roland complained of a sore pitching arm and of mixing beer and rum at the farmhouse. He was like Maureen, able to accomplish most things, and if she didn't break up with him for good, they might accomplish this without planning it.

9   Duck, Duck, Gray Duck

At Antler Lake, sunbathers watched Maureen dive off the float and Roland dive after her. Soon the two stamped across the grass, Maureen heading away from Roland, Roland catching up. They shook words at each other. Then Roland called to Cal and Dave as he went to his car.

"They're going to Hay Valley for pop," Maureen said to Jayne and Louise as she stretched out on her towel.

"I think you fight with Roland because you like making up," Jayne said.

"Roland doesn't like me wearing this bikini here."

"Everyone else is wearing a bikini," Louise said. She thought Antler Lake was becoming an Egyptian strip affair anyway. It was on a highway between towns. Weekdays, teenagers possessed it.

"It was decent of Roland anyway," Jayne said. Steadies in Wanatin stretched and snapped back like trampoline weave.

Maureen had even added a fringe of crochet under her bikini top. "As if I should wear my tank suit."

"If Marilyn Monroe wore a tank suit, it would hardly matter," Jayne said.

Guys in jean shorts chanted on the Antler Lake grass, "Duck, duck, Marilyn duck. Duck duck D-cup. Duck duck, dimple duck."

"It *wasn't* decent of Roland," Louise asserted. "He's an act. He pretended to cry at Dave's party because Maureen didn't like his haircut. Dave asked him what his dad would do if he caught him crying. He burst out crying again."

"His dad thinks he'll act like a girl if he grows out his hair." Maureen put on her round aqua sunglasses. "Roland's father said that if God meant for him to be a girl, he would have put a hole between his legs."

Even Louise had to laugh at Mr. Werff's unpleasant way of putting this. Mr. Werff cut Roland's hair himself, negotiating with his scissors.

An hour later, most of the teenagers had gone. Dee Dee Guccinni and her sister Nina came in from the diving float where they had been browning all afternoon.

"Do you need a ride home, Maureen?" Dee Dee asked. Jayne and. Louise had come in the old Guccinni Desoto.

"Roland hasn't ever stood me up before." Maureen jaunted up to the road while Jayne collected her suntan lotion and her paperback novel. As Maureen stood like a hitchhiker, a shoddy car slowed down. She ran back, excited to say that Roland might be over.

"I've got to work at the Trampoline Center tonight," Jayne said.

"What if they got into an accident?" Dee Dee said.

"Or more likely, they had a flat tire." Louise said. "We'll go to the Trampoline Center tonight, Maureen. Without Roland."

"Well, I hope Roland doesn't go looking for me," Maureen said, knowing it was unlikely for Roland to have either an accident or a flat tire.

"Serves him right. A flat tire." Just as Louise became gleeful at that thought, Roland's Galaxy 500 lunged into the shore drive.

"Get in the car!" he yelled at Maureen.

"I'm going back with Dee Dee," Maureen shot back. She walked toward the Desoto's fins with her towel and her *Seventeen Magazine*.

Roland got out of his car, his eyes like chain links. Cal and Dave stretched their legs and, like a male chorus in a Greek play, they affirmed that they'd been playing pool in Hay Valley.

Near the Desoto, the girls answered like a female chorus, wondering why Maureen had to get into Roland's car. No one should leave a girl in her bikini near a highway.

The guys only gestured at Roland's trunk. Then he opened it to display three six-packs of beer, won in Hay Valley.

Maureen got into the front seat of Roland's car, a steady again.

That summer was like Maureen's favorite Dr. Seuss book, *Happy Birthday to You!* In their birthday suits, Seuss' creatures climbed spiral ladders above cloverleaf swimming pools. Maureen was having a better time than that, going to swimming pools, water holes, and lakes. After she and Roland took a bath together in her house, she accepted any invitation to swim at a public place.

One afternoon Roland breezed along country roads, taking Maureen to the swimming hole on his Grandpa Heineman's farm. His mother was brought up on a farm four miles away from the Werff farm. Roland sang "Jeremiah Was a Bullfrog" along with Three Dog Night until farther into the corn, he surfed up a slope of sand. Sand was stockpiled into palisades around a pond that Roland call Heineman's Sandpit.

"They're getting their tractor repaired," he said.

Inside, the pit was like a huge mixing bowl filled with brown sugar. Storms had shaped dunes and chaise-like ledges. Maureen felt as if she were in a Salvador Dali painting.

The pond was about the size of a twenty-five meter swimming pool and it was so molten with sand that Maureen couldn't swim with her head under water. Grains of sand got into her swimsuit and covered her arms like voile. It was a relief to bathe topless there. Roland sat in his frayed jean shorts and his V-necked suntan, smoking a cigarette. He snorted at the idea of a Heineman sticking their head over the pit like a thirsty camel. But the thought of that kept them apart.

"My brother Arch used to call this place his supercalifragilistic sandbox. The Heineman's didn't have as much farming luck as the Werff's. Grandpa Heineman predicted his crop failures so well that he's the Jeremiah of the family."

"Jeremiah if he finds us," Maureen said.

The Werff's were so loyal to Gethsemane Lutheran Church that Maureen suspected them of being fundamentalist. But Roland's hair frizzed when the weather was humid and he'd also said that his family loved America because they might have gone through the Nazi Inquisition in Germany.

"The Old Testament," Maureen said. She couldn't understand his brand of religion. "Sunday school was enough to make me cry. The teachers made the slow readers stutter through that stuff."

"It was tragic," Roland agreed.

"The people I related to in the Bible were the ones who had dreams. Joseph and Pontius Pilate's wife." Maureen began blowing up her water mattress.

Roland grabbed the water mattress and said, "Your brother's going to be a pastor."

"Yeah. He believes like Louise does. I want to take pictures that are real. I mean, this place is weird. It's like being in the desert. I should have my camera."

"It's just a sandpit. And me."

"Well, maybe that's what I want to see. That it's not weird."

"Take your camera to the beach and you'll have the beach alone. The beach and me."

After Roland finished blowing up the water mattress, Maureen finned to the middle of Heineman's Sandpit. Roland floated beside the mattress but then he grabbed hold of it, making it careen like a crocodile.

"Cal said there might be dead babies at the bottom of this pit," Maureen said. Cal told dead baby jokes that made Maureen want to cry.

"Bags of dead baby cats are at the bottom," Roland said. "Something's chewing on my toes."

They emerged from the pit, streaked with sand, and then they stretched across a ledge, feeling antediluvian.

Louise often chaperoned Maureen after the fight at Antler Lake. From down the block, she watched for Roland's Galaxy 500. When it wasn't in front of the Berwick house, she might find it parked in the alley or on the other side of the block.

Maureen and Roland weren't doing anything. Cal and Dave might show up at the Berwick's where they could play the stereo and say what they wanted. In July, a breeze was like steam and the curtains at many houses were pulled across the windows. Cal chaperoned too. He was obsessed with Vietnam, dead baby jokes, and his father's warning that a teenage pregnancy could turn into a long-term teenage job.

The only other house they could visit without parents turning up was the Werff's. Roland's parents both worked eight-hour days but when Cal came over, he could get Roland's attention simply by tapping on the wall. "Paranoid!" he'd say, lighting up a marijuana cigarette. The fear of discovery was intense. At the Werff's, the crowd knew why it was wrong to spend summer afternoons doing nothing and that the roof over their head wasn't theirs.

Back at Maureen's house, Cal and Louise aired their ongoing argument about marijuana. "Over eighty percent of the senior class tried marijuana last year," Cal said about the school newspaper survey.

"Do you want your picture taken?" Maureen challenged him. He persisted in rolling marijuana into a cigarette paper. "Duncan Nichols would love it."

Cal closed his hand over the joint.

"They just tried it," Louise said.

"It's the cure for alcohol, Louise," Roland said.

"What about your sports careers if you get caught?" she retorted.

"What about it?" Cal said.

"You wouldn't, Louise," Roland reared up. Ever since Roland began having discussions with his German teacher, he considered finks to be the worst sort of teenagers. Roland was just the sort of person who wouldn't be suspected for knowing The Buyer, an older guy who made trips to Minneapolis.

"What *about* our careers? The scouts were here in the spring and here we sit," Dave said.

"You're using Maureen's house,' Louise said.

The word *use* affected Roland like a remote siren. "I used to think you were a nice girl, Louise. But you're in a smog of judgment," he said.

"You argue here because you think I'm used to it," Maureen complained, about ready to take off in Roland's car. She stared at the wallpaper as if its ferny texture would slump from the argument. But the joint was being passed around and soon, the most mundane things would be funny. "I suppose we could watch the Match Game," she said.

"There might be a teacher's strike this fall," Louise mentioned. "Mr. Hammer is going to the bargaining table."

No one could argue about Mr. Hammer going to the bargaining table. He taught history as a complicated intrigue and as if he were part of it. When he lectured, he bent his fingers like a pianist, whispering about politics, and then he rattled off facts as loudly as chords. He was up on Ralph Nader when he talked about Country's Plenty television ads, pilgrims shouldering turkeys in a supermarket stampede. Best of all, Mr. Hammer had so much enthusiasm for the high school baseball team that he drove kids to out-of-town games.

When Mr. Hammer drove Maureen and Louise, he pried, "What are you thinking of taking in college, Louise?"

"I'm not sure."

They passed cows chewing cynically as twelfth graders.

"You're working for a vet. Have you considered pre-veterinary?"

"I just see animals in cages. I don't want to work in a cage when I get out of college," Louise replied.

"I suppose Maureen is going to college or are you going to marry Roland when you graduate?" Mr. Hammer was joking in his political whisper.

Maureen laughed in answer.

"You're going to take pictures of Roland," he egged her to confide.

"That's for the school newspaper."

"You know how to take them." Mr. Hammer's fingers tapped away on his steering wheel. "What about Roland? What are his plans?"

"Roland doesn't want to teach or coach," Maureen said. "There's not enough money in it."

"There's not, is there? Roland's father has a farm, doesn't he?" Mr. Hammer wondered the way he did in class, knowing the answer.

"Yeah, but he doesn't work it. If Roland or one of his brothers farmed, they could have it. But Roland thinks farms are too much work for the money," Maureen said.

"Ahhhh." Mr. Hammer acted as if this were a secret.

When Maureen drove with her father, he often talked about the roads because *his* father worked for the state as a cartographer. But driving in the country with Roland was like being in unmapped land. Landmarks were often cryptic agreements between farmers who worked under a vast pergola of corn silk.

Lost among little-used roads, the old Werff farmhouse seemed surreal. It looked diminutive on its huge lawn. Maureen couldn't be certain of the proportions until she was inside the house and standing near the eyeleted kitchen curtains. Roland had predicted a rain shower the day he had to mow the farm's lawn. Watching him, Maureen worried about getting pregnant. When lightening brightened the lawn into chartreuse and Roland came in, Maureen fixed her eyes on the kitchen's stultifying purple plaid linoleum floor. "I'll bet no one ever said the word *abortion* in this house," she said.

"I'd marry you," Roland said.

The pot-bellied clouds were already turning the cut grass into confetti. Roland ran out to close his car windows. He came back with *Everything You Wanted to Know about Sex but Were Afraid to Ask*, what they had been reading together. They laughed over the tent acts, talked about other ones, and discussed all the birth control methods.

"Werff's put off their first babies until the first alfalfa crop," Roland boasted. There were exactly two recommended years between the Werff brothers. "We usually roast hot dogs out here. Then my parents get out their camp cots and tell us that there's hay in the barn."

"There's hardly any furniture in the living room." Maureen admired the creamy white fireplace mantel. "Do your parents really camp out here?"

"Yeah, we camped here. But I slept on a cot and there used to be a few beds upstairs. Then we quit coming for weekend vacations."

"It must be scary to live out here in the winter. Did you ever stay here then?" The only thing the Werff's seemed afraid of was another Werff.

"When we came in the spring, the rats had eaten the upholstery out of the chairs," Roland said, sitting on an old painted chest. "My parents didn't want to go back to the farm. Even after my dad's war injury got better. He's scared of poverty. That and Nazis. I never saw him scared of the weather." Roland's gray eyes reflected the rain outside.

"When my dad got drunk, he said two things scared him – hell and communism."

They laughed so hard at this that they fell down in front of the fireplace. They were used to any surface. Last week, they snuggled between the stone slabs in a Wanatin cemetery, laughing about how Horatio Persson probably plowed for ten years before he could snatch a few hours of bedroom bliss. Roland pulled a crazy quilt out of the trunk.

In the eggshell-white room, a couple clung to life, producing children despite June flooding, drought, galvanic August storms, tornadoes, frosts, and World War I. They draped the familiar fabrics of childhood around themselves as if they could take tumbles and falls without injury. The countryside was a coverlet of tan and green material, bolts and bolts of it, an argument of plant life that farmers settled with crop lines. On the quilt, the argument quelled and the air was rinsed of cloudbursts.

There was just the bullying from above. The man felt bullied to tears and even when events didn't seem right, he had to be agreeable.

"Ask and it shall be given," they heard after a bombardment of powerful happenings.

They read and burned their marriage manual, feeling as demeaned as barnyard animals.

"It's still raining and the sun's out," the man remarked.

The farmland and the white house were a hyperbole that tricked the eyes. Tomorrow, when Maureen was at a shopping center or when she was drinking coffee with her mother, she would wonder how she could have been passionate with Roland. "I don't know how your father could leave this farm for Wanatin," she said.

"My parents used to get into fights out here. When my mom wouldn't give my dad another beer, he'd get so mad that he'd slug her," Roland laughed. "She could use a cast iron pan like a baseball bat."

"Oh, yeah." Maureen didn't believe that of Mr. Werff, a man who was jolly in the Sunday fellowship hall. As if he would slug a woman who was respectful while helping other women buy girdles.

"I think my dad is still stronger than my brother Arch," Roland mused.

"Are you saying these things because my parents fought so much that the neighbors are probably still talking about it?"

Roland's eyes looked ashen as he stared out at the grass. "My dad slugged me the other night because Arch said he smelled marijuana. I was so stunned that he slugged me again to prove that I wasn't my usual self. That's why my mother would rather live in town."

Maureen thought it was bad enough, being connected with her own family on a long-term basis. The modest farmhouse was now a place where things could be smashed out of proportion and Maureen, being there, was somehow connected.

The week of the school strike, Roland didn't know what came over him.

On Wednesday, Maureen and Louise went over to the high school anyway. Teachers were outside, some avoiding the camera as sheepishly as students skipping class. After Louise interviewed a few favorites and Maureen took photographs of the picket signs, the girls sauntered on to Burt's Burgers. It was noon on Louise's watch. In the background of her hand and wrist, booths were occupied by teachers. Most school days, an adult wouldn't enter the place at lunchtime.

"The air conditioner isn't on." Maureen was wearing jeans and a stretchy long-sleeved body shirt that snapped at the crotch. "Where is everybody?"

"I know. The bowling alley," Louise said.

They walked the few blocks to their own neighborhood, noticing children at play.

"My mom's been sniffing stain all morning, working on a bookcase. She'll probably let me have the car," Louise said.

They stopped at Maureen's house, switched on "All My Children", and drank Kool-Aid, feeling the cross-breezes.

"Where's Roland today?" Louise said.

"We broke up."

Louise got out a package of Hot Tamales as Maureen lit a cigarette, her face moist from a mixture of oil and sweat.

"The newspaper adviser says the strike will be over soon. Mr. Hammer took his wife and kids out of town. Because he got a death threat in the mail," Louise said.

"He did? Is it in the newspaper?"

"Not yet."

The week before school, Maureen was up north with her mother, staying at her aunt's cabin. On the way back, they stopped in Northfield so that Maureen could see the colleges there. Joann Berwick was looking for library work in a different town.

"Roland was doing his crying act last night. He said your mother was taking you away to the college of your choice." Sometimes Louise had to laugh at Roland. "Then he left the party. Anyway, the party started early and ended early because it was on a Tuesday! I guess you broke up again last night."

"There's air conditioning at the bowling alley," Maureen said.

"You've got sweat rings, Maureen."

Louise called the bowling alley but the phone was busy. Maureen was still changing into a long-sleeved blouse when she heard Louise scream. The bruises were explained while they drove the narrow blacktop that led out of town.

Maureen and her mother arrived in Wanatin late on Monday night, Labor Day. The next day, Maureen went shopping for school clothes and then she ate supper at her father's. Her mother went to work at the library for the evening.

After Maureen's father drove her home, Roland called from the party and said he would park in the alley. Maureen met him at the back door where his kiss made her reel from beer instead of the sensations of their first kiss there. She wanted to shut the door on him because he was dragging her by the arm.

"Roland thinks my family has a plan to keep him away from me," she told Louise. "He was mad because I went shopping yesterday instead of waiting for him to call."

In the backyard room, he threw her against the wall, asked her why she came back a day late, and then he grabbed her arms and shook her. She let him drag her to the alley where people might hear their fight. Then she sat on his car seat with the door open but as soon as he started his car and said they were going out to the country, she jumped out.

"He called this morning and it sounded like he was really crying. He said he'd never held onto a girl that way before. My dad used to get drunk but he didn't put marks on anyone."

"I'll lead the cheering if you break up with Roland for good," Louise promised.

Yet if Louise reported the purplish ruffles on Maureen's arms, it would only mark her.

10   Physics Problem

Senior year, 1972. Motion was a trotting horse while the energy from the light lessened, affecting the tendon-bound engine.

"And the price of soybeans."

Roland could plow his way through physics. After Joann Berwick saw his half-moon handprint on Maureen's arm, he wasn't allowed to see her. But he was contrite at the horror flick he became and Maureen, having considered him her best friend all summer, was disturbed at what happened. Joann said that Roland could come over to study.

"I'm taking the class because I want to take good pictures of things in motion," Maureen said. She needed to know about light if she kept on with photography.

"Everyone would be camera-crazy if there was a course in it," Roland said.

"What about the bird and the helicopter?"

It was an unassigned question. Her mother probably expected that Roland would be disenchanted with Clive Berwick's mind in the female gender. But there was also the idea that the women in Maureen's family needed correction. Like physics, a motion caused an imbalance and the need to work things out. Maureen had slept with Roland and that changed things. She had to know if she was kinky, if this was like her parents, especially now that she'd found out something else about Roland. He could comprehend physics more quickly than she could.

"The bird is like a baseball on a gusty day," he said. "The helicopter travels with a 20 mph wind."

Because she didn't have to work out that problem, she mentioned, "Duncan Nichols likes the collage I did of the Trampoline Center. For the yearbook."

"Duncan's a drip, drip."

"You wouldn't say that if you could have a cartoon accepted."

"Yeah, I would. If my parents thought I was going to college to draw cartoons, they would never help me out. Maureen, you don't know it but Duncan isn't like me as a guy."

"How do you know that?"

"Guys suspect stuff."

"Like what?"

"Fag."

"I don't believe that about Duncan. But I probably won't find out, anyway."

Maureen could hardly avoid seeing Roland at the Balcony on the weekend. But now she sat with girls at the tables in the viewing room. When Duncan came by, he stopped to talk.

She was finally dancing with him, the best writer at school. When the local band took a break from shouting lyrics like headlines, he asked her out for pizza. They'd gone to the coat rack, talking about green pepper, when Roland appeared from the Coke bar. And then Duncan, his reddish bangs in his eyes, was being shoved into a coat hook. In the space small as a train car, Duncan deflected a punch, one arm still in his jacket sleeve.

"You really think she wants you?" Roland challenged him.

Duncan wanted to get his coat on. The Balcony-goers had found out that the school newspaper editor didn't like fistfights and that the baseball pitcher could act like Jimmy Hendrix. As Cal moved in between them, Duncan backhanded Roland. "If she doesn't want me, I can go out with someone else."

"How about Judy?" Roland shot back.

Judy Weddle, one of the Lombardy girls, was watching from the doorway of the Coke bar. Cal started laughing and then Roland handed Maureen her pea jacket. "Do you want to dance, Judy?" he said. Judy disappeared from the doorway but this only made Roland laugh all the more.

Duncan led Maureen out of the Balcony but at the pizza parlor, he peered across the green peppers as if she were the anti-virgin. He wasn't intent on her and now she wouldn't ever know if he had passion like Roland.

"Where's Maureen?" Roland asked Louise at Burt's Burgers.

"She's home with a sore throat. Maybe strep." Louise's diagonally cut hair dug at him.

"What'd you think of the movie?" They'd watched *The Grapes of Wrath* that morning for English class.

"I liked reading the excerpts. But I wouldn't pay to see the movie," Louise said.

"Yeah, those chapters really whetted the appetite," Roland said, turning to Cal and Dave. "Are you going to see it? These farmers get shoved off of their land as if Nazis were controlling the weather."

"Better than reading the whole book," Cal said.

"We can get extra credit if we read the whole fricking Frankenstein book. I got to the part about the young couple making it in the back of a truck with the grandmother watching." Roland pulled out some change to see if he had enough for a cheeseburger and a phone call to Maureen.

Cal taunted, "Juicy Weddle's coming in for her malt."

"Judy, Judy, Judy," Dave added.

"Intercept her invitation and tell Maureen what's true," Roland said.

The night before, he called Maureen and told her about Judy. Because he wasn't dating Maureen, Judy Weddle asked him over to her living room, a place with so many slipcovers that Judy's blouse fell off like one.

"Something about you and Maureen," Cal ragged after they stepped outside with their burgers. "Things going bad Kowalsky-wise. It couldn't last."

"We're not picking up Kowalsky tonight, are we?" Dave had to throw in.

Roland had had enough. The demon Kowalsky visited their neighborhoods too, turning men into the lead role from the late movie, *A Streetcar Named Desire*. But neither of *them* had to share a room with a brother named Archibald, speaking of Kowalsky. Even saying the word *bald* made him so mad that he could cover up the old man's back-of-the-truck noise.

"Face it, Roll," Dave said as Roland picked up the pay phone. "You have to be chaperoned at the Berwick's. Does her old man know?"

Roland had been running away to the Battaglia's since first grade. That night, as his father watched Vita Blue pitch and started pressuring him about the major leagues, he took off to the Berwick's. Mrs. Berwick was at the library and Maureen's bedroom window was bright beside the meadowy living room. Inside the second front door, Maureen was kissable though she warned him about strep throat.

"Maybe I'll get to stay home for once," Roland said. He lifted the neglected sick girl and carried her to her bed. The truth was, they were having a physics quiz tomorrow and Roland had the review questions with him. "You have to stay in bed," he said, pulling up a desk chair. "Missed you so much." Her tongue was 101 degrees hot and it teased him. "I don't know why health isn't conductible. Infections are. I could transmit health instead of catching strep."

When he palpated her stomach under her pajamas, she wasn't nauseated. Then he took off his flannel shirt and smothered her fever with healthy heat until, after a tingly sweat was on Maureen's skin, she thought that her fever had broken.

Everyone knew Roland was starting over with Maureen.

"The warming house is open down at Baisley Pond," he said at her locker. Hockey try-outs were next week and he'd been practicing with the other guys before supper.

"You guys hardly ever skate to the music," Maureen replied.

"We could. The Oscillator is down there. He dances around our sticking," Roland laughed. "You should get a picture of him."

"I should. He's part of the winter scenery. Louise, do you know anything about him?"

"Does anyone?" Louise said.

"Rink Man on the Make," Roland jeered.

"I've never seen him skate with anyone," Maureen said.

That afternoon, she walked the few blocks to Baisley Pond, ready to take a picture of the Rink Man. Roland whizzed over to her, his back broad like a bird's. And then the Oscillator strode past, his legs swinging around and back like a washing machine oscillator. No one else in Wanatin could do much figure skating. He had on his dented Levis, the same outfit he'd worn for years and while everyone else let their jeans fade.

"You'd think Country's Plenty is paying him to look like a Norman Rockwell magazine cover," Roland said.

At first Maureen pretended she was taking pictures of the boys playing hockey. The Oscillator's legs wove outside them but when he had to, he swung a leg over the skipping puck. He was a case of perpetual motion, living in his own orbit, especially if someone like Cal shouted at him. The guys also called him Prima Pants and He's Back the Dull Knife. Even with the boys low and whizzing around him, he emerged with his hands clasped behind his back, turning for the camera and launching himself backwards. Then he spun on his haunches, whirling like a Russian dancer.

Roland took Maureen's cold hands and thrust them into the pockets of his corduroy jacket, her camera hanging between them. Then they went into the warming house where Maureen put on her skates. A few regular skaters had come and at the signal, the static of the radio, the boys clomped up the ramp like cattle.

"Hey, let's have a skating party," Roland said. "Friday night."

"There's a party already," Dave said.

"We'll chill the girls and warm up afterwards," Cal said. He was dating Greta this year, a girl in the water ballet club.

Friday, Maureen and Louise walked down to Baisley Pond. If the Oscillator were there, Louise was going to wow the skating party, asking for an interview. "Reporter talks to the Rink Man!" Louise exalted. "He's real!"

They saw Roland's car on the hill. The music was already on at the ice rink and the Lombardy girls were skating with Cal, Dave, and a few other guys. Maureen stood at the edge where Roland helped her with her mittens and camera. The Oscillator was like a Christmas ornament in the chandelier static of the radio, probably the only person alone. While "One is the Loneliest Number," sounded, Maureen fumbled with her flash. Roland put a cigarette in her mouth until The Oscillator approached, swiveling as usual.

"Dare me?" Louise had her skates on.

"Free pizza," Roland said.

Maureen went into the warming house to put her camera in the attendant's care. When she clumped down the ramp again, Roland sailed up to her, escorting her onto the ice. The other boys were swinging the Lombardy girls in rock and roll shoves. As Maureen's favorite, "Tapestry", came on the loudspeaker, Roland hunched his arm around her and led with his hockey footwork. The edges of the rink went by like crystal lace while Roland skated like a beau, making up for last summer. Then he pushed her forward and grasped her from behind, his hands under her breasts until she was riding the ice at hockey speed. Suddenly, she was whizzing alone and then he caught her from the front, hugging her.

Louise was having trouble waylaying The Oscillator. His habit of circling around people confused her and whenever she tried to catch up to him, he swayed to the side, pivoting into his backwards gait. As Cal formed a line for Crack the Whip, Louise waited to take the whiplash position.

"She was going to ask him if he teaches skating," Maureen said to Roland. They joined the whip, letting Louise be last.

Now The Oscillator would exhibit his most daring feat. When Louise shot away from the line, skidding in his direction, he looped around her, his hands clasped at his back. Louise slid down onto the ice, probably on purpose, and then, having obtained his attention, she accompanied him as protection from the whip.

Next, Roland flew across the ice but soon his legs were working on it, channeling his speed so that he was skating next to Cal. Instead of taking the lead and cracking the whip even more harshly, he waited for Maureen to fall off and then he held her up.

The whip was rounding the rink more swiftly. Roland and Maureen went to the front of it, cruising at full speed until Cal was consoling Greta on a snowbank.

In the warming house, Maureen learned about the Rink Man from Louise. Then she and Roland walked on their boots for a more showy shot of him. They tramped on up to Roland's car where Maureen could photograph the entire pond from above.

"Do you think your mother would let you go out to dinner with me?" Roland asked, putting his arm around her.

"I go out to dinner with my father. Last week, at The Poplars, he showed me his new calculator. I think he's more excited about it than his home movie projector. He can only use that about twice a year."

"Did you try the calculator?"

"Yeah. I figured out how much my camera film would cost until Christmas."

"I don't want to sneak to a restaurant. I want to take you to one if your mother will let me."

"I don't know if she will. Or if I want to."

"Probation."

Roland's kissing was more persuasive than his promises.

"The Oscillator works at the roller rink," Maureen said, changing the subject. "And as a night watchman. Louise got that out of him."

"Did she ask if he's married?"

"I don't think he's available."

They watched his cowboy lope while the other skaters etched the ice with starts and stops. Then he wound into a dreamy figure eight as Glen Campbell sang "By the Time I Get to Phoenix" on the car radio.

"He's probably never gotten out of Wanatin," Maureen said.

"Does he teach figure skating?"

"No. Louise said he's weird. Defensive. I suppose it's like photography. The newspaper adviser doesn't know more than the school darkroom."

With Roland out of her life, Maureen had been spending more time with her camera. Tonight, the Lombardy girls avoided her until she let go of it. She endured some malice at school, kids shielding their faces with their coat lapels, and the nickname, Peeping Maureen. They probably thought she was as cold with her camera as her father might be with a calculator. The little box obsessed her in the way she had become addicted to Roland's kisses.

"He never falls," Maureen said.

The Oscillator was spinning with a leg extended.

"That's why he never talks. Hockey players fall all the time. Prima Pants." Roland chortled.

"But it's a picture," Maureen said. "You guys can't skate like him."

"If we wanted to, we could."

From where they were parked, the rink man looked as if he had fallen into the sky. Tonight, Roland was a picture too.

The rose wasn't her color, Maureen didn't say in the car. When she saw the cone of paper at the door, she said a quick goodbye to her mother.

Roland brought the yellow rose into Sam's Steakhouse even though it embarrassed her. He was dressed up in corduroys and a new sweater. For the occasion, Maureen was wearing a wool jumper with patterned pantyhose and her long walnut-colored boots.

Wanatin people facetiously said that Sam's Steakhouse was in their suburb, an intersection of buildings a mile out of town. In the summer, an open air fruit market and a fishing store attracted cars to the few blocks of bluff-like farmhouses. Sam's was a long building, barn-red, and usually crowded on the weekend. It was Wanatin's favorite restaurant though many women hadn't tried the other restaurants in the area. The booths were as high as horse stalls and on their wall was a horse sconce with a lightbulb in the saddle.

"Mrs. Zarvas at Finch's Boutique advised me not to wear yellow. Doesn't my skin look sallow near this rose?"

Roland drank half a glass of water and then he put the rose into it. "It reminds me of your hair. Cornhusk."

When their steaks came, Maureen said, "I didn't come for a rose, Roland. My mom probably let me come because she never makes dinner."

"Brrr. The look she gave me," Roland said. His scaling a hill of glacier would probably cause her glee.

"She thinks you could see a psychologist," Maureen said.

"Nah, I couldn't," Roland said, divvying out butter pats and paper cups of sour cream. "It's only when I drink. No one I know talks to a psychologist."

"I talked to one. About insomnia. You could talk to Pastor Rick."

"God, what does Pastor Rick know? My dad helps around the church. He would think I betrayed him. If they talked about 'Spare the rod', I could lose my car."

By the time the hot fudge sundaes had come in their tulip dishes, one of Roland's legs was resting inside Maureen's knee. "We're going steady again."

At school, guys snooped about Roland when they asked Maureen what she was doing on the weekend, probably because of what happened with Duncan Nichols. Without a steady and carrying a camera, she was like The Oscillator.

A joint in Roland's car helped his syndrome. A syndrome was like an orbit in physics, having no definite start or end. He didn't know why breaking off with a girl only made him think about her. It was like losing at baseball and that led to next week's wind-up.

When he picked up Maureen, her mother said, "I'll quiz you on the late movie." Mrs. Berwick wore baggy pants and she was enjoying butterscotch pudding after a BLT, having broken her own syndrome. "First of all, what *is* the late-night movie?"

Roland acted as if he didn't know.

"*Bringing up Baby*," Maureen replied.

They were double dating with Cal. At ten-thirty, they went with him and Greta down to his basement bedroom, actually an apartment since he had a large sitting room with his own TV.

"I can't believe that your parents don't come down here," Greta said, sitting with Cal on the couch. Were they all so high from the joint or was Baby really a leopard on the loose?

"They don't want their bubble to pop," Roland said.

Cal was a star to his parents. Mrs. McConkey didn't come to the basement stairs when Greta shrieked. Cary Grant was wearing a woman's dressing gown.

"Discussion! Discussion with Mrs. Berwick!" Roland said.

"You'd think they were on LSD," Cal said.

"Maybe they developed the film with it. Californians." Roland snuggled Maureen as she sat with him in a sagging chair.

"There wasn't any LSD in the 1930's," Maureen said.

"Remember that for your quiz," Cal said.

As Katharine Hepburn chased Cary Grant, Cal turned the television towards his bunk bed and then he climbed to the top, teasing Greta. Cal had given girls cellulose treatments in the school halls. Greta climbed the ladder and dove to the top bunk while Roland muffled Maureen's laughter. From the bottom bunk, Maureen watched Greta's toe disappearing as if she were doing her water ballet.

Roland called to Cal, "Some day you'll get struck out by a black man, Cal, and you won't be so dutiful as Cary Grant."

As the movie ended, Cal called, "Hey, you want to switch?"

Roland got up to turn the channel.

"Us switch!" Cal switched regularly as a dating pattern. *Bob, Carol, Ted, and Alice* made more of an impression on him than the movie they'd just seen.

"Curiosity, Cal."

"Alright girls. Close your eyes."

Cal was trying to cure Roland of Kowalsky too. If there was anyone Roland could be jealous of, it was Cal. Cal could get any girl; Cal might get Maureen. With her eyes closed, Maureen felt Roland coming apart from her and Cal bounding down from the top bunk.

"I'd rather kiss you than Cal but maybe that's all there is between us," was Maureen's conclusion. She spent an entire weekend with her girlfriends, going with Louise, Jayne, and Dee Dee to see *Cabaret* and then to Kezia Cohen's house. "We tried apricot brandy and almandine and sherry and then we laughed so hard that we rolled on the Cohen's three-inch carpet. Kezia's parents were in Minneapolis. Her mother wants to arrange a Jewish boy as her prom date. He plays the clarinet too!"

They were lying on Lyle's old bed upstairs. Roland had known Kezia since grade school and all he could do was buzz his lips. "Maureen, I don't know what you're up to, tonight. But it's not what I'm up to," was all he said.

"I was just wondering what it would be like to have parents who arranged dates." She watched the street from the dormer window. Soon, she was pointing at Dee Dee Guccinni's finned DeSoto, probably filled with girls who were unattached from their musical instruments that evening. It was spring break and they knew about a party.

On his back, Roland looked at pictures tacked on the eaves - guys with swimming ribbons and Eugene McCarthy. "So your parents don't approve of me," he said. "And my parents would never think of you. Kezia probably won't think the clarinet player is sexy even if he has enough money for her parents. What do you want? Nineteenth century Germany?" Roland looked more Jewish than Kezia did.

Maureen kept watching the cars going past. "But I wonder if it's even normal. Sex controlling things so much. A person should have control over their life."

The word *control* made Roland grip his right hand. He threw wild balls with it. "Normal! The other guys aren't in love. Ask them!" He shifted his weight, loosening his pants. Then he attempted to turn Maureen over from her stomach. "Why do you think people get married?"

She pulled away, staring at the stars that were coming out, her elbows on a pillow.

"But maybe we don't really cause an orgasm. It's a reaction like magnetic fields and fire. Like physics," she said.

Rarely did Roland become speechless with Maureen yet he had nothing to say to this.

"It's a trick. It's got something to do with God."

Roland punched the pillow. "You think you could feel that with anyone."

"No. I wonder if I'd ever feel that with Cal after kissing him. But what you are. You have a mind but you want to do the physical thing all the time. I mean, if you look at a photograph, you think about it. And yet it's over."

"Shit, Maureen!" Roland rolled over and saw a whistle dangling near sunglasses and snorkels. Lyle Berwick used to be a glamour guy to Wanatin kids, a lifeguard with bleached blonde hair on his brown, well-proportioned body. He was probably a Cal to girls. "What do you know about normal, Maureen? Your parents didn't live together after you were seven."

"I don't think my parents were that much different from some other people. In magazine surveys, only about one in ten marriages are happy."

"What's happy? Marriage is necessary." Roland knew that Maureen liked his family being very regular.

"I don't think you realize that in about ten years, we'd probably be tired of each other. Sometimes I feel tension at other people's houses. When the parents are so polite with each other. It reminds me of the year after my parents got divorced."

"You really don't know."

Maureen buttoned her blouse for the party. They had been drinking orange juice with vodka that Roland took from his father's basement bar.

"You analyze too much, Maureen. I thought you didn't like pictures that were too posed."

"Pictures that look too posed. That's what I'm talking about."

"It's smart to know when thinking is leading to more unhappiness. Things'll just hang in the air."

"Maybe that's what's right for us. It's going to happen anyway. What more is there for us to do?"

She jumped up, collected the orange juice glasses, and started for the stairs but Roland caught up with her and grabbed her arm. Maureen elbowed him, knocking a plastic glass at his face. Not having conquered her tonight with kissing, Roland hit back. Then he stopped her, grabbing her by both arms until she knew they'd bruise.

"You asked me to throw a fast ball at you one day. And I told you it could kill you. You didn't know you'd probably flinch or run. You're like your hippie sister, thinking you can go from guy to guy. It's better to face the knife thrower than to have someone knife you in the back."

"I want to go," Maureen said. "Let me go! I don't know why we would fit together. It doesn't make sense."

He was putting another bruise on her arm and when Roland was angry, his face grimaced with reddened rage as if his face had become muscle. To stop her struggling, he said, "I have plans." But when he told her how he planned to be an executive like her father, she felt as if he'd hit her again. Roland might have been Al Pacino, loyal to the Godfather. "I don't want to marry an executive!" she said.

For a moment, she saw it, how they would accomplish what her parents didn't and that this idea was lurking underneath. They would move to the country and own horses and she would remain as attractive as Mrs. Hutchinson in the society pages. When Roland went over to her father's house for a visit, he mollified Clive Berwick's drunken side, saying how Clive was a great guy when he was sober. The gentleman on the barstool, the Freemason. Roland played basketball with him at the YMCA and found out that Clive hadn't ever beaten up his sons.

"I don't plan to have an unhappy marriage," he said. "Yeah, a couple of horse-kicked bodies under a costume." His hands relaxed and they could finally go downstairs.

"My father doesn't like his job. He wanted to be a professor."

"He wanted to *talk* about engineering?"

It was spring outside and tomorrow, when Maureen saw the bruises, she would say the strong thing over the telephone. They went to the party, out-of-sorts and acting as if they wanted to have fun.

11   Up for Air

In the aqua quiet of the YMCA pool, Maureen pondered how she would tell Dee Dee the truth about Roland. Underwater, Maureen could swim almost two lengths of the tank.

"You'd better be careful, Maureen. Anyone knows that bruises turn yellow," Dee Dee said in the emptied locker room.

"It could have happened when I was taking pictures. I've fallen on the bleachers at the baseball diamond."

Dee Dee could tell that she and Roland were fighting before the spring break party.

"He gripped my arms. Okay, he went wild."

When the bruises were visible and Maureen wanted to break up again, Roland came over to apologize. He drooped on a living room chair the way he did in the baseball dugout except that he began to cry, his head in his hands. Her father used to do that the morning after he drank too much.

That evening, she and Roland snuggled under a throw blanket in the Werff's living room. Dee Dee wouldn't know how this was like the underwater of a swimming pool, slow in the spare Werff house, their "little house on the freeway." While Roland listened to Black Sabbath with earphones on, Maureen felt both possessed and protected in the moonlight that came into their picture window. Yet there were rooms in her head that Roland wouldn't like lounging in. Even if she weren't a virgin, she felt that a whole part of her was someone else's. She wasn't going to marry Roland.

"People from farms have a lot of weather in them," Maureen said, thinking how Roland's mother was a pillar at Sears. Her husband had probably never injured her any more than he would injure a farm animal. "He'd been drinking vodka. He knows we're not going to last."

Dee Dee had never loved a date as much as a party. She searched for a guy with seraphic qualities and then, after the party lights were turned off because of a police car passing, she complained that an admirer rubbed up against her. "So it's swimming during a thunder storm," she said, and then she blasted on the hair dryer, expressing scorn for Roland.

While Dee Dee toweled her hair, she said, "Sid Ciel is going to be home from college the weekend of the YMCA banquet. He's planning on attending."

The YMCA roped off a lane for Sid when he was in town.

"He's probably got a girlfriend at college." Maureen flipped on the hair dryer and watched her hair become tawny. Other girls couldn't believe that Maureen didn't date Sid when she had the chance. She could hear Sid's vague laugh. She dated Roland instead of a valedictorian. But even if Sid appeared like a halo on the lifeguard pedestal, it was because Dee Dee had chlorine in her eyes. Maureen asked him why he wanted to date her and all she got was the vague laugh. He might want a girl that he could be naughty with for a few nights.

"Don't you want to break it off with Roland for good?" Dee Dee demanded.

Maureen shrugged while she pulled at her jeans. "Do you think Sid will notice that I've gained eight pounds?" She also had blotches on her face from eating Cheese Frenchees at King's Food Host. Roland didn't especially adore the extra eight pounds and that was proof of something. If Roland thought that she wanted to see Sid, he would only strive to maintain his position as Maureen's ace date. "Dee Dee, I said I would take pictures at the banquet. And I told my dad that I'd eat with him."

She would look at pictures of Sid afterwards and wonder about college.

Six days after the Wanatin regional baseball tournament, Cal and Dave were looking for Roland. On the seventh day, Maureen told Cal over the telephone, "He just came over." Cal had to find out what Roland did with his anger.

"What'd you do? Take it out on a combine?" Cal asked at Maureen's house.

"Sleep in a barn?" Dave said.

Roland pitched eight innings of the last regional game. When Wanatin was ahead 2-0, the coach sent in a relief pitcher, the star of the basketball team. He was tall and had a tortuous sidewinder that the other team figured out after the second hitter. A three-run disaster lost Wanatin's chance at the state tournament.

"I don't want to talk about it," Roland said.

"At least we can all enjoy a joint now," Cal said. "Do you want to go driving? Maybe we could find a scarecrow to punch."

"Nah," Roland said. He'd rather take a joint than a joke. "I've got to decide where I'm going to college."

They'd all gotten scholarships but according to Roland, Mr. Werff expected the major leagues to finance his son.

"The best team or Maureen?" Dave wondered.

"She has to go to school in Minnesota because of her state scholarship," Roland said.

During one morning of Fill-in-the-Circle, Maureen obtained a scholarship to any college in the state of Minnesota. Her application to Carlton came through, adding another scholarship.

"Too bad about Minnesota," Cal said. He had a double hockey and baseball scholarship at the university, the best deal of all.

"Yeah, too bad," Roland said. His best offer was in Iowa.

"I wanted to visit Carlton too," Dave kidded.

"Between parties," Roland said, going over to Lyle's old record player.

"Chicago?" Cal said.

"Yeah, I might be that far away," Roland replied. He put on the *Chicago* album, which was to say that he wanted to be alone with Maureen. Roland had decided that "Beginnings" was their song.

"Do you carry that album around with you?" Dave asked.

Roland gritted his teeth over a cigarette. "It's her graduation present. Hey, are you guys coming to my graduation party? Then we're all together in our defeat."

"You have to thank the good Lord that we're not going to Vietnam," Cal said, getting to his feet as if he were at the Werff's. He wouldn't bring up President Nixon there, now that the draft was over and no one needed a college deferment. Roland's father feared that professors were useless and immoral people.

After Cal and Dave left, Maureen and Roland went to Lyle's old bed under the eaves.

"Seven days away from you," Roland said. "Look, they left us another joint. I was working out at my uncle's. Thinking about the farm. Arch doesn't want it. He doesn't do the tractor work. It's either turkeys or turkeying around on a tractor here."

Yet after the absence, the marijuana made it possible to pretend they were ensconced from the future in acres of corn. The afternoon was humid, and, like a siesta in a flexible farm schedule, they made love until they were as drowsy as the humidity. There was leftover buttered cornbread for the munchies and Tropical Kool-Aid.

At the dormer window, a roaming breeze ruffled the sheets. Knowing things were going to change gave Maureen a feverishness that had something to do with forever or a picture of that idea. Roland's frame was comfortable as a couch while they planned to spend the summer like this. But as Maureen tapped a cigarette outside the crook of his arm, he suddenly hurled the sheet over her.

Maureen's mother must have done this to her own sons, appearing with her eerie librarian silence. Outraged, her eyes shone the unbearable blue of a ninety-degree sky. She was in a standstill while Maureen and Roland made furtive attempts to dress under the sheet. Roland was different from the men in that house, being broader and his legs muscle-bound. His hair was a shock of dark curls yet his skin was whiter than Maureen's, freckled and susceptible to sunburn.

"For shame! When I'm out-of-town!"

Two days a week, Maureen's mother drove to Mankato for education courses. They could hear her inhaling, fixed in her own emotions. As if the world hadn't been gawking at half-naked bodies since 1960. Or as if steadies didn't fall into these behaviors, seeing each other every day. But this hadn't happened to Joann when she was in high school.

"At least *your* mother knows how to leave changing rooms," Maureen apologized the day of Roland's graduation party. Her mother had declined attending.

"My mother wears a mask," Roland said. In his family, the discovery might have led to a shotgun wedding. But the Berwick's did everything differently.

Werff and Heineman relatives chugged in from the country, anticipating one of Mrs. Werff's town cakes. It was flat, almost as big as a card table, and covered with green frosting. On that, a baseball diamond was piped with a diploma as home plate.

Roland's relatives were such dorks that Cal might have said that to their face. "They'd probably ask what kind of an engine a dork is," he whispered.

Maureen lost any spontaneous speech, meeting them. They dressed as if they hadn't subscribed to a newspaper in the last twenty years.

"Maybe it's for good luck," Dave said. "Nineteen-fifties harvests."

While Mrs. Werff got her spatula ready, Maureen finally voiced a thought. "Are you going to cut the cake so Roland eats his diploma?"

This decision was apparently the dilemma, causing some impatient guffaws until Mrs. Werff dove in.

"No one's on the bases or I'd be a Cyclops," Roland said.

Then Mr. Werff swooped his Cyclops hand down, grabbing the plastic pitcher from his mound of chocolate. He tossed it to Roland.

At the coffee table, Mrs. Werff showed Maureen her scrapbook of cakes. There were birthday cakes, baby shower cakes, and then the wedding cakes. The latter were flat too and decorated in cobwebs of candy confetti and coconut. When Mrs. Werff opened up another scrapbook, Cal stopped eating second base. For Maureen, Roland's baby pictures were shock treatment, his face big as a balloon under hair that was like a toupee. His gray eyes had started out blue, thrilled, and innocent.

"They probably gave me beer when I was a baby," Roland said, driving her home.

Maureen had to wonder how a baby of theirs could fit in with Roland's farm relatives. She was always waiting for her period.

A few months later, Maureen sorted out her college things - her 35mm Canon camera, an Olympia typewriter, four pairs of flared jeans, and a spectrum of turtlenecks and sweaters. Because she was going to live in a co-ed dorm, she bought a new bathrobe.

Some of what she couldn't take to college was scattered on tables in the backyard. Her mother was having a rummage sale and she talked of moving from Wanatin. This summer, she completed a master's degree in education, opening herself up for school library jobs.

Watching the tables with her mother, Maureen saw one of her father's graduation presents out - a book of women's sayings. Adolescent girls were already reading her father's inscription: *Beware of early marriage.*

"Are you and Roland still going steady?" wondered Sandy from down the block. She'd been jaunting around with a camera at her neck and considered Maureen a role model.

"No. We still date," Maureen said, confiscating her book. It might be a dorm ice-breaker.

The girls sighed, looking at novelty beach towels and books that Mrs. Berwick threw out on their ears. When they bought *Peyton Place* from Maureen, her mother stared at her as if she should have hidden the book under a beach towel.

"I suppose they think Roland and I should stay together," Maureen said.

"Shhh," Joann replied as young mothers examined the Corningware and boys' dressers. When Maureen made for the house, she said, "I need your help, Maureen."

"I was just getting something to drink." Parting with memories seemed easier for her mother. When Maureen came back to sit in the hot sun near the trellises where her father once grew green beans, Miss Samperson, a librarian her mother worked with, was in the yard. Of course Miss Samperson was drawn to Mr. Berwick's Christmas presents. "Are you still going out with Roland?" she asked as she admired rarely-used demitasse cups.

"No, not exactly," Maureen said. Roland often met her at the public library when she was looking at magazines or books on photography.

"He doesn't seem like the right person for you to marry," Miss Samperson commented, examining a soup tureen. "Though it was nice to see him at the library."

Finally Miss Samperson bought the demitasse set and an electric frying pan, Clive Berwick's attempts to mollify his ex-wife.

"There's so much junk from the kids," Maureen's mother apologized. They chatted while Miss Samperson collected books that Maureen thought were hers – old Dr. Dolittle's and *Wuthering Heights* with the cautionary woodcuts of Heathcliff. After she left, Maureen's mother said, "She's had a disappointing life."

"I guess she thinks Roland would be disappointing," Maureen laughed. "I wonder if things change with holy love." She collected a pillow with a crocheted cover for her dorm room. "I guess Lydia left this. I gave it to her for Christmas."

Her mother was putting Lyle's set of James Bond near some old National Geographic's. Because she hadn't found Lydia shocking, living with her folksinger boyfriend and her three-year-old from another relationship, Maureen said, "People in your time didn't know what it was to be with someone before marriage. So they thought love was holy when they didn't know each other yet."

"It's not about them, it's about respect for God," her mother replied.

Perspiring, Maureen took a National Geographic and sat on a footstool in the shade. She viewed storks in trees and on roofs. Then a stork was eating an eel. "I don't see how pastors or officials in a city hall magically change things. They don't know how people get together. I mean, how do they know if God put people together?"

"I don't know." Her mother was relieved to see a few housewives milling in from the sidewalk near the cedars.

"Anyone who wants to know about Roland?" Maureen asked.

"Shut up, Maureen," her mother said, using the phrase that preceded exits in their family.

A boy discovered Maureen's Cracker Jack toys from Friday nights watching "The Flintstones." After she helped his mother cart off her old decal-covered bookcase, Maureen sat sipping Kool-Aid. "Dr. Lunn offered me birth control," she told her mother. "When I went for my college physical."

Her mother stared at her, the blue of her eyes like pulsing veins.

"Maybe he was afraid that I'd conceive Frankenstein – Dad's brain and Roland's body."

"You really shouldn't talk like this, Maureen."

It was the way Maureen's father used to talk. "At least Roland puts some value on my brain."

"I don't dislike Roland," her mother said, straightening some relish dishes. "You're receiving money for your education. You should be thinking about that right now."

"I never planned anything with Roland." Maureen had only planned how not to get pregnant. Yet she knew it was going to be more difficult to leave him than her mother. "Roland is like Pippi Longstocking. He's very strong."

Louise Ogland was coming through the garage. "Did anyone buy your old bathrobe?" she wondered. Browsing at the tables, she chose a sun hat that Joyce crocheted. "It doesn't look worn."

"I wore it a few times," Maureen's mother said. "It's too young for me."

Maureen took Louise inside to see her new bathrobe. It was floor-length, its bodice made of dark turquoise flannel and its skirt of polished cotton. "Do you think I can see guys in it?" Maureen asked, modeling it.

"It's a dressing gown," Louise said. "Cool."

Maureen lit up a cigarette.

"Did you smoke all those?"

An ashtray in Maureen's bedroom was filled with cigarette butts.

"She can't kick me out of the house for it now."

But they both jumped at Clive Berwick's voice. "Maureen?"

He was in the living room. Maureen greeted him in her new robe but without the cigarette. "Did you come in the back door?" Maureen asked.

"I had to see if there was anything I wanted. Lyle left some clippings in a book about diving." Maureen's father was also holding the book *Cheaper by the Dozen*.

"Do you think this is OK for lounging?" Maureen asked.

"As long as you're not wearing an engagement ring. I wondered if you'd like to go out to eat? Louise, you're invited if you'd like to come."

With Poppy smoking at Wanatin's Holiday Inn restaurant, no one noticed that Maureen had become addicted to cigarettes in the last month. She assured her father that she and Roland weren't going steady anymore, even if Roland might be more loyal to a woman than her father had been.

PART II

12   Suspension Bridge

At college, 1973. In her new bathrobe and with a cigarette, Maureen felt swanky, freed of burdens in her freshman hall. Other girls were in crises away from their parents and some got drunk for the first time. She was lucky to hit it off with her roommate Valerie. Valerie inspected photos of Roland and paused at his baseball uniform. "How appropriate for high school," she mused. Valerie's high school steady did mescaline while Maureen's had a temper like mescaline.

Having prepared for her release from Wanatin, Maureen had her photography and a reputation for chemistry the first quarter. She studied more than she ever had. When the chemistry professor handed back semi-finals in the lecture auditorium, he lauded Maureen for obtaining the highest score. For a few months, she was a fascination to pre-medical students.

The co-ed that posed continual problems on their dormitory floor was the daughter of a professor. The first thing Amy did was to paint over the plaque on her door. She was changing her name to Hecuba. Eventually, Hecuba painted her wall with messy collage, a fire hydrant high as a column and a man crashing down with a helmet for a parachute. Over her roommate's bed, she painted a thundercloud with lightning words: *Zipporah thou shalt.* Shana, her roommate, was in counseling. She'd come from a small town where her father was funeral director and she had long wished to talk with a psychologist.

Men visited the corridor, often making time, sometimes leaving a woman upset. Only a dispatcher, Sam Smalt, came consistently during the first quarter. He roamed from room to room, giving back massages and information about his floor. Maureen walked on his back but nothing could daunt him because Denise, from Mason City, welcomed the economics major.

One late night, wearing her flannel granny nightgown, Denise told Maureen and Valerie why she liked an easily distracted guy. Valerie, being more interested in feminism than any major, was impressed that Denise's mother kept a college bank account for Denise since she was five. Denise's mother was startlingly feminist, in fact. When Denise said she was too sick to go out weekends with her boyfriend, her mother took her to Chicago for an evaluation and then she arranged for an abortion as if Denise were a suffering cow.

Maureen was far from such worries. She was "in crush" with her chemistry lab assistant. Michael hung around her during lab and often ate a late lunch with her and her lab partner, Kendra. But the senior pre-med student hadn't asked her out.

Valerie was interested in Bret Howard ever since Halloween when she dressed as an American tourist. Wearing a straw hat, sunglasses, and Maureen's camera case along with various instamatics, she talked with Bret about overseas semester programs. So far, they hadn't agreed to register for the same program.

One February evening, Maureen sat with Valerie in the dorm lounge with a stack of photos. Examining one, Valerie held it at arm's length and that attracted Bret to their study table.

Five women splayed on their backs around a stool. Crowded on the stool were Capezios, quilted boots, and the soles of body pajamas. In their nightwear, the women balanced cigarette holders, one with a cigarette, another with a library pencil, another with a fire cracker.

Valerie watched Bret's eyes. "Do you think Maureen can get through college with a photograph for every thousand words?"

Sam Smalt appeared and wondered, "What's Denise got in her holder?"

"A cinnamon stick," Maureen said.

"Where's Hecuba?" Bret wondered.

Maureen pulled out another print in her stack. Hecuba held her paintbrush like a rifle at the painted soldier on her wall.

"Hecuba opened her door when Maureen called out 'Amy'," Valerie explained.

"That's screwed up," Bret said.

"She was mad. But I got the newspaper photos of her room," Maureen explained. "It's tied up between the student council and the administration."

Valerie held the group shot at arm's length again. "I'll remember Maureen in blue, standing over us. She stood on a desk."

Bret peered at the photo. In the group shot, Valerie was wearing a knee-length nightshirt with her Capezios.

"I was nearly a blue baby," Maureen said, keeping up the conversation. "I was born with the umbilical cord around my neck."

The guys glanced at other photos as Maureen spread them on the table. But then they drifted back to their books. Bret and Sam weren't pre-med. When Maureen said she was almost a blue baby in chemistry lab, Michael lingered at her lab station. He was considering psychiatry and she was afraid he favored her because he found out that her parents were divorced.

"You were a heroine at birth. It sounds like David Copperfield. I was born with the umbilical cord around my neck." Valerie adjusted her mohair-like mane so that she could keep an eye on Bret. "I'm strangling from all this studying. We should take the shuttle bus up to Minneapolis one of these dull weekends."

"I'd like to take my camera there."

"I'd like to take Bret there. We could go to the Walker Art Center." Valerie wrote in the margin of her paper on feminism, *Why can't women ask men out?*

Passing Maureen's cafeteria table, Valerie flexed her grin. Rather than stop, she wanted to remind Maureen of their conversation the previous night. "Your crush is graduating," she said. "There's not much time left. Don't you think some divorces happen because women don't choose their dates?"

Maureen was having a late lunch with Michael because she was his favorite lab student. But as usual, they weren't sitting alone. Gordon Kirch held up a gluey mass of corned beef on his fork. He was so critical of the cafeteria food that he wrote about it for English class. "I think I'd rather toast a brat over a Bunsen burner," he said.

Michael swallowed with his head lowered. He was very blonde and husky in build. "We've roasted marshmallows in the lab," he finally said.

Maureen broached, "Valerie and I are taking the shuttle bus to Minneapolis this weekend. Do either of you know of a restaurant near the Walker Art Center? Anyone else need a break?" With the confidence of her Carole King curls, she assumed Roland Werff's casual style of asking. Then she tilted an eye at Michael as if she were about to snap a picture.

"I'd like to eat some decent food," Gordon said.

Michael only offered, "There's a restaurant in the building. Near the Guthrie Theater." But he might have been handing Maureen a container of dry ice.

"Well?" Valerie demanded when Maureen came into her dorm room.

"Gordon Kirch is coming. I never thought of him as a date."

"I asked Bret. And then Sam Smalt came by. He wants to go. Bret can't."

"You're going on a date with Sam?"

"Denise is coming too. And Shana. She needs to get away from Hecuba."

Maureen shut the door. "I suppose Hecuba is interested in modern art."

That summer, Maureen worked so few hours at the YMCA that she visited Hugo and Joyce in the town of Middlefield. Hugo was an intern pastor there, having gone to the seminary after his military service. Their house was a small one-story with two bedrooms and mission furniture donated from the Lutheran church.

Maureen stayed for a week and then she applied for a full-time job at a vegetable canning factory. She preferred Joyce's company to her mother's, especially now that her mother put their house up for sale. It was too big and she was intent on finding a library job outside of Wanatin.

The second Mrs. Berwick was faring better with Maureen's father at their puzzle brick house. Poppy enjoyed sparring words with her ex-employer but when she referred to Maureen as "that unfortunate child", Maureen didn't want to stay on. And Roland was in Wanatin for the summer, working for his uncle. After a few nights out, Maureen decided to subject him to Hugo if he wanted to see her.

In Middlefield, Joyce often picked up Maureen at the factory and then they sunned on the brick patio, a step from the supper they were preparing. Joyce was piqued at Hugo's reticence about his parishioners. During the summer, the town's Lutherans had little time for church projects except for the children's summer program where Joyce taught.

Joyce relished Maureen's blunt conversation with Hugo even when Maureen began the game of miracle riddles at supper. Maureen was a doubter. She pretended she had a camera for a Bible miracle and then Hugo countered her with a Bible-time answer. At the challenge of the fishes and loaves, he speculated that, while the disciples handed out their small stash of food, Jesus knew that some of his followers were prepared to picnic. Jesus had demonstrated sharing, influencing many in the crowd to reveal the provisions in their camel bags.

At this, Maureen showed Hugo photographs that she had developed at the drugstore.

Women bent over green beans, snatching at them as they traveled down a conveyor belt. One of the women wore mascara heavy as high school and another was a Latino. An older woman with crank-like arms stood near a washing tank and behind her, past stacks of boxes, light sprayed from large doors like a horizon.

"If you see one of those green bean cans, thousands could appear from nowhere," Maureen said. "I wonder if Jesus' followers had to pay for their fish and bread."

"There may have been donations." Hugo hunched above Joyce's Homer Laughlin bluebird china, eating chicken sauced with purple grapes.

But he speared his grapes and put them in a pile next to his chicken breast.

Joyce asked, "Would Pastor Beitterman approve of your interpretation of the loaves and fishes for a sermon?"

Hugo shrugged. "Lately, he's been interested in the interpretation of divorce. He asked me if I think divorce makes a woman an adulteress. Married women can be adulteresses."

"Divorce made mom single," Maureen said. Her mother hardly looked like an adulteress.

Hugo scooped up four grapes onto his spoon. "Mom has a boyfriend. Maybe she didn't want to tell you. Anyway, he's a widower."

"Who is it?"

Hugo had said something as solid as a pulpit. And this explained why Maureen's mother suggested the visit to Middlefield.

"Mr. Gleason, a science teacher," Joyce replied.

"He's a widower? We used to call him the missing link man." This was appalling. "Is that why she's selling the house?"

"I don't know," Hugo said.

"I don't know if I approve," Maureen said.

"His wife died of cancer more than a year ago," Joyce said. "He helped your mother put in the tomato plants."

The junior high kids thought that Mr. Gleason's face had always been crestfallen.

"What if she marries him?" Maureen demanded.

"Then who would she be married to at the resurrection?" Hugo quizzed.

"I thought people weren't married in heaven," Maureen replied, pointing out another Bible inconsistency.

As soon as Maureen saved enough for school, she took a train across Canada. At first, there was nothing to photograph except wheat fields. But the moving train room was better than college. And college, churning with laughter and wretchedness, was better than the old house in Wanatin.

In the lounge car, she sat near Yvette from Montreal, a jewelry maker. They were talking about wine and whether water tasted better than a fifth glass of wine. Another of Hugo's riddles.

Yvette held up a dried cherry preserved in shellac. In her workbox were amethysts, glass beads, tiny shells, and findings. "Regardez. Too much wine makes a man look like a prune."

A Saskatchewan woman told about a man who was fooled with a glass of crusty snow after he'd had too many beers. She was a veterinary student, traveling from Ontario. "It'll be nice to see some animals with manners again," she said. "City pets don't know how to make themselves scarce."

When the veterinary student walked with her suitcase to a lone shed in a Saskatchewan meadow, Maureen readied herself for the Alberta badlands. She put a new roll of film into her camera and when the terrain became moon-like, she blurted out, "How long until Jasper?"

A woman counting stitches, there as if she came with the ticket benefits, assured her that the badlands had boundaries. But Maureen, in her childish slip, kept thinking about the train breaking down. A bus broke down in below zero weather when she was seven and traveling with her mother.

Stretching her legs at Jasper, Maureen wandered towards the foothills. The lake there was about as rugged as a waterbed sewn in sunlight, a postcard picture. She climbed and crawled, sliding back to storm gravel as she searched for the chance animal. Then she settled for a view of the nearest Canadian Rockies bluff. Something stirred the whiskered branches on a ledge, a bird flushing out. As it soared, she snapped her camera. It looked like a vulture, not an eagle. She was strangling herself, running after it.

At the tourist haven, someone said, "It was probably a turkey vulture."

She watched couples in honeymoon moods near the hotel, thinking how the guys in Wanatin would laugh at her running after a turkey vulture when she had nothing except a camera.

Through the Rockies, Maureen drank wine with Yvette and a man who spoke Canadian French. She was still amazed that trains didn't break down. "I thought the only thing that couldn't break down was time."

"The Rockies look as if time broke them," Yvette replied. She slipped into French with Raoul until Maureen was struggling to understand that diamonds were under the Canadian Shield.

After a screaming tunnel, Maureen explained that she was staying with her brother in Vancouver. "He said he won't leave Canada even if he gets amnesty. I'm afraid I'll want to stay in Vancouver."

"If one learns a special skill, work that Canada needs, emigration is easier," Yvette said.

"Many people make a marriage de convenance," Raoul smiled.

Unblinkingly, Yvette added, "They will need to excavate the diamonds under the Canadian Shield for all the marriages of convenience."

The tall crystalline buildings in Vancouver seemed to have emerged from seismic movements. Small wood houses were cabbaged in huge shiny leaves. Seeing her brother Lyle stirring kale, water chestnuts, and cashews in a wok staggered Maureen too.

"Have you wanted to go back at all?" she asked him.

"Only to see people. People who took ships to America hardly ever went back."

"When Hugo wanted to be alone, he said that there was a man who was an island. One of Noah's sons."

"And his descendants were shipwrecked in Atlantis. It helps if there's an exotic grocery around the corner."

Lyle met his girlfriend at an East Indian grocery in the Kitsilano neighborhood. He was working on a ferry boat while he studied oriental languages. "Tasha is bringing raita. It's a salad," he said. "George is bringing himself. His wife left him for a science project in Banff."

George was another draft dodger, married two months after he arrived in Vancouver.

Before Maureen saw the Capilano Suspension Bridge, she swayed from one Vancouver ledge to another, balancing her camera. In a park with George, she watched equestrians in red breeches and beanies. Swimming, she tossed from a high wave into a nude bather. The museum totem poles needed a viewing deck.

In Wanatin, the Baisley Park swinging bridge was about twelve feet above the creek. Lyle stepped out on the Capilano Suspension Bridge as if it were a high diving board. At his suggestion, Maureen imagined that two hundred and thirty feet of water were under her feet, not two hundred and thirty feet of air. She attempted to photograph the people reaching the other side; they looked like primitives in search of food. The forest grew vertically there, on the side of the ravine. When she veered to the side rail, she clung to it, sliding down onto the narrow footpath above the abyss. Below, the Capilano River was a thin rushing avenue.

"Hold on, Lyle," George called from behind her. "Maureen's crouching for a shot. We want it to turn out."

In her terror, Maureen tried to take a shot through the pattern of the railing. Finally she said, "I can't move."

A tour guide was threading his way to Lyle. "Do you need someone to walk her back?"

Maureen needed someone to untwist her.

That night, she told George about her photography and that she loved the darkroom, its eerie light, and the chemicals swishing in the tubs. Grasping her tongs, she watched two worlds, a world where time passed so quickly that tomorrow was a blank, and a world where images could be caught like fish and hung up to dry.

Now she felt like a photograph, frozen in time. She would return to college and say that she didn't feel right about kissing a married man even when he said he wasn't really married. Even if he looked like *that*.

But she wouldn't tell her real secret - that she couldn't cross the Capilano Suspension Bridge.

13   Rift in Focus

Junior year, Valerie lived down the hall from Maureen. Another year rooming together might have pocked their friendship. Valerie might have said, "What is your father's mask? Industrial-military or Father of the Hippies?", seeing the photographs Maureen developed after he visited. And Maureen might have answered, "Maybe we don't wear masks."

An older man's white hair waved around a headband. A backpack was reflected in the arching window behind him.

Kendra, the new roommate, took a break from her studying to see Maureen's prints. Having come from suburban Los Angeles, she often pored over *People Magazine* between chapters of abnormal psychology.

"It must have been hard to grow up without your father," she observed in her detached way. She could take on "Candid Camera" at any time and that fascinated campus men.

"That's the backpack he gave me," Maureen said. "He wanted to be a professor. But he left graduate school after one year."

Maureen's friends knew of only one other student whose parents were divorced, Charles Gatterley III, the great-grandson of the Gatterley Dairies founder. Because the Gatterley's funded the college, Charles didn't have to live near anyone that he didn't like. He had ousted disagreeable and drinking students from his floor.

"My father just lived across town," Maureen said.

"Divorce is considered to be nearly as traumatic as the death of a parent," Kendra said.

"I'm thinking of transferring to the University of Minnesota," Maureen told the college newspaper editor, Ed. They were having beers in downtown Northfield. She had said this to her father on the dormitory phone after hearing the girl who answered it say to Kendra, "Maureen's father sounds tipsy."

"What for?" Ed was thin and could thread a surreptitious path through any crowd. If Maureen didn't encounter him with a new idea, he might suggest something offbeat like reading <u>The Thin Man</u>. Discussing his book list helped writers obtain assignments.

"For the journalism courses. For better photography courses," Maureen replied.

"But you're going to be the layout editor next year."

This time, Ed's idea was tempting.

"It's for sure," he said. "Isn't it? OK, *this* week, I want you to take pictures of the *Hamlet* rehearsal and then do the page layout for the article."

Maureen couldn't tell Ed the other reason for a transfer, that the only romance in her life was the delectable blue feeling she had, breaking up with Roland again. She'd spent a weekend at his shared house in Iowa and waking, he'd ordered her, "Let the dog out." Having learned not to argue at such an hour with a man who pitched college baseball, she decided, while leashing the mongrel, never to return.

At college though, her wavy hair and wavy body caused the other photography students to seek her for modeling. She cut her hair so that its waves flushed against the neckline of loose, thigh-length sweaters.

Polonius leaned over Ophelia, his mouth looking as if it had expensive candy in it. He was formidable in brocade.

Newspaper in hand, Polonius found Maureen in a remote library carrel. Valerie knew Gerard from the backstage of the theater. She negotiated with him about his elder make-up and she helped to construct the paper mache mask for Hamlet's ghost. Maureen now knew that Gerard's girlfriend was down at the library foyer, working at her student job.

"Your hair looks like little shells," Gerard said, leaning over her. He acted as if he were on a pleasant reef when he had sneaked through a maze to find her. Ever since the dress rehearsal, he feigned excitement about his photos, as if the production itself weren't more important.

Because Gerard's sudden physical attraction for her might be a dead-end and because she was behind on a paper, Maureen rebuffed him. He looked around, rising from a kneel position, and whispered, "I'll be visiting Valerie when you come back to your dorm."

In the darkened dorm hallway, Gerard continued to be secretive. He told Maureen that she was always in his head, like a photograph on a record album cover. His effusiveness must have come from his hours with Shakespeare but he persisted, "Maureen, I've got to tell Laurel that I've fallen in love with you."

Gerard could get away with this because he was two tads taller than medium build and a tad better than handsome. He had burnished, brushed hair and a vigilant jaw. On another night, Maureen might tell Gerard that her divorced mother was a librarian who, like Laurel, dreamed of being a poetess.

Maureen had to laugh. She was used to dates like last weekend's campus film, *Reefer Madness,* and being kissed by a pitcher of fast balls.

"Why not, Maureen?" Gerard implored.

Kendra supported Maureen's dubiousness after the Friday rendezvous. An admirer of hers had gone public, calling her from the lawn under her dorm window. When Gerard visited, she congratulated him on the play and invited him into their dorm room where she spent late weekend nights dreading her inebriated admirer. She told Gerard how she was saving herself for a serious relationship.

"Why not, Maureen?" Valerie wondered in the cafeteria.

"I feel like the other woman with Gerard," Maureen said at lunch. "Did you tell Gerard that my mother is a librarian?"

"What does that matter? Laurel shouldn't get engaged to a man who says he's in love with someone else."

"But I haven't fallen in love with Gerard," Maureen said.

"Look, here he comes. With Gordon Kirch."

Val always welcomed Gerard because he knew how to please her English professor. And Maureen had to welcome Gordon because he was now the Cafeteria Critic for the newspaper.

Soon Gerard was advising Val, "Start with the idea that there haven't been any heroes in literature since the Viking invasions. Write about a character with base motives."

"No heroes?" Maureen wondered. "Do you know what Gordon goes through to print the truth about this food?"

Valerie applauded Gordon but he made a face, showing with his fork how the slice of ham in his sandwich was as tough as rubber. "When was the last night we had ham?" he said.

"Fence the chef. Of course there were heroes," Gerard said, spreading mustard on his ham. "Some people thought Richard Nixon, Richard the Resigned, was a hero before Watergate. At any rate, the professor isn't one."

"Kendra thought Nixon was a hero. I did too, when he ended the draft," Maureen said, disgusting Gerard.

"So you write about a character who isn't a hero," Valerie said. "Look at Maureen. She can eat all the starch without gaining weight." Even if Maureen came from of a divorce, Valerie considered her lucky in other ways.

"The dearth of heroes is an idea like democracy to Dr. Balmer. He thinks like an aristocrat because he's tenured."

"There aren't many men like Hercules in books," Maureen said.

"They give us mashed sweet potatoes for our muscles," Gordon said. "Flour for our brains. The cafeteria cook is a very busy man, whipping up leftovers."

"The guy built like Hercules did as he was told before 1800. Don't say that anyone like Shakespeare or a lowly counselor was a hero. Servants groveled. Most importantly, type your footnotes with appropriate punctuation. And don't squeeze your text to the footnotes. If your footnotes aren't perfect, he'll drop you an entire grade."

It was easy to imagine Gerard as a college professor, telling huckster jocks what to do. And telling his wife that he had fallen in love with one of his students.

Gordon winced at his bread pudding, wondering if there was mold in it. That helped Valerie to say goodbye to it. After they left, Gerard said, "We could break this thing to Laurel at the cast party. Or I could take you to a movie first. She's in class right now."

Despite the exquisite sense of guilt Maureen was feeling, she heard Gerard out. But then she didn't like being the reason for Laurel's unhappiness. "Isn't Laurel expecting to get engaged?"

"You don't know why I'm with Laurel."

"I don't know if I want to."

"You're not the only person from a disturbed background, Maureen. And you're not the only one on scholarship."

In the emptying cafeteria, Gerard told Maureen how his father died between one siren and another on a gray Chicago street. If a person disappeared on that street, it was often into a bar. After Gerard's mother wandered into the department store where his father worked, looking for him, she kept going to work there.

His mother's friend Dora was in the habit of dropping over. Her husband was out-of-town much of the time and she was consoling, eventually dropping in to make sure Gerard had some supper. She even brought over beers and stayed for Hawaii 5-0 and the White Sox games. Soon, she was showing Gerard how she kissed when she didn't have bad memories of her husband's infidelity. She had to kiss a lot to recall.

It was all a demonstration and a detached performance with the exit door clearly marked. But in the wings, Gerard felt that he was in a tawdry drama that no one would want to watch. Dora's thick matte make-up streaked his face, not lipstick. When Gerard set out for college, Dora was there with his mother, tearful about the separation.

"You're like me," Gerard said. "It's not really home to go back, is it?"

Outside the cafeteria window, roof gutters were dribbling dirty water into icicles that clung above speckled snow. Maureen was fighting off sadness. The gray winter would never end because it would happen again next year. Summer would always lead to it. Gerard was probably a better match for her than for Laurel yet she was reluctant to take a second helping of an unhappy home.

In the summer, Maureen worked a month at the vegetable factory and then she worked for a studio photographer that Hugo knew. In August, she flew out to San Francisco to visit Lydia.

"I helped pose people at weddings," Maureen told her sister. "When I asked my boss if he ever photographed funerals, he showed me his schedule for baptisms."

Staying at Lydia's Berkeley bungalow promised some spontaneity with the camera. Lydia shared rooms with her folksinger boyfriend, her six-year-old whose father was best forgotten, a woman named Flavia, and when Flavia wasn't having her period, her boyfriend Abner.

"Is Mom still seeing that teacher?" Lydia wondered.

"He came over one day to lend her his dandelion weeder. Roland was there and one look from Mr. Gleason was enough for him to work on the dandelions. I don't want to sleep with Roland anymore but it could happen."

While Lydia was at her music therapy classes, Maureen babysat her nephew Lonnie. Flavia was writing a dissertation on absurdity and nonsense.

"When my period is over, I'll show you some of my poetry," Flavia said. "Some of my poems were written during my period. I wonder if you'll be able to tell."

Walking with Lonnie, Maureen admired ivy lawns and plants that seemed to sprout from bungalow walls. The tortoise-like houses contained women who wanted to be different from the hare-like Jones'.

They took children to the coffee house where Emory, Lydia's boyfriend, sang and played the harmonica like a twangy violin. When he strummed bead curtains on the stage, the children made noise, one with a scrub board, one with a tin whistle. Lonnie clapped a small pair of cymbals.

Maureen recalled her first double exposure. "You were standing on the piano, holding a sparkler."

"I never did that," Lydia said.

"I thought it was my best picture."

At a supermarket, Lydia collected mangos and bananas for a rice salad. Abner was coming for supper. He was getting a Ph.D. in Physics, although at first introduction, he seemed offhand and made Maureen think of Groucho Marx.

"Sometimes it seems like nonsense," Abner said at supper, searching with his spoon for a wonton in his bowl. "Looking for dark matter in dark space."

"Is it like finding root vegetables in the ground?" Maureen wondered.

"Yes, but much worse. We're like dogs trying to smell truffles in woods that might not have any truffles."

"Some of us are looking for our home planet," Emory said, cracking open a loaf of sour dough.

Flavia recited a few lines of her nonsense poetry:

"The shaded house we see from the road

has no one in it that we acknowledge.

The painted lady scalloped and rimmed

has too many visitors testing her plaster."

"People my age don't know what they're looking for," Maureen complained.

After dinner, they toured the Lawrence Hall of Science despite a watchman who insisted that the hall was closed.

"I wish I had a photograph of a falling star," Maureen said.

The next night, they all drove away from the San Francisco lights and past groves of avocado trees. No one saw a falling star but Abner helped Maureen set up her camera with a clock drive. Groping at the tripod, she took photographs of the Milky Way, the stars of Sagittarius, and then she focused into a dark area nearby.

"I think you'll get the Cygnus Rift," Abner said.

"You helped Abner prepare for a class he's teaching this fall," Lydia said as Maureen packed.

"I took physics. Believe it not, Roland got better grades in it. He has no intention of using his mind that way though."

"It's a dark matter, Maureen. Falling in love in Wanatin when you don't know what's out there. That Gerard guy sounds alright to me."

As they drive across the Bay Bridge, going to the airport, Maureen said, "I still don't understand what the Cygnus Rift is."

"What did Abner say?"

"When I develop the film, I'm supposed to look for a dark area with swirls of dust around it. It separates stars in the Milky Way. Do you think you'll ever go back to the Midwest?"

"I could go back," Lydia said as she squirmed through San Francisco traffic. "But I never could go back as the same person."

When Maureen's mother picked her up at the Minneapolis airport, she gave her two letters, one from Ed and the other from Gerard. Reading Ed's letter in the car, Maureen exclaimed, "I've got to go back to campus a week early."

Her mother nodded. She'd been known to steam open letters ever since Lyle's troubles with the military.

Gerard came to campus a few days early and with the same effusions that were in his letter. "I missed you so much this summer, Maureen. It was unbearable to think of you affixing labels on cans of creamed corn." He hugged her in the ninety-degree weather and, although Maureen was glad to see him, she pulled away. The hallway shone like an iceberg and when Gerard came into her room, his kisses were so correct that they cooled her. "Summer has made you a gorgeous gilded girl, Maureen. I wonder if your hair glows in the dark." He had her on her bed and that was pleasantly cool too since he was relieving her of her blouse.

"Gerard, the freshmen are here, wandering around."

"I know. And I had a family problem. We'll go downtown and eat in air conditioning. I'll tell you about it or we could see a movie."

"Gerard, I'm here for a reason." She pulled a photo down from her desk.

Between columns were black silhouettes sitting on steps between books. The cutline was below: Is there a cartographer who can direct you to the legendary senior lounge? Four seniors map their campus and yours.

"I have a reason too. I have the missing senior article."

"That's not like getting the first issue of the newspaper out."

"You did layout last year."

"So Ed wrote you."

"Last spring, I offered to write a few articles."

They went downtown for grilled Reubens and deep fried onion rings. Gerard began telling her about Chicago restaurants and Bavarian sauerkraut.

"I really don't have time for a movie."

"We need to talk anyway," Gerard said, nodding at a professor with his actor's nonchalance. "All summer, I thought about being married to you and being married to Laurel. We should spend the night together. How can you be sure? You're so beautiful, Maureen, with your hair gilded."

Maureen could feel oil and sauerkraut mixing in her stomach. She let Gerard usher her to the small town square where people boasted about Jesse James robbing the bank. Then they turned to the back of the buildings. Willows swooned toward the river, their leaves caressing the water. The heat hugged Maureen as she sat on the bank.

That evening happened so much from discreet rehearsal that Maureen let Gerard stay in her room. He was the only man on campus who had mentioned marriage to her, after all. And he was a pleasant floating on a river, one without a heavy current pushing. She could never take him seriously or she couldn't take the idea of marriage seriously.

"I don't suppose I'll have much time now, Gerard," she said. "Now that Ed can swing his semester in England. Didn't you know? He's going next week and after that, I'm assistant editor which includes layout. My head's so full of it that I couldn't think about anybody's engagement. I suppose they wrote up engagements in the college newspaper once upon a time."

14   Picture Yourself

Out of college, 1978. Maureen hadn't meant to move to the Twin Cities. Past the verdigris sound barriers on the freeway, houses were crammed in a monotony that worried people from smaller cities. The Twin Cities wasn't a college graduation present even if Maureen's job as an editorial assistant was.

She lived inside the border of St. Paul, not far from the state fairgrounds. Valerie and Kendra, housemates now, discussed graduate school while Maureen discussed her "real job" at a publishing company. She'd meant to move to San Francisco. Her housemates made the duplex a daydream, tidying their messy bedrooms for their regular men. Maureen read Gerard's dwindling letters in her messy bedroom. He had gone to graduate school in Chicago instead of getting engaged to anyone.

By February, Maureen often spent entire days in a room filled with photograph files. She searched out photographs for books like *The Farmer's Dozen* and *Mornings in Mexico*, nonfiction for children. Otherwise, she spent her time proofreading or cutting up galleys to tape inside dummy books of 32 pages or 48 pages or 64 pages.

When her job was going "swimmingly", as her managing editor Inez said, she re-organized the photographs in the company files. Pictures of Dick and Jane children were among new photographs that editors chose from stacks sent by a photo service. Sorting them into past and present eras sorted Maureen into her specialty area, photography.

Her first year, she established a record of sick days, one for every twenty-five days. Still, Inez considered regularity a positive quality in her editorial employees. "Maybe you should be examined for iron deficiency," she suggested.

Maureen nearly told Inez about the company physician. At her physical, he congratulated her as she buttoned up her blouse. "Thank you," she replied, assuming he was congratulating her on her job. "You have a perfect body," he said. In Wanatin, only a doctor on his way out of town would have made such a statement.

And the company doctor wasn't telling the truth. After a week in downtown Minneapolis, Maureen's acne flared to the extent that she was glad she wasn't dating anyone. A dermatologist downtown took on her case, declaring that her skin was so oily that he would have to monitor a topical medicine besides prescribing tetracycline. Once a week, she reclined under a sunlamp that warmed her like a lover. Her dermatologist was tall, deferential, and brown-haired, just the sort of man that never looked twice at her.

By February, she had dated three men, two that she met at parties and the third a friend of Sam Smalt's, a loan officer. Just as a date became regular and Maureen planned to photograph him, he stopped calling. But while she was riding on the freeway with the loan officer, she saw her first Minneapolis date cruising the next lane. She waved to him in a moment of triumph.

Driving home after a sunlamp treatment, Maureen decided not to tell Valerie and Kendra about the man at the Grain Exchange cafeteria. Noontime, people shifted their feet on the marble floor of the Grain Exchange building as if it were a stone barn. They waited in line for winter soup and an array of salad makings fit for a farmer. Since January, a guy with longish hair, conspicuous near horned-rimmed glasses and wallpaper-plaid coats, said hello when he stood near Maureen. He came to the salad bar for second helpings when she was filling her plate, claiming that he wanted more of what she was spooning up. Last week, recognizing her red-hooded coat in the Schilling Publishing parking lot, he jaunted across it from the sidewalk.

"Hi! I didn't see you at the Grain Exchange today." His round-rimmed gaze was bleary from the cold.

"No, we went over to the Star and Tribune cafeteria today."

"Not for the food! I guess you work at Schilling Publishing."

Maureen nodded, liking his build in his weekend jacket. Then she said, "I had to start my car. To make sure it starts after work."

"Don't let Schilling give you a ticket," he said.

That day, Maureen went to the Grain Exchange with Claire, a manuscript editor. She was seven months pregnant and she craved the second helpings at the salad bar.

The guy was there. After he turned and peered at Maureen in her red coat, he relinquished his place in line. He walked past her but soon, his voice fell inside the furred rim of her red hood. "I've got more time than the other guys in line."

Turning, she saw his masculine dimple, a dent that admitted his interest. His hair was curly but it was fine, unraveled from the wind outside.

"What do you do at Schilling?" he asked.

"I'm an editorial assistant there."

"Can I join you? My name is Milt." His smile was deafening.

Claire surveyed Milt and nodded.

When Claire lumbered towards the huge bowls inside the cafeteria, Milt lowered his voice. "I thought *you* were sticking out in this crowd."

Claire chose a table where she could admire a mural of grain elevators and men with Frank Hart Benton muscles. Maureen asked Milt if he worked downtown, a rhetorical question because he was wearing a flannel shirt under his jacket. Claire cracked a bread stick and pondered him, probably expecting him to be the fourth man Maureen had dated that year.

"I was over at the Trib. A friend works there and I've been revising an article. I didn't feel like eating in their cafeteria today and he didn't have time for the salad bar," Milt said. His salad was piled high. He asked about the work at Schilling but Claire was caterwauling with her fork, distributing the shredded cheese. "Are they publishing your article?"

"I guess not. They're publishing a book review I wrote. The article was about travel in Russia during the winter. They didn't think Minneapolis readers would go for it right now. I don't travel to tell about vacation spots."

"Congratulations on the book review," Maureen said.

"What's the title?" Claire asked, unflappably lunging into her salad.

"*Traveling to Health.* I had a manuscript copy. It won't be in the stores until March."

Maureen asked him the questions she usually asked dates before they dropped her. He went to school at Amherst, spent a summer in Boston, and now he was back in Minneapolis. "Are you Russian in heritage?" Maureen wondered, finding Milt as entrancing as Rasputin.

"I'm a lot of things," he dodged. "Next month, I'm going to Wales and Scotland because no one goes there in the winter."

"I suppose you would go to India during the monsoon season," Claire said. She pulled out a bag from her purse and stuffed cloverleaf rolls in it. While Milt admired her for assuming privilege over policy, she surveyed him as if he had more to explain. "Maureen has to come with me because she usually gets only 45 minutes. She gets an hour lunch with me."

The downtown no longer reminded Maureen of a drained swimming pool.

"Three baby brothers before three o'clock," Claire said, sending Maureen to the photo files. Claire was editing a book on baby brother.

The photo room was painted delivery room green because the color was surplus. Maureen pulled babies from the files, babies that might not be boys, babies too much like the last baby, freakish babies that might be the work of a photographer aspiring to the status of Diane Arbus. By the end of the afternoon, Milt was another man whose attention made her despondent.

At the duplex, a camel coat swayed from the light fixture.

"Do you like it?" Kendra called from the kitchen. On the phone, she was telling her mother about the classic wool coat, a coat Maureen would never buy because *her* mother wore one for years.

On the other side of the coat, Valerie swatted pages of a *Bride* magazine, the newest from her mother's gift subscription. She was marrying

Gordon, the Cafeteria Critic.

Valerie chose Gordon despite his habit of making faces when he was eating. After doing make-up for theater, she thought he was charming. Because her feminist experiment, asking a man out, hadn't worked, she relied on the traditional formula, that of fooling an unsuspecting man. The last semester of school, she planned a party that started with a celebrity game, names picked from a hat and pinned to the back of each party-goer. Senior identity crises were forgotten once a guy had a beer and discovered that he was Mick Jagger or George Hamilton.

While Maureen was being treated like Martha Mitchell, Valerie fished up a piece of dog-eared paper for Gordon. He made faces at being called "Babe" and after his beer, he gratefully paired with the jet-haired Valerie. She took him to her room where he attempted to read his name backwards in the mirror. Gordon was so relieved to be Sonny Bono instead of Yoko Ono that he spent the next three weeks with Valerie. Then he suddenly proposed to her.

Still a feminist, Valerie's wedding plans were like an open sore, in constant need of attention.

"It's just a camel coat," Maureen said to her. "I think my mother's had three of them."

"Kendra's going up to Lutsen Lodge skiing this weekend with Joel. Maybe he'll propose."

When Kendra met Joel at graduation, he was wearing a suit and with the ambiguity of a man who often wore a suit. He was the older brother of Kendra's psychology study partner and an alumnus of Carlton. From the first, Kendra considered him a serious venture, especially since he was finishing law school at the University of Minnesota and could be drawn into heavy conversations about maladjusted human behaviors. His continued ambiguity crumpled her. He had said he wouldn't feel obligated if she became pregnant.

Though Maureen roomed with these women because they could become too busy to make their beds, the picture of Kendra used and abandoned to a doctoral track seemed too maladjusted for either Kendra or Joel. And when Kendra modeled the camel coat with her stomach sucked in and her shoulders thrown back, Maureen saw her with Joel instead of recalling her own mother.

"Maybe I should buy a new coat," Maureen mused. "My red coat was on sale and I liked the fur on the hood. But now I feel like Red Riding Hood. Maybe that's my problem."

"You haven't been crying wolf," Kendra said, turning around in her camel coat. "According to Eric Fromm, Red Riding Hood had a bad attitude about men and menstruation. Maybe you like things not working out, Maureen." She considered Maureen incredibly adjusted for coming from a divorce. "I'm prepared for things not working out," Kendra admitted, taking off the coat. "If my father calls when I'm up at Lutsen, tell him I've gone to Michigan to look at another graduate school. That's what I'll do if Joel doesn't work out."

Kendra's background was one hundred and eighty degrees from Maureen's. Her mother and father looked wonderful after twenty-seven years of wedlock. They had tall Los Angeles builds and when they were in Minnesota, they had second honeymoon moments that prodded Kendra to independence. Peer opinion had little effect on Kendra; she was concerned about keeping up with her parents.

Kendra had advised Maureen about being too much herself on a date. After Maureen greeted the loan officer, she finished the cigarette burning in an ashtray. Kendra heard her talking about her editorial director, Donald Dibbet, as if she couldn't get along with men. "I don't want to disappoint," Maureen explained.

Claire thwacked the racquetball at the white windowless walls. She was winning even though she had given birth to a girl two weeks ago. Maureen had gone to the hospital to photograph Claire's baby with the others born that day. Now the sound of the ball reminded Maureen of her mother flinging bread dough on the counter top. Claire's psychiatrist said that she needed to release the anger from behind her postpartum depression. After the game, Maureen photographed her baby girl rocking in a mechanical bassinet that plugged into a living room socket like a lamp. It was a sad novelty after the precious hospital picture.

At the office that day, Donald Dibbet presented the assistant editor in Maureen's quad with a finished book.

"Look at my baby!" Aggie said about her project. The spanking new pages explained alcoholism to adolescents. Large and softhearted, Aggie had admitted to drinking wine for solace one winter. Her roommate had moved away and her roommate's boyfriend continued to visit, commiserating and drinking wine with Aggie until she was smitten with him.

Claire stepped over to celebrate Aggie's book. Then she said, "Maureen, your photo of the hospital babies might work in the baby brother book. As your first photo credit."

Mights didn't matter at the duplex. Kendra was really getting married. The subject was in-laws and when Maureen mentioned her photo credit, Kendra thought she was talking about wedding pictures.

Maureen called Jayne from high school. Jayne now worked as an occupational therapist and she rented half a bungalow near Powderhorn Park.

Over pie at Perkins, they discussed the disabled feeling of being manless.

"Maybe you'll meet some new men after you get your photo credit," she said.

"The commercial artists are all married," Maureen replied. She hadn't heard from her last date in three months and it had been three weeks since Jayne heard from hers.

Invariably Jayne asked, "How's your mother?"

"She still sees Mr. Gleason on weekends," Maureen said, giving Jayne some glee.

The previous fall, Maureen's mother moved to a town one half hour away from Hugo who was now an assistant pastor in Middlefield. Her mother found work in a school library and was happy to meet people in a place where no one knew Clive Berwick.

"I took my mother to the Riverboat Restaurant when she visited," Maureen said. Her mother popped peanuts into her mouth and gazed at people drinking gin gimlets as if they were on the dust jacket of a new novel. "She thinks I have a crush on Donald Dibbet. One day, I was in his office showing him pictures of wetland ponds and he said, 'I wish we were at this one. But then I might want to ravish you.' I thought she might know what to do but I guess I shouldn't have told her about it."

"At the hospital, men like to discuss the small muscles," Jayne said. "They're always married."

Publishing should have been glamorous for a librarian's daughter. But the plural of *otter* could cause an office schism even when the *The Chicago Manual of Style* was re-opened as if nobody could learn it. Conversations over cubicle walls were as repetitive as those over picket fences. *The Exorcist* was discussed for days. Aggie whispered every time the copyright clerk wore a polyester suit.

Ten minutes before break one morning, Donald Dibbet rapped on the wood frame of Maureen's cubicle. Under his gesticulating fingers, Maureen hid like a woman behind a dressing screen. Donald's fingers strode over manuscripts. His long well-formed hands could be called handsome.

"Are there any photographs of Wales in our files?" he asked.

"Britain is probably the subject." Maureen fumbled for a note to pin on her fabric wall. "I'll look."

"Did you say your grandmother was Welsh?"

"Her parents emigrated from Wales," Maureen replied.

"Hello!" someone said. The voice affected Maureen like a pinprick. Images of Grain Exchange baby corn and croutons were before her.

Maureen stood up to see Milt.

"We usually use a New York photo service," Donald said. "This is Milt Blaisdell. He was just talking to me about a possible travel book. For children. You know, castles and knights."

Nothing made sense to Maureen before her coffee break. She almost said that she read the book review that Milt wrote but she hesitated with Donald there. And Donald was discussing a travel book when so many people wanted to write them, Donald included. Milt was offering her pictures of a frosty Welsh castle and its interior. Donald had accepted them, even when Milt's hair was the most carefree in the building and the top button of his white shirt was undone

"Maureen will show you the photo room," Donald said, adding that Milt could use the back exit.

"He bought them?" Maureen asked, pulling out the B for Britain drawer. "I'll have to make up a file for Wales, or maybe 'castles'."

"I'm not so much of a photographer. Foot in the door," Milt said.

"They're lovely." The sparse snow made the castle look stark.

"Don said you've been sorting out his decade's photos."

"He hadn't noticed how many were out-of-date," Maureen replied.

Only people who had known Donald Dibbet for years called him Don. And then, Milt ignored the exit door. He was joining her on her break after she'd warned him that only editors brought outsiders to the break room. While Milt mystified her, eating a glazed donut, shiny eyes were sticking to his broad back. Regardless, Maureen told him how interesting and well-written his book review was. The book emphasized health habits while traveling instead of depending on a climate for restoration.

"I had a job proofreading health textbooks in Boston," Milt explained. "The summer after I graduated, I lived in an apartment about the size of that photo room. The view outside was like a huge file drawer left out in the rain."

"Is that why you came back to the Twin Cities?"

"My mother was going through some treatments. And I can freelance in Minneapolis."

"Is your mother very ill?"

"Nah, it's chronic."

He told her about his trip to Wales, the pubs, the personable winter castle tours, and the cozy economical hotels where he stayed. At the exit door, his voice creaked, "I don't want to get you in trouble with Don."

"We all call him Donald," Maureen stalled.

"I didn't know anyone used the name Donald since Donald Duck," Milt said, cheery and quixotic. Like a sudden touch, he was gone.

The antidote to anxiety was to invent a trivial worry. Valerie was making her cap and veil a dilemma because she planned to remain a feminist after she married Gordon. Kendra made guitar music a controversy because she wanted to go to graduate school instead of having a baby. "My future in-laws think that Peter, Paul, and Mary were a hippie act," she complained. "They're apostles!"

"How about a headband with the veil swagged on one side?" Valerie wondered.

"You could put parentheses around the name Kirch to be different," Maureen suggested. Lately, she felt as if she had parentheses around her at the duplex. Instead of learning something about smooth marriages from her roommates, their trivial worries ballooned in her mind like domestic stress. She was about to blurt out that Valerie's wedding would be her last stint assisting a wedding photographer when the phone rang.

"Maureen, this is Milt Blaisdell. How would you like to go out this weekend?"

"How did you get my phone number?" she blurted out.

"I have my ways," his voice crackled.

After Maureen told the engaged women how she met Milt downtown, wearing her red-hooded coat, they were satisfied that she was already agonizing about what she should wear to a rock concert.

Valerie and Kendra were waiting with Saturday morning coffee, having watched Maureen drive off in a red Karmann Ghia with a Twin Cities celebrity's son.

Maureen could only say, "Milt might be the coarsest man I've ever dated."

They stared behind veils of inexperience. Dismissing two minutes of last night's evening, Maureen added, "If he calls, I'd go out with him again." Of course, she was in love.

That Wednesday at work, Claire showed Maureen a softcover book. "Do you know this man? Dr. Mort Blaisdell. Mort as in *mortal*."

The picture book about a boy playing hooky was published by Schilling eight years before. The boy somehow found himself fishing near arteries from which he reeled up white blood cells like old shoes. Then he found that he was sitting on a liver instead of a rock.

"Teachers said that they couldn't present the book before or after lunch," Claire imparted. "Dr. Mort is a columnist and he's on the radio with 'Confound the Doctor.'"

Maureen examined a dull version of Milt, Milt without the chip in his cheek. "Why didn't you tell me?"

"Aggie and I weren't here eight years ago. Then we thought you knew. You shouldn't tell Inez about your dates."

Claire approved Maureen's new blouse, a polyester exception because it had a scene printed on it, a country landscape in an apricot sunset. Maureen planned to wear it with jeans and her favorite Prince Matchabelli perfume Friday evening. Now her daydreaming about Milt took on the odd adventure of a night dream, one where she was wearing pajamas in a public place.

On the way to the band palace west of Minneapolis, Milt seemed as jubilant as Maureen felt when she triumphed with a new date on the freeway. His cheerful conversation momentarily creaked when he pointed at an intersection. "There was a hell of an accident here. A decapitation."

While he was in profile, Maureen mentioned his father's book.

"Who told you he was my father?" he said archly. "My parents live off to your right after the Minnetonka sign. My mother's alone tonight. She'd like to meet you."

"She would?" Maureen mused on that.

The dent in Milt's jaw was still dancing after this schmaltzy compliment. "Maybe it's out of a need to protect a woman who doesn't know me well."

"What should I know?"

"Let's see. I used to howl like a wolf across the lake."

Maureen didn't see any houses after the Minnetonka sign, only expansive lawns and terraced trees.

"There," he said. "We'd take a right here. There were once wolves in the woods. There were once woods."

A few miles beyond, the band palace stuck out like a wide silo in the unkempt grass. Inside, people found Milt and they eyed Maureen, knowing that she wasn't following their familiarity.

"It's alright," Milt muttered.

"What's alright?"

"Being seen with you."

Still, Milt spent much of the concert tilted back on his chair. Maureen wondered about her new blouse although the Fleetwood Mac-influenced band was in high hat and motley. Milt was probably adding to the performance, Maureen realized, when she caught him kissing her hair behind her back.

"I haven't seen you wink tonight," Milt said on the freeway back.

"Wink? I squint. It's a habit from using my camera."

She'd decided that she wouldn't deceive Milt the way she deceived most people she met in Minneapolis. His parents' house was coming up again. "My mother spends most of her nights alone. She's been divorced for fifteen years. I grew up with a stigma."

"That sounds painful," was all he said.

Maureen wasn't sure what made Milt irritable at Mama Rosa's, whether it was the waitress who addressed him by name or the restaurant being done in valentine reds. She tried to keep up with his efficient hunger for omelet while introducing various subjects – his father, Donald Dibbet, tetracycline, her college newspaper. But Milt was short with her, treating the frequented restaurant and its wine as if they were a prescription.

In the car, his voice crackled with cheer again and he told her how glad he was to find her. "Same old conversations, same old Minneapolis until tonight," he said.

At the duplex, he slapped her behind while she unlocked the door. Once they determined that Valerie and Kendra were gone and as Maureen's mouth was forming the word *stereo*, Milt kissed her in a mindful way that permitted no interruption. But below her neck, his hands were working at a different speed, briskly unbuttoning her blouse, splitting the sunrise on it, and tugging at her sleeves.

Pulling back, Maureen was startled to see that a window shade wasn't pulled down. This he solved by pulling her to the floor where he splayed her legs open. "Spread!" he urged her. Then he began kissing her ferociously again.

"I need a minute in the bathroom." She had to forcibly push him off her.

On the way there, she buttoned up her blouse and then she wiped her shiny face and stared at herself, deciding not to make the evening uglier. She was an editorial assistant and Milt's father was well-known besides being a millionaire, she had learned at work.

On her return, Milt's voice creaked, "I haven't been out with anyone I liked so well in months." Carole King was singing, "Will You Still Love Me Tomorrow?" "The album had your name on it," he said, extending an arm from the plaid davenport.

The shade was pulled down but Maureen was still cautious. Milt pulled her onto his lap.

"I bought the album for the song 'Tapestry'," she said. "Did you really howl like a wolf across Lake Minnetonka?"

Milt knew he could kiss his way into forgiveness. Then he said, "My little brothers howled with me because our parents wanted to live in the country. After they built their house, people started building around them. We wanted to scare them, howling as if we were sick and suffering."

"My parents talked about moving to the country. I don't know if that cures anything."

Stubbornly, Maureen let him have what he wanted up to spreading her legs. But she had to like Milt for knowing that he could be a wolf.

15   Breakfast in Bed

When Milt called again, he was blasé as blue jeans on Nicollet Mall. Maureen was all nonchalance. She was unlikely to marry the son of Dr. Mort Blaisdell, an often-photographed man. Anyone knew that, even her engaged housemates.

Public moments were the best of men when they had downfalls like other men. Maureen fell for Roland when he looked like a primitive spear-thrower in the sports column of the Wanatin newspaper. After photographing Gerard on stage, she'd found him disconcerting and possibly false.

On a double date, Maureen met Dr. Mort at Chi Chi's restaurant where he was having supper in a sequestered corner with his radio staff. He was shorter than Milt and that made his voice more sonorous, greeting Milt's old friends by their first names. Maureen knew that Lisa Lammerville was the only child of a CEO and that Gary Drake didn't live on a lake, a funny thing to Milt's people. Dr. Mort surveyed Maureen from the other side of Milt and nodded.

He didn't join them for margaritas. After they ordered and their green drinks came, Lisa leaned across the table and said to Milt, "The golf course is all grown in, Milt. Do you want to golf one of these afternoons?"

"I usually golf at the university course. You know I'm not a member at the country club." Milt exhibited the chip in his cheek as if he were a golf ball found outside the green.

"Maureen. How did you get your job?" Lisa inquired as they all dipped tortilla chips in guacamole.

"I sent a resume to the company and got an interview. I worked on my college newspaper," Maureen replied, probably looking perplexed. At her interview, Inez discovered that her parents were divorced. At the time, Maureen hadn't known that a divorced woman hired her.

The colorful Mexican food inspired Lisa to explain why she got a degree in elementary art education. She knew that her chalk drawings of pets weren't anything on which to build an artistic career.

"Do the animals sit for you?" Maureen asked. "I suppose they have pet photographers in cities this size."

Lisa stared at Maureen as if she had interrupted. "*I* sit in a room with the pet. I'm working on a neighbor's Persian cat right now. My art is mostly for teaching purposes."

Maureen knew how Schilling Publishing hired commercial artists but she wasn't sure if that was what Lisa wanted to hear.

"Lisa is building a reputation over in North Oaks. Her parents just moved out there," Milt said. He'd known the Lammerville's since childhood.

"I've done most of the dogs in the old neighborhood," she smiled at Milt. Then she told about her college program in Vermont. "I really don't enjoy artists. The way they indulge their emotions. I wish teachers wouldn't think that art is an hour for them to be relieved of emotionally disturbed children. Or to think those are the children with artistic aptitude. I wasn't trained to work with children who have emotional problems."

Maureen was attempting to prevent a huge section of her first empanada from splintering all over her plate. "Kids probably make messes in this restaurant."

"I start my kids out with chalks, not finger-paint," Lisa said.

Milt rented a small house on Lyndale Avenue in Minneapolis with Gary Drake and another friend. They watched "The Muppet Show" and "Charlie's Angels" with the sound turned off and Pink Floyd on the stereo. Lisa was an integral part of this mix, sipping the tip of a joint. In her designer clothes, she examined Maureen's earrings with concern, knowing that Maureen shopped at campus stores and that her India cottons were borderline at an office.

The three men at the rented house were used to prosperity. Their first skirmishes with money shortage were flirtations with nihilism, they joked. Chronic destitution was a parallel reality, perhaps an intentional nihilism. Lisa challenged their beliefs. Milt felt that marijuana or pills led in most cases to more marijuana or more pills.

Even as Milt made a game of rubbing Maureen's upper thigh when Lisa wasn't looking, Maureen was oblique in conversation. This crowd believed in socializing and that bad social behavior was a choice that prevented people from moving up. "What is that book with Lammer in the title?" Maureen asked.

"Sir Walter Scott wrote *The Bride of the Lammermoor*," Lisa replied.

"You should read it," Milt advised. He and his friends often used the word *should*. They seemed to believe that anyone from a less privileged upbringing would benefit from their counsel.

"I read *The Bride of the Lammermoor*," Maureen mentioned a few weeks later. She was holding a golf club for the third time in her life and again, at a miniature golf course. Her father took her and Lydia miniature golfing on visitation.

"What did you think of the ending?" Milt asked. "It was based on a true case."

"You mean, blaming the old ladies for making the bride insane? Did they charge them with witchcraft? In the preface, it said that the groom recovered from his sword wound but the bride died two weeks after the wedding. I thought that the other man might have gotten into the castle."

"He was traveling," Milt said. Then he left Maureen with the other women, at a hole where an old woman was holding a watering can.

One of Lisa Lammerville's friends said to Lisa, "Have you seen Milt's mother lately?"

Maureen practiced her golf stance, listening for Lisa's reply.

"She's recovering. She asked if I'd like to be the fourth in a bridge game. That's all she was doing. Buttermints and sugared pistachios."

"It's alright to be pigeon-toed," someone coaxed Maureen.

"I thought her bridge partners were from her auxiliary on latchkey children."

"Or latchkey adults," Lisa suggested.

After a few tries, Maureen tripped the old woman into watering her daffodils. Then she hastened towards Milt.

"You shouldn't hold your golf club up like that when you're walking! Put that weapon down," Milt said, still joking about the demented Bride of the Lammermoor.

"I can't keep up with you."

Milt aimed his ball at a lighthouse. "You can go home if you want." Then he shot a hole-in-one, causing the lighthouse to glow. "Shoot or drive?" he said with such friendliness that Maureen considered him false for the first time.

At a suburban bar, the woman sitting at Milt's right blamed her bad golf game on the opal rings she was wearing. An orange-haired beauty, she had an opal ring on every one of her fingers. Milt examined each of the opals, touching her fingers when he came to an Australian opal. On Maureen's other side, a guy said, "I've been collecting Scrooge McDuck stuff since I was a kid. Everyone else here has seen it."

"And the engagement ring," Milt confirmed, tapping her third finger.

"I had the diamond reset," said the fiancé.

The tablecloth was ruffling along Maureen's thigh and then Milt's hand groped for hers. He was still sorting out the rings with his other hand.

"Did anyone bring any buttermints?" Lisa wondered.

Being with Dr. Mort Blaisdell's son romantically was about as private as a hospital bed. At the duplex, Valerie and Kendra wanted to become acquainted with Milt while he and Maureen reclined on the living room floor, watching the late movie *What's New Pussycat?*

Milt suggested a weekend at the guest cottage on the Lammerville property. Lisa was mansion-sitting while her parents were in Key West.

"You two can stay up here if you want," Lisa said after they arrived Friday evening. "We're re-decorating the guest house, you know."

North Oaks was considered more upscale than Minnetonka although its lake was much smaller. The living room of the Lammerville's plush post-war mansion reminded Maureen of a cocktail lounge, its furniture upholstered in burnt orange leather. On the walls were paintings of shorelines that seemed to have absorbed ship spills of Alka Seltzer. Thick deco pillars with crocodile spikes of dark coral might separate the room into three or four conversations. While Lisa was standing behind one of the pillars with a tray of gin and tonics, Maureen heard her say to Gary, "It's so awkward when people aren't used to wealth."

She must have doubted that Maureen was welcome at the homes of Country's Plenty executives. Usually their houses were painstakingly displayable, furnished from examples in *Better Homes and Gardens*. While many people in Wanatin had homespun interiors accented with needlework and carpentry projects, the executives lived in houses that were like packages people recognized and trusted.

Walking from the house to the cottage, Maureen and Milt could easily elude Lisa and Gary, disappearing into pine passageways and crouching when they chased up a rabbit. They couldn't see any neighbor mansions until they were at the dock, watching the tints of dusk across the bay. The sand on the short beach must have been imported and it extended into a sandbar that made the water look pale.

"You don't want to do any cooking, do you?" Lisa said in the guest cottage.

Its decorations were for sailboat enthusiasts. The curtains had swags like sails. A paddled ceiling fan made the rooms breezy. Outside were a deck, a dock, and a boathouse that kept a motorboat, a sailboat, a rowboat, and a paddleboat.

"I'd rather the neighbors didn't know that you're here," Lisa explained.

"Me too," Milt agreed.

Lisa ignored him. "Some of them are very conservative. You probably won't want to use the fireplace. Or the shower. That's what really needs renovation."

"That's alright. I'd like to take a swim," Maureen said.

"The people on this lake don't swim in it. Most of them sail," Lisa informed her. "Do you want to sit out in the rowboat with us? Gary and I love to sit out in the sailboat but there's no wind tonight."

"No, I'll have a beer here," Milt said

He and Maureen sat on the deck, waving to Lisa and Roger. They waved until they heard the pleasant plunking of oars in the shroud of dusk. Then they went inside.

Milt found a box of tinder for building a small fire in the fireplace. Maureen opened a hamper that contained cheese and crackers and seven layer bars. She meandered to the other rooms, curious about the furnishings and the yacht-like woodwork. In one bedroom, she found a drawing of a sheepdog on the wall.

Milt caught her from behind there, as if he were a long-haired dog in Lisa's well-bred home.

"Let's not stay here with the sheepdog," Maureen said.

They shouldered sheets from a drawer to the davenport that opened into a double bed near the fireplace.

"You forgot the pillows," Maureen said.

She found pillows in a room where a chalk drawing of a St. Bernard was on the other side of the door. Milt's parents had a St. Bernard, he had said. "Lisa does chalks of some very untidy animals. Not a hair in place. It's not like her," Maureen laughed, returning with the pillows.

"They're easier to chalk," Milt said, pushing her onto the davenport bed and treating her like a pillow.

The fire reached and crackled while they undressed each other. But as Milt gripped and kissed, Maureen thought she heard oars dripping amidst the rhythm of crickets. She held Milt tensely, waiting to hear Lisa complain about smoke coming from the cottage chimney. She knew that Lisa wasn't serious about Gary Drake. Translating another sound as that of the rowboat heaving, Maureen broke Milt's tight hold.

"You flinched," he said, apparently unperturbed at Lisa and Roger hovering nearby.

Maureen had suggested double dating with Valerie and Gordon but Milt had actually answered that he didn't like Valerie well enough.

"If I'm making you uncomfortable, just tell me," Milt said.

Maureen pretended that their stray clothing was in the way, making a pile of it on her side of the bed. She'd noticed a glimmer of light, probably not from fireflies, coming through the ship shutters of the window on the deck. As Milt began to fit his body over hers, she peered around his shoulder. Light rippled from the kitchen and without warning, barreled towards the fireplace, blinding Maureen.

"Milt, do you want links tomorrow?"

A flashlight beam ricocheted off of Maureen. Maureen yanked at the sheet, not wanting to know how Milt was being discovered. Considerately,

Lisa aimed the flashlight at the ceiling. "Gary wants a beer," she said. "We've just got wine and hard liquor up at the house."

Afraid that Lisa and Gary were going to join them on the bed, Maureen handed Milt his unfinished beer. "Be my guest," he said.

After Gary found a beer and convinced Lisa that they should row back to the mansion, Milt resumed his clasp. He kissed Maureen's stomach, hugged her hips, and murmured, "I'll bring you down some breakfast from the house. Breakfast in bed."

Still, Maureen felt as if she were making love in a rowboat, listening for the rolling and murmuring on the lake. At the brink of abandon, Milt's urging was like a shrug and although Maureen worked forty hours that week, she let him rest. When the only sounds were from the fire and the crickets, she leaned over him. Instead of any goodnight kiss, he had fallen asleep. She inspected his face, a plain and stubborn face, and then she had a cigarette, envying his ability to drop off so easily. She'd been drawn to the dent in his cheek but it wasn't there now, what made him dear to her.

The cloud-sifted daylight gave Maureen a distinct sadness that reminded her of gray aftermaths in her childhood. Milt hadn't awakened even when she tossed with unjustified disquiet.

She wanted to laugh or say what she thought. But she felt bleary and kept seeing beer stains on the hallway wallpaper across from the bathroom in their old house. The fern-green wallpaper was a project her parents accomplished together. Maureen stirred the glue for it while her father stood on a step ladder, holding a panel of wallpaper until her mother caught the shaft below him. Maureen's mother had never been much like other executive's wives, especially after she had stained wallpaper in her hallway.

Maureen could tell that Milt's parents had a problem marriage. She had little confidence that they would have better nights than this. There wasn't too much beer last night; there was just a sense of difference, what depressed her in the morning. Renewed shrugs would make the promised breakfast in bed too much of an event. The gray outside and the davenport looking like a disaster permeated Maureen's inner atmosphere. She was depending too much on the weather, for a break in the grayness, and then for the blithe sound she dreaded and feared, Lisa Lammerville's voice creeping in at the shutters. Soon, Lisa was present and saying, "We want to get out there before the motorboats. There's some wind this morning. Links will be ready soon. Have you ever sailed, Maureen?"

On the drive out of the Lammerville's pine woods, Maureen's remarks were feeble. She couldn't say that things could be better in a different environment or that they got better. This wasn't the way she wanted to spend her time and she couldn't act. Milt was expected for Sunday brunch at his parents' and she had a full week of work ahead of her. She couldn't blame Lisa or blurt out that birth control was hardly necessary with her around.

After all, Lisa's parents didn't have any other children after her.

Talking of the Sunday traffic, she knew that she and Milt were making a pact that put off the intimacy of thoughts. They should have felt the absurdity of their first weekend together. Lisa was like a Lombardy girl in Wanatin; Roland Werff would have joked about her for days. Milt hadn't minded that Lisa apparently never knocked on a door if her parents owned it.

16   Patterns to Postcards

"When is a good time to talk to Inez?"

"When is Inez in a good mood?" Aggie smirked, handing Maureen a sheaf of page proofs.

Because it was Aggie's fourth year at Schilling, she could stand and stare into the glass office of their managing editor. Inez paired editorial assistants with editors, having radar for subject assignments. In conversation, she poked at the sensitive spots of her underlings, using the same radar.

Back in October, Aggie was promoted to assistant editor after she read her work review, what Inez typed on a blank galley sheet. Her review galley invited her to insert questions at the margins. Like most editorial assistants, Aggie let a typo slip into a book, a typo that came off the press and probably made grade school children shriek and exult. Aggie spent too much time talking to the typesetters in their remote office. She didn't always use the color of flair pen assigned to her, orange. She had been heard to say during a discussion about *The Exorcist* that a certain editor might be possessed. Aggie showed artwork to Maureen before she brought it to Inez, artwork delivered by a man that Aggie stubbornly referred to as Apollo. Aggie didn't always see the office as a positive place, and why was she complaining when she was being promoted to assistant editor?

Aggie sat down at her desk. "She's got her X-Acto knife out. It's almost two years since Inez's divorce came through. She was in a bad mood before she got divorced and she's still in a bad mood."

"I think she hired me because my mother is divorced," Maureen said.

"The bat's got radar." But then Aggie said discreetly, "Are you getting married?"

Inez had a dread of editorial assistants leaving her. She never got over a male editorial assistant taking a job in New York. Out of her commitment to Schilling, she kept up on Maureen's dating developments, especially that spring. The department was working overtime, coming in before work or staying after for an hour or two.

"No, I'm not getting married."

Turning to her page proofs, Maureen was touched at Aggie's decency and that she thought Maureen worthy of Dr. Mort Blaisdell's son. But pondering this, Maureen could only see her family showing up at a ceremony like damaged toys donated to a hospital.

"Your parents were selfish," was Milt's opinion.

He had called the Wednesday after the Lammerville weekend and, following Valerie's advice, Maureen had him over for lasagna.

"I haven't had such a good dinner for weeks," he complimented her and then they walked from her duplex to a bench at Como Lake.

Wondering about his mother's cooking, Maureen said that she started cooking Italian food in junior high when her mother worked evenings at the library.

"Your parents had four children?" he asked.

"I have a sister and two brothers. I'm the youngest. My brothers were pretty much gone when I was cooking."

Then Milt appraised her parents as selfish. That stymied her as if he had netted something from the depths of the lake. No one had ever said this and for the moment, he was a hero.

"Of course many adults are selfish. Me, for instance," Milt laughed.

That made him more valiant. Maureen settled back against his arm and said, "Do you think that people should stay together for the sake of their children?"

Milt's eyes glinted like the lake. "If everyone made what you did out of a bad situation, this would be a better world. But you couldn't say it was a good situation, could you?"

Maureen wanted to sit indefinitely in Milt's good opinion. But he might be the illusion that the city lake was to a swimmer. "If the world's so bad, then why do you keep traveling in it?" she asked.

"To shake a pattern, I guess, and to form another pattern. Researchers have found that it's all about patterns. What should I do? Go to medical school? Or enter a graduate program so that I can get paid to talk? So I try to get published, having the gift of gab like my father, afraid of the pattern."

She didn't mind being adrift with him, without a definite destination. If Milt made commitments here, he would soon be as confined as a lake within a public park.

"I had insomnia in childhood," Maureen mentioned. "Does that mean a child of mine would have insomnia?" She was still losing sleep because of him.

"My father would probably give you a pill and regret it later. He's not the best doctor around, you know. But the question is, what would you do if your child had insomnia and you hadn't solved yours?"

"My parents didn't know what to do because they weren't insomniacs. So do the researchers only talk to people in patterns or do they find people who broke the pattern? Like the teetotaler whose father was an alcoholic? Or the guy whose father beat him up learning restraint?"

"The uncharted," Milt said in a pleased, older voice. "That's the goal, breaking a bad pattern. I'll bet you've never met a researcher. I knew there was a reason why I kept calling you."

She wasn't configured in the patterns he was in. "I might get divorced like my parents."

"So they say. So they say."

"I'd wonder about you but I guess that's nothing to worry over."

"Too bad I don't know." Milt scratched her thigh. Then he admitted that his attempt to get published in the *Christian Science Monitor* was out of rebelliousness. "I wanted to see my father's face if *The Monitor* published me. He's a hard man to see sometimes. It was the article about my train trip in Russia. But I was interested in the common cold and that got me wondering about a country having a national disease in the same way they have literature. *The Monitor* doesn't like the word *disease*. The Soviet Union has good doctors but they tried to treat the sick or wrong thing about their society with Communism. That broke other patterns, like their pattern of publishing great novelists."

"That's like saying that Germany is manic-depressive. They make toys and had a mania for music. But their photography is severe and depressing when they aren't an impoverished nation."

Milt laughed at that and then he asked Maureen to go on a trip with him.

"No, Maureen. You know you can't have your week of vacation until after July tenth, a year from the day you started here."

Inez had her X-Acto knife out. When a subject of little importance was taking her time, she often worked on a dummy book as carefully as some women manicured their nails.

"But that's in a few weeks. I thought that the overtime might count. That would give me days off," Maureen argued. "The overtime in one week would be a day off. I'd have four days off and a weekend."

"No. Overtime is not flex time at this company. We need the staff for our fall deadlines."

"I'll tell Milt that. He has to drive his brother back from college because his father is too busy."

"Publishing is a nine-to-five job, Maureen. In Minneapolis, it's an eight to four-thirty job. It's regular work, not a romantic venture." Inez took up her X-Acto knife again. "I predict that you'll marry in the year 1982 and that you might be divorced by the year 1988."

Maureen faltered on her way to the door, trying to laugh at Inez's joke. Many people left her office looking as if they had paper cuts on their hands. Inez wrote up specifications for books and workbooks, their page lengths, paper type, and binding materials, and then she estimated the editorial time for projects. She gave the specifications to Donald Dibbet so that he could calculate costs. Inez and Donald prided themselves on books coming off the press exactly as predicted.

Aggie whizzed over to Maureen's desk on her chair wheels.

"I should call Milt," Maureen said, shaking her head.

Soon she was in a state of vertigo, hearing the phone drop on Milt's couch.

"Reality, Pal. Maureen is on the phone," Gary was saying. After some crunching, Maureen had the sensation that Milt was halfway round the world and that his time was two in the morning.

"So what did Inez have to say?" he said drowsily.

"I don't have any vacation time until July tenth."

"My brother won't wait at college until July. Gary, I'll need that after all the driving."

"What?"

"Nuts. Nothing, Maureen. I want to see you before I leave. Keep tomorrow night open. Gary, what's in the other drawer?"

During afternoon break, Maureen prepared Aggie for her best augury about Milt. Her roommates were getting married and she'd speculated about her and Milt living in the duplex together. But she wanted to keep working at Schilling with school library materials. Evidently, Aggie hadn't heard of anyone at Schilling living with someone of the opposite sex because she was startled. Maureen told her about the Blaisdell's instead of pursuing this question.

The morning after the lasagna dinner, Milt took Maureen over to Lake Minnetonka to pick up sleeping bags and supplies for his trip. Near the Blaisdell's, lawns glistened like gowns and the walks to front doors glittered as if gems were set in them. Terraced trees could be described as shapely. Maureen expected the Blaisdell's house to be as glitzy and that Milt's mother would be daunting or lambent, probably blonder than Maureen, a salon blonde.

On the drive into the Blaisdell's, Maureen was reminded of the road to her grandparents' house in Northern Minnesota. The Blaisdell property was filled with woodland trees. Their St. Bernard trotted to Milt's car, sidling alongside it until they reached the clearing where Dr. Mort Blaisdell's A-frame stood. Steps led up to a second floor deck with window boxes ornamenting the cross line in an A.

Outside, Milt's youngest brother was sitting near a large terrarium jug.

As the dog barked and Milt's brother yelled something, shrieking sounded at the upper deck. A woman had run out onto it, looking as if she had just had a home permanent. Her hair was in disheveled brunette coils and she wore a loose cotton wrapper over slacks. Her final shriek, Milt's name, covered up his heavy sigh as he opened the car door. He went into the front door as his mother called his name again.

After Milt lugged out the sleeping bags, he said, "A friend of my father's from *Medicine This Month* magazine is coming for dinner tomorrow. She wants me there. Do you want to meet her?"

"Do you think it's the day?"

"She does that on purpose. My mother tries to be patient. She's neurotic. We'll just walk down to the lake today." They ambled the shore of Minnetonka where Milt explained, "My mother practically raised us alone. My father was still in practice when he first became Dr. Mort."

At Milt's rented house on Lyndale, there was a croquet game for Gary's birthday. His dog Tucson ran for the balls and then, Maureen helped Lisa with Gary's cake. The third housemate decorated it with segments of tootsie roll because Gary's dog decorated the lawn. Lisa had a charming chalk drawing of Tucson.

"He's going to raise his dog alone," Milt said.

"At least the cake isn't decorated with pastel pills," Gary replied.

After watching clouds and droplets on the weather report with Milt, Maureen was being carried into a bedroom for the second time in her life. The first thing she made out in the murkiness was a black and white photograph of someone in a wolf costume. Milt was kissing her and murmuring, "As if Schilling Publishing has a corner on the world."

Maureen watched the room develop. Across from the wolf was a dragon in Celtic knotting.

"You flinched again," Milt said, annoyed at having to remove her clothing. "I'm not going to hit you. Were you with someone you were afraid of?"

"Why do you have a wolf on your wall?" His fathoming her past relaxed her.

"It's from a Russian production of 'Peter and the Wolf.'" His voice creaked into a chuckle. "You're such a flincher, it would be good to have you in the car. My brother might start an argument." He coddled her as if she were a child, making himself a hero with her as she helped him with his shirt and his belt.

"I don't know how you can be faithful to such a boring office and a boss like Don Dibbet," Milt said.

Maureen allowed him to ponder that. Already, he was outdistancing her so that she wanted to call Inez from the road Monday morning. She needed to say, "My mother eloped, you know." Or, "My sister ran out to California because she was pregnant." But Milt was kissing his way to her stomach and was coaxing her to do the same for him, to act, not talk. After this dizzying assurance and the parting in bed, Milt was silent, holding her hand. She wanted a cigarette.

"It's because of your parents," Milt said as she sat apart, smoking.

He had made their relationship a problem when he knew she had to work. People talked of "working out" their relationships, a phrase she disliked. She couldn't tell where Milt was going. If she went along, she would be afraid of the time or the place where the clouds frowned like an overseer. Probably, they would fight mosquitoes in a campground. The motel they could afford would probably be seedy, a place that would emphasis their unsuitability. There was the gas station mirror three days down the road and the crumpled aluminum can, the thrown wrappers, in the car. Conversations might slam like car breaks at unexpected road signs. An evening could become eerie because of a knocking noise in the car's motor.

Probably the crisis would happen when Milt wasn't sure of a fork in the road. Or it would happen when they were looking for a gas station and became mired in a desolate neighborhood, the nightmare that vacationers know as real life. At a certain juncture, some men wanted to get rid of the woman in their lives. If Milt wanted to get rid of a woman, Maureen wasn't sure how he would go about it. In the Twin Cities, he would simply stop calling.

"I need someone to keep me from eating fried foods on the way," he said, still awake. "And seafood on the East Coast."

"No fried foods?" She couldn't say that it was because of his parents that he had to drive alone. Dr. Mort was almost like a divorced father to his own son, showing up with fanfare and extra money.

Milt told her about his stomach problems and his allergy to shellfish. "You ate enchiladas at Chi Chi's," she recalled. "And tortilla chips."

"That's what I mean. And I need an afternoon nap."

"You're kidding."

"I took one the other day."

"I took a nap once. After a bunking party," Maureen mused.

"I'll send you a postcard."

The next week, Maureen was in a state of happiness, anticipating Milt's postcard and telling people when he would be back. She was invited to parties and entreated to after-work gatherings. Everyone was attentive. That was when she realized how she felt differently about Milt than other men. She was most in love with him when he was gone, happy as a honeymoon when they were apart for a week or two.

17   Look Mommy, No Daddy

Maureen's workdays coasted on thoughts about Milt traveling. At two o'clock, she passed through a county of yawns and in two more hours, she would encounter a city. The cubicles were a stretch of small-town boredom until Inez gave her the specifications for a new softcover book.

"The working title is 'Look Mommy, No Daddy.' Of course we'll probably decide on another title," she said. "I've planned for some photographs. Maybe it's an opportunity for you to have a photo credit."

Maureen drove from Minneapolis to St. Paul where she gaped at an imbroglio of wedding gifts.

"Gordon went home last weekend and brought these," Valerie said. "Oh, God! Where will I put this? Maybe you should take a picture of it here, Maureen." She displayed a porcelain clock from a case of Styrofoam. A nesting bird was tucked in a castellated tower.

That aroused Kendra from the trance she attained, perched on her knees four feet from the television. She stared with listlessness at the French-style mantel clock as if it were another persuasion from Los Angeles. "Your postcard came from Milt," she said. "It's on the kitchen bulletin board."

Maureen made her way to the kitchen as if she were on a trail in the Alleghenies. Somewhere, Milt found a spliced photograph of a wolf with a swatch of red plaid in its mouth. *'Drove up to Newfoundland anyway – then south along the seaboard. Made my sleeping bag and slept in it too. You should have come."*

Maureen recalled their parting words. *'Why don't you do something about that?" "About what?"* He had jutted his chin towards his bed. Realizing that he wanted her to make his bed, she leaned awkwardly over it. His father had seen so many deftly made hospital beds.

"I don't know what I've gotten into!" Valerie said, holding up a linen tablecloth in the living room. "Dinner for eight?"

"Oh, there's a letter from San Francisco for you, Maureen," Kendra said in her trance voice.

Maureen vaulted over more boxes to find a letter from Lydia on the side table. After reading it, she informed her duplex-mates, "I've got to pick up my sister and Lonnie at the airport Thursday night. They're hoping to sleep on the living room floor in their sleeping bags. I can't drive to my mother's until Friday after work." She considered the boxes on the living room floor, understanding now that she could have driven away from all this with Milt. But she would lose her job and then she might lose Milt too.

"At least a person can get divorced now if it doesn't work out," Valerie muttered.

"You're having a Catholic priest marry you." This appalled Maureen, coming from Valerie. Valerie acted as if divorce was like the disassembling of the duplex. Maureen could tell her that if she wanted to plan for a divorce, she should expect the eeriness of a tornado watch for months and months and then when the divorce was over, she would creep out of hiding to assess the damages.

"I'm not marrying a Catholic," Valerie said.

"I'm marrying an Irish Catholic," Kendra said. "I have to get up early on Friday, Maureen. No noise and no marijuana." San Francisco was a place worse than Los Angeles to Kendra.

"Do you think Milt will be coming to the wedding?"

Valerie was probably being wicked. He hadn't answered her RSVP and, because Milt wouldn't double date with Valerie, Maureen expected he wouldn't want to go. Instead of answering her, Maureen spilled her own mind. "I think I'll get married on my honeymoon. I'll send announcements about it. And spend the wedding money on travel."

But Milt had asked her on a trip and she didn't run off with him. Now she knew what she wanted. She wanted to plan running off with a man in the time it took to plan a wedding. She didn't want a wedding and seeing Valerie's preparation, it made sense to have a small ceremony at a honeymoon site.

Lydia spread butter on a piece of swirled cinnamon toast while smoke swirled from a cigarette set in a saucer.

"That's Kendra's cinnamon bread," Maureen warned, having come in from work. Lonnie was sitting in the living room with a glass of chocolate milk, cross-legged and two feet from Fonzie on television.

"Does Kendra count the slices?" Lydia countered. "That Los Angeles lady would probably thank Lonnie for another slim day." She tapped her cigarette on Kendra's stoneware. "Milt called."

"Does he want me to call back?"

"He said it can wait until tomorrow." As Kendra often did, Lydia talked as if she were as far away as California was from Minnesota. "He has to take someone to the airport."

"But I won't be here tomorrow!"

"I wouldn't drive back for a phone call either," Lydia reflected.

"What does Jeepers mean?" Lonnie yelled, breathless at the kitchen door. He was holding out his empty glass of chocolate milk.

"Nothing," Lydia said. "Jeepers doesn't mean anything. It's not a car. Now go roll up your sleeping bag. People don't watch TV on sleeping bags. Not even if they're wearing cowboy hats."

At her mother's house, Maureen took pictures of Lonnie. He could make himself a quick breakfast of cereal with strawberries cut over it. He rolled out his sleeping bag and put out water for the new puppy that his grandmother had obtained for the big yard outside her new bungalow. Wearing Muppet musician pajamas, he turned the knobs of a clock radio.

Outside of the Twin Cities, Milt Blaisdell was just another name to most people. Maureen's mother, puzzled and wary about the son of Dr. Mort, would rather discuss the man that Lonnie called Dad. "I thought Emory was an unusual harmonica player. Why would he want to become a partner in a coffee shop?"

"In San Francisco, a coffee shop can become a center for the arts," Lydia replied.

"Oh Lydia, a coffee shop isn't an auditorium."

"For some music professors, it is. Everyone can't be slick and have their act together like Maureen."

"My act together?" Maureen was puzzled now. "I'm practicing taking photos of Lonnie because I've never photographed children much. I might get a photo credit in a book if I do it right."

Her mother stared with galled blue orbs. They were sitting at the old Formica table where arguments used to be as irresistible as the wooden bowl full of Old Dutch potato chips. The table was smaller, its middle section removed like the dining room table in the softly carpeted area where steps led up to the bungalow living room.

"How do I count myself asleep?" Lonnie said, having heard his name.

"Oh, Maureen! You don't mean you've been photographing Lonnie for an office project? You don't know what it is to have a real child. To make money that way!"

Even though Lydia thought that Maureen had her act together, her mother felt that Lydia's having a child gave her more validity. Maureen's mother was like an inveterate television viewer whose daughter suddenly announced that she was taking a bus to Hollywood. Years in a library made her leery about her daughter's career in publishing.

"Is it alright if I show the managing editor photos of Lonnie?" Maureen asked Lydia.

"If it's alright with Lonnie. I don't know what a managing editor in the Midwest could do wrong. Schilling Publishing is not exactly known in California."

Their mother cut a small slice of rhubarb pie, shaking her head because Lonnie had already brushed his teeth.

"It's pretty crowded in your house, Mom. I feel like sleeping outside near the rhubarb. Did you keep the pup tent?" Maureen said.

"I want to sleep outside!" Lonnie yelled.

"Oh, Maureen!"

Kendra pried a bit of dried jam off of her stoneware plate. "Does your nephew wash dishes?"

"Sorry. Lydia didn't know which dishes were mine. Did Milt call?"

"Valerie talked to him."

"He'll call another day," Valerie said, looking at her wedding list in exasperation. "We should go out today and find a dress for the photographer."

They drove to Rosedale Mall where Valerie became distracted at any reminder of the wedding gifts she'd already opened. Because Valerie didn't mention Milt's RSVP, she probably knew the answer now.

Maureen pouted, "I'd rather know if Milt is coming before I buy a dress."

Valerie mollycoddled Maureen into trying on four dresses before they ate lunch in a restaurant with diamond patterned trellises. Dipping her roast beef au jus sandwich into its broth, she said, "Milt is neither here nor there, is he? You should buy a dress for yourself."

"Should he be?"

Valerie gazed at Maureen's sopping sandwich as if Maureen were the only one eating a messy lunch.

"What did Milt say when he called?" Maureen persisted.

"He talked to Kendra. Then I called him back about the RSVP."

"I could have told you that he wouldn't commit himself," Maureen said.

"I'm glad you know that." Valerie bent over her sandwich again.

"What else did Milt say?"

"It's not what Milt said. It's what the woman said who answered the phone. She thought I was stand-by at the airport."

"Milt had a girl at his house? A girl who was going to the airport?"

"He was in the background."

"So what?"

"Milt asked me not to tell you. But I just did." Valerie started to take a bite of roast beef but the broth was dripping all over her fingers. She took a napkin and gave up, putting her sandwich down and finding her knife and fork.

"I suppose she drove back from the east coast with him. He didn't want to drive alone with his brother. What if Milt had a girlfriend in college?"

Gordon Kirch didn't have a girlfriend until Valerie. Maureen was pretty sure that Milt had someone on his mind because when the song "Midnight Blues" came on the car radio, he flipped down the sound and said that he couldn't stand the song. At Gary Drake's birthday party, she heard Lisa asking Milt if he was going to see someone named either Tracy or Stacy in Boston.

"She had a backslapper of a laugh. A real cackle. She didn't sound much like you." Valerie forked a hunk of disintegrating bread out of her broth. "I think you should choose a dress for yourself."

When Milt called back, he suggested the Guthrie Theater on the weekend. They would mix with other people and then kiss instead of discuss.

"Could we go out and talk? I mean, yes, I'd like to go to the Guthrie. But I'd like to go to a bar or somewhere to talk."

"Oh no."

"What?"

Instead of ordering a carafe or a pitcher, Milt ordered himself a beer and let Maureen order a glass of wine. They were at a student bar where the booth walls were waxy as yellow apples and so high that Maureen was reminded of changing stalls at the Wanatin swimming pool. She used to compete with girls from Twin Cities suburbs when she had no figure and placed fourth in the backstroke.

Milt was cracking open a peanut instead of telling her about the woman who drove back from the east with him. "I don't know what you're talking about, Maureen." His words were as measured as sedative in a syringe. "Valerie said that you went to the airport this week. You've got it all mixed up and Valerie's been on the phone with a lot of people about her wedding and travel plans."

Maureen had to wrack her memories for an instance of Valerie lying or being that mixed up. After one drink, she perched in Milt's car again, continuing the conversation as the city lights probed in at the windows.

"This whole thing has evolved into something that I can't do right now," Milt said. "It's not your fault. It's my problem."

He said this in seriousness when to Maureen, he might have been talking about a case of acne.

"I have some work to do on my own life," he stated.

When Maureen looked at Milt, it was as if another type of windshield had evolved, a windshield between them in the front seat. Outside the duplex, Milt turned off the motor and moved to kiss her, what he usually did. But they stared at each other the way people at Schilling Publishing looked through glass office walls. And then, Maureen wished she were on the other side of a lens because she doubted Milt would call again.

"If you want to do something, give me a call," he suggested. Then he put his hands back on the steering wheel.

Evenings now, Maureen developed photographs in a darkroom on the West Bank university campus where she was taking a photography class. She fished her summer from a tub and hung it on a line like laundry.

Sunlight looked hard into empty fairgrounds. A snow cone cup sat like a spring flower in the grass outside the gates. The shadow of a couple dancing floated on concrete.

Maureen explained to another darkroom student how she positioned the shadow. She and Valerie were showing Valerie's bridesmaid the state fairgrounds, only a few blocks from the duplex. Gordon was driving them all back from a restaurant. For the shadows, Maureen got them to practice dancing, Gordon with Valerie and Gordon with the bridesmaid.

"Some people in this neighborhood charge for parking during the fair," Valerie said. "Can I reserve my old spot?"

She would be back from her honeymoon, living in a rented inner suburb house.

"We could make a party of it," Kendra suggested.

"Are you going to call Milt?" the bridesmaid wondered.

Surveying her prints, Maureen regretted that she didn't have a shot of Milt. He was off and on, not a situation she wanted. She knew that the present happened the way it did in the darkroom. It had developed and couldn't be changed. The image had to be accepted even if it were the ghost of a split second. Milt wanted to take her to the Guthrie Theater until he was confronted.

Even if she would like to see men the way her friends did, she caught a man the way she caught him in the time she met him. There was only so much time and then the facts went into the dark the way an image went into a tub of chemicals, revealing the composition.

The photography students liked the empty fairgrounds photo better than her other photos. It was a picture of disenchantment, the fair being over when the fair was coming again. Everyone wasn't getting married right then.

"Yes, I like this kid canoeing. Who is he?" Inez paused, gesturing to Donald Dibbet.

A boy with longish hair paddled a canoe tied on a long rope to a dock.

When Donald stepped inside Inez's office, Maureen told them about Lonnie visiting from California and about the day at a lake with Hugo and Joyce.

"He's not saying 'Look Mommy, no paddle'," Donald said. "Hmm, I'll take this bookmobile picture."

Towards the end of the work day, Maureen could file three of her prints in the photo room. She didn't have a Welsh castle but she might have a photo credit in an educational Schilling book. Returning to her cubicle, she admired the sunlight tinting the desks in the old building. Outside, it would glare from cars.

She rolled out a parcel of galleys and began cutting them into pages, a task a child could accomplish. Cutting galleys at the next desk, Aggie wondered what she was doing on the weekend. Since Milt, Maureen was dully disappointed at the prospect of starting something new. She was going to the darkroom that weekend.

Between snips, Maureen heard Inez and Donald Dibbet walking back from a meeting.

"Someone will have to make up a separate check for Maureen's photos," Donald said.

"She's in the photo room," Inez replied.

"Did you hear Dr. Mort's last 'Confound the Doctor' program? The one about family patterns? They're wondering if divorce is a family pattern."

Inez's voice was on the other side of Maureen's fabric wall. "Is it? Is that why people get divorced? Because their parents did?"

"Confound it, they're afraid divorce is becoming a pattern too," Donald mimicked Dr. Mort Blaisdell.

"I'm glad my kids didn't hear that. My parents got along well. Maybe my ex inherited his condition," Inez hissed and her glass door closed.

Counting lines on a galley, Maureen was reminded of crochet. In high school, she latched onto her crochet hook the way she latched onto a cigarette. Making purses and shawls with repeating patterns gave her a sense of certainty. She saw her days stretching out at Schilling Publishing, each counted and shaped in a world where women no longer looped yarn for hours at a time.

Wondering how long she would stay at Schilling, Maureen realized that she had never had this choice. She had never had indefinite security in a place where crises were eased and mended. After Milt, routine was a refuge, even a comfort in the asylum of an office. Milt was a prince to her there. He was a person who had better means of satiating himself, better than most men. But he wasn't very secure for her, and he may have intentionally dated a woman who hadn't the tenacity to make marriage out of dating.

18   The Idea of Permanence

Somewhere between the studio arts building and her car, Maureen's blood paused in its pathways. She might backtrack to the studio arts building where she could pick up an MFA application and where a man named Hank was still developing film. Still, she put her new Minolta camera and her portfolio of prints in the front seat. Then she looked across the Mississippi at the steely mist that was downtown.

She began walking back until she realized that a vandal might see her camera. When she about-faced, she thought she should simply drive back to her duplex in St. Paul. But she dawdled, delving for the keys in her shoulder bag. Feeling drawn to something she feared and disliking its vagueness, she opened her car door and slung her camera over her shoulder. Then she glanced at the many windows above her. Students of social science might be observing her behavior. She felt like a two-dimensional carnival figure that turns abruptly every time a shot goes off, a target without volition.

Once inside the studio arts building, Maureen went directly to the bathroom. Her eyes were dilated and she felt like a mass of particles that were becoming unfixed. The darkroom door was nearer the bathroom than the office. Hank was still in the semi-darkness, hovering under the hood of an enlarger. He was happy to tell her how he accomplished the macro he was printing. He had already explained that he was getting his Ph.D. and that he worked part-time at the DNR, the Department of Natural Resources. His brown hair was rough like tree bark and his smile was boyish when he said goodbye some minutes ago.

"I forgot to pick up the application," she began. Talking to Hank was easier than thinking about leaving her job at Schilling Publishing. Maureen was another person here, a woman who wore crocheted headbands and splashy scarves.

She admired the cellular design of orange cup fungi. The boyish smile didn't have much zoom action and it had already encouraged her to tell about her work and her MFA dilemma.

"I've been thinking about a darkroom," she said.

"I've got catalogs at home. Would you like to go out for lunch sometime?"

This was not what she vaguely feared.

"How about East Bank on Saturday? The place with the ranch French toast?' Hank didn't seem surprised at seeing her again.

Months later, Maureen felt like the metal carnival figure, making about-faces as she walked between the desk quads at Schilling. Once a week, Inez asked, "Where are you going with Hank this weekend?" Every Friday, Maureen reported that the trustworthy and possibly brilliant student, as good a catch as a woman should expect, was taking her to an event that was runner-up on the weekend roster. She never told about the unaccountable sense of sadness she had, smoking a cigarette and waiting for Hank to pick her up.

Hank called every Wednesday night, regularly as Maureen had choir practice for the Sunday Lutheran church service when she was a little girl. About as regularly, her mother put her cheek near her father's when she put his dessert plate before him. The year before her father moved to an apartment, he turned away.

"Do you like classical European songs?" Maureen asked Hank as they sat down at a concert.

"I don't know for sure. There's a trout in this program." Hank laughed. "I just want to relax. Maybe something will pull on my line."

Another weekend, after attending an exhibit of robotic assistants at the Science Museum, Hank dutifully walked Maureen to a watercolor exhibit in a nearby St. Paul building.

"I like this one," Hank said, standing in front of a picture.

"Why?" The artist had attempted to color the abstract wind in a boat's sails. Instead of feeling a storm, Maureen saw a huge mosquito. She thought it the worst picture, displayed near a cubic representation of a lighthouse beam.

"I don't know. But I like it."

Either Hank's easiness made Maureen irritable or she had made an awful discovery. Hank had no aesthetic sensibility.

One Friday, Maureen answered Inez's question about the weekend with, "I have to look for an apartment."

"You're not seeing Hank this weekend?"

"He suggested a discotheque."

The new editorial assistant, Jim, looked up from his desk. To him, Hank was a set of page proofs that were behind schedule. Jim was planning his wedding as long as the word *obey* was maintained in the vows. He was proud of bringing the basics back to a wedding.

Inez pondered the discotheque. Then Maureen said, "I can't afford my duplex after my roommate gets married. I don't *have to* go to the discotheque."

Jim turned his chair towards Maureen and Inez.

"Hank took me from one food booth to the next at the State Fair last fall. Then he wanted to go on the rocket ride. The only reason I went on it was because I didn't know him well then. What if men don't know how uncomfortable it is for women to obey in some instances?"

"That's going too far with the idea of obeying. He wouldn't make you go on a ride," Jim countered.

"Eve didn't have to obey Adam in the Garden of Eden. She had to when she was outside of it," Maureen stated, having opened up the Bible since Jim started the debate.

"Most people don't live in a garden where God is walking. She didn't obey God." Jim was watching Inez retreat.

"Shouldn't a modern woman be given her chance?"

"There are too many choices these days. Say that you were pregnant and you wanted to go on a ride. Or you wanted to do something that your husband thought was a risk," Jim said.

"Then he could discuss it instead of ordering his wife around. The standard marriage vows make the fallen world an ideal," Maureen persisted.

Maureen stood up to Jim because she wasn't falling. She had tried to fall for Hank. But at the end of a night, Hank embraced her like a person who was trying on clothing that wasn't flattering or didn't fit.

It was like knowing under the strobe lights that Hank's dancing gave her more perplexity than laughter. It was a relief to leave. When he suggested an excursion to North Dakota where he planned to hunt a rumored albino turkey, Maureen asked him if she could photograph him.

"Guys are betting on it. Whether the turkey was an albino, a domesticated turkey, or a mix," Hank was saying.

He wore a T-shirt, khaki shorts, and hiking boots, standing at the open door of his dusty car. His legs were rounded like an outdated car fender. His car seemed to have endured a storm. Notebooks, paper cups, a duck decoy, magazines, and jackets were strewn on the back seat.

Maureen bet that the turkey was domesticated and then she declined the trip. She wanted a hiatus and, having a photograph of Hank, hoped to find him familiar when he came back. Then they might fall into each other's arms.

Her father drank and divorced but his vacuumed car contained no evidence of that. Roland Werff's car was as spare of extraneous objects as a tractor. The other men Maureen dated could accommodate passengers in going-out clothing. Every time Maureen got into Hank's car and saw the back seat, she felt a disappointment akin to fear. Another woman might have been thrilled at the prospect of putting Hank's back seat in order.

One Sunday morning, Kendra asked, "How long did Hank stay last night?"

"He stayed through Mr. Bill on 'Saturday Night.'"

Hank laughed uncontrollably at Mr. Bill, the clay man, being manipulated by giant sadist hands. That Saturday night, Maureen found out something else about Hank, something Kendra might be interested in knowing. Hank's best friend was a diagnosed manic-depressive. On a duck hunting trip, he locked himself into a cabin and refused to leave the woods. He had been making wild statements about land and threatened to drive from the cabin to Montana.

Nights, Maureen laid awake, blaming Hank for her relapse into insomnia. At three o'clock in the morning, she knew that she wanted to stay at the duplex and that she wanted to set up a darkroom there. A darkroom might solve her insomnia.

"There's certainly free love in the animal world," Hank said after Maureen told him about Lydia and her living arrangements in California. "But that's what makes animals easy prey. The irresponsibility of the male towards its young and the multiplicity of partners. The male competes with his own family for food."

Probably, Hank hadn't ever thought of living with a woman.

Maureen decided to have a party to celebrate Kendra's upcoming wedding. Besides Kendra's friends, she invited everyone she knew, thinking that she might somehow secure someone to share the duplex with her, someone preferably male. Roland Werff heard about it and managed to be in town, arriving with Maureen's hometown friends.

As Maureen said she might do someday, she called Milt Blaisdell. She had run into him downtown and they lunched again at the Grain Exchange, only catching up. At the party, Milt's entrance was announced by the people who listened to "Confound the Doctor" on the radio. He was annoyed, introducing his brother Mick, and then he became engrossed in talking with the only person who didn't seem to think he had met Milt's father.

"Have you ever been out to Montana?" Duane asked the traveler, Milt. At the coffee table where magazines were strewn, he challenged Milt to discover hidden pictures in the photographs. Duane believed that subliminal persuasion and camera tricks were affecting the minds of America.

Having been warned about Duane, Kendra pulled every cat out of her California wedding bag. Her dress could be viewed in her bedroom and a picture of the musicians was near the cheese ball. Presents could be left on Kendra's bed while the coats went on Maureen's.

Hank stood around like a human floor lamp, keeping Duane under observation. He told Roland and Cal McConkey about the albino turkey that was sighted in North Dakota.

"No! It must be domestic," Cal protested. After they found out more about Hank, Roland's eyes, prominent because they could be seen above the other party-goers, became unpleasantly glaring. Maureen caught up with Jayne Magnuson, now dating a man heavily, and Dee Dee Guccini with her date, an IBM employee. Then she ducked around to Aggie from work.

"Hank seems like a good man," Aggie said.

Kendra beamed next to Joel, holding his arm so he wouldn't sneak to the bedroom for a glimpse of her wedding dress. "I don't feel badly about leaving Maureen alone," she said.

But Kendra wasn't so pleased to leave Maureen with Roland at the end of the night. His arm was comfortably around Maureen's shoulders while Cal snoozed in a chair.

"Who's Hank?" Roland asked.

All Maureen could really say was that Hank was a friend. Roland had become a first love twice-removed, an old friend actually. He had fallen in love with skiing and now he coordinated ski trips to Colorado. Milt Blaisdell was going to Argentina in the summer because it was winter there then.

Maureen confronted her bed and her future, an undeveloped film in the dark. Although she knew how a woman could use subliminal persuasion, her stomach was a void. She put a pillow over it, hoping to sleep. On the wall though, she saw the flat form of a carnival target marching back and forth. She tried to count how many times it crossed the wall until finally, she put her pillow and a throw blanket on the floor, attempting to sleep there.

The lens is like an eye without another eye, a wink, a pirate eye. The more Maureen thought that, the more she felt unbalanced and needful of the common cure. If she kept going out with Hank, she would be able to marry him because Hank had a righteous conscience. But she couldn't imagine being a part of him. If she had children, she couldn't imagine that they would be hers. Hank's children would admire him. Since she was attractive enough, people wouldn't know that her relationship with Hank was really adulterous.

She might be tempted to have an affair that seemed like real marriage, an affair that would ruin her sleep. Then Hank would call someone, what he did with the manic-depressive Duane. She would find herself in the fallen world, a bad woman married to a friend.

Sorrow was two o'clock when it wasn't two-thirty at Schilling Publishing. Maureen knew she had no right to this sorrow. One day, Donald Dibbet found Maureen in the break room when it was only one forty-five. She was reading a newspaper and drinking coffee as if she were an editorial director like Donald.

"I wanted to look at this photograph," Maureen said lamely.

A child was living in a frosty tent. His parents waved from outside the oxygenated blimp that extended as a large tube into the hallway.

"It's because of a newly discovered disease."

"Medical science. A wonderful thing," Donald said dryly.

Maureen wanted to deplore the tent but she had strayed from her tether.

For the next day, Maureen should emulate the behavior of the model employee in her department. Even though Maureen could be promoted to assistant editor in the next year, she joked about the editor whose desk was hidden in a corner. There, the model employee could dig into manuscripts inconspicuously. She didn't mind not having a glassed-in office of her own.

The only person who approached the model employee casually was Donald Dibbet. He rapped on her cubicle wall and politely asked, "Can you be disturbed?"

The model employee wasn't unattractive but she was as sensible as her Earth Shoes. During breaks, she walked on her Earth Shoes rather than socializing. If she wasn't a saint already, she maintained a calm urgency that reminded other employees that she had been in the Peace Corps.

"One of these days, that editor might stand up and scream," Maureen said at coffee break. "How boring was her life when she was in the Peace Corps?"

The model employee had been in the Schilling syndrome for six years, reporting to work in one of her ten pants suits, alternated in a two-week period.

"What if her safari suit is a Yves St. Laurent design?"

No one had ever talked with the model employee about her clothing.

"If I put a weird photo in her in-box by mistake, I wonder if we would hear her reaction."

"I'll bet we wouldn't," Aggie said.

When the office was an extension of a sleepless night, Maureen decided that her insomnia stemmed from permanence. Those mornings, the permanence became distorted so that she had a sense of impermanence. And Maureen believed she was becoming unpopular. When the most admired woman employee sailed through their department, Maureen stayed at her desk, puzzling at her gut dislike.

Nell wasn't much older than Maureen but she was promoted more quickly. She wore close-cut suits, vivid as flags, and somehow managed to look comfortable when she sat in her stiff skirt and nylons for hours. Maureen often wore roomy pants with India cotton blouses if she didn't have a meeting scheduled. Nell might have the same barber as Jim, the man who wanted to be obeyed. It was apparent that men liked her style, the pert haircut contrasting her figure which was well-adapted for women's suits.

Ostensibly, the men made Nell their office star because she was editing a new series on the modern family around the world. When she sauntered in one day to shake hands with a graphic designer, the editorial staff gathered to see her project. Maureen stayed at her desk just as the model employee stayed at hers.

After Aggie returned from admiring Nell's work, Maureen said in their quad, "She rejected the photos I sent to her. I guess she doesn't trust my sense of family."

Maureen felt like the familiar floozy. Her co-workers had wondered aloud at the five or six men she dated in her two years at Schilling. Judging from the way Maureen slinked in on Monday mornings, Hank might be another man that she slept with instead of marrying.

One afternoon, Cal McConkey came into the office at lunchtime and asked for Maureen. Cal was obviously athletic, wearing a zip-up jacket, and he had acquired a habit of grinning at secretaries. Maureen was sitting in Donald Dibbet's glass office as Cal waved at her.

"Cal's from my hometown. We're going out to lunch," Maureen explained to Donald. He was staring at her as if she had run into Cal on the street. "He's downtown getting shoes for an interview. He took coursework in public transportation systems."

Donald snatched up some finished proofreading from his in-box, and said, "There are new graduates who would treasure your job."

Donald didn't hire Maureen.

Eating lunch with Cal revived the vitality that Maureen had in high school. She ran a folder of photographs to Nell's division instead of using inter-office mail. Nell was in the main meeting room with a textbook editor.

"I make a lot of noise before I enter that room," their secretary said before Maureen knocked on the door.

Nell sparkled her teeth at Maureen from the best furnishings at Schilling Publishing. Framed illustrations were on the walls and manuscripts were spread across a large table.

"They work together in there for whole days," the secretary said after Maureen closed the door. Her eyebrows were like hyphens. "If I weren't putting my husband through school right now, I wouldn't stay at this desk."

"Under Nell?"

The textbook editor working with Nell was Schilling's idea of an intellectual. His eyes seemed hollowed out behind his glasses and his body was lanky to the point of neglect. Once, he smiled at Maureen and she saw that his teeth, like his hair, were a low priority. It would never have occurred to Maureen that Nell would want a man like that even if his wife wanted him at one time.

Seeing Maureen's satisfaction, the secretary said, "I hear you lunch over at the Star and Tribune cafeteria. I haven't been there yet."

The next time Nell sailed into their department as if the weather were beautiful in hers, Maureen knew how balmy it was getting. This time, she joined the circle around Nell. Maureen had a photograph in her hand and when she held it out, Aggie burst into laughter. The other editorial workers craned their heads to see what caused Aggie's reaction.

"It's an albino turkey. My friend Cal gave me the photo in case I go hunting for the albino turkey in North Dakota," Maureen explained.

Nell's febrile zeal was ruffled and so were Donald's eyebrows. People didn't laugh around Nell. Strangely enough, if Donald learned about Nell's affair with a colleague closer to his age than hers, he wouldn't think she was hard up. Donald probably wouldn't think that Nell was a bad woman. But if Maureen didn't settle down with Hank, she could go from bad to worse.

19 Cracks in the Eggshell Ceiling

Summer of 1980. The sun was really up all night too. Maureen dreaded Sunday morning because she had to look for an apartment. She had only a few hours of sleep before the newspaper arrived, and when it did, she was recalling her mother, vigilant near the telephone. When her mother didn't hear from Lydia or Lyle after they each fled to California, she polished the telephone table, then the hutch, and finally the silver in the hutch. Her mother was almost alone then and Maureen was almost alone, wondering why her mother was polishing the silver. Just the two of them ate at the kitchen table.

At seven o'clock, Maureen began making calls.

"Sorry, it's already rented," the landlords near her St. Paul neighborhood all answered. Apartments were passed down or around in St. Paul. She crossed the column of ads to Minneapolis, feeling portable instead of like breakfast.

Visiting the first apartment, Maureen asked if she could take a picture. She started with the kitchen where the old linoleum was sunken with heel forms. At the next apartment, she walked onto a back porch where she photographed the neighbor's yard. An old beer sign was a patio tabletop supporting cans of anti-freeze and greasy towels. A motorcycle was parked on the lawn.

"Oh, a carpet," Maureen said, and when the landlord wasn't looking, she took a macro worth a thousand odors.

By the end of the day, Maureen had an excuse for spending Friday night in Hank's darkroom.

"How did your macro turn out?" Hank's voice jolted her. His darkroom was a small stall, constructed from a kit. Showing his photographs of lampreys, he one-upped her. She listened to his discourse on the effect lampreys had on duck hunting, mostly because it was a soporific. Hank loved the animals he hunted. He hadn't yet killed a lamprey.

Now that Maureen had a new hobby, photographing apartments, she circled a few of the more expensive ones, curious at what she couldn't afford. Near the arts institutions in Minneapolis, she fibbed about her intentions with her new Minolta. "You don't mind if I take a few pictures to show a friend?" She would like to see Hank's reaction to an art nouveau mantel carved with tree branches. The light fixture was like a migration of geese.

"This might be just for you," a landlord said in another dream apartment.

A darkroom was already installed near a kitchen done in black and white.

"Not the carpet," Maureen said in the white-carpeted bedroom.

The closer Maureen's moving day approached, she felt weighed down, as if she were wearing an X-ray apron. One Sunday morning, she drove over to Irving Avenue and leased out an apartment she hadn't yet seen. She met the landlord in a sunny garden-level one-bedroom and agreed to take an identical apartment on the second floor.

"The tenant is getting married. I'd like to show it but he's in the process of moving," the landlord explained. "The walk-in closet has the same dimensions as this apartment. Room for a chest of drawers so I suppose you might use it for photography."

Maureen admired the front balconies, girdled with wrought iron. Then she walked to the side yard where crab apple trees screened a wide lawn pinned with tiger lilies.

Kendra dropped by the duplex and, letting herself in, found Maureen watching a corner of the room as if the television were still there. Kendra's philodendron plant still dangled from the ceiling, tipping sunward at a windowsill.

"Aren't you going to buy a TV, Maureen? I could bring mine back," she said, ready to turn in her key and to collect the philodendron.

"I don't want to move one. I'll get one after I move."

Kendra asked about Schilling.

"I was thinking about an odd dream I had," Maureen said. In it, Maureen told off Jim, the man who wanted his fiancé to obey him. He probably wanted Maureen to obey him on the job someday. "Jim broke down and said he was in debt," she told Kendra. They went walking with Donald Dibbet in a deep channel where bulldozers were digging up a street. The men were going to help Maureen find a file of photographs in the construction area. Deeper in the dirt, they discovered file drawers and women's boots, embedded like artifacts. Then the sky glowed like the hood of an enlarger.

Kendra agreed that Maureen could use a walk over to Como Park. Maureen ambled out of the duplex with her and once Kendra was driving away, she tried to shake her lethargic circulation. Her legs felt as if silt had settled in them.

There wasn't anything to photograph, only gardens that were as neat as bedrooms. She couldn't reach Como Park because it was too difficult to see affectionate couples near the lake. At a small grocery store, the produce was limp and the Pepperidge Farm cookies were probably displayed on borrowed time. She bought Vienna cookies anyway and then she realized that she would be happier if she drove to the Co-op store on Hamlin Avenue. But phrases came to her like "You are what you eat." She wanted to buy nuts.

All Maureen felt like cooking were scrambled eggs to eat with the Vienna cookies. Then she should start packing. In a storage drawer, she found lavender yarn, crochet hooks, and patterns that dated back to her high school days. She could start a shawl. She could wear her nerves on her sleeve. Her sister-in-law Joyce gave her the yarn at The Lavender Inn, a restaurant near her college. Pictures of sad-eyed children painted on black velvet were sold there.

Certainly she picked up crochet more quickly when she was sixteen-years-old. Now she was afraid that she wouldn't be able to make a shell of double crochets without consulting Joyce. Mercifully, the telephone rang.

Maureen turned on a light and prepared to talk with either her father or Hank. Hank only called for the weekend date and her father, if he was drinking, wondered, "Hank?" He hadn't met the man she'd been dating for months. Her father and mother were alike when it came to her love life. They were supposed to finish marriage but they dropped out and now, if Maureen had questions, they didn't have answers.

"Dee Dee!" Maureen said as she did when she was sixteen-years-old and learning to crochet.

Dee Dee Guccinni had a guest pass to the Meadow Pond Spa. At the party for Kendra, Dee Dee said that the spa wasn't far from Apple Valley, the suburb where she was teaching her first year of high school French.

"When was the last time you went swimming?"

Maureen paused because she couldn't remember right away.

The spa tour was tiring. Maureen had to flex her *no* as she walked through the Jacuzzi room, the sauna, the aerobics area, and the lawn chairs where women drank fruit juice under gooseneck sunlamps.

"You can even get your hair trimmed here," Dee Dee said.

Maureen's face looked lachrymose in the salon mirror. Dee Dee's exuberance at the suburban splendor was bewildering because Maureen remembered her with a bright ribbon attached to her black tank suit. Now her black swimsuit had silky frills at her hips.

"And there's a masseuse!" Dee Dee said.

She was sure that Maureen had been sitting at a desk too much. But Maureen was going to get a workout when she moved to her new apartment. Trying out the lawn chair and sunlamp, she asked Dee Dee about the date she brought to the party for Kendra. He'd almost become a pianist but he switched majors and now he was an IBM employee.

"He's much better to know if there's a piano in the room. Otherwise,

Southdale Mall furnished his apartment." Dee Dee faltered and changed the subject. "Have you seen *Superman*? Let's go to a Saturday matinee."

"Why didn't you ever tell me about your Aunt Elena?"

Maureen and Dee Dee were on their way to South Minneapolis where they would pick up Elena and head for an Owatonna lake. The Labor Day weekend was a sweaty one for packing.

"She's lived in Minneapolis for years," Dee Dee said. "My father had an argument with her. She received a bequest from her fiancé after he died. All these years, she's been like a daughter to his parents. The bequest paid for opera lessons and now she teaches singing. Since I was in high school, she's been seeing a board member of the opera."

They parked in front of an old Victorian mansion that had three mailboxes inside its porch. Elena came out and led them to her yellow Le Car. Her grin rared up with the ignition and when the wind flumped her wavy hair, she didn't bother to smooth it the way Dee Dee's father smoothed his, directing the Wanatin High School Band.

"Did you like *Superman*?" she wanted to know.

"I liked it," Maureen said, having been enthralled when Superman escorted Lois Lane into the night sky.

Dee Dee snorted the way she did in junior high school. "*Superman* reminded me of city men in their success syndromes. I mean, why do they become unreal, leading double lives at IBM?"

"He's a doll, isn't he?" Elena flashed a smile at Maureen in the car mirror.

"Has Dee Dee ever been in love?" Maureen asked from the back seat.

"Elena knows about my semester in France. It was miserable," Dee Dee said. "At least it wasn't as bad as Elena's experience."

"Still it's worth it," Elena said.

"What happened?" Maureen asked.

"He died." Elena said.

"From what?"

"War."

"Oh."

They admired the cornfields south of the city, their tassels grown as high as plumes on old military headgear. Not finding anyone to marry when a woman was in her twenties wasn't any mystery when the only human being in sight was tied to a tractor.

"Remember the Italian restaurant that used to be at the edge of town?" Maureen asked when they reached Owatonna. The lake beach there seemed shrunken with ropes that crowded children in.

"I don't know what's worse, a city lake or this," Elena sighed.

"Lake Calhoun looked like heaven the first time I went there." Maureen told about the slope where she spread her towel and sat for some minutes with Valerie and Kendra. "We were surrounded by handsome men. Just them and us. Then we realized that we were on the gay beach."

"Let's drive around the lake. We can't swim here," Dee Dee said.

They got back into Le Car and rounded the lake until Elena saw car tracks to a boat launch. She parked there and then they undressed to their swimsuits near the patches of goldenrod.

"We'll say we had a sudden attack of hay fever," Dee Dee said.

They ran into the lake, estimating that the beach was about 200 yards away. Dee Dee spurted ahead, swimming freestyle, and Elena bobbed behind her. Maureen turned onto her back. Hearing Dee Dee slap the water and Elena laughing, she lolled under the sky, finding that her limbs were more lethargic than tired. She was like a closed fan lately, disciplined to ignore a man's muscle tone under his work clothing.

A few years ago, when she went to all the swimming holes with Roland Werff, they came to this beach. She and Roland dove beneath the ropes and played underwater for as long as couples got away with things in a movie theater. Now her memory blocked the insolence of their pleasure. Dee Dee had jagged her memory back to the virgin time.

Maureen heard oars and then she saw the hull of a rowboat. Swimming the backstroke, she had veered towards the lake's center while Dee Dee and Elena were headed back towards the boat launch. She ducked into the water, sinking and wandering in its dark green shades, a place that was forbidden and beautiful. Then she surfaced, defiant.

"Can you swim across the lake?"

A lifeguard was no longer swanky. He was a wiry boy wearing a whistle like a pendant.

"You're with those women who swam from the boat launch, aren't you?"

"Yeah."

He was making Maureen feel deranged. She and Dee Dee used to swim this distance as a morning warm-up.

Dee Dee and Elena laughed about him in Le Car. They'd gotten what they craved, an experience they couldn't have in the city. Dee Dee remembered, "Maureen's high school steady got all worked up one day because he thought her bikini was too revealing. He was in town for her party. I never thought he was the real thing."

"Did you?" Elena asked Maureen.

"No, I didn't think of him like that."

They whizzed back to Minneapolis in their swimsuits, letting the air from the windows dry them. After Maureen and Dee Dee put on their summer clothes, Elena stopped so that she could dress for a Mexican restaurant.

It was a hole-in-the-wall, better than Chi Chi's, Elena said. The tables at the restaurant were crammed between walls decorated with pottery plaques and sombreros.

"Hank is such a good man," Dee Dee was telling Elena. "I had a nice talk with him at Maureen's party."

"You're going out with a good man," Maureen said. "He's as nice as the Steinway piano at your parents'."

"He's got awfully good teeth. Like piano keys," Elena agreed.

"But he's not like a Steinway," Dee Dee complained. "We've never even had a fight."

They were eating on pottery dishes painted with bright Mexican musicians. Dee Dee told about a fellow teacher. "Her husband was a university professor. We all thought they were the ideal couple. She said they'd never had a quarrel. Then, overnight, they agreed to get a divorce. It was shocking."

Maureen fumbled in her bag for an envelope of photos. "Here's the apartment building that I've moving into."

"It looks like a building for a boudoir. Look at the balconies, Elena. Elena has a boudoir," Dee Dee said.

"That's a nice façade. I've seen it," Elena said. "It's hard to be intelligent about men," she added.

"Maybe it's better not to be intelligent," Dee Dee said.

"I've thought about getting an MFA," Maureen said.

"I've thought about seeing a psychiatrist," Dee Dee said. "Sometimes I think I'm going crazy."

Even though the women couldn't help each other anymore, Maureen visited Elena's apartment. Her boudoir room had a dressing table and a carved armoire where she kept clothing for singing engagements. Still, it was as if Elena had been told to go to her room in the old Victorian.

Elena seemed to guess Maureen's thoughts. "You're not alone here in Minneapolis. Lots of single women live here."

"Maybe it's our age," Maureen said in her car, driving Dee Dee to her apartment in Apple Valley. They were enjoying each other's company more than the company of the men they dated. The only solution for Maureen was her empty apartment and the possibility of running into Dee Dee's aunt at Lund's grocery.

"Or maybe men can really read our minds," Dee Dee suggested. "They're not exactly what we wanted and we're not exactly what they lost."

They were both twenty-five years old.

Surveying her apartment, Maureen had nothing to say to the landlord.

"You have the view," he said, pleasant as a Saturday hobby.

There was a catalpa tree behind the crab apple trees that hedged her side of the building. Inside though, the shaded apartment seemed designed with cracks near the window frames and on the eggshell-colored ceiling. A black electrical box looked morbid near the door. In the kitchen, the criss-cross marks of knives textured the counter.

"Have men been living here?"

The bathtub had a chipped claw foot and a fracture at its ankle.

"The last renter was a man. He was a smoker." The landlord's nostrils dilated as if he smelled the cigarette Maureen had in her car.

Because he wasn't inspired to re-paint the walls, Maureen gazed out at the trees, thinking how they would tissue her view in the spring. Already, she felt shut into a corner of Minneapolis for the duration of a nine-month lease.

"They're just surface cracks," the landlord said at the doors of the walk-in closet where Maureen planned to set up a darkroom. In the hallway across from the bathroom, it was a large space with clothing racks, shelves, and room for a dresser since it once had a fold-down ironing board inside.

After the landlord made his escape, Maureen could utter the word "Bastard!" She hadn't been out on the balcony. Its door was at one side of the large room that would become her bedroom. She unlocked the door and stood on the platform but what she saw cracked the air like a camera shutter. On the wrought iron railing, she fisted her hands, gaping at a house built with the same architecture as the old house in Wanatin. A million times, she'd looked at the brick and stucco. And there were hollyhocks and hydrangea along the same narrow sidewalk below.

Feeling that she would never get out of the place, Maureen sat on a box in the room. The nine-month lease was a symbol landlords hit on, the symbol of a fate that shouldn't be escaped. She had arranged to meet Hank and a U-Haul at her old apartment where he would help her with the heavier boxes and furniture.

"Don't you like it?" Hank said, touring the apartment and seeing her disappointment.

"It needs more work than the apartment I saw."

"It's not that bad."

Hank could and would walk out of the apartment. After that, he could make her feel vulnerable, something he hadn't gotten away with before. She couldn't tell Hank about the house at the back of the building. All she could reply, when Hank said the neighborhood wasn't a bad one, was that she didn't want to see Hank for a while. Hank wasn't a doll but he was ideal. Hank was unreal. Hank was perfectly agreeable.

20   Over-exposed

Alone in her apartment, Maureen was a restless spirit, pacing. She wondered if she could live with herself and why she didn't like herself enough to enjoy herself. While it was warm, she could sit at her balcony door until she felt exposed. When night came, she hid in her darkroom. Once she had arranged the black curtains inside her walk-in closet, she felt as content as she did in the bathtub.

Her pacing resulted in a photograph from the balcony.

A boy in a backyard waited, his head tilted upward. Sharply in the foreground was a ball rolling behind a chimney.

The boy had seen the restless woman in her balcony seat so often that he didn't notice her taking the photograph. If Maureen sat at the door of her balcony at dusk, four frames lit up in the house across from her. She had seen three women close their window blinds. Maureen wasn't sure if the boy belonged to the woman who wore a poncho or the woman who raked leaves in army fatigues or the woman who had more than one boyfriend.

One October morning, the woman in the poncho exited from the side door with the boy. Outside, the leaves were like excelsior in the sunshine. Maureen was late for work. Neighborhood children, usually invisible, gathered at the school bus stop.

When Maureen played in the backyard of a house like the one next door, she often stationed herself near the yard of a benign old couple. They were polite and seemed indifferent to her parents' problems. The plump old woman used to paint by number on her back porch. Her husband had little to say except, "Cecily, can I give away your painting of the pony, Colors 23-8-12?"

While Maureen's parents fought and she preferred to play in the backyard, she wished she could stay in an uninhabited bedroom of Cecily's house. She imagined that Colors 23-8-12 would be grazing on the wall and that her sleep there would be as untroubled as a horse in a pasture.

Maybe she had gotten what she wanted, Maureen thought as she nodded to the mother of the boy, going to her car.

"Hi. I noticed a ball stuck on the roof of your building. My balcony is next to it."

"You saw my ball?" the boy said.

"I wonder when they'll get it down," Maureen laughed. "It's stuck behind the chimney. Maybe the wind will move it."

"We're moving anyway," the mother said. "Toby wants a puppy."

"Your apartment is opening up?"

"It's a roomy house. People keep to themselves. The women on the first floor are lesbians, you know."

Maureen felt like the old woman painting ponies by number, not wanting to understand what she saw next door. Photographs were forced upon people, photographs in the news, in books, on billboards. But now, she realized that views were forced on people.

When the sun changed its aperture over the house, Maureen recalled from her college days a painting of the god Morpheus, his gargantuan gray arms embracing the world like clouds. Restless, she craved sleep, dreams that offered a different view.

Ducking into work, Maureen heard the editorial assistants talking about the latest. Dr. Mort Blaisdell was doing a new book for Schilling.

With genuine ignorance, Maureen stated that she missed the programs where children called in questions to "Confound the Doctor." "He was discussing father figures the last time I listened," she said, restlessly spreading her work over her desk.

Maureen missed children telling about bumps on their skin, the food they ate before got the stomachache, and the insects they found in their hair. At break, she confronted Aggie. "I heard that Dr. Mort's book will begin with photos of the radio station."

"Because it's clinical, like a doctor's office," Aggie said.

Everyone except Maureen was wondering if they would be assigned to Dr. Mort's book. "I wonder what Milt's doing now?" She had decided to be candid. If Aggie didn't find out, she might flinch in front of her co-workers, hearing about Milt.

Visiting their office, Dr. Mort spoke as if an audience of thousands were listening. "Of course they can't publish anything so humorous in *Medicine This Month*. They'd be more interested in the article my son wrote about the common cold in Russia. Yup, I'll get Milt into medical school yet."

Maureen stared at a photograph pinned to her fabric wall, one that she took near a church in her new neighborhood. *Jesus stood with his hands extended but a pigeon preferred to plant its claws on his scalp.*

Dr. Blaisdell was saying, "In the forties, aspiring doctors had to see something of the world, a world at war, before they could start a practice. I think something is lost if a student goes from college to medical school."

When Maureen went to the photo room, Inez gave her an incisive grin and Dr. Mort looked askance at her. She tried to walk as if she were cured.

On her return, Aggie wheeled her chair to Maureen's desk. "I guess Milt is dating a woman who flies with emergency patients on planes. For her residency. She's got quite a suntan, ho ho."

"He was interested in winter travel when I knew him," Maureen said. Then she attempted to concentrate on her page proofs.

Tam stood at her apartment door while Maureen sauntered to hers at two in the afternoon. A secretary, Tam was usually as neat and indifferent as the woodwork.

"I've found a new job," Maureen smiled.

The new job happened so quickly that Maureen was still unsure of its conditions. She told Tam about the Photographer III position at the University of Minnesota. "It's part-time but the hourly pay is better. I might do freelance work for my old employer."

Tam stood rigidly in the dim hall light, causing Maureen to think about her as a camera subject. But then she said flatly, "I've had an emergency. I'm going to need quiet. Not that you make much noise. I have to organize a wake."

"A relative?"

"My mother. She was murdered. A burglar got into her apartment. Near Lake Harriet."

Her separateness made Maureen feel as if she were looking through a lens.

"When?"

But she had said too much. Tam's door admitted her in a broken way. "Two nights ago."

The door shut and Maureen turned into her own apartment, asking herself what she could do. She couldn't knock on Tam's door and ask that. Thanksgiving was in three days and all she could think of was a sympathy card.

Dully, she remembered that she finished a roll of film before she entered the foyer. The crab apple tree branches resembled tridents in the brusque November wind. She was going to develop the roll behind a black curtain and the double doors of her walk-in closet. But that seemed morbid now.

Her darkroom helped her insomnia. When she went to bed, she awoke when her eyes were closed. Instead of seeing darkness behind her eyelids, faces sometimes drifted into view, images of men or women that weren't familiar, some kindly, some hags or ogres. And couples appeared, embracing and kissing. If she rubbed her eyes, she sometimes saw a perfect geometry, a patterned plane like a textile or an Islamic wall design.

Fearing that the dead were beckoning or that she was made like a machine, fearing the chaos of the dark, she often got up and went behind the black curtain as if a mysterious lover were in her darkroom. She risked film in the economical space.

Although there were many burglaries in Minneapolis, Maureen felt safer in her darkroom than she did in bed. If its door were opened, an intruder would find a dark curtain.

But Maureen had failures there. When a picture didn't develop as she hoped, a smile broke out inside of her, somewhere near her stomach. The satisfied smile also happened at the university when she couldn't find a room where a photo session was scheduled. As her face saddened, the sickening thing smiled in her gut.

Lydia composed a piece of music for her music therapy work, Maureen's mother wrote cheerfully. *It's written like modern music. The children count and then play whatever they want on their instruments. She named it "The Sea Horse", for finger cymbals, xylophone, Mexican ocarina, and maracas. We'll play a tape at Thanksgiving. Hugo and Joyce are coming.*

The smile said, I thought people would like me better if I failed.

"We're eating at four o'clock," her mother said when she called. "Hugo wants to leave his church."

"I've decided to stay here over the holiday."

Her mother was always touchy about Thanksgiving and the turkey that came from Wanatin. "I don't know what to say to Hugo," she said. "He has to get a call to another church."

"I don't know a prayer offhand."

"Maureen, you weren't fired from Schilling, were you?"

"I thought you would like me better if I failed."

The smile was so wide within her that it usurped her appetite.

On Thanksgiving, Maureen thought she might drive to a dusk-eaten lake, hoping to see the cloudy arms of sleep above a city that was drowsy from overeating. But at four o'clock, a light knock sounded on her door.

"Have you had Thanksgiving dinner?"

"Some good restaurants are open," Maureen said, prepared to go out with the bereaved Tam.

"No. I have food from the wake. I can't eat it all."

Moments later, Tam appeared with a china plate filled with turkey, stuffing, dinner rolls, pearl onions in a satiny glaze, Brussels sprouts, and a sweet potato, amber with butter.

"Would you like some coffee? Or wine?" Maureen pulled out the gate leg of her small dining room table.

"No."

Tam was studying Maureen's photographs. Then she surveyed the woven black and oatmeal-colored Peruvian rug that Maureen bought from a secondhand furniture store.

"Do you like tea?" Maureen felt that she was skipping some phrase, ritual as prayer.

"I like your apartment. It's calm." Tam pronounced this as if she knew she was the first person to notice that. Then she disappeared from view. "Just knock on my door when you're done."

It was the first plate of food that Maureen had finished for a while. She could tell Tam that it was the best Thanksgiving dinner she'd ever eaten. Someone taught Tam to add chestnuts to the stuffing and to enhance the sauce and gravy so that they were emollients for the mouth and stomach.

Maureen hadn't taken communion since high school, never having cared for its concept. Her brother's giving communion only made it less magical. Now she sat at the empty plate, seeing a wreath of English forget-me-nots. She understood that she should be thankful to be alive. She should be thankful that she could talk to her mother.

Tam's door opened so narrowly that she took the washed Staffordshire plate like a person in a dish-washing line. Inside Maureen, the smile was relishing what Tam had to give.

Tam was moving at the month's end. The next day, after someone came to take some of Tam's things, Maureen took a drive with her camera. She was restless and she needed practice with her wide-angle lens.

Tam's mother was murdered in a building near Lake Harriet, probably a staid brick building that loomed over the old houses in the area. A street called King's Highway took her near a cemetery. Maureen parked and walked along a lane where she might find a face that needed a mask. There were angel sculptures on high-rise monuments if she could focus between prongs of wrought iron.

Near Lake Harriet and some of the best residential real estate, the apartment windows were murky today, stricken with tangled, stripped vines. Obvious targets. She walked along the lake as it became pearl-gray within the brambly wreath of trees. A few loyal runners passed her before she made her way out from the gardens, full of thorn-like stalks now.

Dipping in and out of lake drives that could confuse a getaway car, Maureen became entrapped in a neighborhood with newer houses. There were pebbly sidewalks with small lanterns lighting them, curtains swagging people who looked posed. Houses blurred into crests as if they were on a journey to the suburbs, to land. Maureen might have obtained a passport from a man. She towed the waves, feeling as if she were looking into portholes, until she spied a perpendicular intersection and then a squared-off, hedged neighborhood.

Forty-fifth Street was ahead and a blinking light was behind her, a police car. At first she thought serendipity was leading her to a photograph but then she was handing hers over to a policeman.

"Thirty-five in a thirty zone. Not a good thing over the holidays. What are you doing in this neighborhood?"

"I didn't realize I was driving too fast. My neighbor's mother was murdered in a building near Lake Harriet."

The policeman was staring at her, her shaggy hair and her everyday yellow leather jacket.

"Last week. Isn't it your job to help women?"

She'd just blurted it out. But the policeman had asked why she was cruising outside of her shabby neighborhood. He seemed to know that she was slipping just as the smile inside her was satisfied that she was slipping.

"Your license tags are overdue. Another ticket. Another word and it's disorderly conduct." he said.

Photographers I and II dropped in with film while Maureen sat restlessly over news releases. Any leftover assignment would delight her - photographing kidney dialysis, a new set of computers being hooked up, or an experimental day care center.

Children were like swimmers, surfacing into a photogenic moment. Their restlessness calmed her even if permissiveness led to behavior modification. Then she was assigned to a psychology clinic where she would photograph patients whose self-image didn't match their appearance.

A young woman's clothing hung in uneven pleats at her ribs and her hips.

The co-ed's psychologist had diaphanous eyes like Doris Day's. "Lynn thinks you've taken the picture at an angle that makes her look thinner. Can she choose your position for the next picture?"

Or maybe Maureen's eyes were damp.

After a few weeks with eating disorders, Maureen visited the session of a therapist whose face had the discreetness of Bela Lugosi's. Now she knew that he screened patients for sex changes.

The patient's shirt was checked with roses. His reddened lips cooperated but his eyes emitted agony.

Maureen wanted to take a department group shot because the

psychologists would look spooky together, one cryptic, another diaphanous, another wearing tennis shoes with his dingy white hair.

It wouldn't help to have the liberal in tennis shoes photographed with his paranoid patient. Afraid of being watched, the patient suspected Maureen of working for another agency and of knowing about him previously. After this photography failure, the department head, the only dull psychologist, approached Maureen.

"I'd like to talk with you for a minute."

He was dressed for camouflage near his filing cabinet, the charcoal gray of his suit and hair matching it. Even when he discussed *affect*, his face had little expression.

"I've noticed that you seem depressed," he said.

"Maybe it's the weather. February is a depressing month."

"Weather shouldn't have that much of an effect on a person."

Maureen gave him a genuine smile, wishing to superimpose his gray head on his metal filing cabinet.

"If you're feeling sad and want to talk with someone, I can refer you."

She had slipped into the bathroom a few times because of the sudden seepage at her eyes. But the department was depressing. At first she felt bad, losing her assignment to Photographer II, but then she was sent to celebrations. A doctor's new treatment for cholesterol caused people in their fifties to wear festive blouses and brave ties. Their faces were full of affect. Then she practiced film speeds and panning, covering a "Nutcracker" rehearsal.

At four in the morning, Maureen was ready to get up from a dream about her bedspread disintegrating. She thought of the old lady who painted by number and how she complained to Maureen's mother that she woke up at four in the morning. Too often, Maureen felt decades older. Later on that day and after a few glasses of Beaujolais wine, she set up her tripod for a self-portrait.

She looks happy enough and her hair has sunny smiles in it. Her expression comprehends.

It took a photograph to convince her that she was in the prime of life. In fact, she'd spent too much time at the mirror, trying not to look over-the-relationship. Maureen had never looked better. She just didn't know where she belonged, not even which box was right for her self-portrait film.

In the high school box was a new photo of Jayne Magnuson, taken the weekend of her wedding. She and Jayne went driving on their old smoking route. They'd stopped at a diamond-shaped caution sign that had stick figures of children on it. Jayne puffed her last cigarette, and then she stood like a scarecrow, with yarrow in her sleeves.

In another box were antique family photographs, begged or snitched. When Maureen put her self-portrait into this box, she took out some of the photographs, determining to mat them and put them on her wall.

A boy, her father, squeezed a bicycle horn while men in lodge hats and sashes drove off in an early Ford.

A dark-haired young woman in a cloche hat, Grandma Rhiann, smiled near a porch balustrade.

Scandinavian women posed in folk dress before a studio screen painted with evergreens and a misty shoreline.

Maureen's ancestors had the stamina to start a new life. She matted her self-portrait and put it on the wall of her darkroom.

21 Game at Any Cost

Winter 1982.

"Hugo is talking about leaving Minnesota. Nearly everyone has now, Maureen. Your old dad knows about people going away."

"People move out of my building too." Ever since Maureen began living alone, her father called at precisely 8:30 on Friday evenings.

"I bought Poppy a house and she's off at an Eastern Star meeting," he complained.

"I know all about it."

"You'd better be careful or you'll become like your mother. She moaned about her problems when there was a war going on! You're beginning to sound like her."

"Mom was married and had children when she was my age."

"You can be thankful that you're not married to a husband who abuses you."

"Oh, yeah?" She wondered how much he knew about Roland Werff. "There's always something to be thankful for."

"I'm going to be retiring early. Poppy can have this house if that's what she wants. I'm going to move to the country and build a condominium. For turkeys."

"At least you have plans, Dad."

"I have drawings of the decks. The turkeys can sleep in the air. I'm going to live where there's plenty of air."

"Call me on a weeknight next time, Dad. I'll be out next Friday."

For the first time in her life, Maureen bought a steak. Men liked steak and she thought she might enjoy it with a sauce, Steak Diane. But on Friday night, the leftover half was the color of liver. Despite what her father would say, she took the half-eaten steak to the garbage bins and threw it on the heap that happened when a tenant moved. The lid was ajar, and then a cat raced into the snow-tipped bushes.

Inside, she collected her camera, leather gloves, her jacket, and a camp cushion. On the peppery snow, she waited. She waited and she waited, readying her flash and experimenting with filters while the red lozenges of headlights passed. Wondering if she could withstand wildlife photography, Maureen went inside to heat water for Russian tea. Then she heard a shriek below her balcony. Soon she was downstairs at the back door of her building, watching cats playing hockey with the Styrofoam dish of steak. A tiger tabby hooked the steak, a charcoal cat hooked the tabby, the dish spun, and Maureen snapped pictures. Then a third cat startled the charcoal cat as it gorged itself.

She felt terrible, like a callous hunter who had gotten game at any cost. When the telephone rang, she was timing a hunk of film in her darkroom.

On Saturday, she examined her prints in bed, having acquired a cough and a low fever. The telephone rang and Maureen sounded miserable. Valerie had been so busy since her marriage. A co-worker of Valerie's other fraction was having a taco smorgasbord and singles were coming. Valerie and Gordon would pick her up next Friday. Be creative!

The tables of taco makings were overwhelming. There were mix and match cheese, chicken, and vegetable tacos, bean and bacon tacos, steak and pepper tacos. And dessert tacos with fudge sauce. Maureen reverted back to the person Valerie knew. Her tomato gazpacho with floating taco chips made her as familiar as tomato soup to the man who offered her a ride home.

Greg was in real estate. He craned his head towards Maureen's 1920's building and inquired, "Nice façade. Do you know what this building sells for?"

Because he had asked her to lunch already, she decided not to ask him in. The only elegance about her apartment was probably the matted antique photos, the work of someone else.

How did it go?

Greg was taking her to a movie, Maureen told Valerie the way she used to.

How did it go? Writer III wondered at work. She met Greg in the office before they'd had lunch.

After the Agatha Christie movie and Greg's speculations about a mansion filled with clocks, Maureen felt like the building she inhabited. Its exterior was inviting but inside, her apartment was warped at the edges, wrinkled, smoke-stained, used up. Landlords let buildings like hers go or they renovated them with economical carpeting. Maureen doubted that Greg would want to renovate a woman who was more interested in photography than in houses.

Because she hadn't been with a man for a monotony of months, Maureen presented the depreciating state of her apartment and cuddled with Greg on her uncomfortable couch. To lessen the tension, she switched on the late movie. Greg wanted to see the exotic sea villa where Richard Burton lived as a derelict writer with Elizabeth Taylor, dressed in unwifely garb. Maureen became so fascinated with the failed artist and Taylor snarling, "Writers write!" that she failed to have casual sex.

How did it go?

He went away.

"I'm burnt out from dating," Maureen said to Valerie, Writer III, and then to her mother. "Maybe I've already met the man I should have married."

She and her mother were at the Black Forest Inn, trying spaetzel on a Friday. But her mother only stared at her. "Look at those!" she said.

On a carved shelf were Bavarian figurines similar to the fresco figures painted on the restaurant's exterior walls, what made her mother eager to eat there.

"When you're in the forest, it's hard to see which tree," Maureen said.

Her mother was reluctant to discuss past romances. "Hugo is talking about leaving Minnesota. Joyce hasn't been the best pastor's wife, you know."

"When you're in the forest. Sometimes a person can't be the best."

"Hugo wants to go to Seattle. There's a job at Lutheran Social Services. It's not a call at a church."

"What's wrong with that?"

On the way to Maureen's apartment, her mother told her about Mr. Gleason. He visited her on weekends but she was afraid of their set lifestyles. Although she only confessed friendship and affection for Mr. Gleason, Maureen's mother might get married before she ever did.

Seeing Maureen's darkroom and her self-portrait, her mother said, "You might have combed your hair."

"We could take a picture of you."

Her mother's cry of horror came from the bedroom. "The house next door is like our old house!"

It was a usual night in the apartment, looking at photographs and magazines and the television. Maureen set up her tripod and her photography lamp as her mother fussed, "I'd rather be photographed near a lake here."

Maureen told her about the Depth of Field store where she bought fabric for her living room curtains. Blue herons stood at a shore. "There won't be a blue heron at a lake here," she teased.

Her maternal grandmother photographed a great blue heron up north. Her mother remembered that and settled in front of the curtain, watching one of the eight television channels. But then the phone rang.

"I'll get it," her mother said, breaking her pose.

Maureen let go of her camera and looked at her watch.

"Is that you, Clive? Yes, I'm visiting Maureen. She's fine. I think. She's trying to take a picture of me."

He's been drinking, she mouthed and held the receiver away as if fumes were coming out of it. Then she reeled because Maureen snapped a picture of her.

That forced a real photo session.

"I'll sleep on the couch," her mother said, watching people in "Second City Television" throw televisions out of windows.

Maureen helped to arrange wrinkled sheets and then she closed off the hallway. She tried to turn in too but with her mother there, she was more restless than usual. She had to find out if she really saw a death mask on her mother's face. It was like a cat's inimical grimace, a ghastly expression that was beyond her mother. Her mother found out that Poppy's husband was drinking alone on a Friday night.

"Don't open the door!" Maureen cried.

"Maureen, it's two o'clock in the morning!"

They sat in the living room the way they did when her mother was separated and Maureen couldn't sleep. The world could change in one night, a night of vigilance because the morning light might not be familiar. When Maureen couldn't sleep after seeing *The Time Machine* long ago, she let her mother think that she was afraid of the machine and her father. But she had a dream then about a black box and someone saying, "You are the only one who knows the answer to this." She usually got the highest arithmetic score of the girls in grade school. Now she knew that her mother frightened her because she didn't have the answer to her father.

If Maureen weren't sleepless, her mother might say that she had thrown away opportunities. Having only a camera wasn't much to her. In the darkest hour of the night, they both knew that they would never spend another night together like this.

After the sun finally appeared, Maureen made coffee and fried sunny-side up eggs.

"But you've made them just right."

This accomplishment in a city apartment seemed desolate.

"That house *is* just like our old house," her mother said.

Maureen pulled out the gate leg of her dining room table and they sat over coffee. Afterwards, Maureen's mother could escape something that almost everyone Maureen knew had escaped.

22   The Black Box

Thursday afternoon, Writer III gossiped about sinecures, sackings, and plans for the weekend. Because the office did publicity, Maureen and her co-workers happily planned for the next job. Most of them had nine-month appointments with a possible extension or promotion.

"Publishing could have been a sinecure," Maureen said. "Jobs like that are like marriage. They can last thirty years and if people get that far, they'll probably have a pension."

Writer III pondered Maureen the way she did at the Uptown Theater last Friday night – like a photographer who has stumbled upon a pitiable spectacle. She'd found Maureen standing in the movie line alone. Then she asked about this weekend's plans, the subject Maureen was trying to stanch.

"I'm burnt out from dating," Maureen said.

She often spent her weekend nights developing film. Waiting for her windows to darken, she might have a glass of wine and switch on "Fantasy Island." Then she had to have another glass to get through "The Love Boat." One Saturday, she stopped marveling at the success of a midget exclaiming "The plane! The plane!", comprehending that she was free.

She'd been feeling like a misfit instead of like the photographer Diane Arbus. Her ability to obtain a subject's natural pose often happened because people hadn't expected her to be a photographer. Before she watched "The Love Boat" again, she put a bottle of capers in her purse and drove to a ninety-nine cents movie theater on Lyndale Avenue. No one led her past the seat she liked, about halfway down the theater, one from the aisle. No one exclaimed when she popped capers into her mouth instead of movie mints. She was anonymous in Minneapolis and didn't have to worry about social mores.

After her first night out alone, she listened to her favorite classical piece on the stereo, Debussy's "The Sea", and imagined that she was like the gracious Greek girl in *For Your Eyes Only*, "between jobs", and in grief because her family was blown apart. In the swaying darkroom waters, she might find a culprit, a new meaning, or someone she might like to know.

The Friday that Writer III discovered her in the movie line, she had gone to a Chinese restaurant in Uptown and asked the hostess for a corner table. Inconspicuous amid the red décor, she ate chicken almond ding and drank a glass of the house wine. Across the street was Lund's supermarket where, because of the lines, she ended up slipping a bottle of capers into her purse. That gave her the courage to stand in the Uptown Theater line for the movie, *Cousin, Cousine.*

"Maureen!" Writer III was beckoning to her. "Are you alone?" Writer III wasn't and she was already introducing Maureen to her date.

"I'd better check. There's been some trouble with the car."

"We'll hold a place," Writer III said.

At the office, Maureen said she had dated a Ph.D. candidate and also the son of Dr. Mort Blaisdell, a celebrity whose photographs were kept in the files.

"Doesn't he have a new book out?" asked Photographer I, Aaron.

Over the months, Aaron and Maureen had become friends, picking out photos for news releases and preferring each other for assignments requiring two photographers. Today, Aaron agonized over the portrait of a costume designer. Then he asked Maureen if Editor I would scoff at the six-foot teddy bear in the picture. The bear was wearing a jacket and bow tie similar to the suit the designer wore except that the teddy bear's bow tie was askew. Aaron often tried to turn an assignment into a picture for his portfolio.

Maureen admired the portrait. "She's in her own world. An adult woman with a pretend friend."

"Defiant possessiveness," Aaron said.

"You're just stuck with the teddy bear's role. It makes you a good portrait photographer," Maureen said, looking at his other prints. "Don't you think faces have build-ups like sediment? This professor's face talks mountains and it looks like he's in them. Older faces are distorted because they keep their happy scrapbook underneath. The costume designer isn't used to being left."

That Thursday afternoon, Aaron was certain that Maureen could write the papers for an MFA. Forethought made his face photogenic though he was balding prematurely. "I thought I'd try nature photography when I came out here," he said. "The scientists love their cameras and f-stops. They're just calling us for demonstrations."

"I was thrilled to get the botanical conservatory assignment," Maureen said. "But once Gardener II understood background flash, they didn't want to add me to their budget."

"At least we don't choose our sour grapes in this department," Aaron said.

Writer III complained, "All the money's going to the new technology building."

"We should show initiative and get photos of the building crew,"

Aaron suggested. "I heard they have equipment that heats the frozen ground."

"What do they call the ground around here? Tempafrost?" Writer III said.

"C'mon, Maureen. We're not in high school anymore," Aaron coaxed her.

She had climbed into the Volkswagen van he obtained for nature photography. They drove to West Bank where they prowled the streets like teenagers, looking for characters near occult boutiques and bookstores.

"Publicity never sends us over here," Aaron said. He found an alumnus in philosophical disarray, an old hippie who claimed a square of Cedar Avenue was his. He had proposed that the titles of dissertations should be engraved in the sidewalk.

At the Coney Island cafe, Maureen focused on a life-size poster of Sindbad the Sailor. He seemed to be offering jewel-like lozenges to students sitting on stools. Aaron deplored the food and that inspired an actress on break from Theatre in the Round to chew for him. Then he caught Maureen yawning. Lately she yawned a lot but her yawns were like sneezes that didn't happen. They weren't satisfactory. Despite the actress, her yawns were enchanting Aaron.

They drove to Aaron's duplex where, feeling like a plant full of carbon dioxide, she yawned, "Your portfolio is so professional, Aaron."

"You should have yours ready," he replied.

Maureen smoked, trying to get the smoke to swirl around her neck like the umbilical cord at her birth. Then she photographed Aaron with a piece of red cloth fixed on his head like Sindbad and wearing a black shirt, open at the chest. He might be too attractive to work with if it weren't for his premature baldness.

"C'mon Maureen, we're not in high school anymore."

Friday was an ordinary day except that Maureen's theory was proven. Everyone could see the sediment of the previous night in her face and in Aaron's.

"Take the day off," Aaron had suggested.

Maureen had craved a magic act, the mysterious lover behind the black curtain. "Watch the birdie!" And then their friendship flew beyond them, what left her with an ordinary day. The flash, Aaron's telling her how sensuous she was, subsided into a yawn. She didn't know why she found men like Hank and Aaron attractive when close-up, she was sure they weren't hers.

In the next days while extensions were being decided, Aaron nobly left his job open. He was going back east. But the department didn't need a Photographer III anymore and Maureen wasn't Aaron. Maureen talked of her alternative plans - the MFA and a freelance assignment at Schilling Publishing.

A colorblind boy posed in a Schilling office with his drawings and his easel. The photo session was for a book with the working title "Disability Ability."

After the session, Maureen walked down the back staircase with Aggie. She told Aggie news more recent than Aaron. Roland Werff had turned up in town, arranging ski packages at a Colorado lodge where he was now an instructor.

"I had to get a picture of the eligible bachelor," Maureen said. "He's becoming as chauvinistic as his father. He and his friend Cal came over. The next day, Cal called to tell me about Roland's new girl, a novice that he met on the bunny hill. She was a virgin. A virgin bunny."

Laughing with Aggie, Maureen was slipping on her new interview boots. She kept sliding down the polished yellow stairs, her camera flailing at the wall like a crow. And then it somehow fell out of its case, crashing onto the steps.

"Maureen, are you alright?"

"Don't worry," Maureen said. "I took the film out after the photo session."

But Inez had just entered the stairwell with Claire and they hastened down to take Maureen by the arm. They were all going to lunch.

The frames Maureen took at the restaurant turned out black.

She was wrong, thinking she had already met the man she should marry. She'd fallen for Roland when he drew cartoons. One summer, his tractor toppled into the rural ditch at his uncle's. When she saw his drawing of it, she had cared for him. His last ditch effort with her had been a threat about her lone career. He found film in her refrigerator. Instead of wondering about her weight loss, he appraised her honed figure. Women slept with him and he expected it. He'd expected to find someone like her for his bedroom. She didn't want to touch him while his chauvinism was as stolid as his father's religion.

When Aggie told her about Dr. Mort Blaisdell's book, *Kids Confound the Doctor*, she assumed that Maureen knew about Milt going away to medical school. His father told the world about it on his radio program. The program Maureen tuned into was about depression.

Yes, depression is like the common cold. But how often do you have this cold?
Every winter, almost all winter, Doc.
So I guess if the cold keeps coming back, you would want to see a doctor. Usually a doctor can tell if the cold needs two aspirins, liquids, and bed rest, or if it needs penicillin. Now what were we talking about? Confound it! I forgot.
Depression, Doc.
Oh yes, we were talking about depression today.

Maureen kept staring at her black frames. They reminded her of the nightmare black box in her childhood and the voice saying, "You are the only person who knows the answer to this."

She was the only girl in high school to own a 35mm camera and lately, she felt knocked out by it, like a person in a cartoon. Rather than repairing her camera, she waited until she had an answer to the black box. Finally, she knew that the answer was outside the box. She had numerous rolls of old film from which she should find prints for a portfolio like Aaron's and unlike Aaron's. And she had boxes of prints.

With a bottle of wine and Carole King playing, she waited for "Tapestry" and its "figure gray and ghostly, come to take her back." Behind the black curtain of her darkroom, she knew she found leave-takings romantic. When her father left their house, it wasn't because he was divorcing his children.

Too many pictures passed her by when she didn't have a camera. Lucky women were everywhere when she was looking for a job and afraid to look for a man. Maureen wanted to change but when she descended from the upper reaches of an escalator, she had a sudden urge to throw her purse over it, just for the picture.

In a neighborhood of old buildings and a crumbling brick street, an Indian picked up a thin branch of spring leaves and said, "Hey, do you want a twig?"

Two Mormon men in dark coats accosted her at her apartment door, men who looked as if they should be in a daguerreotype. They showed her illustrations of Jesus Christ in the Rockies instead of a daguerreotype of him.

She wasn't upbeat enough for an advertising office in Uptown. Wandering out, she considered what would happen to a woman if she left everything to follow Jesus Christ. Following Lake Street to Lake of the Isles, she imagined a twentieth century female lasting about a week and then, walking along the lake, she imagined the woman's death. She should look at Steiglitz and Steichen, she thought, walking back on Lake Street to an old Carnegie library. She could think about the dangerous heights that Anselm Adams climbed because she was afraid to confront Diane Arbus, an artist that death didn't dally with.

Looking for the painting she liked of Morpheus' cloud arms, all she found were sculptures and the story of Aphrodite falling into adulterous love with him. Morpheus was also the god of dreams, of visions that the mind desired to see like a portfolio of photographs. She had taken a picture of the eye on a Masonic temple when the clouds were as dark as Morpheus and another when an eye of light came through them.

Flipping through an art book, she gazed at Egyptian pictures, figures in organized formations, watched by a god's eye. *The Book of the Dead* explained it. As if struck by a fatal attraction, Maureen searched the card catalog and then she put on hold *The Book of the Dead.* It would wait for her at the downtown library like a man she shouldn't take home.

Photographers specialized when they earned a book. So far, all Maureen had were monotonous prints of the Midwest and some nature photographs. There were small-town weddings and baptisms, babies with blue and pink ribbons, fairs that overflowed with blue ribbon beer. Subjects attempted to blend in, resisting the camera's focus.

The slaughter area of Country's Plenty was like a publicity photo, planned by her father and showing what he felt was humane. The poultry was well-cared for on the best farmland. Maureen had to station herself in the early morning to catch a truckload of poultry at the abattoir, the preferred term for a slaughterhouse.

She had shown her apathy in the hospital zone. While a mother brought out her newborn bundle, an old woman was being wheeled through a windowed tube to the next building. Mothers, like meat-eating men, knew a secret, Maureen feared. It was the secret of transferring life from one body to another through a set of tubes that kept life going, without rest, without death. In her apathy, it seemed a desperate process like the processing of animals into food.

The Egyptians, she found, didn't really believe in death unless it was a complete consumption, the end of the wicked. The dead world was another massive organization. An Egyptian might have a body in a sarcophagus, but he also had a shadow hanging around it, a heart on earth, and perhaps a shining self in heaven. If a farmer was a good man, he became a farmer again in the Elysian Fields.

Light, shadow, and the evidence of the heart might take her from one photograph to the next in filling a portfolio.

Feeling like a shadow hanging around her past, Maureen opened up a bottle of wine. She craved to see photographs of ancient times as she sorted out her prints. Sometimes she was unsure of where her subjects were. Probably, they were in a zone that people didn't want to especially see. But that's how she felt about her day when she woke in the morning.

23   And No Tripod

Sorting out her prints on a Friday, Maureen admired her last empty apartment picture, Aaron's apartment. *Gray meadow wallpaper surrounded a picnic hamper and tablecloth spread on a hardwood floor.*

He liked a print she took of a nursing home. An old woman offered a teacup to a soap opera matron on television.

Everyone liked the print from a county fair. Entering the house of horrors, a boy in a cowboy outfit pulled a gun from his holster.

She was on her fourth glass of wine and that made her anticipate her father's phone call.

"It's amazing that you can be so punctual when you're drinking, Dad. You know I don't like it when you call on Friday night."

"That's the trouble, women liking this or that. What are you doing?"

"I've been making prints. And going through old boxes of prints." She heard the liquid shifting in her father's mouth, an image of his displeasure. "I found a picture of you at The Forum cafeteria."

He looked bewildered at a table of empty trays amid other tables full of empty trays. Her father's hair, if it wasn't combed then, could become puffy, almost clownish. At the Forum Cafeteria in downtown Minneapolis, people could go back for unlimited platefuls of food.

"Hugo could eat all evening there," he said. "The Forum is gone now, isn't it? What are you laughing at?"

"A picture of an albino turkey. I kept it for comparison. In case Hank Mickelson found an albino turkey in North Dakota."

"Hank Mickelson? Who's that?"

"Hank's the man I dated last year."

"I already heard the one about the albino turkey. Why are you still laughing? What did you swallow? If you didn't sound so much like your mother, I'd think you were drinking."

The next Friday the telephone was silent. At nine o'clock, Maureen called her mother, wanting to confirm that they didn't sound alike. "I thought I might

178

come and stay with you this summer."

Her mother was appalled. "Where would you work in a small town? The drugstore?"

When Maureen was in grade school, she went to the Lombardy Plaza drugstore on any errand or excuse. There, she bought magazines with her allowance money and, near her house, she sometimes sat on a chain link fence, looking at *Redbook* or *True Confessions*. Sometimes she stashed the magazines in the cleft of an old tree that secured the last link of the fence. After she made a scrapbook of magazine pictures, she hid it in the tree, hoping someone would find it.

A woman distraught about her confession watched the alcoholic in Come Back, Little Sheba.

Elizabeth Taylor and Richard Burton fought near a man building a bomb shelter.

Poultry attended Barry Goldwater, making a speech.

Under the photographs were captions like, "What next?" No one found the scrapbook stuck in a cleft of a tree, bleeding from the rain.

Her mother said, "Every time you stay down here, you're so bored that you test Hugo's faith. He's had too much of that with Joyce. She has people over at the manse when he's not there."

"Joyce? They don't live in a manse."

"They might have. Joyce appliquéd a sash for the church choir director and then the soloists had to be outfitted. The tenor and baritone anyway."

"What's she supposed to do? Have a baby?" Maureen said.

"That's not funny, Maureen. Her table at the bake sale looked like a lodge meeting."

"Why did Hugo marry her?"

"Maureen, you can't date around in a small town. Even if your father got away with it. You're moping like him because you can't have the job you want."

The classifieds were a blindfold without photographs – Editorial, Graphic Designer, Photographer. Mr. and Ms. Right, despite having gotten their jobs, kept showing up for more interviews.

Grandma Rhiann, dark and direct, smiled smartly at Maureen from the wall. In Wales, her father's family was poor.

Your mother knows who you are.

Maureen didn't resemble Grandma Rhiann much.

The others know too. You're like your Aunt Gilly. Wally kept her dressing like a teenager. He took her to Missouri, a place full of caves.

Maureen resembled Aunt Gilly. She'd never thought about that.

Somehow it was alright, having a séance with Grandma Rhiann.

Out of habit, Maureen went to an Uptown drugstore where she might stand all day near supplies of film and cigarettes. A calm woman with long shell-gray hair must have worked there for years. The regular clerk didn't wake that morning from a wine-induced sleep, wishing she didn't have to live her fate.

Drugstores were full of solutions and speculations. Summers, Maureen used eye drops for her allergies when she was taking pictures. In August, she would like to use both eye drops and tablets, despite the side effects.

She dreaded summer, her itching eyes and her aimlessness this year. If she worked at the air-conditioned drugstore, her eyes wouldn't itch and other issues would be solved. Instead of approaching the secure oyster-haired clerk, she went to the counter of a younger clerk whose hair was short and dyed white.

"Allergy season is starting," Maureen said.

"You never know the day or the time." The clerk was practically occult.

"Are you taking applications?"

"If a person has experience at a cash register. There aren't any openings right now."

"Oh." Maureen considered the film but she didn't need any until she repaired her camera.

Near the university, a student at work in a camera shop almost forgot to give Maureen change for her purchase of print paper.

"Not hiring," the student replied to her inquiry.

Photography magazines revolved on a rack, magazines Maureen should examine. The movement distracted the eye. Film on a nearby display fit into Maureen's hand like a bottle of capers.

Grandma Rhiann was still amused when Maureen set a canister of film and a bottle of capers on the coffee table.

What a sight, little Maureen making off with her brother's camera.

No one could catch the shadow Maureen had become.

People often ignore the poor. A grandmother couldn't ignore a little girl who thought she was poor.

When people visited Maureen's apartment, the first photographs they studied were her photographs of the dead. Even if the pictures of dead relatives were the best photographs, probably because of that, Maureen took them down and put them carefully in a cardboard box. She hadn't had a man since the dead were watching and Grandma Rhiann was the only one grinning.

Someone might need Maureen.

Over the telephone, Joyce said, "Hugo and I are moving to Seattle. Very soon, in fact."

Maureen drove out of the city with the desperation of April. Passing a gas station, she saw a woman holding the gas pump like an obscene gesture. Near Northfield, she found a full-service station and basked under the courtesies of the attendant's windshield wiper.

"Are there still any old Pegasus stations around?" She was clumsy finding a pen and paper but the attendant stared over her car hood at the sky.

"It's crumbling from storms. Golf-ball hail today, they say."

Because the young man found that Maureen had no foresight, she told him that she was visiting her old college. Then she fulfilled her lie.

In Northfield, the college students appeared distorted, their strength and health a short-term encasing. The girls would do the right thing if a friend were moving away. Aware of being small since a weight loss, Maureen ducked into a gift shop where she struck the pose of an attenuated professor. At first she examined things without comprehension but then she realized that she should give Joyce and Hugo something portable.

"I'm waiting out the storm," she said as a saleslady wrapped place mats appliquéd with birch trees.

"I think it's passed over," she replied.

Maureen believed the tranquil woman in the tucked-away town. She drove south on 35W but then, gazing west, she saw nimbus clouds moving like a tremendous frontier over the black fields. Her car swerved off the road as the sky discarded an icy avalanche onto the freeway. A traffic jam of hail encircled her and then a sound like boxes being kicked around made her think she was being rear-ended. Listening to her car's hood being battered by hailstones, she felt vulnerable without her camera.

When a large hailstone hit the windshield like a hallucination, Maureen recalled that she had only a few hours of sleep the night before. Images between sleep and daylight caused her to crave a document of reality. When she began driving again, swipes of wind rocked her car as if she were on an uneven trail. Her car was estranged in the stretch of a weekday. Decades ago, only men traveled in the isolation and ice.

Her Grandfather Berwick was a surveyor and a cartographer of roads that were forged in his time.

On the narrow road is the old land.

Thinking she heard this, Maureen pulled to the roadside and got out a map. Old highways looped around the freeway. She found the route to the old Pegasus station, what would make her happy and unhappy because she didn't have her camera.

The worn blacktop dipped and rose, its secret people driving rusted cars and trucks. The land really rode on gargantuan plates under the straddling soil.

Rich soil.

It tilted and as Maureen drove, she felt how the West was once steep and terrifying. The farmhouses tipped as if they were precarious, having no point of reference. Car graveyards used to thrill her. Now the cars were from her high school days, looking ancient from winter's desiccation. She had skimmed over news about farmers selling out, reports of foreclosures, all of which reminded her of Roland Werff's last visit and how he boasted about his father selling his land.

When the sun gleamed, she wasn't so startled at the ancestor lens, seeing the fields like a negative, the houses makeshift and tattered, leashed to the ground like the muddy dogs in the yards.

People moving here, moving there, nomadic as Indians.

Her thoughts were like a tintype. An old gas station had tombstone pumps but it wasn't the whitewashed Pegasus station. Inside its clapboard shack, Maureen became disoriented at the old graduated shelves displaying candy. The attendant leered during her conversation at the wall telephone.

"Hi Hugo. I'll be later than I planned."

"Where are you? There could be ice on the roads."

"Where am I?" she asked the attendant.

His answer was slow, as if he weren't sure of his answers.

"Joyce can wait to fricassee the turkey," Hugo said. "Mom's here. You don't have to snap it."

Hugo's double meaning about her camera wasn't the reply of an assistant pastor. He was going away and Maureen wasn't sure of her perceptions.

A Last Supper candelabrum arched over the dining room table furnished by the Lutheran Church.

"I didn't bring my camera," Maureen announced.

"That's not like you, Maureen!" Her mother pouted above Joyce's bluebird china, probably fearing that with her own camera, Hugo's eyes would turn out red.

"We've got a camera," he said. "Someone else can say the prayer."

Maureen's mother sniffed, began the "Come, Lord Jesus" as she used to do, coughed, and took a sip of water. Joyce took up the next phrase. Bluebirds flitted as Maureen scavenged for the words. It was easier to talk to Hugo.

"I don't see why Mom thinks you've leaving the ministry. Isn't Lutheran Social Services a call?"

Hugo replied like the Sunday Kyrie. "I think I can work with people that others don't believe in."

"I don't know why you couldn't do that in Minneapolis," Joann objected. "Look how mixed up Maureen is there."

"I've cut off my camera to make prints for a portfolio," she explained. "You know, 'If something bothers you, cut it off.'"

Hugo sighed.

"If Jesus Christ was photographed saying that, you'd probably see his sarcasm," she went on. "Otherwise, he was suggesting suicide."

The bluebirds were hanging in the air.

Her mother said, "Lutherans don't read the Bible literally, Maureen. That's why there are ministers."

"And Bible studies," Hugo said.

Maureen felt more like talking than eating. "That's because the Bible was full of prize-winning photographs. It's hard to find them in Minnesota. When Elijah wanted to die, he floated to heaven."

"There's cheesecake with cherries for dessert," Joyce said in a floating voice.

"No one would believe a photograph," Hugo murmured.

"Why?"

"Because you want a prize."

"If you were Elijah, you might mount a Pegasus horse at an old gas station and ride off into the sunset."

Joyce tittered but the blue eyes darted like the bluebirds flying off the plates.

"Are you feeling alright? Or are you trying to diet?" Hugo asked her.

"I snacked in the car."

"How much do you weigh?"

"I haven't had any colds," Maureen protested. "You don't have to practice social work on me."

"The bathroom scale isn't packed," Joyce said. "Let's go stand on the scale, Maureen. C'mon."

Maureen followed Joyce's trilling Christianity.

"She weighs 106 pounds!"

"*We* didn't stand on the scale," Maureen said.

"Why, Maureen?" Hugo demanded.

Maureen had no answer except that she was craving her apartment. "Dad is buying a house somewhere between Rochester and Lacrosse. For his early retirement."

Her mother said sternly, "I wouldn't fall back on him for money if I were you."

"You wouldn't, would you?"

"I'll give you a name and an address, Maureen," Hugo suggested. "You know where you can go if you're having trouble, don't you?"

Somehow, Hugo never looked sarcastic.

"Away in a car like everyone in this family?"

There were more frames to print, people Maureen photographed and left the way that wildlife photographers left animals in the wild.

Never before did we. We did not know what we were traveling to.

The dead opened their mouths somewhere because they were never really put away in a box.

Maureen repaired her Minolta and then she dropped off her portfolio and her MFA materials at the university. Most years, she went to school, away from her family.

At the university, she wandered around, thinking about the film and print paper that she needed. Colors outside dimmed into tints but that wasn't from her being downhearted. People were opening umbrellas that she could photograph from the campus footbridge. She had a zoom lens with her for the unprepared people, people who might be robbed of their dignity. Maureen made her getaway but at the bottom of the footbridge, a hooded windbreaker blocked her. When the man sidestepped and turned with her, she snatched a look at him.

"Hank, is that you? I worked over here for months and didn't run into you."

"Where were you working?" Hank led her along the sidewalk.

"I was a Photographer III for Public Relations. I got laid off."

"And now you're back."

The silver rain was fooling with Maureen's opinion of Hank and his deceptive attractions.

Her darkroom still beckoned like a lover who was wiser than her. Most of the people Maureen knew in her prints went the traditional way. The dead had somberly stared at a photographer's black drape as if they were being reasonable about what was before them. They were only looking for a better place. They didn't expect ecstasy on earth. If Maureen kept looking for it, she might have to talk with a man like Hugo. Or she might drink a bottle of wine and talk to a man like her father.

Hank wouldn't suspect that she drank two glasses of peach Reunite before she called. She wanted to do some wildlife photography before going back to school.

"How about a movie Saturday night?"

The wine almost made her say, "Friday would be better." Somehow, she still hoped to fall in love with Hank.

Her friends did what was expected of them. Most seemed more unbalanced than passionate before their weddings. She could at least make things look right when Hank had a naturalist's tolerance. He didn't care what she did during the week. So far, he hadn't done anything very wrong with her except that he usually chose the wrong movie.

24   Great Blue Error

The fall of 1983. Waiting for an innocent man, Maureen thought about what was gone inside, what grew and controlled her. Two years ago, it smiled sadly, turning like an image in darkroom waters, like the subconscious. But it sank into her gut and became demonic.

Outside somewhere, children ran in the striations of leaves red as brick, orange as the hearth. A Robert Woods print hung in her childhood living room, a picture of a man raking leaves. As a toddler, Maureen thought the man was in their neighborhood and that he looked sad. When she came into possession of a Brownie camera, she took a picture of her father raking leaves, a fuzzy picture overcast in black and white.

Hank was visiting a wistful woman, not one with the idea of family turning inside.

"You've been a good friend." Maureen said. "But that's all I can see."

"I knew you were uncertain. I've gone slowly with you. Because of your childhood."

Maureen lit up a second cigarette because this man claimed to be more sensitive than her other boyfriends. Still, it wasn't fair to want the security of a brick house more than him. And Hank didn't choose brick houses. If she thought about the house he chose, she saw herself as a wallflower wife.

"I've had other relationships," she said.

Hank might ponder that for another month. Maureen would rather have died than have these moments stretch on until death. Wallflowers crinkled and cracked.

"So have I," Hank countered. "I didn't tell you. The months I wasn't dating you, I went out with a woman at work. She had an awful argument with my mother."

Maureen had never been so pleased with Hank. His mother's best accomplishment was Hank's Ph.D. Behind bifocals and lapels, Mrs. Mickelson blurred Maureen into Hank's background. ""Hank loved his night school photography course. I wish he would enter his pictures in the State Fair contest," she said at their introduction.

"I started with my grandmother's Brownie camera," Maureen said. "She was a bird watcher. Her best picture was of a great blue heron up north.

That's where she lived." Being like her maternal grandmother was to have life sorted out.

"I've rented a house in West St. Paul with an option to buy," Hank told her. "It's near the old Soo Line and woodsy around there. My dog likes that."

"I've been accepted into the MFA program."

A camera was opened at the wrong time and all was exposed. Not that it mattered. Maureen hadn't taken a good picture for a long time.

Evenings that summer, Maureen drank wine and added twenty years to her life. Some middle-aged women hankered back to their weddings; others made plans for sunset grandchildren and funerals. She was already like the second type, looking to a future that would release her from unhappiness.

She came home from a job that should have made her thankful. All day she sat in a little cell of an office where she examined negatives that she might crop into photographs of child abuse. A professor hired her to help with his manuscript. The photographs were from the police and from hospitals, photographs that Maureen altered so that children with bruises, fractures, and burns couldn't be identified. Typing case studies was easier.

The wine at 5:30 p.m. was from a family pattern. Since she'd been accepted in the MFA program, she had no desire to touch her camera.

Don't open it!

When Maureen took pictures at the wrong time, her sister Lydia reversed the Pandora 's Box, opening the camera. Her father bought a movie camera so that he could see his children in the evenings. But the movie camera became another stipulation for his visits.

There wasn't much to photograph in a town that avoided the troubles of the world. Maureen examined the inside of her 35mm camera as she went from calculus to trigonometry. She found that she could coldly synchronize it the way her father synchronized machinery and employees.

One year, she could sense a picture before it happened and then she was said to have talent. But now she couldn't see ahead, especially after August. The calibrating went on in her head and August was part of a formula. In her mind, it was an abstract splicing of oppressive humidity, wine, darkroom chemicals, her X-Acto knife, and phantom film negatives.

Only light enthralled her lately. She gazed at it, studying the escape of colors from ceiling fixtures, from raindrops. The light made wood and other dead things look as if they had feelings. She wanted to follow it. She was through with being fooled. The light that she splashed on her print paper was like the background light of the universe.

When she didn't care about buying groceries in Uptown, she admired a cockatiel in a pet store, its feathers spurting around its black eyes. She took

Glinda home and then she took out her camera to record Glinda's clipped wings growing out. The bird posed under an umbrella plant in a cookie sheet of sand, looking as large as a great blue heron in the print.

"I want to photograph a great blue heron," she said to Hank on a weekend night. The great blue herons on her living room curtains pleased him.

For the first time, Maureen went out-of-town with Hank. They stayed with a married couple near a lake where the men either shot or photographed duck, depending on the season. The first evening, their foursome sat below the white bellies of matted ducks, listening to Joan Baez. Dogs slept at their feet.

But Maureen was on the other side of a blind, watching the contentment of the other couple. She felt like a euphemism, a bagged girl. She fidgeted, eager to play an old-fashioned game of checkers after losing at backgammon.

"They've decided to go back tomorrow morning. We can stay," Hank said, picking up one of her red checkers. They were sitting in front of the fireplace, friends again.

"I've never felt like this before," was all she could say.

She had the sensation that she'd swallowed an anchor. Hank made her think of her maternal grandmother and how women in her time weren't allowed much fickleness about a man's physical style. His game was that of men who used guns, one of waiting and sudden action, flirtation, and flushing out. His hands were uncertain, undoing her blouse and bra and this gave her a sense of doom. She even felt indecent since her attitude was callous in return.

Trailing Hank the next day, she remembered how she might have walked away from the class she had with him. She had contrived a conversation.

A ruffled sound came from the lake and Hank's spotted hat veered towards it. He might forget her while she kept on the woods trail, taking a fork that shrouded her in green transience. She was with her camera now.

The leaves laugh and they frown.

A primitive person was inside her, a desperate person who wanted to wander in the wilderness. People by the thousands disappeared into woods instead of returning to cities.

A nest was moving on a branch. A porcupine. Moving off, she sat in a thicket of fern, waiting for a full view. She could camp out. Porcupine quills were probably the worst danger in these woods. Except Hank was coming, slashing the brush somewhere. She couldn't call out to caution him because he might not sense her whereabouts. She wasn't right for him. But he called her name, meandering on the trail and then, as the porcupine began moving on the branch, she called out, "Be quiet."

"Why did you walk away?"

Maureen pointed at the porcupine hugging the Jack pine and then Hank could take his photograph first.

"I'm an artist. You're a selfish..." she said on the way to the cabin.

"I don't call what you did unselfish."

Close up, he was an annoying boy in a man's body, his teeth knocking into her lips. She covered herself with pink calamine lotion.

"I don't suppose you came here to stay overnight."

He was smug, charmed at her pink embalming. He had found a woman who thought she was an artist but she had an emotional problem. Possibly she was nearer being a virgin than other women her age. She wanted something, a glass of wine. There was something she knew, the sexual power that a wrong relationship could acquire. Hank's being transformed was ominous, like a blizzard being marriageable. He was the kind of man who was willing to work through anything.

Coming from Maureen's bathroom, perhaps for the last time, Hank said, "I don't think I could use my sink for a birdbath."

"It looks like toothpaste when she goes there." If Maureen emphasized her craziness, Hank could justify going back to the woman at work. "I guess I never had much of a nesting instinct. Great blue herons hate their stinky nests. They're like cats, aren't they? Glinda is the only bird I can photograph so far."

Maureen felt crazy when she lied. Someday, she would photograph a great blue heron. Having failed at that, she showed Hank the photos she took instead. *A fiddler in a tank top dueled with an electric guitarist.*

"That's the only wildlife I could focus on up north. I must be allergic to everything."

Friends told white lies so that they wouldn't upset friends. Hank had to take his dog out for a run instead of saying goodbye. Maureen didn't say that she wouldn't try to get married again.

Hank wouldn't have to know much about her August trip except that she intended to photograph a great blue heron. She had talked about it the way an alcoholic banters, thinking about the next bottle.

She didn't fight what kicked underneath any more than she fought showing up for work or going out with Hank. In early August, the professor came into her clinical office and said, "We're going to celebrate today and watch a movie. I've received more funding. You can stay on here."

Maureen sat in a classroom with staff from his department, watching a movie on alcoholism in families. Afterwards, she was invited to the coffee argument. A man with an Irish name argued genes, a man with military experience argued state controls, a battered woman specialist argued against men, and a man with two women in his house argued because he couldn't stop being in an argument. When someone mentioned Dr. Mort Blaisdell, Maureen skulked back to her office, thinking how Hank would argue about survival.

Even if people with dark childhoods tended to lower the lights when they were adults, Maureen poured herself a glass of wine at home. She hadn't done much wrong until a few years ago when she became a big blue person. If she died tomorrow, there wouldn't be a lot to punish, she believed. When she did things wrong, that was done with confident carelessness. She swam most summer days as a child, so often that she ate before swimming. Now she drank at night and in June when the pollen was high, she took allergy pills.

She might do everything wrong at once if she were waiting for a great blue heron and found, as usual, that her wishes were illusions. A bird went into the beyond because something inside was driving it. Her preoccupation at the shore of disaster was as stubborn as other women were about weddings. Hank might as well find out how she could wreck things now that he had a house in the suburbs.

From her office, she called the DNR one afternoon. "Hank was going to get some maps for me," she said to the woman who answered the phone.

"This is Hank's day at the university." Surprise said that Maureen might have known that. "I'm looking at his desk."

"It's the map that has Chisholm on it and the lakes west of there. Lakes with heron sightings marked."

Shuffling sounded like reeds.

"Or maybe he found a fisherman's map. I wanted one with lake depths," Maureen said.

"You mean shallow areas. Some people take toads with them if they want to see herons."

A long beak seemed to probe through the telephone.

"Or a shoreline where herons are nesting," Maureen conversed.

"You mean deciduous woods where the trees are protected from wind. They don't nest on cabin roofs like storks."

Maureen felt like a dead fish revolving instead of like a great blue heron.

On schedule, she gathered up her camping gear, maps, thermoses of wine, and a hamper of food. She never drove and drank because, since she began drinking, she often visualized death. A car accident was too mangling for her. Doggedly, she kept to her triptik.

Driving, Maureen only cared about leaving Glinda, stuck in her cage down the hall. Glinda's leaps in the sunshine would always be on the other side of glass. Maureen's first memory was of crying at being left on a hard sunny surface. Her mother walked away and she couldn't walk with her. The sunshiny floor was of no comfort and neither was a toy that an old woman brought to her. Her mother remembered the neighbor's yellow linoleum floor. Today the yellow fields were only a refulgent surface, apart and of no comfort.

Maureen spent hours in the sunroom at their next house, looking at books and adult magazines, comparing Thurber cartoons and the funnies to photographs. One day, she noticed that some photographs were probably better in gray than in color. That year, Minnesota made the magazines for its high quality of life. Her father toted that to Sunday dinner because her mother had plenty and he had an apartment. Usually on a Sunday, the congregation at church hadn't sung her favorite hymn, the only hymn she believed. "Immortal, invisible, God only wise / In light inaccessible hid from our eyes..."

Every day that March, the sky was gray as a black and white photograph. Maureen thought she would rather die than be stuck or suspended in the gray zone. All that year, she hadn't wanted to go home after school. Her parents' divorce made invitations more obtainable in a town where people needed relief from the sameness. Nobody ever said, "Do you want to go home with me?" They said, "Do you want to come over to my house?"

Maureen watched spaghetti being ladled in a kitchen where a woman had to turn like a fork and wind herself around. At another house, a girl had a tall dresser with loads of folded pants and tops but while her toys were kept in condition, her baby brother had a heart operation. The pretty girl in the mansion with the spiral staircase whispered and remained the unknowable girl who had a spiral staircase in her huge stone house. One girl slept behind a curtain in an apartment rented by her widowed mother. In a small house as old as the downtown, a girl with thick braids sat near a wood stove because her father wouldn't turn on the heat. Most mothers were worn-down and excitable except for the most depressing mother of all, the one who inconsolably watched television amidst strewn clothing and toys.

"I feel homesick," Maureen actually said at one house.

The doctor's houses were the best because they had sprawling rooms and yards that could be explored because the father wasn't home.

Their town was better off than most places because turkeys were slaughtered in it.

Thinking about that kept Maureen from ordering more than coffee at a roadside restaurant. She drove on towards Chisholm, past obsolete railroad tracks and evergreens that reminded her of unfamiliar pagodas. She didn't make any wrong turns from the highway to the blacktop, and that made her feel as if she were in an eerie dream, traveling without volition. Without confusion, she found the dirt road marked by an arrow with the words *Logren's Resort.*

Gerta Logren was ready with the arranged canoe. She was over sixty, a resort owner who catered to fishermen. Her calves in pedal pushers bulged like shiny fish. Dogs rose from patches of wildflowers and followed them past a *Bait* sign, written in an unsteady hand. Under a *Store* sign, Maureen stood near a soft drink machine, breathing the smells of gasoline and lake water.

Gerta returned with three children. "We'll have to bring the canoe down. There's a cabin open that you can have for less. The roof is leaking but we're working on it," she suggested.

It was easy, unloading her equipment, except that Maureen's sunglasses slipped. "The campground is over there, isn't it?"

"On the next bay. Most don't camp alone."

Not wanting to get acquainted, Maureen waved the children away from her camera bags. They walked under the canoe, seeing which of their fingers could reach the overturned keel. Carrying the bags, Maureen kept her eyes on the uneven wooden steps that led to a dock where a large tackle box blocked the way. Rowboats thudded in the boathouse.

"Has anyone seen a great blue heron lately?" she asked.

A fisherman was staring at her but the children answered. "Last week, someone saw one!"

"Over there!"

She looked from their bare feet to the bays that spread out like sky above the city. An arching island obscured the shore in the next bay.

"Around the big house on the point," Gerta said. "Do you fish too?"

"I've done more swimming than fishing. I might do a little snorkeling."

She went back for her other bags while Gerta handed the children lifesaver cushions for the canoe.

"Would you like a Coke first?" Gerta asked when she returned.

"No. Here, I'll take that."

She rescued the knapsack holding the thermoses of wine, letting the children carry her food hamper to the canoe. Gerta helped her with the tent bundle. Then Maureen could push off with her paddle and slide away.

On the other side of the boathouse, she hugged the shoreline until she was hidden among outcroppings of birch. All summer she had been self-centered, concerned about how she appeared. She needed to look competent in her sunglasses and the designer visor that flattened her sandy hair. Her gray T-shirt blended with the canoe. She had to appear cheerful on the surface when muck and weeds were underneath.

The initial bliss she felt was soon blunted. Even more crushing than a city's opulence was that of this lake. Everything was for the eyes.

She was like a boat, drifting along and obviously off-course. Yet, aware of a jabbing inside, the anchor she swallowed, her listless paddling paved her plan. The people at the point had cooperated with it. Wooden shades covered the windows of a recently built stained wood house. Its boathouse doors had a lock on them.

She steered to the shore side of the shaggy island where she was concealed from boaters and fishermen. No one inhabited this cove off the bay, marshy land once owned by a mining company. Herons were sighted here, and the water was comparatively shallow, full of seaweed. At the shore was a garden of spadderdock.

Digging her paddle into the water, Maureen floated until she was twisting the stems of water lilies. What churned inside never matched what she saw. She had accepted every invitation from Hank, usually disguising her unhappiness so that she fit in with the weekend entertainment or his friends.

Here the lilies on their green platters gave her acute pain. They were for frogs, for children, for real lovers, for themselves. At night, they closed like fists, assured but mean. Or that's how things seemed to her.

Finally, she dragged her canoe up onto the reedy shore, set her things within the trees, opened a thermos of wine, lit a cigarette, and let the sweat on her skin find the air. She stared at the moss, noticing its intricate patterns. Then she looked at a dead log, its shelf mushrooms, poly somethings. Words she learned from Hank and forgot.

She doubted that a great blue heron would come near her. People sensed her unhappiness and maintained their distance.

The air was torpid, matching her mood now. The wine wouldn't taste good until it had some effect and then that would be evanescent, short-lived as a dragonfly. Indians in Minneapolis drank Irish Rose wine. She bought a bottle to try it. The Indians hung around libraries the way she had when she was on unemployment.

She ducked into the antiseptic-smelling forest where a toad skittered. There weren't any trails. She could collect tinder but it was pointless. She hadn't ever built a campfire and was equipped with a huge flashlight.

Yellow tiles of light cascaded across the lake but the smell of algae was like the doorway to a cellar. Gnats aggregated like dust. Maureen found the bottle of allergy pills in her knapsack.

The waxy Jarlsberg Swiss cheese and hard roll went down with the second thermos cup of wine. There were cashews, bananas, Bugles, and Pepperidge Farm cookies. As usual, the anchor in her stomach poked at them.

Rubbing her eyes, she needed the allergy pills. Then the water lilies began to interest her, their petals seemingly coated with shellac. Restlessly, she waded into the water and considered setting up her tripod in the mud. She could try a time lapse.

When she planted the tripod on the bank, it swayed and made her feel like collapsing. Between gulps of wine, she took light readings. Then she put on the snorkel to take a reading of herself. She didn't bother to remove her T-shirt and shorts. The dank green led to drowsy underwater woods.

When she first burst into the air, a cord twisted around her neck. Even as a child, she wondered at her bad fate, almost being hung as she entered her family. They had watched her for signs of brain damage. Afraid of doing anything wrong, not wanting things to get worse at home, she knew that even if she weren't wanted, there was no turning around. She waited, waited for improvement, waited for Jesus Christ, waited for aliens, waited for love to work out. Only light came from the sky.

When the water was sleepy and the seaweed was like shrubbery, she knew her preoccupation had been stubborn and unthinking. It was like the mind of an embryo that rebels from being born, a creature writhing. This wasn't anyone's fault when even she couldn't understand why she couldn't go on. Her mind worked in jags and sometimes her short term memory evaporated. Setting up her tripod had become as difficult as cooking when she had no desire to eat.

On the bank, she slouched in the moss, drank more wine, and then tossed out the rest. The spadderdock sat hard and on top, doing nothing on its own. She set up a long exposure and noticed that the water was peaceful, the woods pleasant. The thermoses had to be washed out and then she tottered to the shore. Her plan was in control again like any farce of planning. She stopped the time lapse, took the camera from the tripod, and waded into the water. The water lily had begun closing like an observatory.

Then she pulled the canoe into the water and, after sandwiching her camera in the cushions, fell into it. It rocked and as she found the paddle, she floated haphazardly into the shimmering dusk.

This was all she wanted. Everything would lead to it. Beyond the wavering seaweed, the lake glowed orange, receiving the horizon. She looked fine, paddling a little and leaning towards the water as if she were a part of the lake. When the island cut off the sun, she stood up in its shadow, reached

194

down for her camera, and stumbled over the side of the canoe.

Letting the water overwhelm her, she closed her eyes and thought of the seaweed as an eiderdown. A light was still on. She had to pull the water off of her, take a breath, and wait for the deity that made her worship sleep. In her apartment, she reeled from wine but her feet still worked involuntarily. She had to sleep in a bed. Capsizing again, she saw that the water was full of deep sleep, dark sails that wafted her up again, up to the surface.

A great blue heron was standing on the shore down the cove. Strong wings flapped from it. She was blubbering in the water, she was kicking. The heron was flying and her canoe was floating in a cloud, the island she was trying to see. It might be less than fifty yards away.

A sign could be a photograph but this one would only be in her head. The plan was past. She had to swim like any coughing, exhausted swimmer. She had to save herself because it wasn't just a doctor who saved her at birth. She had to breathe. Though she never swam the sidestroke much, that brought her nearer the looming canoe. Hoisting an arm onto its rim, she tipped it until she could grasp the paddle.

The paddle was a kickboard. She could lay her head on it and kick her way to the island, thinking how nature had outwitted her. The island rocks rose from the deep water, sudden and knocking against her toes. She dragged herself up to one, then pulled herself to another, then to the rock shore.

Her lungs were making a terrible noise. Chugging was the sound of a motorboat. The heron was gone. She might have photographed it. Stupidly, she was sitting the way she did in her apartment. But her chest was heaving as she saw a rowboat and a man riding in the direction of the canoe.

"Help! Help me!"

She waved the paddle but it clattered on the rock. The rowboat was coming and the man had long brown flapping hair. His flapping shirt was open on his broad brown chest. She was still crouched on the shore when he pulled his boat up onto it.

"Are you breathing alright?"

He fell down beside her and, when she didn't say anything, put his arm around her. He exchanged air with her but then, she pushed him away. She hadn't tasted such competence for some time.

"You're alright," he laughed, rearranging his shirt until he found a pack of cigarettes in a pocket.

"I fell out of the canoe. There was a great blue heron on the shore over there." She tried to turn but she was beached.

"A woman photographer came out here with some snorkeling equipment."

Her T-shirt stuck to her breasts but she felt insubstantial, her stomach still in the water and her limbs numb.

"What's your name? Mine's Stevo. Like stevedore."

"Maureen. That's my canoe."

"Did your camera fall in?"

"No."

"My old lady fell in with her guitar once. She hasn't strummed in a rowboat since."

Maureen would rather photograph Stevo than get acquainted.

"Do you smoke?"

She accepted a cigarette only to prove that she could inhale. But it stirred up waves inside of her. She pointed at the canoe with the cigarette and Stevo went to his boat. He pushed off with an oar. Then he yanked on his motor cord and yanked a grin at her. Soon he was tying the canoe to his boat.

After he steered to the island again, he yelled, "Where's your other stuff?"

"Over at the shore."

"I'll pull the canoe up. Get in my boat and ride. You can't stay here overnight."

"No, I'd feel better if I stayed with the canoe."

She wasn't ready for any gasoline smell or bumping. As soon as Stevo's hair was flying, she pulled the canoe into the water, put the paddle in it, and pushed off. Her stomach swelled and then it settled ominously. The paddle stumbled in the heavy water. When Stevo was beyond her sight, she leaned over the side and heaved a pink-tinged vomit into the tinted lake. It was the final failure.

Turning the canoe so that it would ride over the mess, Maureen paddled in a tranquil way, thinking how herons were finicky about water purity and that a nature photographer would set up a blind.

Soon Stevo soared up beside her. "I'll pull the canoe. C'mon. Ride in the boat."

"No. Please. I came here to canoe and take pictures. I'll pick up my stuff at the Logren's." She took her camera bag, remembering that her money and car keys were in it.

"Have it your way."

Regaining her self-possession, she paddled past inert trees that calmed her intermittent quivering. The water had darkened and she was craving sleep by the time she reached Logren's Resort.

It was just a spill, she told Gerta. She didn't think she needed a doctor. When she went to the bathroom in Gerta's cottage, the water she drank traced its way to her stomach. Her face startled her the way it did on crisis nights in her childhood. The mirror reflection was pretty when she felt frightened.

"Stevo said you saw a heron," Gerta said.

"Only for a minute. I tried to catch it with my camera, standing up in the canoe."

Gerta showed her the available cabin and then she said the sauna was still warm. Feeling nervous, Maureen went with her for a 7-Up and then to the sauna. Finally, she sat at the end of the boathouse, drying her clothes. The wavelets lulled her and the boats creaked like Venice. She watched for the Northern Lights.

"Is that her?"

Maureen's head was throbbing. A woman her age stepped onto the boathouse dock, her hair swagged with two sticks. Her earrings were like fishing lures. Then Stevo appeared at the door of the boathouse.

"My old lady. Here's dry and spry Maureen." He crept in and soon they were all seated near the water, Stevo sitting in a boat.

"Can you take a photograph of a band?" Stevo's old lady asked.

"Sure. I've photographed performers."

"It's one of our favorite bands. Have you ever been dancing in Chisholm? All I have is an instamatic."

"It's only a few miles from here," Stevo said, his chest covered now. "The best dancing around. We'll buy you drinks and food. There's only hot dogs, stuff like that."

From the back seat of a car, Maureen followed the spectral trail that flowed between the masts of trees. Stevo lit up a joint and passed it back to Maureen. The odor made her sleepy and then she was at the bottom of a lake. Soon a bleary brightness radiated from a tall pine building around which cars flashed like fish. Maureen sat up and hung her camera around her neck.

25 Yesterday's Undertaker

In the dance hall, Stevo was known to the Northerners. Maureen was his catch for the day while he recounted his rescue.

"Only St. Jude would re-roof that Logren cottage. Maureen, that's old news."

She was studying the carved commitments on the pine table where they sat with their beers. When she looked up, people writhed in the splattered lights like seaweed. She had never been in this condition when she was expected to use her camera. At least she was prepared for the dusk atmosphere with her light meter and flash.

"C'mon, Maureen. I'll take you out on the floor, nearer the band. The old lady is waiting to talk to the band. Over there."

Once Maureen floundered into the waves of dancing, she could enjoy the floating lights, the bare arms, and the sensuality that sank and kicked and rose again. The band was on an island, what she was supposed to reach somehow. She followed Stevo through the undulations.

On the steps to the stage, his old lady said, "They're taking a break pretty soon."

"A lot of people are wrecked here," Stevo said, lighting up a cigarette and stretching his legs on the steps. Maureen fumbled with her lenses.

"I told them she couldn't stay long," Stevo's old lady said.

Near the stage, the music pounded above them. Maureen stood up and photographed the musicians with their instruments flapping in the strobe lights. Then there was a current of clapping. Summoned up the steps, she made her way over cords and boulder-like cases.

"The band is wrecked too," Stevo said behind her.

Living up to her claim of being a Twin Cities photographer, Maureen surveyed the scene. The guitarist wanted to stand on a tree stump with his head between the points of a moose rack. Then the fiddler dueled him for this honor. Maureen folded herself to the floor until the drummer seemed to have paws and his drums were like moonlit rocks.

At last, they posed for the next song, the singer marking his spotlight territory with the microphone. Stevo helped her back to their table where she endured a fierce kiss. As if it were etiquette, Maureen put her head on the table where the smell of pine and beer were as stagnant as a sleeping bag.

"At least the new lady isn't from around here. Look who Stevo's dancing with now."

I'm not the new lady, Maureen said but she didn't hear her own words. Chairs scraped and smoke encircled confidences like a campfire's.

"Stevo acts as if his old lady is going to run off with the band. She's never had her guitar hooked up."

"She waited too long for her turn to live with him."

"I hope she didn't drive. Hi! Maureen! Stevo-o! Come here! This one's had too much."

A firm hand was pressing Maureen's neck.

"Price of an eight by ten glossy. She risked her life to get a picture of a great blue heron today."

"Someone should get her out of here. Someone other than you, Stevo. She's got pills in her bag."

"Those are allergy pills."

"Yeah. Kiss her goodnight, Stevo. Hey Maureen! Do you need a doctor?"

"She's trying to talk. Shut up!"

"You didn't give her anything, did you?"

"She practically drowned tonight. I don't medicate people."

Maureen was breathing. A bed was under her, solid and soft. She felt for her camera cord but it wasn't around her neck. "Where's my camera?" she said, flopping over and finding windows that framed stiff branches. Turning the other way, she saw people standing around a raw wood counter. Nightlights glowed from the wall and cigarette tips dipped like fireflies, tinting faces. Then a silhouette obliterated that view, Stevo, his dark torso so near that Maureen could see beads at his neck.

"Do you have a bad allergy?" a female voice asked from the dark.

"It was in my eyes. Where am I? Where's my camera?"

"Are you breathing alright?" Stevo inquired.

Maureen averted her head, remembering his resuscitation efforts.

"I took care of your camera. Here it is. There's a surprise picture in it. Did you ever take a picture of yourself sleeping?"

Maureen remembered that she was wearing shorts and a T-shirt over her bathing suit and that she was probably a mess.

"Did you ever see yourself in my arms?"

"Thanks for warning me."

"She's alright. Just crashed. Not a sick woman, hey, Maureen?"

Two women were sitting in a shadow. Hearing the trees shuffling outside the windows, Maureen dozed off. When she awakened next, she was in a house with people, what she hadn't experienced for a few years.

"Maybe her pills wore off and her allergy hit her. People don't know all their allergies. The night Ferd got so drunk that he hit a wasp's nest like a piñata, Luann didn't know she was allergic. They had to bring her into the hospital, stoned and all."

"People like her everywhere in the Twin Cities. Camping alone!"

"I wonder if she fell for Stevo."

"Who hasn't? Stevo's not challenged."

"Stevo's no good. Why does God make men like him?"

"When they all do it alike."

"They all do it alike."

Maureen drifted away into sleepy woods. Then she heard a shriek. Shaggy feathers were hunched near a pool of blue.

"Stevo! Turn off the TV. You're sleeping through the weather."

Maureen was lying on a rock and then it was the stone bench in front of her apartment building. Water the color of concrete lapped at her toes. She feared that her toes would become set in it when a man in a black suit came up the sidewalk.

"Hey, Maureen! I'm going to sit on a roof today. The old lady is here."

"What time is it?"

Stevo was standing near a brown couch that looked as if it were molting. He was wearing a verdigris T-shirt with cut-off sleeves. Behind him, the man in the black suit was watching them both.

"He's not scary."

"No, I'm not scary, Maureen. Just an animal in the woods."

"No, I mean the man in black."

"The man in black."

Maureen looked around Stevo but the man in black vanished.

"He's waiting for me to fall off a roof like a shingle on acid. The old lady's here. Sleep it off."

He was just a business-like little man, there the way she sensed a picture before it happened. His dark head was like a camera, the undertaker of yesterday. She felt his presence as she watched a soap opera in the house that would seem poverty-stricken if the sumptuous woods weren't outside the sets of windows.

"Stevo ate all the bacon. He doesn't touch Krispy Critters. There's a table outside. It's not so hot under the trees."

"What time is it?"

"'All My Children' is done at twelve-thirty."

"Oh, yeah."

"Say, don't take a picture of Stevo's house. OK?"

The bungalow was typical of Northern Minnesota lake dwellings, once painted red. Now the old paint peeled out like petals from under the newer brown coat.

Maureen offered, "Maybe I could treat you to dinner." She was hungry and happy with the cereal and milk, sitting under birch trees.

"That might be nice. Stevo just has to give a Tarzan yell today. They think the guys don't work as hard when the sun's hot."

Maureen didn't ask what else Stevo did. The mining companies hadn't left much for last night's partygoers.

"I can play a little guitar. I'd like you to photograph me here with the trees behind me. Stevo knows a lot of people in the T.C. but no one who spends money on photography equipment."

Stevo's old lady sat on a high-backed black rocker that had a wreath of yellow flowers painted above her head. Maureen coaxed her to say her name, embarrassed that she didn't know.

"You're not 25, are you, ..."

"Twenty-three."

"Should I write 'Stevo's old lady' on the back of the print? Stevo must be thirty."

"Thirty-two."

"I'm younger than him."

"It's hard to feel young with Stevo."

"Sing something."

"I'll just hum and strum."

"Does Stevo sing?"

"Don't make me laugh."

She wore a dimity blouse over jeans and a bead bracelet that brought out her hands. The tune was "Muskrat Love" while Maureen made chords of the illuminated leaves. Then they walked into the woods where Maureen could photograph her on a trail, the guitar frets at her shoulder like a gun shaft.

"Cold beer! It's cold."

The words nearby startled Maureen.

"Who'd you expect? The man in black?"

Stevo's gnarly arms and his lichen-colored shirt blended in with the foliage. He held out a can of beer as his old lady came for a cooling kiss, what Maureen remembered as bristly and flavored like pine. Then he had to give Maureen and her camera a hug.

"We're going to Chisholm again tonight. Don't worry about food," he said.

There were meat pasties and sausage pizza on the outdoor table.

"Send us the pictures, at the Logren's," Stevo said. "How much? Or I could take the roll to a drugstore. But then you won't see yourself sleeping."

"I'd better get back to the Logren's," Maureen said.

"Say when you're ready. It's only a few minutes from here. Unless you think you can take better pictures of the band tonight."

"I'm running out of film," Maureen fibbed.

"There's a drugstore in Chisholm."

Maureen wondered if there was a clinic in Chisholm.

"Aren't you feeling alright? There aren't enough doctors to go around during the tourist season. You want to tell him about the man in black?"

"No. I'm just worried about the allergy pills."

"We didn't give them to you."

Driving into the clutter of marsh marigolds and vehicles at the Logren's, Maureen wanted to wipe out the previous day.

"I rented the canoe for today too," she reminded Gerta. "I won't be taking any allergy pills."

As they went down the crooked steps to the sauna, Gerta said, "My grandson can canoe with you. He wants to be a guide someday."

Stevo helped to carry her things along the overgrown trail to her cabin. Inside were two twin beds, a small refrigerator, and on the kitchen wall, a few photographs of fishermen with their trophies.

"Don't sit under the leak. We just got started on this cabin," Stevo said, looking towards the ceiling with his hands locked into his jean pockets. "Do you want to drive behind us to Chisholm?"

"No, I'm feeling pretty well here. Thanks."

Maureen put a bag on one of the beds but then Stevo's arm blocked her.

"Wasn't it special, what happened?"

"I can't tell you how special it was, having someone come when you did." But this was like telling a tree to move a branch for her.

"You'll be here and the band might play something that reminds me that you're still here. I could drive over."

"There will be plenty of girls if you want to break another heart, Stevo."

She attempted to duck under his arm but his hand grasped her shoulder, trapping her near the bed. Besides his classic kiss, Stevo's mystique, being a grown man who didn't compete for fish because he won with women, made her laugh. The women liked his longhair allure because he evidently knew his limits.

"It keeps the girls primed. Otherwise they let themselves go."

"The man in black might be watching."

Stevo stood back and said, "Do you think you could photograph him?"

"It probably wouldn't impress anyone if I could."

"I don't know who you know in the T.C. but I'll think of coming down for those photos if you don't send them."

It wasn't the first time Maureen had seen something before it happened. The man in a black shirt, his hair neat as a camera, sat in front of a white-painted brick wall explaining his role as her MFA adviser.

"You've already been taking courses at the 5000 level. Are you planning a full load?"

Maureen wasn't sure if she would be staying at her summer job.

"You'll have to decide. Now. Here, I've got you down for Color Techniques. And for Advanced Darkroom. It's hard to juggle classes once you're signed up. Have you gone to the student loan office yet?"

There was another student waiting.

On the lanes between the looming buildings, Maureen kept seeing silhouettes. But they were students wearing black. When she became confused about the location of the student loan office, she remembered where the drop-in counseling office was. There, she was given tests before being assigned a psychologist.

A woman in a dark suit was watching her. After speaking to the receptionist, she walked in squash heels down a hallway. Maureen felt as if she were at a wake where she would appear irreverent in a jean skirt and a loose blouse. Then a lanky man sauntered into the office, wearing an open beige jacket and Hush Puppies. He was discreet with the secretary before entering the hallway.

Maureen crossed to the receptionist and asked, "Is he available?"

"We usually assign the walk-in women to women psychologists."

"I would like to talk with him."

"If you think you can talk with him more easily."

Having chosen the man because he wasn't her type, Maureen waited until he came out again. His long arms were like paddles as he showed her a chair in his office. On the wall, a naked sculpture man was looking through a telescope at stars that made a constellation of his form.

"I see you're entering an MFA program. People usually come here because they don't know what to do next. Why are you here?"

Maureen faltered, not wanting to say that she knew too well what she was doing, taking pictures of people or creatures that were alive when she felt fated.

"It's alright to be confused," he encouraged. His name was Simon and his voice was yappy and soft. The thinning hair on his head was like parched grass.

"I guess I'm here because of plans not working out," Maureen replied weakly. "I was supposed to talk to a woman. It's all just plans for me. I don't want to go on this way."

"You've signed up for a Plan B program." His eyes were a warm brown. "You're afraid your Plan B program is just a plan."

"I hate to waste money."

Simon leaned forward as if Maureen were really in a blur.

"It's kind of dead to plan on life," she said.

"Tell me, what plans didn't work out?"

"Let's see. I made plans to do something on a trip and my plans didn't happen. I planned to fall in love and that didn't happen."

Simon drooped, watching her.

"So I did something stupid that seemed to be a plan of fate. Now art is like a relationship. It's hard to plan."

"Wow. You sound overpowered. Throughout history, a lot of art has been commissioned." Simon crumpled back into his chair, his long fingers hanging from the armrest, fingernails oval as eyes. "Can you tell me what stupid is?"

"Oh. I drank wine to sleep. Then I did that about three nights a week."

"You *drank* and that was stupid."

"Yes. But since I broke off things with the man I'd been seeing, I've been sleeping better. You might think it's stupid to say this but I stopped drinking." She couldn't tell this man about her plan to do everything wrong at once. It was like talking about a dead person's foolishness after the funeral.

"You say you don't drink if you're sleeping well," he said, writing on his clipboard.

"That was like drowning to sleep. I had to breathe. Most people think it's stupid to go back to school instead of concentrating on a man who is steady."

Simon pulled the papers up on his clipboard. "You've taken an MMPI. We'll discuss that next time." Then he took a faceted paperweight from his desk, a clock. "I usually ask people who they wish to be like. Or what sort of person they want to be."

Maureen floundered and then she remembered that she wanted to photograph a great blue heron because her grandmother did. "I haven't thought about that much. I guess I wanted to be like my grandmother. My mother was divorced so I didn't want to be like her."

"Ah!" Simon had made a discovery.

Maureen diverted him, saying, "I didn't grow up around anyone who knew anything about artists like Georgia O'Keefe. I suppose most women MFA students would like to be like her."

"Why your grandmother though? Or Georgia O'Keefe? Most women who come here don't bring up Georgia O'Keefe."

"Because their lives are a picture for me."

"Wasn't O'Keefe photographed in the nude? What about your

grandmother? Was there anything unseemly about her life?"

"She died when I was in grade school."

"Ah."

Maureen felt like saying "Ah" too because he wanted to hear more about this. "At her funeral, my brother told me her casket was a train car and she was traveling to heaven. No one remembered her doing anything wrong."

"You won't always be taking pleasant pictures for your MFA, will you?"

"No. I want to take true pictures."

"Did your grandmother drink wine in the evenings?"

"No," Maureen said, thinking that her other grandmother, Grandma Rhiann, may have drunk socially.

"So you haven't been making a good impression on yourself, knowing the truth about yourself."

"That's why I'm afraid my plans won't work out."

"We'll make an appointment and if you need a treatment or a prescription, I can refer you to a doctor."

"I can't afford a doctor."

He kept writing on a form, making plans for her.

"Have you noticed that students are wearing black this year?" she said.

"What makes you say that?"

"I was wondering if I picked them out or whether you noticed."

"Toughs wore black leather when I was in high school. Many of my college classmates elected to wear dark suits when I was entering a Ph.D. program."

"Do you know many people who live like their grandparents?"

"Now you're asking questions. That's where we'll start next time. Do you like fruit?" He put his clipboard notes in a file and then he opened up a plastic bag with purple grapes in it.

"No, thanks."

Simon got up, popping a few grapes in his mouth, and opened the door for her. "What kind of fruit do you like?"

"Bing cherries."

"Do you ever go to museums at night?"

"Sometimes."

He toppled beside her, walking to the receptionist. "Let's see the calendar. Can you come in the evening at seven? We have evening hours Tuesdays and Thursdays."

The leaves changed color and drifted around people who didn't want to live in a black and white world. Fathers everywhere bagged leaves that crumpled like dollar bills. Children shoveled through books so that in the spring, when they poked up higher, they would be admired and examined and photographed for their biological identification. Everyone was in a long romance with the earth, especially the piece that they would eventually grasp for themselves.

Maureen might fool the psychologist, changing color and not needing him to remind her that she wasn't really dead. She could be like a camera, adjusting when the world changed but not having to be faithful to the changeable. If she drank too much or couldn't sleep, she could see the psychologist. But now she wasn't faithful to either alcohol or sleep because she couldn't count on either of them. The psychologist was probably too popular to be counted on.

She went back to school because she could count on its consolation. She only had to impress people with photographs, develop rolls of film, and get her prints in on time.

Before Stevo turned up in Minneapolis, she sent prints in care of the Logren's. Then she examined a dim photograph of a girl sleeping. She loved this girl who was really a woman, loved her exhaustion, her pinched eyebrows and the hair that wanted to sail somewhere. No one could tell what kind of life made this person curl and hang onto a pillow as if it would keep her from falling off the bed. No one would suspect her of a morbid plan. She was a waif, not a wife, wandering around and looking at other people's lives. Maureen wanted to take care of her.

She liked the girl in the photograph as much as she liked Glinda the cockatiel. Glinda's clipped wings were growing out. She leapt around the apartment, wearing a hat because she was made to be above the wrestling and the running.

On her balcony, Maureen drank warm milk and stared into a darkness that couldn't overpower the stars. Even if she were self-centered, she needed to have a childhood. In the morning, she might not do what was expected because she didn't understand what that was anymore. She would be taken up with the remarkable.

PART III

26   Thursday Darkroom

Coming off the cracked, gummy walls was a calendar of the months after Maureen's lost summer.

"I won't have filth on my walls," her new landlady said.

"Filth?"

Gail was examining adhesive strips on the wall. "The sticky filth left on the wall. Once these walls are painted, I won't have any more nail holes either."

During Maureen's first encounter with the disgruntled Gail, Gail and her mother sat like toll-takers on the steps leading to the second floor.

"You must be the one with the darkroom in your apartment. I'm Gail Flaherty. The new owner." Her hair was tinted dark cherry.

Maureen slurped an ice cream cone, bought because she had just photographed an ice cream truck.

"This is my mother," Gail said about the woman with bumpy blonde hair like Joann Berwick's. They made a small aisle so that Maureen could set one of her Bass shoes between them.

"We're going to paint your apartment," Gail called after her.

Maureen was one of the older tenants. Between her photography job for a suburban newspaper, freelancing, and trips up north, she liked to picnic on the grove side of her building. She tossed trail mix to baby squirrels that chased each other in the crab apple trees. In August, the crab apples attracted cardinals and the piebald pigeons that camouflaged themselves on shingles next door.

One afternoon, Gail joined her, sitting on a bench near Maureen's throw blanket. She stretched out her knobby legs and mused about pruning the crab apple trees. Then she said, "The guys are coming to paint your apartment on Saturday." She opened up a large clutch purse that bristled with applications. Offering Maureen a fancy mint, she asked, "Why do you stay here?"

"I was in graduate school."

"You don't want to stay here, do you?"

Not knowing if Gail meant the apartment building or Minneapolis because of its rising crime rate, Maureen allowed her to persist.

"What do you want to do?"

Questions like this were not unusual if a young woman had the looks to marry. Maureen mentioned something about teaching photography. Sympathetically, Gail nodded until her hair, moving in one mass, seemed too heavy for her head. "I can understand how a hobby turns into work," she said.

Then the ice cream truck began clanging its hollow bell on the street.

"That ice cream truck," Maureen sighed. Its bell sounded flat and dejected, like a child lost in city traffic. Maureen ran out one day to see if she could photograph the sound of the toddling vehicle as it encountered traffic at an intersection.

Gail straightened her dress in a deliberate way, knowing that in her tenant neighborhood, tall children with grebe-blue hair were likely to stop the truck. "I have to show you how your furniture should be moved for the painters. They don't move furniture."

Maureen followed Gail with her throw dragging like a security blanket.

"I want my tenants to be happy," she tossed at Maureen. Once Maureen unlocked her apartment door, Gail trounced in ahead of her.

"Did you put these hooks in the walk-in closet? I mean, your darkroom?"

"They're for the curtains. I need to shut out the light when I'm working."

Gail trawled the photographs on Maureen's walls but when she turned, she pronounced what she saw as filth. "All of these men," she added after Maureen protested. Then she shuffled the photography magazines on Maureen's coffee table, saying again, "I won't have filth in my apartment building."

"Those aren't my photographs."

"The pictures you took of this building. You took them for your last landlord. They were good."

"I freelance. And it was convenient for me to take interior shots after tenants moved out."

Gail's tantrum, its implication that the men in the wall photographs were in Maureen's apartment, waned. "Maybe you could photograph my mother's house. It's in the neighborhood. We're going to be putting it up for sale."

"Sure," Maureen said.

"You could come on Saturday when the painters are in your apartment. If the weather cooperates."

The yellowed wall brought back a giddy sense of transience. Maureen grasped the first photograph she took after starting over, what led from one picture to the next until they should have led out of the apartment.

Three phantom faces jostled in shadows.

The litho subjects were the Thursday darkroom cronies, Anna, John, and Vic. "We're the spooky ones," Anna said.

Entering her program with credits behind her, Maureen signed up for darkroom evenings with older students, some who had experience in photojournalism. The Thursday cronies seemed to sense her recent crisis.

She had made an ascent from destructive thoughts, and now she felt as if she were floating with her photography. So she fixed herself to a schedule. Mondays, she checked in at a suburban newspaper for freelance assignments. Tuesdays, she saw her psychologist. On Wednesdays, she assisted undergraduates in the darkroom, and on Fridays, she sat in the YMCA sauna, rinsing the city salt from her pores. Saturdays, she bought groceries, often at a neighborhood Coop. Sundays, she studied.

The bird trainer held a cockatoo near a candelabrum of birds.

"Where was it taken?" John asked in the darkroom murk.

"The upper floor of Southdale Mall. It's Fred, Biretta's bird, and his trainer. They were in town now that Fred's retired from TV. My newspaper editor wanted me to attend."

"It's hard to imagine this man working with a police show," Anna said. "The way you've caught the light, it looks as if he's in the air too."

Anna followed people who had to follow – farm workers, religious cultists, people in line-ups for welfare or rock concerts. John drove to weather events - tornadoes, hurricanes, and Mount St. Helen. Vic stalked shorelines, oil spills, and the industrial stew that Lake Michigan served up. Maureen had rolls of film from her descent into the nether zone of Minneapolis. The best were morbid.

A crushed wing had capsized on city pavement.

"I didn't say fisheye lens when I saw it," Vic said.

"A dead bird," John said.

"I must have a dead bird on every roll I took last year," Maureen apologized.

"Where were you?"

"Here. They were like omens. A bad day if I saw one."

She might find the reason for them if she developed them all.

"People who look through rose-tinted lenses might be more depressed," Anna welcomed her.

A man of indeterminate age sat like a septuagenarian on a bench in the hall of the library. He had Indian stamped on him.

Like driftwood, he wedged himself next to Maureen on a bus the day her car wouldn't start. But the liquid that honed him was alcohol. He muttered that he didn't have the bus money to get away from his caseworker. "She makes me take a bad drug," he said.

Maureen paid to take his photograph at the public library. She wondered if he was once tall and strong like the young Indians that jaunted the sidewalks of Lake Avenue, usually in a threesome.

When her Melitta coffee pot broke, she stopped at a Nicollet Avenue café. At nine in the morning, customers sat with strangers at the tables. Returning, Maureen found willing subjects, actors who were planning next summer's Shakespeare in the Park productions, a black man distributing religious materials, a man from a typewriter repair shop that was becoming an antique typewriter shop.

After discussing sticky rolls and sticky relationships with the woman actor one morning, Maureen let her boyfriend have the seat at their table. There was an open stool at the counter where Maureen could order her second mug. A young man next to her gazed at paintings mounted above the coffee machine.

"Which do you like?" he wondered.

The first was abstract with shapes like limbless humans and the second was of a tipsy vase, throttling flowers.

"They both remind me of tottering bowling pins," she said. "They're not bad."

"I like the abstract better." The man wore a jean jacket and he was sturdily built as common sense.

They talked about which coffee was best on a rainy day. Maureen saw his dark ponytail streaming under the collar of his jacket.

"I'm an art student," he said to Maureen's inquiry. And then cocky, he asked, "Would you have gotten into this conversation with an Indian?"

"I used to know kids who were part Indian up north. When I visited my grandparents." He nodded slowly and she said, "In fact, I've wanted to photograph the Indian men that walk in threes on the sidewalks here. Why do they walk in threes?"

He shrugged and said. "It's a good number. I came down here from Duluth. Wanted to see the world."

"Do you paint?"

He brightened, a taciturn brightness.

"I'm still not alive," the woman actor said. She was getting another mug of coffee.

"She doesn't feel alive if she isn't on stage," Maureen said to the Indian man. "So I photographed her."

"Does a photograph prove that she's alive?" he wondered.

"I guess not."

"To those who believe that all the world's a stage," the actress said, raising her empty mug.

After she got her refill, Maureen said to the Indian man, "Sometimes it's too easy with people who can pose. I like to photograph people going about their lives."

"Maybe I'll see you around."

His name was Ben Dufour, she learned the next time she saw him. He was waiting for a few friends of his to come by.

Three Indian men, tall and wide-shouldered, strode near a clogged coffee shop on Nicollet Avenue.

At home, Maureen played with filters and double exposures when the frost was on the windows. She nailed a birdfeeder platform just under the outside balcony door windowpane. Then Glinda could perch on a chair back and encounter blue jays, chickadees, and a huge crow. A circus of squirrels swung up to see Glinda. She was a bird incarcerated behind glass like a television screen. Glinda was a sad case or Glinda was spoiled.

Because Maureen was unaccountably sad for too long, she spoiled herself. She ate ice cream for supper, took candlelit baths, neglected people from her past. Sometimes, after hearing crime reports, she stayed up until four in the morning and slept until noon. Passing a mirror one late night, she panicked. She thought she saw a dark man in the mirror but it must have been her own shadow.

She often had a sense of things coming and along with that, a need to stop time. Continuing to spoil herself, she made the shadow man into a pretend man. When she was out, she knew people imagined she had a man somewhere and because she used to, she played along.

"Is there anything wrong with sleeping from four until noon? It's eight hours of sleep," she asked Simon, her therapist.

"Can you come to your appointment at nine in the morning next week?" he replied.

On her MMPI, Maureen showed some depression but she wasn't

near the drowning line.

"Let's talk about your passive-aggressive scale tonight and your weighing on the passive side. This can mean that you have a private side and a public side that you present to others. You must know what that means in photography."

"Photographing well-known people is much different from photographing people who aren't used to posing," Maureen said.

"Gosh, when I think of photography, I think of a wonderful exhibit I saw at the Walker Art Center. It included some nudes and our little girls saw them first. That was alright as long as they could admire the other pictures."

"Swimmers and wrestlers are almost bare in their pictures. It's how the photographer and the viewer look at nudity. This is what I've done lately."

Forms like wrapped mummies were crystalline at a shore of intense gold.

"You must have been up early to get these."

"That's what happens when I don't sleep."

She was stranded in Duluth during a blizzard and instead of driving on to her aunt's, she stayed at a motel near Lake Superior. Early the next morning, she waded to the peninsula, Park Point, for the wind-sculpted drifts. "I was supposed to help decorate a Christmas tree," she told Simon.

"You sure saw some decoration!"

"I added some color to set off the snow forms."

Simon treated her photographs as inkblot tests. He stretched his legs so that his Hush Puppies were at one side of her chair. He must have been gawky in high school. Maureen hadn't expected to feel any affection for him.

"Do you like having to keep your distance when you use your camera?"

"I'd rather be on the outside this year," Maureen answered.

"Most people need to pull back at times. I've heard that in my own life."

Simon probably knew that Maureen was content to see the frozen drifts when she was supposed to see her mother and her aunt's family.

"What church is this?" he wondered, looking at the next picture in Maureen's small stack.

"It's the church of the silver cars."

Four silver cars were parked near stained glass.

"Did you attend?"

"No. I don't own a silver car."

Simon dandled the picture on his knees, leaning over it.

"You can have it if you want. I used a star filter for it. A little too twinkly for my professor."

"Isn't it stuffy in here? How about a turn in Dinkytown? We could get better coffee or some hot chocolate. I could use some advice on matting."

Simon helped Maureen with her coat and then they walked past a student to the dank staircase.

"Have you eaten this evening?" Simon asked.

Under the peaks of the university, a lanky man and a woman carrying a large satchel were far from the brooding suburbs. Maureen often saw the picture she was making. Cognitive therapy had taught her that grief was a guise like a hat. Even when the days weren't inclement, she had grieved about inevitable partings. She had even grieved the parting from her past self. Her being stranded in a below-zero bus with her mother more than twenty years ago wasn't necessarily a traumatic event. Last summer was the summer before the next summer. Maureen didn't take pictures because life was dying or because she could put people back together. Still, she was irritated that she was spending Tuesday evenings with a married man.

She stopped and Simon leaned, his arm prepared to steady her. "On second thought, Simon, I'd better go home. I'm getting ready to go out to San Francisco to see my sister and her new baby. I have to call my mother. She's paying for the trip."

"Should I sign you up for the Tuesday after Christmas break?"

"No, I'll call if I need an appointment."

"You're thinking you might not."

"I'm thinking."

"You can pull away."

This was like a benediction as Maureen took another lane at the next lamppost.

A baby surfed waves and its mother's billowing breasts.

Lydia sang while nursing Roxie, "'The genie of sleep from the seven seas.' Jenny only takes seven children at a time. I signed up with her for day care before Roxanne was born."

It was Maureen's third day in California. Lydia still talked as if Maureen were planning to have a baby too.

"Jenny signed us up for the baby swimming classes."

"Do you want Roxie attached to water?" Maureen wondered.

"The theory is that babies are traumatized, being born, and that water helps them to adjust. Upsy daisy, Roxie. Not another upset day." She let Maureen hold Roxanne instead of her camera. "Mom keeps asking if Emory is going to marry me. Not if I'm going to marry Emory. Women in Mom's time used to get married in a traumatic way."

They gossiped about their brothers, both still childless and living in future vacation spots.

"Vacation spots are work opportunities for me," Maureen hinted.

After she played another game of Dune with eleven-year-old Lonnie, they took a walk around the neighborhood. Elves sledded under real holly and Lonnie pointed out bus stops where Maureen might ride into San Francisco.

At Emory's coffee shop, Emory explained to Maureen, "The time you spend with Lonnie is special to him. He's really proud of his picture in the Do-It-For-Yourself kids' book. He's a regular Do-It-For-Yourself man now. One of these days, we're going to have to tell him about his father."

"Does Lydia know where he is?"

"It's natural for Lonnie to know where I am. Gig or no gig."

Emory welcomed another customer and then a guitarist sat down with Maureen. Bill's receding mane of hair was combed back as neatly as a businessman's. The beads above his shirt line were as well-chosen as a tie.

In a daytime drizzle, Bill took Maureen around the city that inspired his saga of the Sixties. "There's the apartment building where I met Alan Ginsberg."

"I don't recall any photographs of hippies in the rain," Maureen commented.

Bill's recollections formed double exposures in Maureen's mind. He saw sunshot hippies in parks where Maureen saw forlorn panhandlers standing under monkey puzzle trees. At the site of a concert, she saw a parking lot and a fashion parade of rain gear. A commune house was lovely with fresh magenta and green paint. In front of it was a "For Sale" sign.

"The painted lady's taken a shake," Bill said. "Friend of mine came out here in '67 and one day, tripping, he saw the concrete crumble and a new San Francisco rise like Gibralter. Then he wrote his theory. He thinks the sheer weight of a city could bring it down. He's probably home."

Bill's friend sat on a foam futon, drinking from a plastic tumbler under paper lanterns and baskets holding paperbacks. On the wall were the words: *Thou Shalt Fear and Love Gravity.*

At a Chinese market where Maureen took still lives of aphrodisiacs, Bill said, "Lydia said you might have a father thing."

"That's because Lydia didn't. Maybe she's got a mother thing."

"She thought you might like going out with someone older."

On Bill's paisley sofa, Maureen looked at photos of his recollections and then at the lyrics of his song saga, a manuscript of over a hundred pages.

"Would you like tea, wine, beer, or marijuana?" Bill asked.

Maureen took a glass of Liebfraumilch and said, "I'm off men."

"Oh?" Bill's voice was tinny and tame.

He was a secret romantic about himself as many men were. Maureen prowled with her camera as if she were initiating foreplay. She put a dried flower garland on a lamp's rim and took pictures of his memorabilia.

"I went off the deep end," she explained. "Don't tell Lydia but I drank too much wine last summer."

"Lydia wouldn't like that."

"Men have been like wine to me. Happy and high for a few months and then the hangover." She waded towards Bill.

"I had two marriages that didn't work out. But that was after they worked out for some time," Bill said when anyone could see that.

Maureen admired men, especially the ones on her wall. The shadow man in the mirror observed that none of the men on the wall had grabbed her. In the darkroom, Anna admired Bill and asked, "Are you going back to San Francisco when the drizzle lets up?"

Anna and John were planning a trip, probably through an ice storm on their way to the Mexican border. Vic came and went from Chicago where he had gotten work with a magazine. Maureen was going places in the darkroom. She filled notebooks with exposure times, results with dyes, the effects of textures on negatives, and her experiments with Sabbatier shadows. Vic said her timing was transcendental.

Glinda's encounter with a blue jay at the frosty windowpane earned Maureen a page in a regional bird calendar. One of her blizzard forms was bought from an exhibit for an office complex. She could take these achievements to her mother's besides the pictures of Roxanne. In exchange, her mother had kept up on the farm auctions near her town.

"Can I borrow your snowshoes?" she asked her mother after a March snowstorm. She took trail mix and a thermos, driving at dawn to a vacated farmhouse. Deer grazed in the barnyard. Cats inherited the farmhouse kitchen.

Her mother demanded, "Are you trying to catch pneumonia? A picture isn't worth that!"

Maureen put on another sweatshirt over her thermal underwear and left for the drugstore to stock up on Vitamin C. Then she attended a farm auction where hog number 38 wouldn't separate from trough number 87.

She usually knew people through her camera these days.

27   Bird Sanctuary

Late summer in 1985. Taking down the next wall of photos for her landlady, Maureen reluctantly dumped her new friends in a heap.

Brianna's dress was a block print of her cockatiel, Glinda.

During the darkroom course Maureen assisted, a student asked for a negative of Glinda the cockatiel. Brianna designed fabrics for her MFA and wanted Glinda for a block print. They went out for a late lunch after class.

"I still pick up my crochet hook sometimes," Maureen said. "It's good for anxiety. I went to a psychologist but he was like other men. Insinuating."

They were trying newly invented sandwiches, chosen from a West Bank restaurant's chalkboard.

Brianna agreed, "Once men become wage earners, they look at women differently." She lived on and off with a man who wanted to do film.

"Psychologists really believe that a woman has enough power over other people to transform her life," Maureen complained over her BLT - baked bean curd, lettuce, and tomato.

Brianna concentrated on the sprouts extending from her turkey-avocado sandwich. "As in, I get what I want because I overpower people. You should try a woman therapist."

"Maybe we would talk about men more. I admire men when I'm not involved with one."

"My therapist would help you to see why you're comfortable with that. My father traveled for his job and unwittingly, I've found a man who isn't home all the time."

Maureen recalled, "After my parents divorced, I could admire my father when he visited. I used to think break-ups were romantic. The great romance, I expected, would be reconciling with an old lover."

"Could you?"

"No. I guess it's like divorce."

They decided to browse at Depth of Field, the store where Maureen had gotten the blue heron fabric for her curtains. Brianna said as they walked, "I'm working on intimacy versus familiarity with my therapist. Maureen, do you know that guy?"

Ben Dufour, the Indian from the coffee shop, smiled as he

approached them on Cedar Avenue. "How are you?" Maureen asked him. She'd run into him in the studio arts building and given him a print.

Ben was having a painting exhibited in Duluth. "It's made my grandmother proud," he said.

"What is the subject? Or is it abstract?" Maureen asked.

"Most people would probably recognize the ceremonial drum."

"I have to see it," Maureen said. "I haven't been up to Duluth since I photographed a blizzard."

Brianna interrupted, "Do you know people who do quill work?"

"I know many people at the reservation near Cloquet," Ben said.

Maureen was ready to drive the weekend that Ben would be in Duluth.

At the Duluth museum, Brianna studied old Ojibwe dresses adorned with elaborate beaded flowers. Maureen took Ben's picture near his painting and then they drove to the Indian community center in Cloquet. Lately, news pictures of Indians were of clashes over fishing rights, frames they shared with policemen. It was the first year that the community center in Cloquet had a government page telephone number.

While Brianna observed quill and bead-work at the center, Maureen took pictures and looked at photographs taken earlier in the century. Then she and Ben drove to the maple sugar trees where Ben's grandmother was helping to collect sap. Later, Maureen could see a few of the people at the community center in their Native American pow wow dress. Ben remained as refreshing as their conversation on coffee shop stools. He wasn't given to insinuations.

Vic looked at Maureen's photo essay drying in the darkroom. "Native American women don't dress up at all in Minneapolis."

A jeaned woman bent over needlework. The same woman was transformed by jewelry and feathers.

"I've been trying to obtain a concept with people photos," Maureen explained. "Ever since I read about the ancient Egyptians and their four selves - shadow, heart, body, and shining self. They called them Ka and Ba souls or something. With Indians it seems more pronounced. Too many shadow selves in Minneapolis."

"This one here. I could show it to the magazine editor in Chicago if you want," Vic beamed.

Ben's grandmother sat on a log near a birch bark tub, her face stitched like it and pleased as if sweetness inside her had been tapped. A boy was bringing her a collection can of maple sap.

"The future of these people and the future of maple trees," Vic said. "That's the magazine's direction."

They were going to finish their degrees, ending the shining time when they could concentrate on photographs they wanted to take. Vic was moving to Chicago to take a photography position with his magazine, *The Midwest Forecast*. John was reporting to weather scientists. He and Anna were planning to roam the Caribbean during the hurricane months, print negatives in Texas, and then spend some months in New York City.

Maureen developed a few more pictures for her Native American essay. An apricot sky over Lake Superior, taken last December when a mist of frost swirled over the ice, would fit the theme. At the Native American community center, an old man told about spirits that made mirages on the lake, according to tribal legend.

While Maureen removed the matted Indian photos from her apartment wall, she remembered telling Ben about her attempt to photograph a great blue heron. Herons were soon indifferent to their mates. They abandoned nests that became noxious as garbage dumps from regurgitated fish. Then they groomed themselves obsessively even when they were solitary.

She wore a camera like a false beak now, a woman with idiosyncrasies. But she'd earned the photographer's pass, having waded through the physics of light and the ticks of a stopwatch. Sometimes, passing her mirror, she thought she saw the shadow man. Even though a shadow spouse didn't pay rent, she imagined what he might think of her photos, the clothes she wore, the cigarettes she smoked, the bruises and colds she inflicted upon herself. A shadow man could be perfect sexually.

When she no longer received her stipend for assisting in the darkroom, she took her birdfeeder photos over to Schilling Publishing and sold three to Inez. Then she thought of doing a food essay, having grown up in a town that advertised food in magazines.

Green-topped carrots at the Co-op were the best for still life shots. The manager there, Carl, examined her photogram of a gilled mushroom and said that he hoped to start a newsletter.

"Do you have broth or bouillon?" Maureen asked while Carl looked at her card.

"Animal products are sometimes the worst part of the animal story," Carl replied. "That's what's usually used for bouillon." He was lean and brambly, his hair tied back in a red kerchief. "The poultry and cattle aren't prime. Chickens simmer in buildings as if they're already in kettles."

"That must be why the prices aren't rising," Maureen observed.

Carl told her about calves living in cages and egg-producing chickens that never saw the light of day. To Maureen, this was surreal because she had never seen a photograph of such a scene.

Her father, taking early retirement, moved to the edge of a small town near the Mississippi. Behind his aspen-ensconced house were a woods and a small lake. In his new office-like living room, Maureen discussed the phone calls he made from his desk.

"Your brother Lyle is out at sea," he said.

"I thought he was working in a bookstore."

"He's on a salmon boat. Practicing languages with the Oriental men on board. Maybe he'll like that industry." Her father spoke concisely and with discomfort because of his dentures. "And your sister-in-law Joyce entered the seminary. By the way, have they baptized Lydia's new baby? Poppy and I are planning a trip out there."

Maureen showed him her San Francisco photos. "Are there any abandoned farmhouses around here?"

"Our neighbor, Mr. Bovely, would know best."

Poppy set down a tray of coffee. "Mr. Bovely is the county mortician."

As was still his habit, Maureen's father switched from coffee to beer at five o'clock. Then he became increasingly boisterous until Poppy announced that it was time for a game of casino.

"She wants to make a beggar of me," he said, showing the lining in his pocket.

He was supervisory in the morning, waking Maureen early so that she could photograph deer that came for apples he put out. "There's something I'd like to show you in the cemetery."

Thinking that her father had chosen a grave site, Maureen asked again about Mr. Bovely.

"We'll stop there."

Past marble markers framed in frosty stems, her father took her on a stone path. Sometimes he wiped it with his windshield brush and then he wiped the snow off old headstones, standing like a hedge.

"Hadrian Berwick," Maureen read.

"My grand-uncle. He died in 1932." Then he brushed at the loaf-shaped stones until she could read out Priscilla Berwick and Baby Rose Berwick who died in 1886.

"Do you have any pictures of them?"

"No. Hadrian was a surveyor. That's how my father got interested in map-making."

A fox sniffed near the knock-kneed struts of a chicken coop.

From an old tractor seat on a pile of tires, Maureen watched the fox and then her father's car crawling the nearby road, checking up on her. At his house, she drank hot brandy and water and then Poppy went upstairs to her sewing room.

"Are you doing alright with your photography equipment?" her father asked. They were watching a Judy Garland special and the narrator was telling about Judy's susceptibility to bad contracts.

Maureen could always use one of her father's helpful checks. He went to his desk as Maureen told him about the small expenses. "I buy trail mix at the Co-op. But it's still expensive."

"Like penny candy."

"I thought you were going to build a turkey condominium," she said.

"The plans are here in the desk." He pulled out some papers from a drawer. "The shelter would have decks and ramps. Turkeys could sleep on the roof." He went to the kitchen with his empty glass.

When he returned with it full, Maureen said, "At the food Co-op, the manager said that chickens are being kept in warehouses without windows. They never see the sun."

"Who's he?"

"His name is Carl. He manages a Co-op in South Minneapolis."

"A what? What is a Co-op? A farmer's market?"

"It's a small grocery with organic foods. They buy directly from farmers and guarantee against pesticides." When she was young, Maureen got along with her father because she never bothered with him after he drank. But that was the only time he complained about his work. "Do they keep turkeys that way now?" she asked.

Discreetly, he leaned towards her and said, "I loved your mother."

Maureen did what she did as a child. She laughed in his face, laughed at what a drunken man couldn't say when he was sober.

"But do they keep turkeys that way now?" Maureen persisted. She could see the green wall of their old house in his eyes.

"Who do you mean? They? I don't work for *them* anymore. No one listened to me. Your mother. The young men. Men I trained in. Poppy doesn't want turkeys in her backyard. You don't listen! You just look."

"Poppy wants turkey in a package."

"Poppy wants a garden."

"What do you want?"

"Oh, God! What does it matter? Poppy's kids are going to make sure she gets what she wants."

On the Saturday that her walls would be painted, Maureen took down pictures of her father flipping his last card and of the fox in the barnyard. Surveying her blank wall, she prepared to hike over to Gail's house.

It wasn't far, a Thirty-eighth Street brick house with salmon-orange trimmings, a bay window, and a pedestal entrance. Gail gestured from the bay window, a telephone at her ear.

She let Maureen inside and left her to admire a surreal picture of Jesus, swaddled at the hips in a sunbather's sky. Photographs lined a credenza – a studio portrait of Gail, her long hair all cherry-colored; Gail as a bride; Gail's mother with her hair in pincurls under a sleek pink hat.

"The way houses are going around here, we'll have plenty of time to re-paper the walls," Gail said before she hung up the telephone. "I'm going to re-paper so I'll just need outside shots," she said to Maureen. Then she led her outside where they drifted away from each other, crossing the street. Maureen set up her tripod.

"Do you have somewhere else to stay tonight?" Gail snooped. "The paint is going to smell for a day or two."

Maureen was stymied, not having dated anyone lately.

"Where do your parents live?"

"Not in the Twin Cities," she replied.

"The painters might not be done until six. They had another apartment before yours today."

After taking views of Gail's house, Maureen folded up her tripod, said goodbye, and began walking away.

"Where are you going?" Gail demanded.

"It's so nice out, I thought I'd take a walk along the lake."

Past King's Road were older homes with crumbling flower vases, bricked walks, and perennials that encircled lawns like charm bracelets. Wishing for a neglected mansion as her next real estate assignment, Maureen headed for Lake Harriet.

The Shakespeare in the Park players were on the lawn. They were doing *Twelfth Night* and finally, as promised, Maureen could photograph her coffee shop actress when she felt lively. She played the part of a meddling maid. Then Maureen basked with other spectators until a Shakespearean cloud appeared overhead. The actors begged people to return for the last act as the rain made its entrance, flourishing a few swords.

Rather than sit in the coffee shop until dinnertime, Maureen told her actor friends that photographers got rained on all the time. But she ran past the Pan fountain and the fairy candles, hurried through the rock garden, and, on the other side of a turn gate, took shelter in the bird sanctuary. The foliage there was thick, especially near an elderly tree that was scrolled like a mantel.

Birds shrieked in pinwheels of vine that made pergolas between the diamond willow and the maples. Maureen prowled a trail, having accepted that she wouldn't feel at home within blank, bright walls. A cedar waxwing settled on a low branch while the rain tapped above. Hearing voices, Maureen turned back on the trail and then she took another, probably what lead to the lake paths and people who might be walking in circles again. The cloudburst had passed.

Coming to a clearing, she felt blinded by a basin of sudden sunlight. It was prairie grass, tall gold-green spires, cattails, teasel, a metropolis of grass that seemed to go on and on. She felt she had stepped into a photograph but this was the optical illusion of a park planner. Previously, she'd taken the trails through the bird sanctuary.

She could photograph the prairie here as if there were no neighborhoods or skyscrapers for miles. Wading, she was soon thigh deep in the thatching stems. She sank into the grass, noticing butterflies cruising. A ladybug made its helicopter ascent. Wildflowers were deposited like gems – gentian and lupine.

She turned with her camera and saw in her viewfinder a man strolling the edges of the grass. Holding her breath, she encapsulated her panic in the cavity of her lungs. What seemed sinister and dark was only a pair of slick running pants on a tall person with a pair of binoculars hanging on his V-neck T-shirt. Ever since Maureen began snowshoeing up to empty farmhouses, she had prepared herself for a man appearing from behind a barn and also for the confrontation, churlish and probably insinuating.

While the man walked, Maureen readied her telephoto lens. He was walking towards her, looking beyond her, when she snapped his picture. She veered in another direction and focused on more prairie grass. When she turned, he was backtracking on the trail.

Alone again, Maureen grasped the straps of her tripod bag and emerged from the grass. When she reached the misshapen, elegant old tree near the entrance of the bird sanctuary, the man was standing nearby, his binoculars raised. He pointed them at her, hearing the stir of her steps, and then he lowered them.

"It flew off," he said. One of his eyebrows tufted.

"Sorry."

Maureen maneuvered her tripod case, going through the turn gate. On the other side of it, she examined the man. He wasn't sinister but he looked like a strong runner.

He approached the turn gate. "I'm waiting for my photographer friend. Guess I got in the way."

"Maybe the bird flew in your friend's direction."

"That's the idea. Sorry if I intruded on you." The tufted eyebrow was quizzical. Though he didn't look much over thirty, he was probably a professional who lived near the lake and ran around it.

"Anytime in this park," Maureen replied with sarcasm. Such men went around without wedding rings though they were married, amusing themselves with insinuations.

Maureen loped along the rock garden, noticing the shooting star flowers, and then she saw that the sky had turned golden. Its filter was alchemy, unbefitting above a lake where roller skaters chugged along. She sat on a bench, considering the sky and expecting to see someone from the university or her freelance work. Usually, she ran into someone here. While taking light measurements, she noticed that the man from the bird sanctuary was seated at the next bench.

"Sorry to be in your way," he said.

Then Maureen heard someone call, "Eugene! Hey, look who he's found. There's Maureen!"

Vic was coming down the slope with a woman Maureen recognized from his photographs. Her tied-back hair made a natural bouffant.

"Nose like a telephoto lens. That's Eugene," Vic introduced him.

"You're back in town," Maureen greeted Vic. She hadn't seen him often outside the darkroom. He and his friends were in jeans, what made Maureen instantly aware of what she wore to Gail's session. Her crepe slacks and India cotton blouse weren't anything for the Thursday darkroom. "My new landlord roped me into taking real estate pictures today."

"Have you met Eugene? This is Carrie," Vic said. "We need another head shot of Eugene."

"Are you a writer?" Maureen recalled more than one article by Eugene Cameron in the Chicago magazine that hired Vic.

Eugene jumped from his bench and extended a hand, large enough to encircle Maureen's wrist. "She might already have a picture of me in her camera," he said.

"You *would* walk right into a picture. What? The trees or the lake behind you?"

"What's it for?" Maureen inquired.

"The magazine."

Eugene was an easy subject and his hair, backlit, had a tint of auburn. He had good teeth or a good dentist, an asset that nettled Maureen. Women walking on the path admired him instead of the two with their cameras. That gave Maureen a sudden feeling of wistfulness.

"You might like her shots better. Oh, c'mon Carrie."

"No, I've had enough," Carrie protested. "It's time we got something to eat."

They drove to William's Pub, taking routes along Lake Calhoun and Lake of the Isles for Eugene's benefit. Settled with a pitcher of beer, Vic told Maureen of Eugene's promotion as the Minneapolis editor of the magazine. They asked about Maureen's real estate pictures and she told them about Gail and the filth on her walls. Vic laughed and said, "Eugene is going to make my old apartment into an office."

"That's downtown, isn't it?" Maureen said.

"It's nearly downtown," Carrie affirmed.

Vic hesitated and then he said, "There's a darkroom position open in Eugene's office. It reports to me."

Carrie found something amusing about that but Eugene turned, considering Maureen. "There's some photography with the job," he said. "It's only part-time. But we need consistency with freelancers. I've got to interview." He was sitting beside her and peered with eye contact. "What are you doing besides real estate right now?"

His eyes were a murky green. Maureen concentrated on the eyebrow tuft, telling about the suburban newspaper where she developed photographs for the reporters.

"Vic calls you the darkroom midwife," he said, and then he took a bite of his cheese and bacon burger.

Maureen nodded. She concentrated on her Reuben sandwich. Her editor at the newspaper office was a wide-eyed, sardonic woman. Usually she greeted her with "The reporters are restless."

Then Eugene said, "We liked the photos of yours that Vic showed us. And the way you toned Vic's harbor water so that it looked like tomorrow's pollution."

"Good. I'm glad," Maureen said and then she took a slurp of beer. *This is it*, flashed through her mind. A raccoon stood with its hands on a farmhouse railing. Clouds hunched like a god. A great blue heron spread its wings. But then, disbelief followed.

"I was planning to call you," Eugene said.

They always seem to care at first. Admiring men now, Maureen was in the habit of stanching enthusiasm. Eugene might be Vic's age, three years younger than her. And what she immediately admired about Eugene was the build she preferred, tall with prominent shoulders.

Roland Werff was strong and clean-smelling but his German shoulders sloped and his legs were like tree trunks. Hank was broad and hairy, ironically boyish. She had admired Indians for their builds and knew it was easier to think these thoughts than to follow Vic's discussion about the book *Future Shock*. She hadn't read the book, what had inspired *The Midwest Forecast* editor in Chicago.

Eugene accepted her smile as an answer about *Future Shock*, probably knowing that she would get the book tomorrow. When he explained why he often interviewed subjects without bringing a camera, she could simmer into the conversation.

"Do you send a photographer over after the interview?"

"They usually arrive about the time I'm leaving," he said. "Vic's likely to have car trouble."

"Or I eat my lunch in the car," Vic said.

Maureen was uneasy at fate arranging things. The man sitting beside her was apparently used to things working out this way, or his way. And he had a side that she involuntarily disliked, a stubborn blandness, what was in his eyes under the tuft.

"I needed that food. Not the smell of paint," Maureen said. "I should check on my birdie."

"She really has a birdie," Vic said.

Eugene lit a cigarette and said, "But she hides in the bush. At least your duplex already has a darkroom, Vic. I'm trying to see its future."

"Eugene's misunderstood, you know," Vic said. "He's generated so many letters to the editor that he's taken responsibility."

They know you can't say no, Maureen thought. She was staying for another pitcher of beer and wasn't protesting, afraid she would cheep.

28   Static Electricity

December 1986. Disappointed yet satisfied, Eugene often said, "If it's all the same to you, I'm going to lock the door for the day." Maureen learned to time the darkroom to that minute.

Here it was her second year with *The Midwest Forecast,* and Maureen was afraid he would never say that to her again. Perched on her high stool, she waited for him to conclude the worst day she'd had at the magazine.

Paragraphs were being retracted. Her mistake, driving to a vacant farmhouse, might be expected. Eugene knew she photographed abandoned farmhouses when he hired her. But the prints in the darkroom were a discovery. Although the cages in an unused barn were fuzzy as the snow tonight, Eugene thought they were laying egg cages.

Worried, Maureen shuffled through the seven magazine issues she had worked on.

The day of her interview for the Photography Assistant job, she came with her camera. Eugene wanted her to take a picture of a new condominium under construction down the street from his office. It appeared in the November issue. Tonight, young professionals and yuppies, the new downtown dwellers, would go home to the condominium. Vic's old duplex was shabby enough for the magazine to rent. The article on urban renewal confirmed its presence in Minneapolis.

That day, the duplex was empty except for the bedroom. On a massive desk there, a new computer loomed, looking as out-of-place as an iceberg. Vic had taken his air conditioner with him. At the desk, Eugene perspired as he explained the part-time position that would entail darkroom, layout, and some photography. Vic's darkroom was near the kitchen. The magazine would open up further space with the removal of a decrepit stove. Once a layout table and files were brought in, the photography assistant would work there. Maureen could easily imagine the living room as a reception area.

The humidity was so cloying that Eugene suggested they discuss the job over lunch. Then he removed his tie and, because he wanted her to take a picture, she undid her vest buttons. She could tell that Eugene preferred her.

"You know where it is," he said. "The restaurant where I might take interview subjects."

Turning towards Nicollet Mall with Eugene's voice lurching above her ear, she felt fine. He was disarmingly direct, wondering why she hadn't absconded from the darkroom the way her classmates had. Did she really prefer the latest tricks there to fieldwork?

The darkroom was her forte, she replied, glimpsing their reflections in store glass. They might be mistaken for summer visitors. The top button of Eugene's shirt was open and he was wearing track shoes. Maureen had pulled her hair back with combs. She wore foam-heeled sandals with her swaying skirt.

"So what's the name of the restaurant?" he said, producing a pack of cigarettes and pausing at Orchestra Hall. Musicians were playing on the patio. "They're going to tear it all up. This mall."

Puzzled at the brick parquet being replaced, Maureen mentioned a mall-side restaurant where Schilling employees went for celebrations. Le Jardin offered both French and Italian dishes and it had a second story view. Or they could walk the other way to Esteban's if he liked Mexican food.

"I've been there and to the Arab place too, Abdul's," he said.

At Le Jardin, Eugene good-naturedly insisted on a table near the wide windows. The hostess sat them at a clutter of dishes.

"It's a challenge, finding photographs of tomorrow," he said. "Somehow, the reasons behind the mall renovation should be apparent."

"What are the reasons?"

His eyes, without the glasses he wore at his desk, were a mixture of green and hazel. But then, looking past Maureen, they became bland, as if he didn't see anything. "I don't know," he said.

The aim of *The Midwest Forecast* was to reduce future shock. Its articles prepared the public for long-range changes while they were in the planning stages.

"Non-smokers have the five-star view," he said, turning towards a labyrinth of dividers that separated them from smokers. "I wonder if we could have dessert and cigarettes at a different table? Can you see us repairing to the smoking room?" Eugene hunched over his trout almandine.

"Not exactly," Maureen said.

"Your eyesight is probably better than mine."

Maureen liked his grin but it subsided almost instantly. He had to inquire, "What do you see yourself doing in ten years?" She smirked at the question all the employers were asking, already having another bite of quiche on her fork.

"You don't want to say," Eugene said. "But you could. In ten years, you might order the lobster salad if you wanted. Whatever the shock value."

"I hope so."

"Right now, you'll want to look for the thing that won't be here tomorrow."

Considering she had a talent for that, Maureen said, "This restaurant probably won't be here in five years. Restaurants come and go in Minneapolis."

The eyebrow that didn't smooth out reflected Maureen's perplexity. "The difficulty is to see tomorrow. You can change the color of water in a photo. Could you add more particles to the air in one?"

"Sure."

"What do you usually do? A double exposure in your camera or a montage in the darkroom? For example, a forest extending into its future deforestation."

"It depends on whether the second scene is the next shot."

"I never got that far with photography. Making sandwiches of negatives."

"I never met a writer who wanted to learn those things," Maureen said.

His smile was wary and his hair was still cobbled from the humidity. In her apartment, she had studied her photographs of Eugene, satisfied to find that he wasn't really handsome. What she found attractive was a wry expression, the hollowing of his cheek, what made him look somewhat abject. He was immediately handsome to her because of his build. Not wanting to bring up their backgrounds, Maureen imagined that he was from a Chicago suburb.

"Next time, let's drive over to Mama D's. She came up here from Chicago," he said.

The following week, Maureen sat on the other side of Eugene's desk, going through the classifieds. She found a lawyer's office sale where they obtained furniture for the reception area - a midnight blue couch and chairs, a coffee table, and a desk. Eugene knew where to get second-hand horizontal files and the light table for the layout room. Then Maureen's friend Brianna came by with a hooked rug that had a Northern lights motif.

Early the next week, applications poured in for the Administrative Assistant position. Maureen sat in on the final interviews with candidates who could proofread, handle advertising, and manage the reception area. One of the applicants had taken the darkroom class she assisted, Linnie.

The next time Maureen came in to work, Linnie was there. Her stealth and seal-like movements soon demarcated Eugene's office from Maureen's area as if one was land and the other, water. Having been tempted, Maureen became submerged in choosing equipment for the darkroom. If she kept track of her own supplies, she could use the darkroom for her own projects. Bring her bird in, fill up the counter fridge.

Just as she was basking in her new position and developing prints from her first photo shoot, the fall deadlines began. A man had never given her what she wanted before and now she was committed to pleasing Eugene.

"I guess it's what Vic said," he commented when he examined one of her prints.

In it, a man fed grass into an apparatus. On a garage door was a chart with a chemical conversion and the word *FUEL* under it. The other garage door opened to a view of a car passing on the road.

As promised, they celebrated their first *Midwest Forecast* issue at Mama D's restaurant.

Eugene asked, "What did the inventor tell you about the large scale feasibility of producing gasoline from switchgrass?"

"I don't remember exactly. I was concentrating on the demonstration."

"I typed it up," Linnie said, her nose tipping. "But I couldn't quote it."

"In order to take photographs, you need to understand where the article is going," Eugene reminded Maureen. "I thought you might remember the chemistry. It doesn't hurt to have two of us hear it."

The wine and dinner brought on less intense conversation. Maureen talked about Jacques Cousteau, one of the few nonfiction authors she had read thoroughly. "I don't know if he still believes this," she said. "Some years ago, he speculated about human beings evolving gills. He thought they might."

"Seriously," Eugene jeered.

"Most of his inventions worked out."

"Did he estimate the millennium that the gills might be developed?"

"Sounds like Atlantis," Linnie said.

After the fennel fragrant lasagna, they admired Mama D's celebrity photographs. People embraced each other in her restaurant.

By December, Eugene's nice lunches were with other people. When advertisers, insistent women writers, and freelance photographers loitered in the reception room, his voluble side emerged. He could appear gullible, stooping at a wall.

In Maureen's area, he often acted as if it were all a letdown and as if Maureen and Linnie were part of an office limbo. He wracked his shoulders over page layouts before they were sent to Chicago. It was a kind of chess game, his moving a block of copy and then changing the position of the photo that Maureen placed on the page.

One afternoon as they pondered a page, Linnie came in and said,

"The medical resident called. He has time for the hospital photos."

Eugene strode out and returned with a handful of pens. "Your Christmas present. It's all we can afford. Take notes for the photo captions. Ask him about cataracts growing back after laser surgery."

He hooked one pen onto the strap of her camera bag, a *Midwest Forecast* pen with his name on it. Maureen was now part of his cost cutting, being less expensive than a freelance photographer.

By Christmas, Eugene had established an office with austere boundaries. He limited his conversation to work issues. Yet he used the bathroom for shaving and kept a toothbrush there. Because Maureen had to scrub the bathtub after she mixed chemicals in it, she also kept the bathroom presentable for visitors. Sometimes Eugene left a ring of mouthwash at the sink drain and one day, when she mentioned that, he informed her that the magazine couldn't afford a custodian. He was learning computer maintenance.

Even Linnie couldn't find out what Eugene did with his holidays.

Mornings, Maureen sat on the couch in the reception room and opened the mail with Linnie. They sorted out apocalyptic predictions from announcements of household inventions. On cold days, Brianna's rug produced static electricity but what startled Maureen more was Eugene's ill-humor at that. He swiped his mail, ignored Linnie's laughter when Maureen jumped back from a spark, and then his office door slammed.

"Sometimes he doesn't answer when I knock," Linnie complained.

"I've been slipping notes under his door. He acts like Eeyore the donkey if he opens it," Maureen sighed.

After that, Maureen and Linnie warned each another if Eugene was having one of his Eeyore days. Whatever menaced his moods could be attributed to his journalist's cynicism, they hoped. Linnie became less squeamish about showing Eugene antagonistic letters to the editor. And though Eugene reminded them that their magazine was not one about weekends, Linnie dated one of the men who visited the reception room, an MBA with an article about flex hours and job sharing.

When Eugene was at the public library one late afternoon, Aggie from Schilling Publishing visited. Schilling was planning a wildflower identification book for children and Aggie had a list of plants in case Maureen wanted to submit photographs.

"I've got photos of trillium and coralroot," Maureen said. "This spring, I could work on this, weekends. What's the deadline?"

"The book is slated for next year. You have the summer."

"Perfect."

Then Maureen saw Eugene standing at the door. Instead of his usual five o'clock message, he went over to the coffee counter and said with visible irritation, "You left a bottle of developer over here again, Maureen."

Used to editors, Aggie began getting her coat on. But she was exulting at Eugene's being single, attractive, and irksome, what she could report to Maureen's old co-workers. And he answered their introduction by handing Aggie her purse.

After she left, he went to the refrigerator, got out a beer, and complained, "There's film, Vaseline, and distilled water in this little fridge. Is your darkroom refrigerator full?"

"New supplies came in," Maureen said.

"Do you listen to Dr. Mort Blaisdell on the radio?"

"No, not often." Maureen went to the kitchen fridge and began removing her supplies.

"Our article might look like a follow-up of his last program. He's already planning to have laser surgery. His mother had cataracts."

Eugene was sitting on her high stool, drooping into his Eeyore mood.

"Dr. Mort can't show pictures of laser surgery on the radio. Maybe it will stir interest."

"Is it all the same at Schilling?" Eugene inquired.

"I haven't been over there lately," she replied.

Drinking his beer, he watched her as she stacked her supplies in the darkroom fridge. She had to walk around the stool until he said, "If it's all the same to you, I'll lock up."

With her coat on and her car keys out at the horizontal file, she felt her hair floating. Yet she flinched from a shock of static electricity. This made Eugene smirk when he could make interview subjects comfortable.

"Goodnight, Eugene," she said, not having thought of a better phrase.

On another darkening afternoon, Eugene sat on the stool with a beer again. "I've been reading *The Book of the Dead*."

He had demanded to know her philosophy about photography one day. She quoted one of her MFA papers, the ancient Egyptian ideas about the body, shadow, heart, and shining soul, and how they caused her to look at people differently.

"The book's a soporific," Eugene said. "The Book of the Slumberer. Did you know that astral projection is based on the Egyptian Ka-soul?"

"No. Has anyone ever photographed astral projection?"

"Levitation has been photographed. I guess people believe the photos the way the ancient Egyptians believed the three-headed snakes in that book."

Then he mentioned a region in the Egyptian underworld where a god with a butcher knife reigned. Continually, the dead slaughtered animals there. The newly deceased, if they weren't warned, could be trapped by the food of that region and made to slaughter meat instead of progressing toward heaven.

"It made me wonder why there wasn't a similar situation with brewers in the underworld. The Egyptians invented beer," Eugene said.

"I was more interested in the Elysian Fields. And the part about turning into a heron," Maureen said. "Are you learning hieroglyphics?"

He leaned over her table and sketched a picture of an owl.

She was ready for his questions about Wanatin and turkeys. But then he assigned her the photographs for an article about future cemeteries. She was to feel grateful, driving to a family catacomb where cloisonné urns were ensconced between pots of lilies and sprawling jade.

By spring, the days stretched with equilibrium even if the magazine thought in the future. Maureen laughed in her apartment about her strained relationship with Eugene.

"Picture quality looks almost the same as Vic's. The new freelancer is good." Eugene brightened for a moment.

Away from the magazine, Maureen felt glamorous. She took lavish baths, looked at other magazines, cooked dinners from recipes in them, and planned short trips to state parks and Northern Minnesota. Sometimes she went out with men who happened into the office, usually to see a print, but then she went back to it the way she came there. She didn't ask Eugene about the trips he took. The magazine existed on surmises.

Weekdays that spring were warm and auspiciously sunny when most Fridays, the rain began. After drenching herself near woodland blooms, Maureen expected the Saturday rain. At the end of May, she spent Saturdays at the office, developing prints.

Lately, she'd been sleeping better than she ever had, what may have caused the feeling of equilibrium. Eugene was like static electricity to her and she was probably in love with him. At any rate, she was contented, coming out of the darkroom to the dimness of the rain and the luminous radio. Then she heard a tearing sound, not lightening but paper. Something like a thunderclap sounded, a file drawer slamming or the wastebasket being kicked.

She heard him in his Eeyore mood, loathing his load. "Where's the ego pimp? Not in the pending, Linnie! And the closet hussy."

The second epithet might be about her, Maureen thought. Smelling smoke, she realized that she liked the falseness between them. She went to the door and saw Eugene standing over a wastebasket with some papers. Usually, he never smoked in the reception room.

"The fallacies of this most feeling fella," he said.

Maureen returned to her projects, doubting that there could be any romance between her and Eugene. He was probably reminding her of that. She often dreaded his arrival in the morning, his expectation of coffee, the swarthy supervision, and the door slam after he got his messages. It was the man in the mirror, her clairvoyance.

"What are you working on? Wildflowers?" He was being patronizing while he took a beer from the refrigerator.

"I was at a park in Duluth. It's vetch."

"And cascading water behind it." Eugene shrugged at the print and took his beer to the other room. She heard something heavy fall and the waste basket teetering.

"Want to see the last of this fella?" He was at the door again.

Stalling, Maureen thought how Eugene would never do this during a workday. He was holding a lighter to the photograph of a man who wrote a manual on living and loving.

"There's usually another side to a face like that," Maureen said, following him to the reception room to see if he was really going to burn the photo.

The side-burned avuncular man brought materials to the office that he used at a condominium for single parents. Their rent was defrayed with community projects - landscaping, plumbing, child care, and interior upkeep. The tenants attended his workshops and therapy groups.

"We're not here to expose guys who start fires," Eugene said. "I checked out a few of the women who returned to a normal neighborhood. I hope it's not *the tip* of the iceberg." He tossed the photograph and a thick file into the wastebasket.

"Are you going to leave that wastebasket for Monday morning?"

"Linnie's got some letters to send. I'll dump it if you scrub the bathtub. I might be having a few girls over tonight."

Maureen retreated from his gamesy grin. When she heard the files moving at a reckless speed, she wondered if Eugene had been drinking before he came in. He was probably having a rejection fest, judging by the envelopes stacked on Linnie's desk.

A song Maureen liked, "Dog and Butterfly", came on the radio. She turned up the volume. The song went with her weekend photography, its words absurd and breezy.

Dog and butterfly.... in the air they like to fly.

"Do you like that song or that volume?" Eugene yelled while the female dog found it couldn't fly.

She roll back down to the warm soft ground laughing to the sky.

Maureen returned to the darkroom as the song told of a woman who couldn't be transported. She hung up her prints and prepared to leave. But at the door, Eugene's frame blocked her exit.

"If I brought women here at night, they'd turn up in the daytime."

"Maybe they have."

Eugene leaned towards her as if he were going to grab her. But her camera eyes could dare and all this time, he had hardly touched her. Smugly, he stepped backwards as if he were proud of his discipline.

"What are you afraid is going to happen?" he said.

"Fire. A four-letter word."

"What else?"

"I don't know. I haven't been afraid lately."

"I suppose not. Photographing wildflowers."

A few hours ago, she might have credited him for her newfound confidence but she was taken for granted.

"You're afraid of something all the time. What? You're not really afraid of men."

Maureen considered the irrational fears she had when she couldn't sleep. Lately, she'd fallen asleep thinking about Eugene and how he was afraid his articles wouldn't sell the magazine.

"Crowds scare me if I don't have my camera with me," Maureen replied. "Too much life scares me. And then it scares me that I stop life in action."

"I think life should be analyzed," Eugene said, offering her a beer. "Why does it scare you?"

"Because it goes on and on. It's like insomnia. When I was a kid, I used to have insomnia from movies."

His riled eyebrow probably worked in interviews. He looked as if he were trying to understand her. "What movies?"

"*The Time Machine.* And even a comedy like *It's a Mad, Mad, Mad Mad World* horrified me."

"Did you ever want to do film?"

"No. I think it fascinated me. But it goes on and on."

"Those movies weren't produced for children. But what did you want to stop in action?"

"I don't know. People being ravenous, I guess."

"That's like saying the sky is falling. Movie makers purposely try to scare people."

Maureen didn't know why they were talking about movies. Eugene was sitting on her stool, lighting a cigarette, and he didn't really understand her.

"Perhaps artists are afraid of life," she said. But that sounded feeble.

Feeling her beer, she went on, "Did you know I grew up in a town that slaughters turkeys? The whistle blew in the morning, the way it did in *The Time Machine*, and then the animals were slaughtered. My father said he took the job because he was sure my mother would hate that town. Then he could return to graduate school."

"Not a good plan."

"Anyway, photographs told the truth. Movies were like my worst nightmare."

"Tell me about it," Eugene said.

"My worst nightmare?" She didn't want to tell him about the black box because he wouldn't think she was the only one with the answer. "How about the second worst? It might make you laugh."

"I'd like to laugh."

"In the nightmare, a lawnmower went out of control and took off by itself. It was chasing me near a grassy pond and it was so dangerous, no one could get near it. It was going and on and on."

"Did you lead it to the pond?"

"I woke up," Maureen said.

Eugene smiled so that his eyebrow tuft seemed suggestive. But then he went to his stack of files and hardly looked at Maureen when she went out the door.

29 The Eggs Came First

Hunched over the September issue, Maureen admired her photograph of a grebe. It rushed across a lake as if it had to keep up with the fashion of grebes. If Maureen could fathom what the naturalist feared, then she could turn a trip into an assignment. She hadn't feared for her job then and now, she wondered why she didn't see this day coming.

Eugene was snatching the magazine from the counter. Then he furled it and pointed it at her. "Why did you take so long to show me those frames? And why didn't you tell me what you did after you left Grevis's farmhouse? Print the frames again with more contrast. This is a tray for eggs! A laying hen cage, *not* a range shelter."

Maureen stared at the fuzzy picture, what she took from outside a barn window, standing on crates.

At the fall office party, one of the writers admired her abandoned farm prints. A matted photo of cats in a farmhouse kitchen was on the wall near the fridge. On the darkroom door, fruit bats were hanging in a barn. That farm was near the town where Maureen's mother lived. A corporate farmer acquired land nearby for a poultry operation. Eugene thought this could constitute an article but when he called, Farmer Grevis said he wouldn't consider an interview until after harvest.

Once the snow came, Grevis insisted that the photographer visit with Eugene. There were already stacks of photographs, routinely taken, at the farm.

Maureen drove there in her car and parked near the rose-red main barn. New additions stretched behind it, garages and stables. Farmer Grevis was in his forties, sturdy with the vigor of an athlete, his face almost orange from a fading tan. He wore jeans, flannel, and a flung-on jacket. Having grown up near a western Minneapolis suburb, his business interests first took him to California. Nat, his farm manager, came back to Minnesota with him. They showed the main barn and the prize animals in it first.

A dozen pigs with starch-white ears.

"You're going to have to do better than my favorite photos of this clan," Farmer Grevis said, allowing the pigs to jostle as Nat readied their feed.

After they admired the sow and prize cows, they went out to a pick-up truck. Farmer Grevis seated Maureen in the front seat between him and

Eugene while Nat sat on a bale of hay under the topper. They drove to a large aluminum building on the other side of a field. Inside, the view was whiter than the snow outside and flurried with throngs of leghorn chickens.

"You'll want to focus on the feeders," Farmer Grevis said to Maureen. "What you're seeing is a small town of chickens, about three thousand."

Because Maureen's immediate response was to put her camera between herself the confusion, Eugene led her over to the feeders. She heard how the windowless hen house had the most sophisticated of ventilation systems. The chickens seemed to revolve at the circular feeding station, waves of them making a shrill chaos around her footsteps. Dust from the feed bleared Maureen's lens. She held her breath because of the acrid odor. "I thought the chickens would be sectioned," she gasped to Eugene.

He glared at her comment and waited for Farmer Grevis' reply.

"They can go all over town this way," he said. "Each chicken has three-and-a-half square feet. That's better than most coops. Birds on the seashore crowd more than this."

They had to stand together, Eugene writing and Maureen leaning over to snap a chicken pecking at Nat's shoes. He involuntarily kicked it away and said, "Birds at the seashore can crowd worse than this."

Eugene crouched with Maureen and said, "Grevis is going to choose the photos so you might as well follow the farmer."

She was following chickens while Farmer Grevis maintained, "State of the art." At the roosts, Nat found egg after egg. The word "art" and the sight of the eggs didn't abate Maureen's feeling of seasickness. The whitecaps of chickens rose and fell as she readied her camera. In this place, Farmer Grevis' face looked as orange as a fox's.

"Broody!"

A hen intent on hatching her eggs squirmed as Nat picked her up. The broody hens were the only ones shut into the wire cages.

"That's one of our range shelters," Farmer Grevis said. "We set them outside in the summer. If we don't put the broodies into a cage, they'll go back to their eggs. And they don't eat as they should."

Behind the large shelter cages were a pair of low doors. Nat unlocked one and then they went out into the vast silence of the snow.

Farmer Grevis explained, "This is the acreage that we'll seed with clover and a special blend of grasses. The pullets do best in the yard. Older hens get attached to the feeders. The temperature inside is more dependable than the sun so they like it there. Are you ready to see the broilers? They're another drive from here, housed about the same way."

This time, Maureen and Eugene sat on bales of hay under the truck's topper.

"That looked like rush hour, not a small town," Maureen said.

"Don't comment, Maureen. Ask questions."

The broiler house was an overwhelming sight, chickens at a continual feast, toppling about in slower waves.

"We're still experimenting with our feed recipes," Farmer Grevis said. "These get the best. This one here will be in the supermarket within hours." He carried the rotund and "finished" broiler to a scale in another room. "My wife has some goodies and eggnog. And of course, we have our own rotisserie."

The Grevis's newly built farmhouse, white with brick trimmings, was behind a brick wall and a windbreak of poplar. Karen Grevis asked Maureen and Eugene if they would like eggnog. When Eugene inquired about egg collecting, she asked him if she could take his ski jacket. Then she wondered if Maureen would like to see the farmhouse kitchen. Eugene lowered an eyelid, reminding Maureen to ask Karen more about her role at the farm. Her bleached jean apron protected cashmere.

After the hen house odors, the smothering smells of baking only made Maureen queasy. She put her camera to her nose and focused on a crockery bowl that contained a dozen cracked eggs.

"Did you collect those eggs, Mrs. Grevis?" she asked.

"You can call me Karen. I had to get the business office ready for our little party today. The eggs are collected in shifts, of course."

"How do you tell how much a hen is laying?" Maureen asked.

"Of course it has to do with the hen's age."

"How do you tell that?"

"It's odd but a little like women. When they're laying a lot, their feathers are dull. Just a minute. I need to find Nat's wife for these trays."

Maureen prepared for a shot of Karen with the rotisserie behind her. Then Nat's wife came in and said, "Hens that aren't laying much molt their feathers. Their feathers are much shinier than the hens that are laying."

"June. Maureen," Karen introduced them.

Karen was the shinier of the two, her tinted hair gleaming like the egg white that she was beating. When she turned off the mixer, she said, "Sometimes when the hens are removed, they find broken eggs inside of them."

This information, what seemed to affect Karen, coincided with a sharp urgency in Maureen's abdomen. The thought of broken eggs, their yellow yolks bobbing inside one of the chickens in the crowd she saw, made her feel as unbalanced as an egg. She snapped Karen opening the rotisserie and asked, "Is there a bathroom nearby?"

"Down this hall," June replied. "It's near the back door."

When Maureen saw that the toilet cover was the yellow of egg yolks, she began to get sick. Reeling from towels that had edgings like rooster combs, she turned on the faucet water, opened the toilet seat, and threw up.

Rinsing her mouth, she thought about what was under the wire flooring in the hen house. Her face had gone pale.

She wandered to the back door and cracked it open. An aggregation of boots was on a yellow linoleum floor - cowboy boots, hiking boots, and orange tie-up boots like the ones Farmer Grevis was wearing. *Grevis Farms* hats hung at the wall near photographs of horses. Admiring the horses, Maureen examined a photograph with a jockey. Then she saw Karen Grevis with the platter of roast chicken, ready to lead her to the other refreshments.

"You have a stable, don't you?" Maureen asked.

"Our horses are for personal use. We have children too but they're at school today. We'll show you their pictures."

"Do you have a racehorse?"

"That horse is a friend's. We stabled Squire's Tail - pun intended. He ran at Canterbury Downs. Were you there? That man Eugene watched him race."

"No, I wasn't at Canterbury Downs."

"It's not far from the old Grevis house."

"There must be dozens of photographers that attend the races."

As they entered the business office, Eugene said in Maureen's behalf, "Maureen can do wonders with fluorescent lighting."

Farmer Grevis was pulling print-outs from one of the county's first farm computers. He looked eerie in the fluorescence because a fire was burning at the other end of the room. There, a few farm workers were gathered near a table where Karen carved the chicken and June set the pitcher of eggnog near cole slaw and a pear pie.

Seated near the filing cabinet, Eugene asked, "What is the percentage of chickens that have been de-beaked because of cannibalism?"

Maureen's stomach groaned.

"More often, it's done for prevention," Farmer Grevis answered. "We think prevention here. Pecking and cannibalism happen on small farms too. It doesn't matter about the size of a farm. Small farmers overcrowd these days."

"You are preventing what?" Eugene persisted.

"Chickens that crowd anyway. Aggressive chickens."

"Three-and-a-half square feet a chicken is better than standard. Are you going to standard?"

When Eugene looked up from his notebook, Farmer Grevis was studying a print-out for the benefit of Maureen's camera.

"Our next shipment is broilers," Nat answered. "Replacements."

"Three-and-a-half feet and no cages?"

Farmer Grevis nodded. Maureen backtracked to rouse the farm workers from their plates and coax them into conversation.

"I suppose you want one of Mrs. Grevis and me," said Farmer Grevis, behind her. "Look, she's got the scrapbooks out. We'll have an eggnog near the fireplace."

The Grevis scrapbook was probably a send-off. And the Grevis's had a package of photographs for Maureen besides a carton of eggs tied up with yellow ribbon. While Eugene munched a chicken thigh, Maureen said, "Are there any more pictures? I think I have a touch of flu. And I told my mother I would drive to her house afterwards."

Eugene announced that Maureen had trouble starting her car last week. Because the temperature outside was slipping below zero, Farmer Grevis gestured to his mechanic, a man who would escort Maureen to her car.

Maureen verified the directions to her mother's town but once on the road, she saw the vacant farmhouse where she photographed cats in the kitchen. She was surprised that it was still standing and that its drive was plowed. The kitchen window had been replaced. There were no vehicles. She supposed that it was now a Grevis farm.

Wondering what happened to the cats, Maureen walked to the barn. Its doors were still scabby but there were locks on them. On one side of the barn was a high window, what Maureen might reach from the crates that she carried in her trunk and back seat. Even when she stacked them, the smaller on the larger, she could only look into the window by raising her arms and taking pictures.

The interview photographs and Farmer Grevis' photographs went back and forth in the following weeks. Maureen puzzled over the pictures she took at the barn window. The negatives revealed a network of chicken wire inside. She assumed the pictures were of range shelters like the one in the hen house. One day, she printed one of the negatives and Eugene erupted.

"It used to be the abandoned farm with the cats."

"Yeah. And you know who owns that barn now."

He'd had her develop all the pictures. Leaning over them, he said, "Maureen, there isn't any wood in these pictures. See? This is a tray for eggs."

"I thought they were range shelters."

"Maureen, shut up." Eugene stared her off and then he put a magnifier over a print. "You don't know the difference between a laying hen cage and a range shelter!"

His undecided eyebrow had never been so out-of-sorts. He demanded the negatives for the prints and then he said, "Farmer Grevis is not happy about the changes in the copy. When I couldn't tell him why I cut his quote about cages, he accused us of snooping. He thinks we're trying to make his farm look wrong. I had to say that I couldn't be certain about its future."

"But he's not being exposed."

"You weren't hired for investigative journalism. I can't believe you did this and didn't show me the negatives." Eugene's voice had taken on its Eeyore timbre, defeated. "What I cut out, the omission, will expose him to some readers. That fellow is more certain about the horse races than he is about his poultry plans. He'll be wanting his horse to win the cup, that's all."

"Farmers were never very rich in this region," Maureen said from the darkroom. She cringed over her negative carrier.

"Crop this rotisserie pic to 3-1/2" x 4". Then bring me the Xerox. I have to send the revision in overnight mail. I suppose you don't know the cost of that."

Maureen locked the door before she cleaned up. She could barely see Eugene's car crawling under the blizzard that was beginning. Besides her darkroom being out of its routine, there were burnt pizza rolls near the microwave, dirty cups, and a crunched beer can on the kitchen counter. The radio announcer said that cars were moving at snowshoe speed on the freeway.

Maureen tried to cheer herself, wishing she had a photograph of Eugene when he was angry. The asymmetry of his face seemed to have cracked it. She was exhausted from his ferocity and knew that this altercation with a man was unlike others. She couldn't leave here on her own.

Tomorrow, the downtown would probably be deserted except for the poor and the pioneering yuppies in their downtown apartments. The blizzard looked like thousands of leghorn chickens falling from the sky.

Eugene had sacked out on the reception room couch before. A beer, pizza rolls, a tangerine, and some trail mix were soon on the coffee table. When the telephone rang and she heard his voice on the answering machine, she picked up the receiver.

"What are you still doing down there?" he demanded.

"I had to clean up." She didn't dare tell him that she decided not to fight the traffic. Tomorrow, she would photograph downtown Minneapolis after a blizzard.

"I was trying to leave a message for Linnie on the answering machine."

"I'll hang up and you can call again and leave it."

"You need to hear this twice. If Farmer Grevis calls, have Linnie tell him that I'm on my way in. Only that. *Do not* pick up the phone, Maureen." Eugene exhaled either smoke or exasperation. "I don't like to say that I was unprepared. You said that you felt like the flu and that you were driving to your mother's. You *did not* do what you said you were going to do."

She sniffed the way her mother used to sniff, never crying out loud.

"You can crawl, kneel, climb on your crates. But I didn't think you were a run-of-the-mill chaser. And your snoop work with Mrs. Grevis. I already knew they were keeping a racehorse."

"I really didn't feel well after that poultry building."

"You're trying to get something out of me every time I look at you."

Even on the telephone, she saw his shoulders before his face. And now he was doing his Eeyore again. "This assignment should have brought out your best. If you would only prepare yourself better. Read what I give you. I didn't use a freelancer because I wanted Grevis to trust our magazine. You're drinking my beer, aren't you?"

"But what if you printed his quotes about cages and someone else found out?"

"Then they might write a letter to the editor. At this magazine, I have to do what I say I'm going to do. I can only be stupid if I'm ignorant!" Eugene hung up.

She didn't have to acknowledge Eugene when he came in next. She could see him the way he saw her drinking his beer. He'd found out about a few of her horrors but not the thing she was always afraid of - a relapse into inertia, the feeling of being stuck in old photographs.

Eugene never said that he was afraid of change but he must be. He could find someone better than her but he was probably suspicious of a superwoman. A few years ago, she couldn't have guessed that the shattering inside her and its insistent pain, like a broken egg, would heal and that this job would happen.

30   Walls Away

The year of 1987. It wasn't difficult for Maureen to focus on the day's foreground, her chores. She kept her eyes from Eugene after she noticed what he was wearing, a jacket and tie or a vest with jeans. He didn't have appointments if he wore a dark T-shirt.

One day, he threw on a shirt over his black T-shirt, mentioning an outing with a woman reviewer who had offered him freebie theater tickets. Before he left, he checked on Maureen's afternoon work. She was surmounting her skill level, worried now that things wouldn't work out. She loved her work even if she was confounded at Eugene's being her boss. He must be younger than her.

Secretly, she despised her dependence on him, having to ask him about gas money, about special supplies for photographic techniques, about the dental insurance that she needed more than medical insurance. People dropped in after he lunched at the Star and Tribune cafeteria. She had to be amiable though she winced at the semblance of domesticity, the beer and banter after the office door was locked.

Eugene was almost two years younger than her, she found out when Vic visited. He and Carrie reminisced in the converted duplex, the place where they made love and ate together. Near the darkroom, they swatted each other as punch lines. Maureen and Eugene hadn't any rejoinder. There was only a list of Maureen's expenditures for Vic to approve.

Maureen knew that Vic was supposed to have a talk with her. Eugene sent them off to the Spaghetti Emporium, Carrie's favorite restaurant.

Vic was brusque, wanting to get his talk over before the food came. "Writers can be self-righteous. I've heard Eugene say some awful things because he feels he's right. Sometimes he doesn't see the picture that's right in front of his eyes."

"I thought he might want to know about the abandoned farm," Maureen said.

"He lets his photographers go on their own and then he comes down hard," Carrie said.

Vic replied, "He puts work into the articles and expects cooperation, not contradiction. It's a lesson in reality, Maureen. I suppose he reminds you of how much it costs to call me in Chicago."

Maureen surveyed the baby buggy and the Boston ferns dangling above them. They talked of Calder and mobiles. It wasn't a place for a conference. Then Vic started in about Farmer Grevis, peering as if he had just walked into the restaurant.

"You took some good pictures in that hen warehouse but the guy would only allow partial views and close-ups published."

Maureen said, "He coddles some animals as prizes while he treats others as if they don't feel anything. I wanted to see what was in that barn. He wouldn't show us his horse stables, you know. I still don't understand what was wrong with Eugene knowing about the cages. Well, I thought Grevis was a fox. Eugene knows he's mainly after profits."

"If you had told him at once about those pictures you took. Maybe you don't understand Eugene's attitude about the magazine. If he could publish Grevis's quote about not caging the chickens, then Grevis might wind up doing what he said. Eugene's knowing about the cages suddenly made him part of Grevis's lie."

"Maybe he has moods because of disillusionment. I wanted to see if cats were still living in the farmhouse. And then I wondered why the barn was locked up."

Because the antipasto was between them, Vic said what he had to say. "Maureen, you don't have the background in journalism. Just do as you're assigned. Doing freelance on Grevis property wasn't part of that day. Eugene knows how to investigate. You have to report to him."

Maureen nodded. But then she was curious. "What newspaper did Eugene work for?" She hadn't found any dossier in the office. Eugene only talked of the present and the future.

"Which newspapers," Vic corrected her.

"Eugene has a lot of experience," Carrie said. "He's been a science reporter for the Chicago Tribune."

Afraid that hearing more would be too much with her spaghetti, Maureen wondered, "Does he like being in Minneapolis?"

"He needed a break. He was getting Orwellian in Chicago. Government actions on scientific advances, that sort of thing. And then, his book is coming out this summer."

"It is?" Maureen feigned to have heard about his book.

"You bet. My photographs are in it."

"They're going to be a surprise, I guess," Maureen said.

"I suppose Eugene didn't tell you much about it. He researched Chicago families from documentation - what they expected, what became of them, that sort of thing. Sections on neighborhoods and how they changed."

Stymied, Maureen asked, "Who's publishing it?", and started in on her spaghetti.

"The magazine publisher. Eugene had personal reasons for leaving

Chicago, of course. He'd been there since graduate school. If he wanted to approach Farmer Grevis by jumping over fences, he could do that. He was a pole vaulter in high school."

"He used to joke about the streets where only runners dare tread," Carrie said.

"Be careful about burn-out, Maureen," Vic warned. "Eugene's already talking about moving his office to Milwaukee or Kalamazoo. I hear you're doing some wildflower pictures for a book."

Not that Maureen ever knew much about Vic outside the darkroom. She accepted another level of contentment, considering herself lucky to get experience with the magazine. Her dependence on Eugene turned tepid, a routine that periodically broke into irritation or frank flirtation, nothing to take seriously. The bustling of the office satisfied her and while it continued, she readied herself for the day that it couldn't go on. She had moments when she despised Eugene, his dreary offhandedness, his measured welcome to men much older than him. Seldom did she hear exuberance about an appointment.

"Call her back, Linnie," he said at nine o'clock one morning. "I have an hour. Here, I'll talk to her. Yes, Beth! How about 11:30? Of course, bring the curriculum."

Usually he was loath to schedule anyone on a Monday and that morning, he planned to go over a page layout that Maureen was working on. Twenty minutes before Beth's appointment, Maureen made for his office. But when she entered the reception room, Beth had just come in the door.

Maureen was baffled, seeing herself as the subject of a photo and disliking Beth at once. Beth's hair was a shade blonder and her figure less pronounced by a degree. She hung a trench coat on the coat rack while Maureen admired her fashion suit, a short waist-length jacket with a seersucker skirt.

Eugene greeted Beth as if he'd never seen anyone like her before. Fascinated, Maureen watched him unburden her of a curriculum package and steer her to his office. Usually, he would be reading the top page as he walked with his appointment.

A few minutes later, Linnie came into the kitchen to get coffee for the meeting.

"I'm going to lunch. The page is in the top drawer of the horizontal file," Maureen said.

Linnie's seal-shrug was naughty today.

"Isn't it about company day care? I didn't think he was very interested," Maureen said.

"She tests out educational computer programs that her company is planning to distribute." Linnie concentrated on balancing the beverages.

Leaving for lunch, Maureen could hear Eugene thanking Linnie for the coffee. He sounded as if he had just found Eeyore's lost tail. "You think a company day care program might be extended to a privatized company school?"

Beth's voice sounded confidential.

Maureen went to a new lunch café where she could order a baked potato with toppings and a plastic glass of wine. She recalled photographs Vic took of her, wondering if Eugene had seen them before they met. Because Eugene brushed near attractive women every week, she couldn't have guessed his taste. Neither could Linnie. Linnie usually discovered women callers to be writers and, less frequently, photographers or lawyers he knew from Chicago. Maureen had even wondered if Eugene was gay which made Linnie laugh like a seal.

After her lunch, Maureen wandered among people eating on terraces. It was spring and the sound of musicians wavered like the sunlight. She reached for her camera, carried everywhere in its tomboyish bag. On her flat walking shoes, she found Eugene and Beth at the layout table, discussing lunch. The page Maureen worked on was at the checkmate stage – *this* photograph should be across from *that* ad. But Eugene had made another exception, allowing a visitor to see a page before it was printed.

"Where did you go for lunch, Maureen?" he asked.

Introduced, Maureen could study Beth's face while learning about the company day care program. Beth's excitement was subtle; a photographer would have to wait for her preening lips and her quick smile. Maureen couldn't help but curdle, not feeling as pretty.

Looking from Maureen to Beth, Eugene's conversation was uneasy. "We'll probably have Maureen come out for a photo session. She photographed day care over at the university." He was hunched against the wall, sipping the last of his coffee. Beth didn't turn to Maureen. She was smug with new knowledge, that she would follow Eugene out to lunch.

The day after Maureen visited Beth's suburban corporate office, Eugene demanded, "Exactly what sort of fiasco happened out there?"

"The fiasco? I guess it's in the frames you're looking at."

Having arrived there before seven in the morning, Maureen photographed employees bringing their children to the day care rooms.

Perhaps the fiasco was at the play stations where the children were impatient to be promoted. Two little girls took their geographic dolls to an aquarium where a boy said he could take them on voyages in a plastic boat. Instead of photographing that, Maureen focused on an outcast at a computer.

Beth said in her ear, "Wait until he's off the computer games. He's the president's son. The other computer has an educational program on it."

When the executives came in, some of the children asked for cameras. One of the mothers had an instamatic and soon, Maureen went everywhere with a satellite photographer. She photographed a few children pushing buttons at vending machines and sent her satellite to the playground picnic tables. Soon there was a crowd of children at the vending machines, wanting their photos taken.

The educational computers were behind cubicles that, while Maureen worked, were being scaled by the younger children. Children standing on chairs peeped over them.

"Beth's coming to look at the prints," Eugene said. "I hope you know which frame is the fiasco."

Eugene's siding with someone who could make a fiasco of the office disillusioned Maureen. She hadn't kept track of his irregular meetings with Beth. "I think it's hard for Beth and her assistants to manage those kids when their parents are management," she observed.

"Maybe we'll make an assignment change here," Eugene said. "You should drive to Milwaukee and see another kind of experimental school."

"I'd like that."

For once, Maureen would stay overnight at a motel and eat out with the writer. On the drive there, she envisioned Eugene's future with Beth. Beth was an instant answer for his Eeyore complex, probably mixed up with his love for his computer. Coming from a company that handled computer programs, Beth had a kind of dowry, a veritable source of funding for their small publisher. There was already talk of her company advertising.

Maureen might go on with Eugene the way people like Inez and Donald Dibbet went on over at Schilling Publishing. It was odd to imagine Eugene with a woman physically like her. Maybe he'd like her style of play, the permissions he would need and regressive games like "Button, button, who's got the button?" Maureen supposed that Beth was chilly as giggling but she would probably love Eugene's long strong legs and his pouting comebacks. Still, Maureen couldn't see Beth putting up with tantrums or being oppressed. If she could tell Eugene what to do, he might one day find himself writing computer manuals and not knowing why. Then he would send an article to the magazine on the east coast where Maureen had gotten work.

A few weeks later, Carl from the Co-op came looking for Maureen at the magazine office. She offered him a mug of herbal tea and scheduled a tentative appointment for him with Eugene.

Eugene stormed after it. "You showed Carl the picture of the cages!"

Eugene arrived a half-hour late for his appointment with Carl and Maureen couldn't keep her temper. "I wanted his opinion and you were late. Does the magazine own that picture? Carl will keep it confidential."

Eugene stooped over her, reminding her of his position. They both knew that another confrontation was coming. "I'm not sure that Carl is the man for the proposed article. He's not the only person being considered for the organic side of the subject. You shouldn't have led him on about his writing."

For the first time in weeks, Maureen laughed in Eugene's presence.

"Carl's a confident guy but he's full of technical language and doesn't know how to write for the lay person. And he's capable of cloddish attacks."

"I thought you edited people like that."

"Don't talk to Carl about *his* article. Talk to him about *the* article."

Maureen desperately held onto a string in Eugene's wind. The kites were in the darkroom.

By summer, it didn't matter if Eugene was in the office or not. Maureen went into the darkroom on Saturdays, readying prints for the Schilling wildflower book. They wanted her wild gentian, wild columbine, and lady slipper orchid.

Just as had happened a year ago, she emerged from the darkroom to hear Eugene yanking file drawers and kicking them. But when Maureen saw files tossed on her counter, she quietly slipped back to her enlarger.

"Fifteen minutes!" she yelled after a knock shook her door.

Next she heard a yell, "Fifteen minutes or did you lose track of your timer?"

This knock was at the level of her ears. She could see Eugene's hand cramped the way it was at his keyboard, hitting the fruit bats on the darkroom door.

"You made me spill," she said in greeting.

Her file drawers were open. Photographs fanned the layout table.

"I thought you added to the historical files," he said. "There's not much here."

In the last year, the magazine ran a column called "Harbingers and Humbug." Blurbs from old publications were featured – inventions, speculations, and laughable predictions that never came to pass.

"I sent you to the Historical Society and what do we have here? Green gooseberries increase bile. Blinders help children to learn. It's an advertisement. Is that all?"

"Nobody grows gooseberries anymore." Maureen acted as if she had blinders on.

"And this stuff blocking the work files!"

On the layout table were her prints of grebes, wildflowers, the terminal corner grocery, and a clock shop.

"I'll take them home," Maureen said, righting the picture of the clock shop.

"I need more than this to send to Chicago. I don't like to admit how good that column is for sales. But I suppose you haven't read the sales report lately."

Putting her own photographs in her satchel, Maureen refrained from blaming the last issue. A freelancer took a picture of Beth for the cover. *The Midwest Forecast* resembled other magazines that month instead of having a wily researcher or a wind power generator on its cover.

"You're not supposed to be caught unprepared in this office."

Maureen sensed Eugene standing stubbornly near her, sizing her up as if she were a hurdle. "Today is Saturday," she reminded him.

"I don't want to be another look book."

Maureen didn't dare to laugh, not while he was heading for the refrigerator and a beer. He was wearing stretchy shorts under his T-shirt. She was afraid that if he wasn't firing her and decided to touch her, she would be enslaved, even on Saturdays.

"The people out there. They shouldn't look from photograph to photograph. That's how they're unprepared. You need to read more."

If Maureen gave him a glassy stare, Eugene might admit that he wanted to replace her. But then he said in his Eeyore weariness, "You're not prepared for the fact that no one's fighting you. It's only direction, Maureen. You borrow trouble."

"I thought that's what you do."

Eugene put his hands at his temples like blinders. Then he grabbed his beer and strode to the doorway. "When you've figured out what your little war is about, maybe you can declare it."

She was afraid that if she heard about Beth again, the little war would be declared. But she laughed when she returned to her apartment, what she often did after tension with Eugene. She knew it was from sadness and the suspicion that if they had dated, they might not have known each other for so long. They'd become the picture on the wall to each other, there for visual pleasure and for musing upon. It had little to do with whether they liked each other.

When Maureen left that Saturday, Eugene handed her a file. "Let me know if you like reading this," he said.

It was a piece of futurist fiction. The writer imagined a time when applications were required for pregnancy. A woman had become illegally pregnant. If she were discovered, her child would be aborted or adopted by the state. The pregnant woman's first months with her husband were extraordinary because he was a refugee from the frontier of the expanding ocean. Because of that, he was low on the applications list. It was too risky to have the child aborted because the state paid abortionists well. The couple would probably be turned in and sterilized.

The government regimented swarms of people and encouraged them to think like fish. Children from application parents were added to a school rather than a family. Marked and ostracized people lived underground like crustaceans while the government soared shark-like, having complete control of aircraft. What were once mountain ranges had become archipelagos. Boat people moved from one outpost to another, living off of fish and seaweed.

The couple searched for two marked people and obtained new identities. Because the marked people were allowed to subsist at the ocean frontier, they began to live like boat people. In the end, they floated in their boat like the child in the womb.

Monday morning, Maureen perused old magazines at the historical society. When she came into the office, Linnie said, "Eugene's gone to Chicago for a few days."

Two files jutted from Maureen's in-box, one for her "Harbingers and Humbug", the other for the futurist story. On the second file, a Post-It note asked Maureen to type her reaction to the story and to fill out a form inside the folder.

"Do you think he means type?" Maureen asked Linnie, not having a typewriter in her office.

"He means type," Linnie said. "He said he was going to see if we'd like reading the fiction that came in. I think he's paying by the story. Peanuts."

In Eugene's office, Maureen sat at his typewriter on a straight-backed chair. Facing the wall, she attempted to type her reaction. But she felt self-conscious with Eugene's desk and computer behind her. Writing with a pen, she said she would have read the story to its end whether she was being paid or not. But what intrigued her was the old flood story. Wasn't it that? She liked the futurist descriptions but the woman seemed so weighed down by her fate that she didn't seem as strong a character as the refugee husband. Perhaps it was because of her totalitarian upbringing. She liked the ending but people might want to believe that the flood would recede.

In the folder was a form with a list of adjectives that she could circle if they expressed her response to the story - *compelling, confusing, contrived, crazy, depressing, disturbing, fanatic, ominous, predictable*. Then there was space for her to type.

At the bottom was another yellow Post-It note: *Maureen, read the*

CENTENNIAL folder in my computer. EC

    Linnie had Eugene's computer going. Maureen had learned the basics for the office at Linnie's computer where she typed cut lines and letters to people she'd photographed. Sitting in Eugene's bucket-like chair, she read the folder titles, none of which were mysterious. The chair was too low for her and made her aware of being surrounded by Eugene's handwriting on his blotter paper. That prompted her to look in the folder concerning Beth's day care article. There wasn't anything unusual except for Eugene's enthusiastic correspondence.

    A few years ago, Maureen left a relationship to concentrate on her camera. Today the computer made her feel small. Her work, from Eugene's viewpoint, might be as limited as a laundress's, a matter of colors and starching. A White Sox magnet on Eugene's computer annoyed her. And so did Eugene's pens with his last name Cameron on them, a name that made her ear jump to attention because it sounded like *camera.*

    In the CENTENNIAL folder was a series of letters between Eugene and the mayor of a small town, New Glasgow. She read them, letters from teachers and retirees, and then letters about plans for a centennial book. It was to be commissioned by the town and published by their magazine publisher. The town no longer had a newspaper but they could hire freelance writers and photographers to document their centennial and the town's history.

    One of the early settlers, arrived with a few cows, chopped into an elm tree and was greeted by bees. Honey was still a product in the area but its manufacture had declined along with the population.

    In the CENTENNIAL folder was a MAUREEN file. This contained another note from Eugene.

    Maureen, I'm hiring a few other writers and photographers for this project. Besides the book, there will be an article about the future of towns like New Glasgow. I'd like to get some photos in other small towns on the way there. Can you agree to drive with me? EC

    It was just another project but Maureen doubted that she and Eugene would return the way they left. Separated from him by two walls all these months and having resorted to cowardly notes, Maureen would have to make herself agreeable on the trip.

    Linnie gazed at them when they discussed it. Maureen felt something go slack inside her when she and Eugene made plans over the layout table. She avoided thinking about that, buying new clothes and underwear, having her teeth cleaned, and choosing food for a snack hamper.

    At the hour when farmers began their work, Maureen piled her equipment in Eugene's Ford Escort. She felt as if she were going out for an evening. The lambent horizon ahead, she fell back into the enigma of letting a man drive with his intentions. They escaped the city, passing stores that carried their magazine. When daylight delved in at the windshield, Maureen could see Eugene clearly and although that wasn't startling or wrong, they both put on sunglasses.

31   Field Work

"What are those fields?" Maureen said, letting a sigh escape. Eugene often started the day with the question "What's in the cup?" rather than asking for coffee.

"Soy."

He probably wondered how often Maureen photographed a view without knowing what was in it. "Oh, yeah," she said. "I used to wonder why there were so many soy fields."

"For feeding the pigs."

"The same soy that's in soy sauce." Breaking the tension, she offered Eugene a piece of banana bread to eat with the coffee they'd picked up at a gas station. After that, she learned that she would be staying with the Wicks in New Glasgow. Eugene must have matched her name with a host in the way he wrote headlines.

"Do you know anything about them?"

He sneered. As if he wouldn't know anything about them. "He's the town dentist and a hobby photographer. He's afraid that the town won't find a dentist to replace him."

"The dentist." Maureen gritted her teeth.

"I have to stay with the mayor."

"My bedroom, growing up, was a dentist's drilling room before we moved in. He had his office at the front of the house."

Eugene seemed puzzled, his sunglasses peering at her. Then he said, "There was something I wanted to ask you about." He waited for her to nod. "How would you feel about moving the office to another city?"

"I've been in Minneapolis a long time."

"You're at home there?"

"No. I never was. I'd like trying another place. New photographs and all."

"Good."

Elated, Maureen put her hand on the radio knob, waiting to see if he would mind. His hand stopped hers, a finger sliding onto her nail hardener. "We'll listen to the country stations later. There are some tapes on the back floor."

She set his summer jacket swaying in its cleaner's wrapper.

Examining the tapes, one after another, she looked at Eugene for approval. But all she saw was that they were now driving through cornfields. That only made Eugene pessimistic because the crops had failed last year. "They should have seen it coming," he said as he often did. "Play something without words."

She found Dave Brubeck, sitar music, Nixon in China, and then some space music that she put in the tape deck because she didn't know what it was.

"What's tart in the bread?" Eugene wondered.

"Bits of apricot," Maureen said, happy that he'd never eaten the *Joy of Cooking* banana bread recipe before. Nostalgic, she admired the corn under an avalanche of sunshine. It was enough that Eugene understood why she liked a landscape and why she held onto a camera instead of someone's hand. He had probably gone on road trips with dozens of people.

"I like to empty my mind of words," he said. "Then it's easier to use them for the thing itself. Does the darkroom cause you to see better?"

"I think so, now that you mention it. Sometimes I see images when I close my eyes. It might be from image overload."

"With all this corn around us, you should notice how the next town is shrinking. I like to ask at a drugstore if they carry *The Midwest Forecast.*"

It was Wednesday, a workday. Parked at a town café, Eugene buttoned on a shirt with purple and gray stripes over his charcoal T-shirt. Maureen was wearing a wrap-around skirt over jean shorts for her camera work.

They drank orange juice and ate eggs under a fan that dangled the latest softball victory. While Eugene read the local newspaper, Maureen looked at his map. Four towns on their route were marked because their population signs had changed from four digits to three in the last ten years.

"New Glasgow, for example, lost its honey contract with a cereal company because their bees are unreliable. Roads and public buildings are the giveaway in these towns. It doesn't look as if this town has built anything since 1930."

They hiked near crumbling curbs and visited the dime store because the drugstore had closed. Boys followed and when they found out that Maureen was photographing the town, they ran off. Then someone yelled through a megaphone, rounding up tournament players and a county fair princess. Eugene found the town's first welfare office in the building that used to be the drugstore.

Maureen wanted to photograph the nearest water tower. Eugene obtained directions for that and for a football stadium where livestock were waiting to be auctioned. Rebuilt woodstoves were being sold there.

At the town edge, they met an old woman whose calico dress seemed to have grown back on her like the gladiolus in her garden. She directed

Eugene to a church that was seventy-five years old and in need of repair. In her neighbor's yard, young women in bikinis were listening to Crosby, Stills, Nash and Young. Their children played in a footed bathtub set on the lawn.

Often, they were recognized as city people. The threat of afternoon torpor and the abandoned buildings brought on conversations about the folks who left and why. Farmers griped. Maureen was thrilled to see an old Pegasus station. Climbing a tree, she left Eugene holding her wraparound skirt. It had been too hot for slacks, she complained, even if he wore long jeans. She often layered her clothing when she went on her camera trips.

In a town where a bottling plant sprouted more bars than the other towns tolerated, Eugene wanted a beer. He left Maureen in a booth and straddled a bar stool, joining spectators of a pinball game. While the player treated the pinball machine like a car in a rut, Maureen heard the words *shift* and *Missus* between the ringing of the bumpers. When Maureen got up, she was leered at for not being Eugene's Missus.

She and Eugene played a game of partner pool, what the locals were confident of winning because of the pinball noise. But when Eugene and Maureen dunked their balls, it was only of passing interest that Maureen could figure out camera angles. The locals began arguing about the year of *their* town's centennial.

"Some people make me feel like a Jehovah's Witness," Eugene said, ignoring Maureen's offer to drive. He insisted that he talked more than he drank. But he was talked out and, reaching into the backseat, fished out a wide paperback book.

"It's your book!"

"The proof of it. It won't be out for a few months."

The cover was plain but inside, Maureen had to admire Vic's photographs.

"I wrote it after doing too many articles on genetics, test tube babies, DNA predilection to disease, and other controversies. The newspaper didn't want this as a series. It's a scientific look at family histories. My research started at a genealogy center's data base." Eugene was hunched over the car wheel, his forehead glossy. "Never call me Gene."

A whole book of Eugene's writing mystified Maureen. He'd interspersed stories about family expectations with statistics about neighborhoods, schools, factories, *The Jungle's* packing house district, and business districts. The analyses became predictions about the slums, the suburbs, and the economics. Eugene's words were carefully chosen but fluent, vaulting occasionally, a different person than he was in conversation.

Maureen doubted that he shared her elation at their becoming friends. She absorbed the text near an old photograph of a Victorian house and Vic's current photograph. "I wonder if this is happening in Minneapolis. People buying a few rooms of a house for what the entire house cost at first."

"Houses or housing were the most concrete expectation that people had. The chronicles concerning marriages and children in this country show why genetics is an imperfect science or why it should be. We're continually getting article ideas about the future of marriage. Would you like to work with that?"

Maureen shrugged and kept turning the pages of the book. Men often toyed with her on the subject, probably because she had no sound ideas about it and another woman would have a lot to say.

"What sort of picture would you find for the future of marriage?" Eugene wondered.

"I don't know. There are as many types of marriages today as there are people." Exasperated, Maureen reminded herself that she could be paid for her answers. "I'd look for weddings where traditions were blended from different backgrounds or where the wedding made a new family because of children in previous marriages."

"I wonder if weddings would outwardly express the future of marriage? What about people who are already married? Which would signify the future?"

It was nearing seven o'clock but Eugene's tone was still at its interviewing level. Bonnie Tyler came on the radio with "Total Eclipse of the Heart" and while she lamented, Maureen could pause the conversation.

"Let's see. I'd find people whose clothing revealed their lifestyle. The clothing and hairstyles of couples might not match, the way they used to."

"A woman lawyer married to a florist?"

Maureen mused, "Maybe spouses would be better groomed because of the divorce rate."

"That sounds like the Fifties. Do you think they dressed like that because of affairs?"

"Did they? I think people might express their feelings more for the camera in the future. And then, people living alone might be the future of some marriages."

She had earned Eugene's scoff. The sun was sinking towards the flat horizon so that a cloud near a silo was apricot at the edges.

"And some might live with the same sex," Eugene said. "So you think married people will look sexier in the future?"

"I'm not a Rodin with the camera."

His scoff was less sure. "What made a woman like you wait it out?"

"I didn't wait it out. I didn't happen upon that relationship, I guess."

"There's more to it than that, other women might think. I meant a woman *like* you."

This reminded Maureen of Beth. And that Eugene was a man she had to please all that day. She just stared at him, noticing how his sideburn was reddish in the evening sun and how the nuisance of his beard made him seem vulnerable.

"It's hard to see ahead if you do things through serendipity," he said. "In our time, we were taught to marry that way instead of through arranged meetings. There it is." He was grinning at a billboard advertising the Rainbow Falls Supper Club. On it, a building flowed into a river of silvery dancing. "That means we're about an hour from New Glasgow. It's recommended for a good steak. I'd rather say I've eaten to the mayor and get some sleep. Steak sound good?"

They'd been snacking all day on their own pocket money. "I could eat something," Maureen replied. Beyond the billboard, the clouds in the distance were splendid as the Taj Mahal after her day of water towers. Houses near the roadside seemed lonesome.

The supper club had a curving exterior, probably 1940's. Inside, Maureen freshened up on a powder room chair and then she wandered along velvety wallpaper, a bold French empire pattern from the 1970's. At a table under the glittery champagne shades of a light fixture, Eugene studied the county newspaper. He was sitting as far as possible from the dance floor.

"Come for a bite to eat?" understated the waitress. She might have been in a beauty salon while Maureen was hustling after Eugene in the teeming sun.

The other diners were middle-aged, the women in stardust acrylic and the men in summer jackets. While Maureen and Eugene concentrated on bread sticks and glasses of wine, younger people arrived. Tables were re-arranged while greetings muffled the music that precipitated from the ceiling.

Eugene was evidently famished for his steak. "They make ice cream here," he said.

The music brightened and the glittery lights dimmed except at the dance floor. Then a sprinkling of applause sounded. A couple sashayed to a Four Seasons tune with the awkwardness of exercise. The woman's skirt was pleated like an accordion, which drew attention from her husband's portliness.

"I guess our generation won't be going dancing in the future," Eugene said. "They go to concerts."

"We didn't learn steps." Maureen sliced her corn on the cob while Eugene buttered his lips, biting in.

"I wonder about the custom-styled vows at weddings. Whether couples keep them."

Maureen was just going to tell Eugene how her teeth were capped and that she hadn't bitten into corn on the cob since childhood. But she answered, "Women aren't obeying husbands the way their mothers did. I never understood how the world began with words. Like in *Genesis*."

"It's the idea that words have power however people change," Eugene said.

"Maybe those couples rewrite their vows."

"Rewriting is often a good thing."

Maureen watched the older man on the floor pointing his index fingers at a younger couple. A percussionist had appeared with a trap set and he was adding brush strokes and cymbal to the piped music. The young woman's halter dress swayed to the lyric "Wouldn't you like to fly in my beautiful balloon?"

Maureen giggled.

"Basic as high school," Eugene said. "It's a Wednesday night. What would your camera see here? People working out vows? Permanent felicity? An obligation to express vows like remembering birthdays?"

Maureen pushed her plate of T-bone, a chunk untouched, towards Eugene. She wasn't big on steak. She remembered how Linnie announced her birthday when Eugene's must have passed by. "What my camera sees might not be as positive as what other cameras see," she said. The portly couple reminded her of her father and Poppy. She started on a cigarette and then, snapping her lighter, said, "Why ask me?"

Eugene fell back to his plate, satisfied. "You must have strong ideas about marriage."

"I can't think of any right now. I'm not one to interview on the subject."

"But you suggested that the words other women require aren't as meaningful to you. Even if God wasn't really quoted in *Genesis*, scientific law suggests that there's commitment in the cosmos."

Confused, Maureen turned toward the waitress as she approached. Eugene quickly ordered two plates of strawberry shortcake with ice cream. Then he cut the leftover chunk of T-bone and began eating it.

"Sorry if you're sensitive. There are going to be dozens of family reunions in New Glasgow."

"I like being on the outside," Maureen retaliated. "If a scene is positive to other people, the camera will capture that. I enjoy assignments that aren't for proving a point. But how should I look at a beekeeper? If he lives near a future ghost town?"

"It depends on whether he has ghost hives. Some of the beekeepers aren't doing well."

Soon Eugene was delving into shortcake while Maureen appreciated it more than the previous fare. Then he lit up a cigarette, crossed a leg over the other, and watched the dance floor. After the waitress came with the bill and he had paid with a credit card, he led Maureen towards the dance floor where they stood for a moment.

"Traveling through?" said a man at a table.

"We're on our way to New Glasgow," Eugene said. "For the Centennial."

"Are you from there? We're going to the festivities."

"We're hired to work for it. She's the photographer."

Maureen already had her camera out, ready to obtain permission for a few shots. But Eugene grasped her arm and sauntered with her to the dance floor. "Let's not work anymore today," he murmured. Then he was bending over Maureen in a slow dance while Neil Sadaka sang, "Once a story's told, it can't help grow old..." They shambled between the couples and for once, Eugene's shoulder was an armrest. His hand crept along her back but the other hand was playing at the knot of her wraparound skirt. As they rounded the floor, he closed the space between them and set his lips at her neck until they had reached a path to the exit. Gasping, Maureen released her breasts from him.

"Homegrown strawberries," Eugene said in the parking lot where crickets choked off the music.

"I'd like to drive," Maureen said, feeling forced into a farce.

She went to the driver's side. Eugene relinquished his keys and then they drove through the county seat where on Main Street, teenagers hung from the windows of honking cars.

"Homegrown excitement," Eugene said. "I'd better review the itinerary."

Maureen rubbed an eye and when Eugene peered at her with a tubular flashlight, she explained, "My allergies."

"Are they very bad?"

"I've got something for my eyes."

He bent over papers as they swung onto a gray highway. "What's checked on the itinerary is a must for you. You can assign the other events to the freelancer or do them if you have time. He was hired for the bee stuff, you know. Vic will initial whatever he wants to cover when he comes for the heavy day."

"How much should we join in? I've danced with my camera before but it wasn't my best work."

"Sometimes that makes people comfortable. Soon, I hear, I'll be able to take my computer around with me."

"How?"

"They're going to make them portable. Smaller and with batteries besides cords."

That reminded Maureen of Beth. "You'd think they could make computers smaller for children. At Beth's day care, their hands were too small for the keyboard."

"Beth."

Eugene said her name reminiscently and as if he had forgotten that her face was on magazine covers in the back of his car. "She's already prepared a pre-nuptial agreement."

Maureen had just attained her usual atmosphere with this man, Eugene at his papers and the moon like a safe light.

"Skunk!" Eugene's head was at the window. "Ifs and thens. Beth's pre-nuptial agreement is mostly about children, of course." A skunk spraying must grin the way Eugene did. "It's preposterous to write such an agreement without discussing it first with the other party. She wrote it into a graduate paper, I guess."

"Maybe that's the most honest way." Maureen rubbed her eye again and Eugene watched her.

"Her agreement crashed, of course. Do you need something from your bag?"

"A cigarette." Maureen couldn't ask about Beth's fiancé.

"After Beth showed the agreement to her fiancé, a computer programmer, it was twice as long and full of options," Eugene said, reaching into Maureen's purse.

Maureen tried to recall a man at Beth's company who lit her up as much as Eugene did. "Beth is marrying someone from her company?"

"From the company that created the educational computer programs."

"Smoking helps allergies," Maureen mentioned.

"Smoke keeps bees off," Eugene replied, handing her a lit cigarette. "There are risks to any assignment. What do you think about pre-nuptial agreements?"

"I never thought about it."

"I forgot. You don't put much stock in words. You would take a picture as an exhibit."

He was just a silhouette in Maureen's landscape at the moment, his inquisitiveness probably selfish. He mused, "Still, the picture would refer to a previous agreement."

"Maybe you should be checking out your own case." She'd retorted and regretted that she hadn't inquired the way Eugene was doing.

"That's the problem women don't anticipate," he said. "Men think in terms of licenses, not promises. I don't find so many men wanting to re-invent marriage."

Maureen smoked, too disgusted to answer that.

Eugene kept musing, "As Beth interpreted, marriage has much to do with having a family. But oddly, there aren't licenses for children. Only certificates. Yet men license their dogs so that they don't spend a night on the street. I wonder if licensing children will happen, as that futurist story posed." He shifted a leg as if his was on the accelerator.

"But the licenses in it were to *have* children."

"These days, a woman like you could have a child without marrying. I don't see where marrying first would change the situation if a woman ends up bringing up a child alone."

"Why do you say, *a woman like me?*" Maureen had to laugh. At work, this conversation could constitute harassment. But Eugene often used hypothetical situations instead of trapping a person he interviewed.

"OK, a single woman," he said.

"A woman photographer isn't a person to have a child on her own. Not unless she does darkroom work all the time. In the past, a woman could become a widow with young children. Why ask me? You're just interested in the subject because you see yourself having children. Most men do."

"I've been reading article proposals. You have to admit, if we could do something dynamic with the subject, people would pick up our magazine."

Eugene began telling her about the courtship habits of Indians in the Midwest. A Catholic priest documented how the men visited women in their tipis at night and were either accepted or rejected. If they returned to the same tipi night after night, they were considered married. "It's as if the land itself had something to do with mating," he said. "That's how college kids go about things today. Did you know that they haven't found a legal document about marriage in ancient Egyptian papyri? Yet marriage was an important institution there. So is this a case of the future repeating the past?"

"I suppose they were considered married if they had a child."

"They gave gifts when a couple began living together," Eugene replied. "But they could divorce and women could file for divorce. What if marriage has become so confusing that society will dispense with it? We're just minutes from New Glasgow. I'll drive the rest of the way. Do you have the New Glasgow map memorized?"

Maureen readied herself for meeting the town dentist. But she was realizing that she hadn't thought about having a child since she tried to do away with herself.

32   Rural Remedy

New Glasgow's main street shone like a sliver of amber under a city of stars. A few people appeared from behind yellow shades, the mayor with the key to a defunct office where Eugene would work, the dentist with deft hands for Maureen's equipment and luggage.

Reunions flared at the end of gravel driveways. The houses were shaggy, some with crowds of moonlit sunflowers in the yards. The dentist's white house was polished by comparison. Inside, a renovation of paneling exhibited Dr. Wicks' photographs - bees soaring from the queen's command, geese small as bees in the sunset. Decoupage photographs were "Mom's hobby."

Sitting at their Duncan Phyfe table, Maureen rubbed her eyes and apologized for her allergies instead of her tiredness.

"Hay fever?" Dr. Wicks said, his manner still wily in its welcome. Otherwise, he was sedate with only one yellowing strand of hair out of place.

"Every year."

Mrs. Wicks set glasses of iced tea on the table. "Do you eat honey every day?"

"No." Maureen realized that she hadn't bought honey as regularly as it was on the breakfast table in Wanatin.

"Local honey helps some people with allergies. A few tablespoons every day," Mrs. Wicks said.

Their daughter, an x-ray technologist, was celebrating her first pregnancy with friends that night. She had come for the Centennial.

After Maureen tried a slab of raw honey, she went upstairs with Mrs. Wicks to her room. Cream-painted furniture and mauve papered walls framed a front window. Maureen took a quick bath, watched fireworks, and, though the rockets waned like cars in the city, she fell asleep. Dreaming that she had smeared honey on her camera lens while riding a Chicago El, she woke to find Eugene's book beside her. Lena, the Wicks' daughter, was in the hallway, talking about driving Maureen in the morning.

After breakfast, Maureen and Lena went to the town's old newspaper office where Eugene was already working at a portable typewriter. They walked to a family reunion. The great-grandmother complained that the young people in town used to marry each other; the grandfather conceded that working in the honey refinery wasn't for everyone; the middle-aged parents explained their reasons for moving away; and the children asked why they couldn't stay all summer.

Mid-morning, Maureen met the freelancers at a café. Eugene went off with Andy, the photographer whose portfolio crawled with hymenoptera. Maureen accompanied Danni, a feature writer, to a house where an old woman of 102 years lived with her 84-year-old daughter. The house was a centenarian too, built with small high windows and filled with memories. Maureen admired a kerosene lamp that was corded for electrical current and a cathedral radio that still played one awful station, "not the one with the sermon." Old photographs functioned as flashcards while Danni toiled with recollections of the worst winter, World War I, and the first grandchild.

Then they drove in Danni's car to the farmhouse of the ancient woman's fourth grandchild. Bee-friendly clover, squash, and apple trees formed an oasis between acres of barley. "The farmers used to make agreements with the beekeepers," was the general complaint.

Near an old schoolhouse, a sidewalk ended in a pasture and a set of concrete steps led to a barbed wire fence instead of a front door. Their farmer host showed them inside the school. Desks still had obsolete texts under their lids. But nails were in the inkwells, a pitchfork leaned in the cloakroom, and grass was growing between the floorboards.

Driving around the town, they easily found Lena Wicks. She took them to see Aimless, an old man in search of wayward bees and their new hives. In slacks and the advised scarf, Maureen caught bees in rafters, garage window frames, and in storm-struck trees.

"I need you!" Eugene called from his car.

Downtown, they ate hamburgers in a bar with the freelancers, finalizing assignments for the opening festivities. Andy was covering the hive mite issue with local beekeepers. Eugene wanted Maureen to accompany him on interviews at the safer, deserted hives.

First thing Friday morning though, they stopped at the air-conditioned home of a woman who gave up gardening. "See those bees on the screen?" she said. "They'd swarm my living room if I didn't keep the windows shut." After that, they bravely knocked on a door surrounded by honeysuckle, checking the rumor about a man keeping bees in his basement.

"It's the pesticides, not the mites, that's doing it," he averred. "Every time the wind blows from the new barley fields, another colony splits and no one can find a queen."

They ventured into his garden, a meadow of strawberries, dandelions, and bee balm. Eugene asked about the bees hanging near the cellar doors. He and Maureen both took a sting before Eugene could coax out the story of the cellar hive.

Then, counting air conditioning units at house windows, they set off for a farm that the bees deserted. It took the yells of children to bring the beekeeper to his door. The large gruff man said he hadn't read much news since he lost a court case to the barley farmer. Through a forest of coneflowers, he took Eugene and Maureen to the hives. He talked of the New Glasgow people as if they were bees, saying that it did no good to send his son with his bees in the direction of California. His son had deserted, telephoning his father to say, "Nirvana is the nectar."

"I don't take long distance phone calls," he said to Eugene.

That evening, the Centennial staff ate honey-cured ham at the mayor's house. Eugene asked if bee pollen really helped men keep their hair. While the mayor chuckled, Eugene assigned Maureen the task of counting heads at the banquet for a percentage.

The night was filled with festivities and fireworks, leading to the midnight marking of the Centennial. At one in the morning, Eugene drove Maureen to the dentist's house where she expected to sleep like an insect caught in amber. But she sat at the window, rubbing salve on a bee sting, and watching white moths float around a trellis of clematis. She paged through Eugene's book, studying Vic's photographs until she turned to a page that was blank except for Eugene's handwriting.

Then there's the book I hope we'll do, Maureen. You hardly ever disappoint.

She was weeping. If he had said this in their Minneapolis office, she would take it as a taunt. She hardly ever amazed Eugene.

In the morning, stories multiplied with the arrivals of people.

"You're needed!" Eugene yelled if Maureen walked alone.

Events for an entire year were crammed into a few days – church bazaars, carnival games run by class reunion committees, recipe contests where young people offered baklava and honey granola bars. Maureen photographed pet contests, commemorative speeches, a beer-bleary pig roast, and a dance where grandmothers wore bee bonnets and their daughters wore beehive hair. Vic had shown up to photograph the honey refinery.

The day of the parade, a clown strolled into Maureen's composition, blocking a float made of honey jars. Then the clown blundered into her shot of a re-painted melodeon announcing the Queen Bee. The Queen's float was a network of hexagons under cornucopias of flowers. As Maureen followed it, the clown sidled on stilts towards the float. Then he vaulted himself onto the golden plush.

Maureen was sweating again and, having marked her initials for a sideshow of music, grabbed a front bench. An old woman played a Wurlitzer organ behind a bagpiper dressed in a kilt and tam o'shanter.

"I'm going to be on television," Maureen heard. Eugene's voice was coming from the clown. "You're signed up to go in a helicopter for an aerial view of the town."

Maureen was so enthused at this that she played along with the clown act. Eugene had settled one arm around her while he scratched at his yellow plaid vest. Soon, he had a notebook in his hand.

"You really join in, don't you?" she said.

"It's easier for a sad sack to hear about the skeletons in the honeycomb. Someone should protect you from admirers."

Inebriated helpers had been offering Maureen an unsteady hand with her tripod and bags. They found crates for her to stand on and showed her the way to second floor windows on Main Street.

She wondered what Eugene heard in his tramp hat. Bees were painted near his emphasized lips.

"The identity of the old Queen Bee. She was regal, telling about her eight children, a dead husband, an ex who left her, and her husband drinking at the outdoor bar. When I went to talk to him, another bibulous man told me about drones that impersonate queens. No tiptoeing in his honeysuckle for me. Then I listened in on a controversy about the hive shooting contest. The guy who could put a bullet in an old queen's cell was nearly charged with manslaughter a few years ago."

Maureen and Eugene stayed on two days after the celebrations were over, Maureen collecting old photographs and Eugene delving into the town's records. After a morning thunderstorm, they drove out, sneaking to the blacktop nearest the Wicks' house. Once routed, Eugene itemized the food he ate and the order of it, what sickened them both. The back seat was stuffed with food in jars and tins, carved bears, and souvenirs.

"The farmers were telling the bee keepers to move north near the berry swamps," Eugene said about the bar talk after the banquet. "It almost came to fists."

At least he was wearing a long T-shirt and running shorts. They wouldn't be stopping in any small towns. But Maureen was aware of his thigh muscles tensing and releasing with the accelerator. He stared at the road as if it were coming out of his printer. "How was it at your high school?" he asked abruptly. "Did anyone expect to like their work or did the work ethic prevent such a hope?"

"People never talked about liking their work in my hometown. If I liked photography too much, I might not make a living at it. It was either studio photography or food ads."

"How did your people come to the Midwest? Did they come out of hunger?"

"Land, probably. My mother's family was Scandinavian. My father's came from the east to mine."

"Iron ore? I guess they tried for gold first."

"No. They were near the Mississippi, looking for copper."

"And gold. Did they give up?"

"I suppose they farmed. One was a surveyor. My grandfather was a cartographer. Road maps."

"That's where you got your talent! The trouble was that many weren't prepared for farming. Work became an ethic. Pride was in the ethic, not the work. Do you have plans when you get back to Minneapolis?" Eugene hunched at the wheel as if he were riding a bicycle. He snatched at his cigarette.

"Tomorrow's Sunday. I was planning to recupe."

He mused and she wanted to ask him about his high school days. But his recalcitrance was like the office door that she couldn't poke her head past. Curious about moving the office to another city, she became capricious. "Do you see yourself staying in the Midwest? Where do you see yourself in ten years?"

He laughed at the stale question. "I should say the magazine will make it until then. And that I might be writing *2084* in my spare time. Just thinking about that makes this day seem special."

She had to agree, dreading the return to a rapport marred by stress.

"One of the guys in the town with the bottling company told me about a small lake. They use a vacant farm building as a duck hunting blind there. Do you want to stop and photograph another abandoned farmhouse?"

"Why not?"

"We could eat lunch there. The food's in the back seat."

Closing her eyes, she remembered going to the Wicks' homey bedroom after Eugene dropped her off. As she undressed that night, she toyed with small town consequences. Near him, she usually felt uncannily apart, aired of any imaginings. "Do they swim in the lake?"

"I didn't ask. Probably not. It's a wetland."

She inspected him during another silence, the rim of moisture above his eyelid, his jaw emptying as he smoked. His best side was his profile, the quizzical eyebrow merely curious. At the wheel with his intentions, he was like the men who didn't work out for her.

He rarely told her about disappointments, only that too much friction from her was more than he would take and that it was her privilege to see his Eeyore side. Because men were not all alike, they took the same laconic pose. Even if that were rude or brash, it was considered masculine.

Eugene swung into a liquor store on the main street of the town with the most bars.

"What's in the sack?" Maureen asked as he put his purchase in the back seat.

"Tomorrow's Sunday. And the next day is Monday."

In his notebook, along with information about the bottling plant, were directions to the wetland lake. A dirt road followed chicken wire to a pasture and then, beyond a coppice of aspen, shoreline came into view. The house at the end of a drive was so old that the inhabitants probably used lake water in their kitchen. Its porch was bandaged with tarpaper; the fluted pillars were frail. Most of the windows were boarded up under worm-eaten eaves.

They surveyed a broken barn.

"How long do you hang around a place like this, getting pictures of animals?"

"I put food out," Maureen admitted. "Usually, I'm staying somewhere nearby. Then I come back at dawn or dusk."

The barn was a husk, its window enlarged and covered with a curtain of tarp, probably left by the duck hunters. Beyond the window were high grasses and a bank.

"They may have kept ducks or geese here," Eugene said.

Lugging gear and lunch fare to the bank, they settled near a diamond willow. On a throw blanket, Eugene unwrapped ham sandwiches, prepared by the mayor's wife. Maureen set out cheese, bread, honey mustard, pickles, homegrown tomatoes, strawberries, and bar cookies. After they laughed at the food, they listened to the swishing of the shore reeds. Maureen ate half a sandwich and then she quenched her thirst with beer. But her stomach had compressed like a huge eye with tears behind it. The extension of her work relationship with Eugene, cooperating with him, taking a beer when she saw wine in his sack, made her dismal. The last time she confused a man with nature resulted in a lakeside disaster.

Eugene slouched on the blanket, his bare feet in the grass. He was eating with real hunger. They watched the calligraphy of insects on the water but when he confronted her with frank amusement, she noticed sounds in the willow above her. She picked up her camera, took measurements, and focused on Eugene.

"A minute ago," he said, throwing a bar cookie on a napkin. "And this minute." He stared at her grimly, knowing she hadn't resisted photographing him. "In a minute." He moved to get up. "It didn't happen."

"What?" Her voice was cranky, predicting this day and having her exhibit.

"Things stay the same. Yet it lacks reality."

"You were looking real enough."

She felt Eugene's hands near her, fumbling for something. The leaves were rattling and then she glimpsed a bird with beige and cream feathers. As she attached her telephoto lens, she saw that Eugene was sitting again, lighting a cigarette and watching the water.

"I think it's a veery," she murmured, looking into the leaves.

"You want a picture. Something that will stay the same."

She stood up and caught the bird flittering to a farther branch. Then she took another beer from Eugene.

"From the first, I wanted you around," he said. "I had worked with so many people, contentious people, and finally got to the place where I could arrange things the way I wanted. You were inexperienced. Admittedly, I was surprised that your darkroom skills were what Vic said they were."

Maureen stared again at the fronds of willow. They were like protective emotions – powerlessness, hatred, expectation, dread, gratitude. "Those skills mean a lot to me. It all seemed too perfect."

"It wasn't wise. Vic had pictures of you."

"You ran into me at Lake Harriet."

"We saw you when the rain was starting. After we followed you into the bird sanctuary, I found you." He smiled as if he was seeing her for the first time and yet the moment stretched. "We could go back and be the magazine, maintain the appearance, and do what we want outside it." Now he had his binoculars with which he viewed his car and then the lake. "Or I could tell you what I thought would happen." His words prowled. "If you're really the type to put your job first."

Maureen began putting the food back into the box they brought. She wondered if she was normal or given to self-sabotage. He was as desirable as a shade tree on a downtown boulevard. Still, she was angry, saying, "Are you threatening me with what you wanted to happen? I have to give you credit for not harassing me until now. But that said something else, you know."

"Harassing you! Look, I'm just being honest." He'd given up his covert tone, what he used to dominate. "I'm confessing something. Otherwise, I have to be unreal. You and I are becoming like a couple that does things for show. Not like those people back there." He put the box to the side of the blanket and crawled nearer. When he was in the shade beside her, he peered at her, seeking her opinion the way he did when he was shaved and wearing a shirt. She laughed at his untidy eyebrow and how he worked things out.

"You want me to be unreal," he accused her.

"Not really. But there are things about me that you don't know."

"Touché. Surprise me!" He slurped his beer.

"For one thing, I've been like this lake for some time, not exactly a place of action."

She liked the way he was easily sidetracked and how he usually said what he meant. Getting up to sit near the water, she said, "I'm still not sure I want to hear what you thought would happen."

Even when her feet were doused, she watched the refreshing water more than she felt it. She couldn't be honest and tell him that men hadn't worked out for her and for that reason, she couldn't walk away from him. His shadow was respite from the sun. But he was removing his T-shirt.

"It's interesting," she said, confiscating the conversation again. "Your saying that we've been unreal. I'm not being unreal right now. I get along when I'm a little dead to life."

His foot was in view, his toes pronounced and arching, a man's foot. "Did someone murder you?"

She couldn't disillusion him, remembering the shellac-hard water lily and the wish to sink like the demonic smile that used to be inside her. She hadn't destroyed herself, only her limited capacity for family life. "How did you become unreal?" she countered.

He set his beer down and said, "There's a lot of temptation to dismiss reality. To desert it."

She didn't prevent his arm from leaning across her back but then his hand was finding the waist of her shorts. His face said that this was out of discomfort. He pulled her toward him but she said, "There's the risk of our not feeling the same way afterward."

"Isn't the question of that spoiling work? Those townspeople don't like being let down."

When she couldn't look at his face bending to her, his tight running shorts were too near. "They'd match me up with anyone. Nothing has worked out yet."

"I could say that too. You're just being a child. A child expecting her father to go away. People are always going away from each other. Your heart never stopped beating. Or has it?"

She stopped his hand from finding out and let him grab her wrist instead. She could never try to get married again. "My father never went away. He lived in the same town."

"You were involved with someone who could write a magazine article once in a while. I guess you liked Dr. Mort's son better. He went away though."

She might have given him a lively jab but he held her hand down. "There's no reason to bring that up," she said. "I haven't thought about him for quite some time. He was too fortunate for me. It was a physical…" He nearly smothered that except that she blurted out, "I thought you wanted to go off with Beth and get rid of me. Or maybe that's still a plan."

"Let's not get into that. I told you I'm tired of being unreal. You know I planned *this*."

If she maintained that her plans with men never turned out, they might go back to the car dispirited and leave this stagnant place. But he was right. They would be like the shallow lake, hiding fly-by-night feelings that came like ducks and conflict.

"You really aren't very lively. What could have killed you?"

"Having no certainty that happiness could last."

"You haven't seemed unhappy. Are you taking a drug?"

"No. But this could upset my equilibrium. I earned it. And then, there's all that work."

"There's all that work! And you don't think I've been disrupted from doing my best work?"

"I've disrupted you!" His sternness towards her had never seemed romantic. "I'm just convenient. And not responsible for the problem in your pants."

His beard was on her cheek. He had construed her last statement as liveliness. "I'm so used to you helping me. Some things aren't so easily solved as they say."

He was kissing her and ironically, it cleared the murk that weighted her. In her mouth were words that couldn't get out, words lovers didn't usually say – that she had been sick a long time. She had disciplined her body into an unnaturalness that became natural to her. But she had never been with a man who had already assumed responsibility and now Eugene couldn't get out of it. He was kissing her for every conversation they'd had, her resistant lower lip, the tilt of her unreal smile, the tongue that resorted to teasing.

He scooped her up by her shoulders and prodded her back to the blanket. When he grasped her, remembered sensations sprang up, the same ones, there like a wetland even though it had been drained. "You didn't seem very happy with me," she managed to say.

He was scrawling something on her stomach with his finger. "I had become serious. I liked having authority over you but then, it was no longer fun."

He ended up erasing what he had scrawled on her breasts and thighs. He was still without power, the next moments precarious as a canoe. She felt she would drown, that he could kill her, but then she was breaking the waves and surfacing. Beyond him, the view was shaken up, a kaleidoscope of green and blue, the new pieces falling into place. Then it was still and she was afraid that she had seen a rare sight and if things didn't go well in the darkroom, it might not be found again.

"You must feel alive now." Glistening with sweat, he walked to the shore and splashed the heat from his face and chest. The great blue heron. When he came back, he perched on his knees, and then they stretched their legs under the drooping branches.

"I feel washed up," she said but it came out brightly.

"Venus washed up to shore. Even seashell melted on her skin."

That made her roll to her side and cry.

"What's wrong? It was simply something that was going to happen." He offered her a cigarette, lit from his.

"I thought we were becoming friends." Men played dumb, being obtuse. Now that he was a man with her, he would gain more power.

"The trouble happens when people don't face a truth they already know. Marriages don't start with people being friends. The trouble was, I could see us married."

That didn't say anything, she knew, and he was brisk and energetic again, not admitting how he tired of other women, the truth she could face. They gathered up the rumpled blanket and then she wandered after him to the weathered old barn where she focused with her camera on its rotting boards.

Eugene wanted to find a motel or a bed and breakfast. They sat in his car where they laughed about the articles on the future of marriage. He'd received proposals from classicists to homosexuals.

"I learned that Venus, or Aphrodite, started the Trojan War," he said. "When she wasn't in trouble for adultery, she bet about marriage with Athena."

"I thought Paris started it."

"I used to think Helen's husband did. No, Aphrodite was out to divorce Helen because Paris was her perfect match. But in those B.C. years, Athena won."

"Were you calling me a troublemaker?"

"I suppose so. I'd been wondering what you were fighting."

Their conversation was easy now. Eugene talked of coming back to this place, what was already a wetland issue for the town with the bars. But as they drove away, Maureen knew that later on, he might not have time to find it again. He still had no past for her.

33   Bed and Breakfast

Out of Pope County, they sailed along Highway 71, passing a string of lakes and signs for resorts.

"This is the other side of the small town," Eugene said. "A resort cabin might be nice except for kids running on the trails."

"Sometimes cabins are set away. I could go for a swim," Maureen said.

Eugene followed a resort sign but as he expected, the cabins were full.

"We could have camped where we were," Maureen said.

"You *are* a photographer. Well, I heard about a Bed & Breakfast in a town coming up. A town that's growing. The third floor rooms aren't quite ready because the owners were living in them. Or we could drive to Redwood Falls and try a motel. Richard Sears was born there."

"As in Sears catalogs?"

"Yup."

"We could look at the Bed & Breakfast."

"Why not?" Eugene's tufted eyebrow now looked comical. He drove with one hand on the wheel and the other on her thigh. "I should call first." Then he parked at the next gas station and, while fumbling in the glove compartment for another notebook, began making out with her like a teenager. "Don't get squirrelly," he said.

A half hour later, they were on a street that rounded a lake. A block from there was the Bayview Veranda, an old brick house with meadow-green trimmings. Lanterns were strung above wicker porch chairs. Spirea and rosebushes scalloped the lawn. At the door, a woman in her thirties appeared in a jean skirt.

"I'm Eugene, Ramona. This is Maureen. It sounded like Christmas."

Ramona explained that it was their first year running the B&B. "My husband's still in New Glasgow, taking down the celebration lights."

"He did the lights?" Maureen asked.

"He does their Christmas decorations."

Maureen agreed with Eugene that the celebration lights were spectacular. "We've been going all week," she said as they walked back to Eugene's car. "Is there a beach on the lake?"

A girl had joined them and she pointed down the shore of the lake. Then she took Maureen's suitcase.

"If your father's not here, we won't make you carry our things," Eugene said.

"He's my step father," the girl said stubbornly.

Inside, Eugene told Ramona that he and Maureen were used to sharing a bathroom. Maureen admired the lily light fixtures in the dining room. Ramona was preoccupied with her regrets about the third floor being unfinished. Upstairs, she deposited Maureen's camera bag into a small bedroom, saying that she and her husband had just moved out of the rooms on the third floor. "We live down the street now. Sorry, we took the air conditioner."

When Maureen opened a drawer of the blonde dresser, Eugene set a box on top of it. "We'll keep our work stuff in here," he said.

There was a ceramic doe lamp near the single bed, what a child last occupied. More blonde furniture was in the larger bedroom. But one of the lamps had Gone-With-the-Wind globes and the chairs looked newly upholstered in variegated blue. Their view was on the town side, prosaic businesses along which a few tourists roamed. Then the blue organdy curtain fell to the front of Maureen's face and Eugene was unbuttoning her blouse again. A bottle of wine was on the dresser.

They had never been alone in a room for more than an hour. They pulled back the bed covers and treated their nudity as if it were elegant dress. This time it was a special occasion, the long torture transformed into exquisite relief. A landscape captured, savored without a camera. The great blue heron was in the room.

It said, "I couldn't let you burn with your ideas about harassment when I could get your voluntary involvement."

"You won," she conceded.

The afternoon was dimming behind the curtains but Eugene's eyes weren't going out. "There's no reason to feel at risk. I'm unutterably happy," he said.

"I am too," she said though she was vaguely disturbed. "I was afraid it would be like my first picture of a rainbow. My first picture of a gray sky." She told him how the clerk at her high school drugstore wondered why she was photographing gray clouds.

"Some things are meant for eye witnesses only," Eugene said.

"There isn't even rain in some grayness. Gray isn't even a climate."

"They might not say that in Seattle."

"I became selfish," Maureen said. "And I began liking that."

"I'd been in a desert. Worse than dunes of manila folders." He had liked hearing her splashing with her darkroom baths and seeming very alive when she came out. He suggested a trip to the Caribbean in the winter.

Wouldn't she like to go scuba diving? "Too much of what I did before was a feat or a race. What makes a person thirsty," he said.

Deciding whether to eat more New Glasgow food or whether to order a pizza, they loitered at the mirror above the dresser. She'd had a presentiment of him and now he filled her shadow man perfectly although he would likely become a puzzle.

He didn't care that she didn't know what to do with her hair, nougat-colored underneath and showing the weather. Even better, he liked her not wearing clothing that flattered her figure.

He leaned on walls, shrinking his height and he knew she called him Eeyore. Mensing Maureen was regular, he believed.

"Linnie called me that too?"

"After I guessed. It's pretty obvious. Still, I've had to tell a few people that you're real."

"Who asked that?" She despised being treated like a model instead of a photographer.

"Let's see. Someone who looked an elf. And a woman writer who needed her facts checked."

"The one with the free theater tickets? Did she do hotel reviews?"

"I don't think you're that confused."

Having more wine, Eugene switched on a tape recording of an old man in New Glasgow.

"During the Depression, I went on the road with my bee boxes. Tramps were everywhere but with my bees, I could camp at the fruit orchards. And I earned reward money! A moron held me up on the road. He pulled out the drawers at the back of my truck. Girls thought I was brave, working with bees and having turned in a bee-stung wanted man."

"Did you get married then?"

"No. My wife Esme was back in New Glasgow. She went to live with her parents after she rented out our house. When I wired a buddy who got laid off at the honey refinery, he told me that the renter was an old admirer of hers. He'd been selling jars and paraffin besides honey.

"I'd married Esme after he went to Des Moines, looking for a job. So I was getting dinners at the orchards while the jar man wheedled dinners from Esme.

"She wired, wondering when I was coming back. I started back, thinking I'd catch another robber. That jar man was appearing more and more like an outlaw to me.

"What about hitchhikers?"

"Everywhere. When I got back to New Glasgow about ten o'clock at night, I

parked my truck in the old schoolyard and tramped in. A woman's apparel was hanging on my clothesline. I guessed the jar man gave Esme some fabric for a new dress.

"'I should have known you were back in town,' he said at the back door. 'When Esme sees you, she sends me packing.'

"I thought he might want to step out. Turned out, he'd caused a stir in town that very day. It had to do with the garments on the clothesline too. Esme had been over, wanting him to leave. But his new wife was inside, sobbing to fill a jar because she'd had to get married without the trimmings."

"Who was the wanted man that held you up?"

"I'm puzzled about going back to work Monday," Maureen reminded Eugene.

"Let other people be puzzled. There's no reason to shock them."

"They wouldn't be shocked. There are mistresses all over Minneapolis."

"Mistresses but no mattresses in the offices."

They could watch each other in the mirror, sitting together on the large newly upholstered chair. "It means I might be getting married again," Eugene said, his smile connecting with her open mouth in the mirror.

"Are you married now?"

"I feel like it. No, with you. I was going through a divorce. I thought you knew, calling yourself a mistress."

Maureen went to the other chair, her skin crawling as Eugene put on his T-shirt. "Maybe we should go out for pizza," he said.

"I guess I really understand what I see," Maureen said.

"I didn't like people knowing. It was humiliating, my not seeing what I was in for."

Two days ago he was younger than her and now he stood there, as old as any man, saying that he was married. But she couldn't tell if his divorce was from his life being hexed or from his habit of rejecting people. Fastening her hair back with combs, Maureen watched his movements, realizing that divorce wasn't anything but an embarrassment for him.

Then he said, "Something made you deadly to me. Not dead." He grabbed her hand and pulled her to the chair again. "One of the writers on the future of marriage quoted Balzac. I knew I was in trouble when I got interested in those article proposals. Balzac wrote that if a man can't make his wife his mistress, he's a nothing. Today, I don't feel like a nothing."

"I don't even know where you're from."

"Linnie could have told you. A town in Iowa with farmland in our classifieds. When one of my friends went through there, he wished that 'My Kinsman, Monsieur Molineux' hadn't already been written."

Not having read that, Maureen said, "Are you French?"

He lit a cigarette and talked about himself as if it were an article that he would reject. His father bought the local newspaper when it might have folded, mostly to print agricultural catalogs. Eugene worked there summers when he was in college, taking pre-med. Some readers blamed the newspaper for the first foreclosures as if it were a part of the process. Two evening fires broke out at the office. Rumor had it that his family started the fires in order to collect insurance. It was his first investigation, tracing the rumors in reverse. He was a nothing to a girl in town and, because he smoked, people didn't see him as the doctor type. He'd been damned careful of his cigarettes at the time of the second fire and he wasn't home for the first.

When he got involved with an insurance evaluation about a barn fire, he completed the rumor circle. One of the sons got all the livestock out after lightening hit. The parents admitted that he got the John Deere equipment out too. And there were other odd things he saved, a transistor radio, a couple of saddles. Quite a tough too but there wasn't much to prove he'd started the newspaper office fire. After college, Eugene went to grad school for journalism, deciding to become a science reporter.

"I'd covered so much controversy, I thought an assignment at a genealogy center would be a sweet thing. That's where I met Corinne. I suppose I was trying to prove I had some spontaneity, jumping into marriage."

"Do you have to tell me about her here?" Maureen said, getting up to look out the window. The sky was opalescent, causing the street below to look tarnished.

Eugene turned on the television, seeing the sky and the stillness outside. "We'll go out."

Maureen took her camera though Eugene didn't discover any tornado warnings. They walked to the lake, fluorescent now, and then turned towards the downtown again. The flowerbeds in a park square were tinctured like a Renaissance painting. The trees were holding their breath.

Corinne was the intake director at the genealogy center. She persuaded Eugene to do some research on his genealogy. He already knew that his ancestor was a lumberjack in Maine and that he answered a clergyman's ad about starting a colony in Iowa. The lumberjacks thought they were going to settle among forests. When they saw the plains, they wanted to leave but with land inducements, they were persuaded to learn farming.

Corinne was from a north suburb and a normal American family, scaling Chicago. But she was fixated on an ancestor from Alsace-Lorraine, trying to prove that her family was connected to aristocracy. Eugene didn't know about that at first. She was attractive, almost in a hybrid way, but that probably had to do with money. She stupefied him with her favorite phrase, "Obviously, Eugene." He began to think that with her certainty about him, he might write something of significance.

"You must have been in love with her to get married," Maureen said.

"Of a fashion I'd never experienced. Corinne convinced me that I couldn't get married without her. Once she got hold of it, my future was like suction. When we're off, Maureen, we're still breathing the same air."

A siren began blaring and then a police car stopped in front of the bench where Eugene and Maureen were sitting. "Tornado watch!" the policeman shouted.

Maureen stood where she could see the lake and photograph its chartreuse color.

"Any sitings?" Eugene asked.

"So far, no. You should be taking cover. Do you have somewhere to go?"

"The pizza parlor. We're staying at the Bayside Veranda."

They stood at the pizza parlor door where Maureen watched the lake, relieved to forget about Corinne. Then the proprietor opened the door. "My customers are going to the basement," he said.

After they emerged from it and their pizza was in the oven, Eugene played with Maureen's fingertips. "It's starting to rain," he said.

"It sounds as if you worked with Corinne before..."

"Nooo. I did a story on the genealogy center but when I went back to research, she didn't work there. She went to law school our first year of marriage. We honeymooned in Europe where she looked for her aristocratic relative. As soon as we got back, I spent excruciating evenings arguing with her about LSAT questions.

"To make a short story short, she went to law school and I was supposed to work on a promotion. When the promotion didn't come through, I began my book. It was becoming clear that Corinne and I shouldn't have a family."

Eugene blew the hot air from his pizza slice towards Maureen. She considered hers, not wanting to burn her tongue that day. "Lots of people have trouble during the first year of marriage," she said, quoting someone. "You're bound be biased."

"That's why I don't talk about her. I'm totally slanted. Corinne and I wouldn't have lasted a week if we worked together. I found out that she helped a politician jump genealogies to look better. I invited people in for interviews that she couldn't countenance in her living room. And I'll admit now, I probably won't stop drinking if I don't stop at once."

"Some people have patterns." While Eugene's favorite red pepper and sausage pizza tasted good, it was singeing Maureen's stomach.

"You don't believe I thought about this all these months? Do you have a girlfriend who understands everything if you need to stay overnight at her place?"

"No."

"I know you don't. Corinne was a good sport after she got the status she wanted. And she taught me to say an unequivocal 'No.' She succeeded in turning me into an editor."

They ran through the rain to their room and the scented candles in it.

"Don't you want to supplant the old memories? We'll take that trip in the winter," Eugene said.

"Just don't promise a horse."

"A horse is something to plan, not something to buy all of a sudden. You must have had opportunities to marry, Maureen."

"I promised myself I wouldn't try to get married again. I tried with someone who didn't work out, especially on a weekend away."

"Dr. Mort's son?"

"No. Milt was too fortunate for me. Someone more dependable. I couldn't fall in love with him."

Waking to Eugene the first time, Maureen was incredulously content. She'd gotten used to waking and wondering, an improvement after waking and feeling desolate. Something could happen in a frangible moment, the moment today when she wanted to risk a picture. Eugene was as oblivious as vacation scenery.

When church bells aroused him, Maureen mused about navals. Her pain when she was depressed was concentrated behind hers.

"Oriental medicine centers on the naval," Eugene said. "If it was psychological, you may have wanted separation or you were suffering separation. I hope it's not an ulcer."

Better than contemplating this was to have her stomach covered and pressed upon. She couldn't tell Eugene that she would rather have died than marry a man who wasn't really wrong, except that he was wrong for her.

Missing his morning run, Eugene got dressed for Ramona, the Sunday paper, and a pot of coffee. "Don't bother about the other bedroom," he told Ramona in the hallway.

He was right about the tornado warnings, showing Maureen a photo of storm damage in New London. Unmoved at her having a few bad years, he offered her some news to read. But his hand at his temple screened her out.

"You remind me of Jack Benny with your hand that way," Maureen said. "In New Glasgow, a woman had pictures of him, all at the age of 29."

"My duplex could use the attention of someone over 30."

She was pretty sure he was 29. Then she asked if he had heard an ice cream truck in his neighborhood.

"Do you chase ice cream trucks?"

"They sound so sad in the city. I followed one to see what the picture would say."

Ramona had to tell them where the local churches were as they sat at a table near a lace-draped window. She offered them walnut waffles with blueberry syrup. When her husband appeared, Eugene discussed the centennial lighting. Ramona was sunny, asking about their magazine. "My daughter was baptized in the Catholic church," she said. "The B&B gave me an excuse not to attend. But I guess they're accepting my divorce. Times are changing."

Once they were eating, Eugene said, "My mother used to say that there should be something new to learn at church. The minister became concerned when she taught Ezekiel's UFO angels in Sunday school. She liked the stuff about prophets."

"I think the reason my brother wanted to be a pastor was because he wanted another father," Maureen said. "I prayed for my parents to re-unite and put a dollar bill out as a present to Jesus one Christmas. Like the offering plate. I waited with our Brownie camera and flash but he didn't come."

"A confirmed skeptic at what, ten? I wonder what this town will look like in fifty years."

They swam and then in their room, they uncorked the last of the wine.

"You're in a rush," Maureen said, her bathing suit still sticking to her. "What does that mean?"

"You'll find out."

He'd gotten her to do tricks, surreal frames and color toning until he couldn't afford them. Now he was relieved that she couldn't stay on top for long even if her fingernails grazed the shoulders she'd been under for so many months. Dully, they lugged their loads downstairs as if they'd been working.

Once on the road, they could laugh about Corinne, Milt Blaisdell's naps, and how Maureen tried to marry a man like Hank.

"He sounds a little like me," Eugene said. "And Milt's not a bad writer."

Maureen told him more about her family; Eugene had met her father fleetingly at the office. When the song "Dog and Butterfly" came on the radio, he turned it up as she had on their bad Saturday downtown.

"Odd lyrics," he said. "A dog had to keep up with a butterfly. She had to try."

"That's how I feel with a camera sometimes."

"Admit it. You tried to get along with me. It's not that easy."

When they started the trip, they were like a couple that wasn't on speaking terms. "That Saturday downtown was just one of the days when I was sure you disliked me," she said.

"I hated the fact that I was attracted and had gotten myself into an awkward position."

"Did you predict it?"

"I was going to tell you what I thought would happen. I thought it would be worse and that you wouldn't do the job right. That I might use you as a freelancer after I got to know you. I couldn't see how it would work."

"You don't think it'll be awkward now?"

"Maureen, a good prediction isn't about wanting something. That's the danger I like to investigate. I don't see this going out like the smoke of an old flashbulb. We have too much work in the next months to risk that. And I hope it's not one of those pictures you take to stop life from going on and on. You with a trophy."

Guiltily, Maureen wondered if he knew about the picture she took of him sleeping. And next he said that lovers often confessed.

"It doesn't matter what's confessed," she said. "People live in the present. I didn't believe that my high school steady's father beat up his wife and his boys until that became my present."

"His father beat you up?"

"No. He did."

"You don't mind being beaten in the normal way," Eugene said, and instead of caressing her leg he held her hand. "Some things shouldn't go on and on. But you shouldn't use a bad experience as an excuse."

They went on like that until they reached the snarl of the city again. But instead of it's being all the same, he took her to his apartment.

34 An Honest Quarrel

When Maureen appeared at the office two days later, Eugene's door was shut as usual. Linnie's greeting was uninformed.

"Eugene said you were having one of those days. After a heavy week."

Mensing Maureen. "Luckily, when the PMS started, it was an easy road day," Maureen said, having their usual little joke.

A day in Eugene's duplex was delicious but somewhat oppressive. When they came in, moonlight was teasing the treetops above Lake Harriet and Eugene was a shadow, embracing her. After he turned on the lights, his living room was in a treetop. Stacks of paper splayed his desk and books were strewn on modern blocks of verdigris furniture. The photographs on the wall were taken by someone else and a painting might have been the cover of a rock band album. In the hallway, though, Maureen found one of her futurist photos.

Before work the next morning, Eugene had to run around Lake Harriet while Maureen warmed up a New Glasgow breakfast.

"Take the day off," he supervised. Then he opened boxes of New Glasgow photographs for her to sort.

Maureen sat on the floor with them. After Eugene was gone, she crawled to a glassed lawyer's bookcase because she saw a scrapbook. It was filled with clippings of articles. He kept stacks of magazines that he used to intimidate her.

She took a break with an early *Midwest Forecast* on his bed where a sugar maple on the sloping yard fanned her. Then she had to explore his bedroom desk and open a drawer. Fan mail from his mother was in the center drawer and also, pictures of his family, flourishing like those in the Lombardy neighborhood of Wanatin. Eugene kept up with a foreign correspondent and a woman in St. Louis, she found.

Typed manuscripts were more amusing. He wrote about clones that aliens possessed to revolt against the cloners. In another story, a young woman who grew up in a futurist school, based on a concept of Socrates, unknowingly fell in love with her natural father. And the futurist flood story was his.

Maureen found papers concerning Eugene's divorce in another

drawer. He agreed to support Corinne until she finished law school or until her class graduated, whichever came first. A letter to his lawyer described her blackmail, how she almost perjured an interview subject and how she ruined an average of ten nights of sleep per month, asking him to rewrite her law assignments. He thought he could sue for adultery because of her nights with a woman who had a lesbian past, even if she denied that as a breach of fidelity.

Behind a metal divider, Maureen found her own picture with some pictures of Vic's. Satisfied, she looked into another folder only to find professional photos of women - models in futurist clothing, ascetic women, and a few who might have gotten a job at the Playboy Club. Corinne's photograph was there too. Maureen was glad Eugene spent so many evenings with her. Her raglan style, laced hair, and tallying smile probably veiled her real self.

Falling back on her work as security, Maureen resumed her relationship two walls away from Eugene. They often ate dinner together and went out some nights, taking in the Dudley Riggs Theater, a concert of electronic music, a movie. When Maureen slung on her camera, people preferred to treat her as if she were on assignment or as if she were the robot girl in *Metropolis*, a favorite movie of Eugene's. People found him at the Canterbury Downs race track and at occult bookstores, expecting him to leave her for an exotic coffee or a drink. He had a knack for finding a direct pathway through any crowd, a small-town obliviousness.

Eugene feared his own prophecies, what led him to track down geniuses and ground-breakers. His vaulting into issues and his exhaustion distressed Maureen. Sometimes when he drank, he asked her outrageous questions. If she countered him about the photos in his desk drawer, he said that men bluffed and women spread out their losses until someone spilled the ace up their sleeve.

In Minneapolis, people were always predicting the fates of couples. Maureen walked around Lake Harriet while Eugene ran, leaving her and catching up again. Sometimes he acquired a running partner and often, Maureen encountered acquaintances. In the way that he eased surprises, Eugene hung his arm over Maureen's shoulder and steadied the camera on her chest. He was now nearly the person Maureen expected him to be the day they met, a professional man living near Lake Harriet and already attached.

Talk about their future was intense but without certainty now that the trees flared with leaves that would sail off on their own. Maureen couldn't talk much about having children unless it was to prevent them. She abhorred the possibility of being a single mother and appreciated Eugene for thinking about the future of a child before having one.

The puzzle of their lives took up so much conscious thought that most days were like the layout pages, Maureen suggesting the dinner block and Eugene making his moody chess moves. But afternoons ended with more levity. The New Glasgow freelancers popped in like firecrackers, vying for Eugene's attention as the book was compiled. Maureen was tutoring Andy, the arthropod photographer, on her darkroom techniques.

On irrational days, Maureen feared that she would never get over Eugene, even for a day. She arranged a weekend up north, promising to take pictures at an apple festival for the organic issue. Afterward she went to Logren's Resort and, while canoeing, she rehearsed telling Eugene what she had been capable of doing to herself.

"I really thought a great blue heron saved my life," she told him in the room where she broke up with Hank. "I needed to face being alone then because I was alone. I don't know why I'm well with you."

Eugene's smile was wry but he was won over. He aired a theory, that hormones had no intention of being modernized. Teenagers were set up for first love at a formidable level. Her depression probably included a timed onset of hormones, frustrating her the way he was frustrated with Corinne. He was afraid that sex was imprinted from first experiences. It was all set up, a burgeoning teenage garden. In past history, men married virgins, sometimes years younger because they knew those things. She probably didn't think he loved her if he didn't have an emotional erection every time she went away or came back. He could get used to someone who wasn't always thinking about his future. He might really believe that she preferred her apartment as a retreat some nights, and that she wasn't having anyone over.

She'd taken a self-portrait, a woman in a wraparound skirt embracing a tree, done in Sabbatier shadowing. She did studies of the egg, how it looked on a couch cushion or on a bookshelf. An egg seeped like lava in a toned time release. An egg bobbed between toes in the bathtub.

While the organic farming issue was being edited, they ate out with Carl from the Co-op. Maureen asked him, "Did they dye chicks in your town? At Easter, kids kept pink and lime-green chicks in their garages. They always died. I haven't touched chicken since our visit to Farmer Grevis' poultry buildings."

"Beware of diving egg prices," Carl replied.

He was working on copy about traditional European and Asian eating habits. The ancestors of most Americans ate a fraction of the meat in a contemporary diet. Eugene broke it to Carl that Maureen grew up in Wanatin, the turkey town.

One evening, Eugene showed up at Maureen's apartment with a six-pack of beer and deli submarine sandwiches. Maureen had just come in from taking a picture of a bird's egg on a dead Dutch elm stump. She was waiting for a sunset of spilling clouds as the backdrop for an egg balanced on her balcony ledge.

"Andy, your assistant, brought in chocolate covered grasshoppers," Eugene said. "Danni offered me a supper of seaweed."

Maureen had already eaten. She reminded Eugene that she had chocolate cheesecake in her refrigerator but she stayed in her chair at the balcony door.

"Here, Maureen. I typed this up today. I want you to sign it. Linnie saw it as it came off the printer."

Maureen read her notice to move out of her apartment at the end of November.

Sitting intently on her bed, Eugene said, "Linnie wants to know what she should say when people ask about us."

"She gives them a sleek smile and shrugs her shoulders."

"Deadlines are hitting. You should move in before winter. You should spend your money on something else. Our trip."

"I told Carl that I'd be available if he finds maltreated animals. He thinks I can handle the people."

"Andy handles wasps pretty well. You're doing freelance for Carl?"

"I want a picture like that for my portfolio."

"Along with a picture of the maltreated mistress, cramped in with other downtrodden women. I could be criticized for carrying on in the office."

"Now that your book is published, I suppose you should do what looks right."

"Cohabiting? Look, when you're not around, it's Chicago all over again. There's a vacancy for someone to fill if you don't fill it fast. I've had so many invitations to the Gay Nineties bar that I could honestly say that I've already seen it. Women think that there's something wrong with you and they can guess what it is. Or they think I really want to go out with someone else and can't say so."

"I thought you were the man who could say no."

"Maureen, your happiness is being pursued."

All she could see was that after the colorful clouds, the night would come. Eugene was ready to confine them to quarters where they could lose the happiness they'd found. "You don't know what will happen if we see each other all the time," she said.

"I have an idea."

Maureen put her camera to her eye and began adjusting the stops. She had to sit at the door of the balcony for her shot.

"We'll probably do what those two birds of yours do when their cage door is open. They chase each other from one perch to another until they become so annoying that they have to be put back in the cage." To prove his point, Eugene left the bedroom, shutting the door, and then Maureen heard him slapping her photography magazines around. He was on her phone and opening drawers, turning on the television. They were like cat burglars in each other's lives. He was the shadow she thought she glimpsed in her mirror, what made her jump. He was there when he wasn't there, there after she had become stubbornly single.

When the television news was on, Eugene knew she was sitting in the dark. He knew that the house facing her balcony was like the one where she grew up. But he didn't realize that she was petrified, like a person in a photograph. She couldn't move because of what happened before between them. They'd already put a place in order and established their territory in it. Then there was something wrong with the routine. Even if he thought she was a generation ahead, coming from divorce, he was like other men.

He had turned off the news and then she heard metal clanging on wood, a beer can hitting the coffee table, the door being chained. Then the toilet flushed and Maureen heard water running. He was in the hallway and at the bedroom door, needing to be cared for at once and again in the morning. She couldn't try to get married because that was bad luck. The tragedy to her was trying. It depressed her to hear about people working on their marriages. Her eagerness had flown from the balcony, her exclamation weak. Paralyzed, she couldn't understand Eugene's marriage.

He gripped her chin, kissing her, and then he said, "Your book is coming out!"

"My book? Wildflower pictures in a Schilling book?"

"What if people found out that one of the flower photographers is living with a man?"

"That's not the reason."

"Do you want to get married first?"

"Do I act as if I want to?"

"Not tonight, dearest. People never ask much about photographers. Only photographers want to know who photographers are."

"Stop making fun of me. People are afraid of photographers. The way they're afraid of dentists."

Eugene sat on the bed again. "You are at an impasse, not a place. You know this is optimal."

"Optimal. You talk like one of the people you interview."

"From what you've told me about the men you've known and then, your independence, it's optimal for you."

"I can't make a personal decision because it's optimal."

"Maureen, you sit there in the dark, not seeing what your problem is. You didn't watch a woman preparing to go to bed with her husband. You have no idea, the legal varieties of seduction, coaxing, simpering, and manipulation. Even if you mope, the motive is probably the same. I've never seen you so stumped at work. I've seen other women acting this way there."

She didn't watch him wrestling his way out of his T-shirt and his shoes.

"It's as if you were brought up in a convent," he said.

"The rest of the town wasn't that way."

"You're like a matron crying at a wedding. It wasn't just you that witnessed an unhappy marriage. You're so sure that you know what marriage is about."

Because the balcony door was open, he kept his pants on. But now he was pulling her chair back, towing it as if it were a wheelchair. Her birds were out, he told her, handing her the wine glass and the ashtray that were on the floor. Then he slammed the balcony door. Because he hadn't turned the lock tumbler and because of his anger, glass was splintering and a piece shattered on the floor.

"What did you do!"

Maureen went to look at the cracked window but he held her back. Then he pulled the curtains across the window and turned on a lamp.

"What am I going to tell the landlady?"

"That I'll pay for it. Better that than a burglar. The next time you look at that house next door, you can see it cracked, the way you want to see it. You might as well put a crack across your lens and look at everything that way."

"This. This is what could happen," Maureen began crying. "I had learned to get along alone."

"Oh, did you? What about me? I can't stand to go back there alone. Do you feel broken? It sounds to me as if your family broke up. Do you want to break up?"

"No."

"Those lesbians in that house don't feel cracked, if you didn't know. You feed on it, your kind. You allow people to look at us that way. You know what you're doing, looking at me the way you do when you can see me the way I want you to see me."

He knew she couldn't resist him when the light was on and he was no longer like other men. And he had stepped on glass.

During all the jolliness surrounding Eugene and Maureen as they moved in together, Carl's habitual leeriness calmed Maureen. Before any feast, he was already fed up, ready to discover that a maltreated animal or a chemical risk made the feast possible.

The organic farm Carl preferred for photographs wasn't far from the Grevis acres. On a crossroads in the area was a rural bar where Grevis employees socialized with their high school friends, Carl told Eugene. If Eugene wanted to follow up on Grevis Farms, he might learn more there.

"No, there's no follow-up," Eugene maintained. "The magazine is a tocsin in this case. Maureen, I thought you had boxes that you wanted to take to your mother's house. Her mother's house is in that county too. Just go to the organic farm and take pictures."

Ever since the night that Eugene corrected her view of things, Maureen had to criticize him at times for treating her like a child. She was still packing and, because many of her possessions were unnecessary at his duplex, they were a stash like canned food if she had to set up a single apartment again.

Maureen's mother brought on a traditional dread in Eugene. Her incredulity caused her to meet his Eeyore side. Maureen postponed telling her about their living together. Now she would do that alone, spending a night at her mother's while Eugene was in Chicago.

When Joann curbed her congratulations by noticing that Maureen was rundown, Maureen drove off as she had done years ago, vague about the hour of her return. At the organic farm, chickens were out pecking in the hen house yard. These hen houses resembled a garage row behind an apartment complex, a village of chickens. Harlow, the farmer, built the feeding stations himself.

She photographed the composting system, the vegetable plots, a barn with dozens of pigs in it, and a silo where soy was stored. When Carl arrived with Darcy, his Co-op assistant, Harlow and his wife Jeannie walked them all to the farmhouse where windsocks shaped like vegetables blew from the porch.

Jeannie put on the uniform she wore for her winter work at a canning factory and called her children in for their photographs. After she changed back to corduroys and a sweater, the family sat on new granny squares covering old furniture.

Despite her mother's worries, Maureen saved her appetite for the potluck – vegetable and bean soup, a French gougere filled with mushrooms and made with fresh eggs, homemade bread, apple butter, Maureen's nut bread, and her mother's rhubarb pie. Afterward, Jeannie left her fourteen-year-old with the younger children while they drove to a business that rented farm equipment.

The rural bar Carl visited was nearby. From its parking lot, the moon was nearing its harvest fullness. Having beers there, the men talked about farming, Jeannie talked about children, and Maureen compared the risks of a magazine to that of a farm. Harlow introduced his old friends and chairs were pulled up.

Maureen displayed for Darcy her new ring, a diamond and an amethyst set in a double frame of silver and gold, admired at an art fair. Stoking a new subject, Maureen talked of its modernist style and the artist who handcrafted it.

She hadn't expected such intent interest at this. Pausing, she waited for someone at the table to discuss modern art forms. But then, the heads at the table bent towards the television above the bar. Only one conversation was heard over the antics of the talk show. Someone named Brent was telling about the baling work at Grevis Farms.

No, I'm just hired for the harvest. I'm not getting suckered in like my brother. Don't have a wife and taxes to pay…Yeah, my brother did some baling but he's still on nights in the poultry building…You heard right. That's how much at harvest but it's not that much an hour to start. Grevis dangles the regular shit work if you're good enough, trying to make you want it…It's almost my last day, that's a fact. I told Nat this afternoon about heading for Texas. Know a guy who got into an airplane mechanics program and most of it paid. Now there's some money. Soon as my pay's figured, I'm cleaning out my locker.

"Farm Beautiful," Carl prodded Brent at the bar.

"Yeah, fucking farm beautiful. The bastard featured in a magazine."

"Does he really keep those chickens pretty as a picture?" Carl sat on a bar stool.

"Like hell he does. They had a load come in and everything's in a temporary situation during harvest, they say. Grevis is always complaining about the egg numbers. So now he's found better layers. Says he can find better workers too. He's already got some temporary Latinos, you know, maybe to stay *if* they're good enough. Cages? Now they're saying that the chickens like the temporary cages and that they fight to lay in them. Yeah, like they just noticed that and were going to take them out after harvest. I don't know how my brother got used to it but he got used to Nam."

"You saw the chickens in the cages?"

"Yeah. Maybe they want me to get used to poultry. Keep things inside, more like. I wouldn't spend my time in that stinking place."

"Grevis said he wasn't going to cage the chickens," Carl said. "I've got a camera."

Brent's companion said, "You said it, Brent. Grevis isn't expanding. He's just bringing in replacements. I'll bet you the gas money to Texas."

Hell, I could drive the truck back in to collect some stuff from my locker. Everyone was beat today and has to be up working at dawn. What time is it on? My brother's alone after ten and he'll want a breather. Dying to have a smoke, maybe a joint.….Now that I'm done with this county, I'd just as soon help the organic guys. I've got a new tape my brother might want to hear and then I'll tell him what the manager said today.

Appalled at what she might see, recalling Eugene's clippings, Maureen could be persuaded to duck under a truck topper as if it were a high school party. Carl wasn't used to adjusting his camera in the minutes they had.

Brent knew a route that was all but swallowed in the night. At a corner of the poultry building, he dropped off Carl, Darcy, and Maureen. Once his brother was outside and using both hands to light a cigarette, Brent said he was going to be sick. He ran to the grass, his arm around his stomach, and pretending to retch, showed Carl the ring of keys to the poultry building. Then he yelled that he was going to be sick again and that the truck was on the far side of the building. After unlocking the door of the poultry building, Brent went to the truck to keep his brother on his fifteen-minute break.

Eugene studied the pictures, frames so crowded with chickens, chickens in cages, chickens in confusion, that even the feeding station seemed tarred with their feathers.

"Carl's pictures weren't very good," Maureen said. "He was reeling from the stench. I guess he's not used to holding his breath. No one could recognize this as the place I photographed last winter."

"Have you ever been charged with trespassing before?" Eugene stared out at Lake Harriet, not looking at her.

"It could have happened at one of the abandoned farmhouses. It could have happened at the place where we were first together. Did you know who owned the land?"

"This is different. We weren't doing anything there that would affect the owner." He held a picture at arm's length. Maureen's birds chirped from their cage. They had spent more time in it lately and now she felt like a trespasser in Eugene's duplex.

She and Darcy and Carl ran to the truck after Brent's brother went back into the poultry building. Because they heard a dog barking, Brent let them off on the road shoulder, about a half mile from the bar. Maureen put the roll of film in her bra. Walking near the ditch, she admired the moon, balanced like a golden egg in the sky, not yet full. Precarious. Then Nat drove up, informing them that they were trespassing and that the sheriff was on the way.

Eugene rubbed his temple, blotting Maureen from view. "Can you lie in court?"

"Photographers aren't good liars."

"You're not in the *practice* of it. It's one thing to trespass in Eden and another in Hades. Grevis is talking about suing the magazine."

The room was dimming but neither of them bothered to turn on a lamp. Rather than push her block of the couch away from Eugene's or move the papers and books from the chairs, Maureen slumped onto the rug.

Eugene was supposed to sort the papers because people were invited over on Friday night.

"You were out for yourself last night! I told you that Carl is cloddish and capable of attacks. He was using you."

"He just wants everyone on his side. It's probably a picture of the future."

"Oh, don't! Don't try to make my decisions for me."

On the floor, the dusk light crept over Maureen's feet like shore water. Eugene's calf muscles were clenched inside his sweat pants.

"It was some old party. You can't plan on anything with me." Her voice sobbed when her eyes were dry. "It's better to get this over with. It's better to get Grevis over with. I wanted that picture because I could see it happening." A few days ago, she worried about being too complacent, too accommodating.

"I said that the magazine is a tocsin, a warning mechanism. When I say I never assigned any investigation, I won't be lying. After the organic issue, we're planning an article on egg grading and government inspection. That's what coming. You knew that."

"So I'm a catalyst. You can keep on telling the truth."

"Maureen, I've known plenty of women who went out looking for such an opportunity. You say you didn't plan on spoiling things but you took the opportunity because you think things will spoil eventually. What *did* you have in your mind? A confrontation with Grevis? You!"

Maureen took one of the pictures and then the liquid came to her eyes. "Grevis is tarred and feathered even if no one knows about it. This isn't the world we knew! How can anyone plan a life when things change so fast? In Wanatin, they always said the poultry was treated well."

"People are always telling their plans and a year later, they plan an excuse," Eugene said with bitterness. "As you said, this doesn't look anything like the pictures you took at Grevis Farms last winter. Yes, Carl got him. I don't care if I published Grevis's promises. He has to think about living up to them. The three and a half square feet. You're going to think twice about being a spoiler." He leaned his elbows on his knees. Then his foot lined up with her hand.

At the art fair, he said they should tell the truth, that they were already married. Now she took the cigarette he offered, knowing that he must be seeing ahead. When she didn't please him it wasn't because she was wayward, it was because she didn't please him. Eugene had little interest in people who were complacent, what she could become because she couldn't walk out.

"I didn't know what to do," she said, getting up to let her birds out.

"You're waiting to get kicked. Now you want a lambasting when the fight is out there. What you're fighting is your own future." He pulled her to the couch and said, "It doesn't seem like it but I notice what people are doing today. I'm living with a woman who spoiled a magazine forum. What you did was freelance if you pride yourself on those photos. You could have some hours opened for yourself. More time for the food you said you'd prepare tomorrow, more time for our sex life. You could work for people who have more money than us."

She struggled with that, struggled with his hands on her, what would resolve the evening. Words had strength when a place became familiar.

"You've been living in the dark too long, Maureen," he said in the darkness. "I guess this happens once a year, about as often as you see your father. Like Grevis, you've been found out. You act as if you're such a chicken that you're rather say the sky is falling than understand why these things happen to *me*."

www.ingramcontent.com/pod-product-compliance
Lightning Source LLC
Chambersburg PA
CBHW030319200626
46816CB00006BA/1847